MIDNIGHT DESIRE

And then he snuggled her even closer and gave her the kiss that until this moment had been possible only in her midnight dreams. The demand of his lips...the heat...the passion....

Marilla trembled as she became further alive beneath his kiss, the pleasure pulsing through her like roses spreading their sweet scent through the air in the early spring.

Almost melting from such wonderous sensations, Marilla twined her arms about Kohanah's neck and sighed when he lifted her fully up into his arms and carried her to his bed, to lay her on it.

Marilla was ready to protest, fear sweeping through her like torrents of rain drowning her, when his mouth bore down upon hers, hot and demanding, his hands setting her skin on fire as he touched every secret part of her.

She drifted toward him, shaken with desire.

To her now, at this moment, the word "no" did not even exist....

SAVAGE WHISPERS

CASSIE EDWARDS

LOVE SPELL NEW YORK CITY

LOVE SPELL®

September 1996

Published by

Dorchester Publishing Co., Inc.
276 Fifth Avenue
New York, NY 10001

The name ''Love Spell'' and its logo are trademarks of Dorchester Publishing Co., Inc.

Printed in the United States of America.

With admiration, I dedicate *Savage Whispers*
to my talented editor Hillary Cige, whose devotion to
my Indian series is greatly appreciated

and

to Donna York of Hobart, Oklahoma, and her Kiowa
brave husband Morris, and their lovely Kiowa children,
Andrew, Rachel, David, and Michelle.

Alas, how easily things go wrong!
A sigh too much, or a kiss too long,
And there follows a mist and weeping rain,
And life is never the same again.

Alas, how hardly things go right!
'Tis hard to watch in a summer night,
For the sigh will come, and the kiss will stay,
And the summer night is a wintry day.

And yet how easily things go right,
If the sigh and a kiss of a summer's night
Come deep from the soul in a stronger ray
That is born in the light of the winter's day.

And things can never go badly wrong
If the heart be true and the love be strong,
For the mist, if it comes, and the weeping rain
Will be changed by the love into sunshine again.

—George MacDonald

Prologue

The treaty of 1865 between the United States government and the Kiowa Indians left the Kiowa with the southwestern part of Oklahoma, then called Indian Territory, and the Texas panhandle, which fortunately included the best of the traditional buffalo-hunting grounds. The Kiowa were promised annual presents of hunting rifles, staple foods, utensils and tools, seeds for planting, blankets, and clothes.

The Kiowa did not understand the injustices of the treaty. In their minds, they still had the best buffalo range and supplies, and were content. In their innocence, they had committed themselves to life on a reservation.

The Kiowa soon became embittered by their government rations of pork and cornmeal. The foundation of their native culture was undermined by the incursion of the white man into tribal territory while *their* people were confined to the limits of a reservation. The whites were planning to build a railroad through their reservation! The Kiowa Sun Dance was scorned and condemned. The white buffalo hunters were swarming across the plains, stripping hides and leaving carcasses to rot. The mainstay of Kiowa life was being wantonly destroyed; their complaints went unheeded.

1

They had no choice but to have a tribal meeting to decide what should be done. Had the Kiowa forgotten they were warriors? Was it to be peace, or was it to be war? Should the Kiowa emulate the white man, building schools and houses, planting and plowing fields?

Their decision was to fight for their rights and to show the stuff the Kiowa were made of! The raids against the white man began . . .

In 1874, General Sherman of the United States Army, advised President Ulysses S. Grant that steps had to be taken against the Indians. The army then pursued and punished all hostile Indians. Every Indian capable of bearing arms had to answer to a roll call at the reservation once a week. If any Indian failed to report, he was to be declared hostile. All hostile bands would be run down and exiled. President Grant said, "Settlers must be protected, even if the extermination of every Indian tribe is necessary to procure such a result."

After a bloody fight at Palo Duro Canyon, the Kiowa came in, a few at a time, to surrender at Fort Sill in Oklahoma. Their horses and weapons were confiscated and they were imprisoned. In a field just west of the post, the Indian ponies were destroyed. Nearly eight hundred horses were killed outright. Two thousand more were sold, stolen, and given away.

On April 28, 1875, seventy-two Kiowa, young and old, identified as ringleaders in recent raids against the whites, looked upon their families at Fort Sill for what they thought would be the last time. Then guarded by troops, they set forth on a twenty-four-day journey by wagon and railroad to Fort Marion, a decaying Spanish-built strongpoint in St. Augustine, Florida.

My story begins there, at Fort Marion. . . .

One

Florida, May 1875: It was *pai-aganti*, the time of hot weather soon. . . .

Though the Florida sun was hot, its rays reaching out like clutching fingers through the open spaces of the knitted shawl draped about her head, Marilla Pratt walked across the Fort Marion courtyard with several other women, carrying baskets of food to the Indians confined in the hot dungeon. Having been given instructions not to go near the dungeon by her father, Lieutenant Pratt, commander of Fort Marion, Marilla kept her head bowed, trying not to disclose her identity to the other women.

Slipping the handle of the basket over one arm, Marilla lifted a hand and drew the shawl more protectively about her face. If her father discovered that she had been disobedient, what might he do?

Yet Marilla felt some comfort in knowing that her father sympathized somewhat with the Indians. He treated them with dignity and respect, for he admired their pride and courage.

But Marilla's attention had been drawn to one Indian in

particular, as he had seemingly been drawn to *her*. He, Kohanah, was a young warrior at his age of nineteen, she an admirer, perhaps even one in love, at her age of seventeen. From the moment their eyes had met on the day of his arrival in Fort Marion, they had been mystically drawn to one another.

Sneaking into the dungeon as often as she could to be with Kohanah, Marilla impatiently waited for the guard to unbolt the heavy door that opened into the dungeon. Shifting her feet nervously in the sand, she felt her pulse race. This was always the most dreaded moment of all, when she might be discovered by the guards and sent to her father, to be scolded.

So far, she had been lucky.

But each time she took a chance. . . .

"Hurry along with you all," the guard said, nudging the door aside. He stepped out of the way as the women moved into the semidarkness of the damp, stinking dungeon; small cells lined both sides of the long walls.

Sunbeams fell in streamers through the few small grime-covered barred windows, settling on filth-laden floors that were crawling with all sorts of insects. Perspiration laced Marilla's brow beneath her shawl, her nose twitched with the foul, unpleasant smell of human waste and body odor. In her basket she had included a jar of perfumed water for Kohanah, so he might at least partially bathe himself. Even now he should still smell sweet from his bath the night before with the gift of perfumed water she had brought to him yesterday.

Marilla's heart swelled with love as she hurried her pace past the barred doors, seeking one in the far distance. Already she could see Kohanah's silhouette against the wall of his cell. She could see the long, lean fingers of his powerful hands circled about the rusty bars and now, as she came even closer, the dark pits of his deep-set eyes as he recognized her in her hideous garb.

Oh, how badly she wanted to toss the shawl aside so that her hair could hang golden and flowing to her waist. He had told her often how he loved her hair . . . its color, its softness, calling her Tsonda, light-haired one.

When she had almost arrived at his cell, she would loosen the shawl enough so he could see that she had made herself as beautiful as possible for him.

But damn the dreaded bars that separated them! Could it ever be . . . different? Was it even moral for her to care for him? Kohanah had surely slain many white people. Why else would he be there, imprisoned?

Somehow this did not come to mind while she was with him, and she was certain it could not be true.

Out of the corner of her eye, Marilla watched the other women move to the cells and begin their daily kindness of handing bread, fruit, and cheeses through the bars to the captives. The guards would come later with the Indians' ration of water.

Afraid that someone would get to Kohanah before she did, Marilla broke into a half-run, then smiled bashfully up at him as she finally stopped at his cell.

"Again you have come," Kohanah said in a voice deep and resonant for his young age of nineteen. He spoke in broken English, having learned the language during the treaty talks with the white men and now, more and more every day, from Marilla. "Each day I wonder if the day before will be the last. Your father still knows not of your visits? The *yapahe*, the soldiers, do not know? You pass by them so easily?"

He laughed huskily, his eyes sweeping over Marilla. "*Ho,* yes, why would you not? You dress like a woman of forty winters instead of one who has just blossomed into a woman. Your shawl and ugly cotton dress betray what you truly are beneath them!"

His face became a mask of seriousness as his smile faded. "*Guapeto*—I am afraid—that one day you will get caught. What then, *manyi*, woman?"

Marilla was always touched by his concern for her and delighted that he referred to her as a woman. So often she still felt like a gangly schoolgirl. Only recently she had begun to experience the feelings of a mature woman and Kohanah was the cause. He had stirred her in ways that she had only read about.

Being near him caused many tumultuous feelings to invade

her senses. These were feelings that she feared, yet they were so wonderful. How could she *not* want to experience them?

The fact that an Indian caused them gave her reason for concern, not because he was an Indian, but because she did not expect to ever be able to totally share in these feelings *with* him.

Kohanah was to be in prison indefinitely. . . .

Marilla stepped closer to the bars and spoke up into Kohanah's face. "*Tsan*, I come, regardless of what anyone says," she murmured. She smiled proudly. "Did you hear my use of the Kiowa phrase? I said 'I come' in Kiowa, Kohanah. So you see? I am learning your language as you are learning mine. Isn't that *zedalbe*—wonderful?"

Kohanah smiled down at her, nodding. "*Ho*, yes, that is good," he said, his eyes now moving slowly over her as she placed the basket of supplies on the floor, freeing her hands so that she could slowly ease the shawl back from her face.

Marilla arranged the shawl loosely about her shoulders. She twined her fingers through her hair, easing it out from under the shawl, only enough so the soft, long tresses lay across her breasts.

Kohanah felt his heart begin to beat like a drum within his chest, having grown to love Marilla in the short time of their acquaintance. She was different from all other white people he had ever known. She was gentle. She *cared*. She was beautiful, not only in her appearance but in her heart as well.

Marilla's lustrous blue eyes seemed to reach clean into his soul, arousing something almost unidentifiable to him. He wanted to remember that he was a Kiowa warrior, not a weak man, run by feelings for a white woman.

But Marilla's hair, golden as the sunshine, soft and glossy, made his fingers ache to touch it again, let it caress his callused fingertips.

His eyes continued to devour her, knowing that she allowed it. He noted how petite she was, yet knew that outward appearances did not mean anything at all. Though he did enjoy viewing her loveliness, the pink oval face,

her full, ripe mouth and straight nose, and her sublime,
long neck, it was her inner self that meant everything to
him. She was filled with much courage and strength! If not
for the pale color of her skin, hair, and eyes, she could be
Kiowa!

Feeling suddenly timid beneath Kohanah's searching
eyes, Marilla looked downward bashfully. In doing so she
saw the basket of food and was rudely reminded of why
she had come.

Kohanah had not eaten since yesterday!

Shame washed through Marilla . . . for the way Kohanah
and the other warriors were being treated. Prison life was
intolerable. The climate was humid, the white man's food
was strange to the Kiowa, and the cells were filthy and
uncomfortable. *No* one deserved to live like this. Marilla
was convinced that these Kiowa were wrongly imprisoned,
for they had only fought for their rights, the same as any
man who was guided by values and pride!

Forgetting her shawl, letting it flutter away from her,
Marilla went to her knees on the sandy floor and threw
aside the napkin that covered the food in the basket. "I've
brought you fresh bread." She grabbed a slender loaf still
hot from the oven.

She had become quite a skilled cook since her mother's
death a year ago. Her father was pleased more often than
not with what she presented him each evening on the
supper table. She was just as pleased, though she wanted
more out of life than to be a substitute wife for her father.

Marilla longed to teach. One day she would. . . .

Getting to her feet, Marilla pushed the slender loaf of
bread through the bars and looked heavy-lashed up at
Kohanah, who towered over her with his six-foot height.
"It's still hot, Kohanah," she said softly, an eagerness in
her voice. She also secretly wished to please him in every
way. "Eat it now while you can enjoy it the most."

Aware that she was still being scrutinized by Kohanah,
Marilla felt a blush rising to her cheeks. She refrained
from turning her eyes bashfully away this time, instead
returned his gaze, seeing in him what she admired . . .

and, yes, loved. He had fine classical features. A striking figure of a young man, he was tall and lean, yet powerful and fully developed.

He was lithe and surely knew beyond doubt of his great strength and vigor. He stood perfectly at ease. In his face there was a calm and goodwill, and intelligence. His dark hair was drawn close to the scalp and his braids were worn long down his perfectly straight back, and wound with strips of colored cloth.

Kohanah wore tight-fitting, fringed leggings and a fringed buckskin jacket that went over his head. His high moccasins were made of the softest, cream-colored skins. On each instep there was a bright disk of beadwork—an eight-pointed star, red and pale blue on a white field—and there were bands of beadwork around the soles and ankles. The flaps of his leggings were wide and richly ornamented with blue, red, green, white, and lavender beads.

Deep-set and so brown they looked almost black, Kohanah's eyes were filled with many sorts of passions, so many that Marilla had yet to experience. There was a look of bemused and infinite tolerance in his eyes, and Marilla had to wonder how any white men could have ever hated him, or those like him. Their hatred was so great that they tormented Kohanah and his people until the Kiowa were forced to fight back . . . to kill. . . .

It had taken only the meeting of Marilla and Kohanah's eyes for them to know the destiny that must somehow be theirs, no matter what had drawn them together. That they were together was all that mattered. . . .

Marilla felt ill at ease, with Kohanah yet to accept the bread. She dropped to her knees again and gestured toward the rest of the food. "If you don't want the bread, perhaps the cheese, or grapes?" she said, her voice soft, her eyes pleading. "Kohanah, you must eat *something*."

Kohanah sat back on his haunches, balancing himself on his heels, Indian-fashion. "I will take the bread," he said thickly, smiling at Marilla when she quickly thrust the bread between the bars again, his hand grazing hers as he accepted the warm loaf.

He could feel her flinch with the touch and knew that it was not because of any distaste for him, as an Indian. He knew that it did not matter that their skin color and customs were so different. They had learned quickly not to let such differences stand in the way of their friendship . . . a friendship cherished now and, hopefully, forevermore.

When she reacted so to his touch, he knew that it was because of feelings being ignited between them, as does lightning charge the clouds!

"Your father did not see you take the bread?" Kohanah asked, lifting it to just beneath his nose, where he enjoyed its fresh aroma. His gaze fell upon the other foods placed neatly in the basket. "Did your father not see you take the other foods? He would not approve, Tsonda, my beautiful light-haired woman."

Marilla lifted a bunch of grapes from the basket and let them rest in the palm of her hand, having grown accustomed to her Kiowa name, Tsonda, thinking it so lovely. She adored Kohanah's name, which meant "swift" in English.

"I brought only the bread from my own kitchen this time," she said, placing the grapes back in the basket, seeing that Kohanah was content enough for now with the bread. "I did not dare take anything else from our supplies or father *would* begin to notice. This time I went to the fort kitchen and mingled with the rest of the women as though I were one of them. I took food that is prepared each day and given to the women who bring it to you who are imprisoned. There is less risk this way, Kohanah. The other times I sneaked in while the guard had carelessly slipped away, it was at a high risk. If the guard had returned, I could have been locked in the dungeon without him even knowing it."

"Kohanah finds it hard to understand why the women were assigned such a task of feeding those of us who are imprisoned here," he said in a growl. "This terrible place is not fit for women to enter! It is not fit for the Kiowa!" He bit off a chunk from the bread and began chewing it angrily.

A flush rose up Marilla's neck, causing her face to become hot with renewed shame. Her gaze moved about slowly, seeing the rot and decay, the dampness oozing from the pores of the stone walls. She could feel the dampness. She could almost *taste* it!

"The women asked to do this for you," she finally said. "It is the *least* the women can do for you. It is not a pleasant thing to think about . . . all of you placed here like a . . . like a penned in pack of wild dogs."

Kohanah swallowed the bite of bread. Its taste was not as pleasant to him as its smell, but it eased the hungry, gnawing ache at the pit of his stomach. "From the very first you were not afraid," he said. His eyes filled with fire as he watched for Marilla's expression to reveal, perhaps, more truths to him than her words. "You did not look upon me and my warriors as 'savages'? Did not the other women? That ugly word has become a brand, burning clean through to my people's hearts."

Marilla paled, hating the word "savage." It sounded even crueler coming from Kohanah. "I am not sure about the other women," she said softly. "Perhaps they felt that you should be treated more kindly because they are Christians."

She willed her eyes to stay locked with his, though she was not sure if she should say what was only moments away from being said.

But she knew that he must already know her feelings for him. *Saying* them should not be all that hard. Between them a trust was already formed.

Surely even more than *that* . . .

"As for myself?" she murmured. "Why do I do this? It's because I see you as someone special. I see a gentleness about you . . . a *presence* that says you are no criminal!"

She lowered her eyes. "I am not explaining myself clearly enough," she murmured, his steady gaze having unnerved her. "Though I plan to be a teacher one day, I find it hard to put my true feelings into words while with you."

Marilla's insides became suddenly warm when she felt a hand on her cheek. Kohanah's hand! Never had he touched her in such an intimate way. Always before it had been by pure accident, when their hands would touch upon exchange of food.

But he had never touched her because he wanted to.

Slowly lifting her chin, Marilla scarcely breathed as she allowed herself once more to look into Kohanah's eyes. There was such warmth . . . such kindness . . . such understanding. Was there even something more? Something akin to passion? Did she . . . *could* she . . . arouse such excitement in him?

Yet even if she did, weren't such emotions futile, even *wrong*?

She did not wish to have to draw his hand away just yet. She could not deny that she enjoyed his touch, which stirred such delicious sensations within her! She wished such feelings could last forever!

"Tsonda, you care," Kohanah said thickly.

"You know that I do," Marilla said, her pulse racing.

"Kohanah thinks you are beautiful," he said, leaning closer to her so that his words did not travel any farther than Marilla. He feared showing his feelings for a white woman. He feared being chided by his fellow warriors . . . being shot by the white man.

Marilla was taken aback by his confession. She was at a loss for words, then smiled adoringly up at him. "I hoped that you would think so," she whispered, drawing her hair back from her face, having momentarily become careless by revealing her true identity to the other women around her. A scolding from her father was the last thing on her mind. Kohanah had sole possession of her thoughts, as well as her heart, at this moment.

"You are beautiful not only outside but inside as well," Kohanah said, smoothing his thumb beneath the softness of her chin. "You understand the Kiowa and that warring is a sacred business. It has always been that way among my people. But the white man has changed that. In peace councils the Kiowa were lured by the promise of gifts. Because we accepted them, the very foundations of the old way of life of the Kiowa were shattered. That is why we tried warring just one more time with your people. So much depended on it."

"And now?" Marilla dared to ask. "What of those of your people who are not imprisoned? What will happen to them?"

Kohanah eased his hand away from her face and drew it back through the bars. He picked at the bread, his eyes troubled as he watched crumbled pieces fall to the floor where roaches scrambled after them. To the white man he was no better than the insects, and this made an emptiness assail him.

One day . . .

"*Atanta*, I am disappointed with how my people are now coping with the loss of their better warriors," he said hoarsely. "It is the beginning of the spring moon, which the Kiowa call *pai-aganti*, the time of hot weather soon, the time when the Kiowa begin making plans for the sacred Sun Dance."

Kohanah spoke in a monotone, trying not to reveal his deeply hurt emotions. "But the great tribal ceremony of the Kado, Sun Dance, which is commonly celebrated annually when the down appears on the cottonwoods, will surely be postponed with the best of the Kiowa warriors imprisoned. The Taime, the sacred idol, the Sun Dance doll, must be kept hidden from the white man, or it, too, will be taken from us. Without it, the vital element in the Sun Dance ritual, the dance cannot be performed."

Kohanah's words trailed off as he saw that Marilla was becoming troubled, continually looking over her shoulder. Seeing that many of the women were leaving the room, his insides grew tight. Marilla would have to leave soon, also!

Marilla had listened intently to Kohanah, touched deeply by what he had said, but out of the corner of her eye she was seeing that the women were departing. She did not have much longer. And once she left, she could not return again until the next day.

If even then . . .

Her eyes searched desperately inside Kohanah's cell,

wondering where he might place his food so that the bugs would not devour it before *he* did. She eyed the checkered napkin that she had used to cover the food. Anxiously she spread it out and began placing the food on it, then drew the corners together and tied them.

"Take this," she said, shaping the bundle so that it could fit lengthwise through the bars. "The napkin should protect what I have brought you for a while at least."

She reached for the jar of perfumed water. "This is to refresh you," she said, handing it to him.

Glancing across her shoulder, she saw that only a few women remained in the large, airless room. "I don't have much time, Kohanah," she said solemnly.

She lifted the shawl up from the floor, cringing when she saw a black water bug clinging to its fringe. Until she moved to Florida, she had never seen such huge bugs. In New York, where her father had taken a hiatus from his law practice to do his duty with the United States Cavalry, the bugs were large, but never *this* size.

Giving her shawl a quick shake, she sighed with relief when the bug fell to the floor and scampered away.

"Must you leave already?" Kohanah asked, his eyes silently pleading.

"If I am to be able to come again tomorrow I must leave before I am caught today," Marilla said, placing the shawl about her face. She watched the scurry of roaches and water bugs at Kohanah's moccasin-clad feet and became sickened at heart. She set her jaw firmly, suddenly seized with a determination never felt before.

"Damn it if I am going to worry about being caught this time," she said, jerking the shawl away from her shoulders. "I am going directly to Father to argue your case. The fort grounds are large. Surely arrangements can be made for you to be outdoors at least *some* of the time. These conditions you live under are . . . are deplorable and *inhumane*!"

She stomped her foot with this last remark. "Kohanah, I *shall* go to my father. Now!" she insisted hotly.

Kohanah's insides grew cold. He placed the food and

water on the floor and reached through the bars and grabbed Marilla's wrists, gently holding her in place. "No. You must not do this," he said dryly. "You will endanger our times together. Your father will be too angry with you for having disobeyed him to listen to your plea."

He glanced over his shoulder at the wall that was shadowed by dusky gloom behind him. "But tomorrow when you come, could you bring a small piece of a buffalo skin and paints in your basket? *Gyaguatda*—I make pictures. I paint," he said, his voice cracking with emotion.

His eyes implored her. "The worst of this imprisonment is the inactivity. While I was free and was not on my horse riding the plains, I was in my dwelling, painting. I long to paint now. I love painting almost as much as warring."

He again turned his gaze toward the wall. Marilla looked in the direction of his vision, and as he released his hold on her wrists and stepped aside so that he could give her a plain full view, she was able to make out some roughed-out sketches in the shadows, on the walls, looking as though they had been done with the chalky fragments of fallen stone from the walls.

She stepped closer, seeing so much talent in the drawings of a horse and an Indian sitting proudly astride it.

"My word!" she gasped. "You did this? You have such *talent*. I did not notice before—"

Kohanah interrupted her. "It was not there," he said thickly. "I did this today. Now I hunger for true paints and skins!"

Marilla still marveled over the sketches. "You are a true artist," she said, her face beaming. "I shall arrange for you to be able to draw *many* paintings. Somehow I *shall*, Kohanah."

She delighted in having something special to do for him besides plead his and his warriors' case with her father. She circled her fingers around the bars of his cell. "Are you the only artist in your tribe?" she asked anxiously.

"No. Many have such talents," he said, looking beyond her, from cell to cell, feeling a deep sadness for his confined comrades. "Through good times and bad, the Kiowa have always been keenly interested in keeping track of our history, to reinforce a sense of tribal identity. Calendar histories are painted on buffalo skins by an artist of the tribe. Each year-long saga is depicted in two panels . . . one recalling an event of the winter, the other showing a summer incident. Wintertime entries are drawn above a black bar symbolizing a dead blade of grass. Summer occurrences are depicted above an image of the sacred medicine lodge in which the annual Sun Dance is held.''

"That . . . that is so beautiful,'' Marilla said in a low gasp. "Kohanah, tomorrow you will have paints and skins. Even perhaps a hope of some sort of freedom. I will do the best that I can.''

"I only ask for paints and skins.''

"I know. But that is not enough for *me*.''

"You will endanger everything by asking.''

"I know. But chances must be taken sometimes.''

Aware that time was passing much too quickly, Marilla knew that she must say another farewell, but hopefully this time for only a short while. Surely her father would listen to her pleas for the Kiowa. He had already toyed with the idea of having them released from the dungeon to build their own barracks in which to live.

Marilla would just have to slip in a firm reminder. . . .

"Kohanah, I *will* bring you skins and paints,'' she once more reassured him.

When he reached through the bars and grabbed her hand and momentarily held it while his eyes spoke so much unsaid to her, she felt as though she might melt right on the spot.

"Kohanah's heart will be lonely until you come again,'' he said huskily. "The night will be long.''

Feeling a blush scorching her cheeks, Marilla stared up at Kohanah for a moment, then eased her hand free, grabbed her basket, and hurried away from him. She was filled with much wonder.

Wonder of him . . . wonder of her*self* . . .

Then something grabbed her full attention, making her footsteps falter. From somewhere close by, an Indian was praying aloud. It tore at Marilla's heart . . . at her inner *being*, for there was something inherently sad in the sound, some merest hesitation upon the syllables of sorrow.

The prayer began in a high and descending pitch, exhausting the Indian's breath to silence; then again and again, and always in the same intensity of effort, of something that was, and was not, like urgency in the human voice.

The Indian seemed beyond the reach of time. . . .

Marilla swallowed hard, moved almost to tears. Ducking her head, she rushed from the dungeon, sadness overwhelming her, yet reaffirming to a fevered pitch her determination to help Kohanah. . . .

Two

The fragrance of apple pie was sweet in the air as Marilla eagerly set the dining table. She had placed a faded tablecloth on the meager oak table used for dining, and had set the table with the odds and ends of tableware supplied by the United States Cavalry for those who lived at the fort, the Pratts' expensive belongings having been left in New York and their house closed down until their return. Two candles were lit, their soft light shimmering in the room just now shadowing with dusk.

Her golden hair drawn back from her face, secured with a blue satin bow to match her blue cotton dress with white eyelet decorating its bust line and the cuffs of her sleeves, Marilla went to the parlor and lit a branch of candles. She turned and eyed the door eagerly, awaiting her father's arrival.

"Where *is* he?" she worried aloud, going to the window, to draw back the sheer white curtain.

She peered into the gloom, forcing her eyes not to look toward the high walls of the dungeon. She hated to envision Kohanah there, confined. It tore at her heart. Hopefully after tonight he would have some hope of partial freedom!

Looking in the opposite direction from where the dungeon sat looking like some dark sentinel, she could see many log cabins such as the one in which she and her father made temporary residence, those occupied by the other cavalry officers and their families.

Looking farther still, she saw the soldiers' barracks on the far side of the fort, built close to the high fortress walls that closed everyone in from the ocean on one side, palm trees on the other. She leaned closer to the window, hearing the steady beat of the ocean, as waves washed up onto the shore close by like some mighty pulse beat.

Of late she'd had fantasies of one day walking along the sandy shore with Kohanah.

Hand in hand they would walk . . .

"Daughter, are you daydreaming again?"

Marilla's heart lurched as the familiar voice of her father drew her quickly from her momentary thoughts of Kohanah. Letting the curtain flutter from between her fingers, she turned slowly around and smiled at him. After tonight he would know whom she had been daydreaming about the several times he had caught her.

Marilla's eyes swept quickly over him before she responded to his sudden appearance in the room. She again saw her father as so tall and masterful, with only a faint sprinkling of gray now appearing at his temples where his hair hung dark to the unbuttoned white collar of his shirt. His blue eyes were friendly, his face narrow and thin, with a nose quite crooked from having been broken during a fall from a horse during his youth.

He wore no set uniform because Florida was too hot for such attire. He wore a white shirt with loose flowing sleeves, and snug gray denim breeches, sporting belted pistols at his waist. His black boots shone as though freshly waxed.

Oh, but if only he would understand what Marilla was about to ask of him! He *did* have a heart of gold. He wanted the best for everyone, even the Indians, for more than once he had voiced this aloud to her. Now was the time to see just how much he *was* concerned!

But first she would serve him the special supper she had prepared for him.

Trying not to show her nervousness about what lay just ahead, when she would reveal her innermost feelings and thoughts to her father, Marilla lightheartedly rushed across the room and embraced him. "Father, you're finally home," she murmured, always cherishing his closeness. Since her mother's death, he was all that she had.

Except now for Kohanah . . .

"I've been late before," Richard Henry Pratt said, amused. "Why is tonight any different? Why, Marilla, I can even feel your heart pounding quite pronounced against my chest. Can my daughter miss me that much?"

His nose twitched as he became aware of the aroma of apple pie drifting from the kitchen. It seemed that his daughter had something up her sleeve to have gone to the extra bother of baking a pie today. He knew the recent heat had kept her from the kitchen more oft than not and he had understood.

Why a pie today, then, when it was hotter than usual?

Surely it was enough that she had awakened earlier this morning to prepare the bread that was needed. In this heat, pie was a damn luxury, to say the least.

His mind drifted back to the dungeon. He had just left it and its stifling heat, and the nape of his neck bristled with shame. The Indians were suffering more than was necessary in that damn hellhole. Something had to be done. And soon!

Marilla drew away from her father, knowing that he was too intelligent a man to fool for too long. Being an attorney by profession he seemed to know how to look into one's mind *and* soul. So the charade she was playing would be short-lived unless she behaved much less anxiously than she was at the moment.

Swinging the skirt of her fully gathered dress around, Marilla began walking toward the kitchen. "It is only that I am hungry, Father," she said, giving him a quick glance over her shoulder. "Shall we eat? Surely you are as hungry as I. Has it not been another busy day for you? You are not one to sit idly by, doing nothing."

"Nor are you, I see," Richard Henry said, chuckling low, now *knowing* that she was up to something. She hadn't acted so nervous since the day she had sneaked a baby skunk into her bedroom at age six, while living in their palatial mansion on the outskirts of the city of New York, on a great stretch of land where wild animals prevalently roamed. The smell of the animal had given her away that time.

But *now*? At her age, surely anything could be on her mind. She was restless. She needed to be back in New York.

But not quite yet. There was much still to be done here in Florida! Starting tomorrow!

Marilla sensed her father's mind working overtime, now surely suspecting that she had more than food on her mind. It was hard to keep anything from him. She smiled to herself when she thought of the time she had sneaked the baby skunk into her room. Lordy, she had smelled for weeks! He had *never* let her live *that* down. Ever since, he had teased her into more mischievous acts than not!

But this time there was nothing mischievous about what she was up to. What she had planned to do for Kohanah was being done from the heart!

In the dismal, small spaces of the kitchen, light from the flickering candles on the table her only guide, Marilla plucked the pot roast from its pan and arranged it along with carrots and potatoes on a platter and set it in the middle of the table. She poured a cup of coffee for her father, feeling suddenly nervous beneath his watchful eye as he stood in the doorway, unbuckling his gun belt.

Slowly she turned to him. She smiled sheepishly up at him, then went and pulled a chair from beneath the table and offered it to him. "Father, did I not say that I was hungry?" she said softly. "Pot roast sounded grand, so I prepared it. It's good that it is not only my favorite but also yours."

Draping his gun belt on a peg on the paneled wall, Richard Henry nodded in agreement. "Yes, our favorite," he said, easing down onto the chair. "Just like apple pie is our favorite? Honey, you've never taken more than two bites of apple pie in your life. You detest it. And if my nose is right, isn't that an apple pie sitting on the window-sill, cooling?''

''The oven was heated up from baking bread so I used the opportunity to bake the pie for you,'' Marilla said, moving smoothly to her chair, to sit down. ''I had the apples a neighbor had brought to us. I had to use them, or they would spoil in this wretched heat.''

She spread a napkin on her lap and looked in an annoyed fashion at her father. ''And besides,'' she said, ''why do you question why I do something special for you? Don't I enough times so that you would not wonder so about it? I do try to make you happy . . . make you miss mother less.''

Richard Henry's smile faded at the mention of his wife. His lieutenant duties had not entirely filled the gap left by her death. But Marilla! She *had* been a godsend. No daughter could have ever been as attentive. He would see to it that she got on with her life when they returned to New York. He was trying to find some time each day now to tutor her in the skills of eventually being a teacher. She would be the best! It was her heart's desire to do so!

''You do yourself proud in everything you do,'' he finally said, spreading his own napkin on his lap. He led them in a small prayer of thanksgiving, then carved the pot roast and placed a slice on Marilla's plate, then his own. The first bite proved that she was, well, *almost* as good as her mother in the kitchen!

He smiled over at her as they consumed the meal in silence, yet with an air of strange apprehension lying heavy in the air. It was in the anxiousness of Marilla's eyes as she kept glancing over at him. It was in the nervousness of her smile and in the stiffness of her shoulders.

None of this was like Marilla, unless she had mischief up her sleeve . . . and she was becoming almost too old to behave in what one could define as a mischievous way. Whatever she was up to had to do with something a girl of her age would be about.

If they lived in New York, he would believe that she had found a young gentleman friend of whom she had become enamored. But this was Florida! There were only soldiers, and Marilla had not spoken openly of any of them. None had come forth, asking about her.

And then there were the Indians!

Richard Henry stopped his fork halfway to his mouth, his insides growing numb, now recalling the strange daydreaming look that Marilla had carried around with her these past few weeks. It had begun just after the arrival of the Indians!

But she had not been allowed to go into the dungeon, and they were not allowed to venture out. How, then, could it be that a young Indian warrior had caught her eye?

Laying his fork down on the table, apprehension growing inside him, Richard Henry was recalling a time when Marilla *had* fully viewed the Indians. On the day of their arrival in Fort Marion! And he was now recalling an Indian whose attention had been openly drawn to Marilla, and hers to *him*. The young Kohanah! Upon first viewing of one another, there had been something written on both their faces. Richard Henry had seen it and had grown uncomfortable from the knowing. But he had cast thoughts of it aside after Kohanah and his comrades had been taken from view!

Had Marilla . . . seen him since? If so, when and how?

"Marilla, you did not spend this entire day cooking," Richard Henry said, drumming his fingertips nervously on the tabletop. "What did you do to pass the time away? I don't recall seeing you at all. Tell me. What did you do?"

His sudden question stirred guilt within Marilla, jolting her so much she dropped her fork. The clink it made against the plate, and then the shatter of the china as it split in two, made her grimace and gasp aloud. She had never been as jumpy! But she had never planned to plead an Indian's case before. And not just *any* Indian's . . . Kohanah's!

"Damn it," Richard Henry said, pushing his chair back with a start as the bits and pieces of the plate flew into the platter of meat and vegetables. "'Marilla, what on earth *is* the matter with you?"

He went to her and urged her from the chair, then

implored her with his eyes. "You may as well tell me now. No sense in beating around the bush any longer. My dear, has it ever been all that hard to confide in me? Why is it *now*? Did something happen today? Did some soldier . . .?"

He couldn't find the nerve to say "Indian."

Marilla's eyes widened into two pools of blue. "No!" she gasped, placing a hand to her throat. "Father, it's nothing like that. And if it were, I am very capable of taking care of myself. Though small, I pack a mighty punch!"

Richard Henry's eyes twinkled and his lips quivered into a smile. He took his cup from the table and went to the stove and poured himself a fresh cup of coffee. "Let's go into the parlor," he said, giving her a half-glance over his shoulder. "Let's sit by an open window. Just perhaps the night breeze blowing in from the ocean will give us a respite of sorts from the heat."

"Yes, perhaps," Marilla said, relieved to be able to leave the table mess behind at least until she composed herself and got the nerve to speak openly to her father.

She moved on ahead of him into the poor excuse of a room that was called a parlor, and went to the window and eased it open, then sat down on a faded overstuffed chair. She watched her father sit down opposite her, stretching his long, lean legs out onto a hassock, taking slow sips from his cup, his eyes never leaving her.

The candles were slowly dripping wax. The candles sputtered . . . sputtered. . . .

"Well?" Richard Henry finally said, lowering the cup, placing it on a table beside him. "Let's hear it. I think you've suffered through worries of what you want to tell me long enough."

Marilla's fingers worked nervously with the white eyelet that decorated the bust of her dress, only minimally aware of the cooler breeze now blowing through the window onto the upper lobes of her breasts where the dress dipped low in front. She felt cornered, yet it was of her own doing. If she did not speak openly now, she had only herself to blame. Her father was patiently waiting, quite attentive to her and her sudden strange mood.

Pushing herself up from the chair, Marilla began to pace the wooden planked floor, the petticoat rustling beneath the skirt of her dress sounding eerily much louder than it should in the strained silence of the small room.

"Marilla!" Richard Henry said, rising quickly to his feet. He placed his hands on her shoulders and stopped her and forced her eyes up to meet his. "I've had enough of this. If you don't tell me what's bothering you now, then I shall take it that you never intend to. I only hope and pray that whatever is bothering you isn't as bad as you are making it out to be. If I hear that someone has . . . has—"

Marilla saw that he was at his wit's end and that his patience had run thin. And she did not like it that he was again implying that perhaps someone had taken advantage of her.

Stopping him in midsentence by gently placing a hand to his lips, she squared her shoulders and looked boldly up at him. She had an idea that she was pale from her nervousness, but in the dim candlelight, surely he could not see all that much!

"Father, no one has approached me wrongly," she said softly. "Please believe me when I tell you that."

She eased her hand down from his lips and went to the window and stared through the darkness that had fallen in its black shroud, toward the dungeon. Perhaps if she continued looking at its hideousness she could get the courage to begin her argument for Kohanah and his comrades. Just envisioning Kohanah there, hot, uncomfortable, and fighting bugs and rats, was all that she needed to blurt out the reason for her behavior! He depended on *her*. She could not let him down.

"Father, I have not been totally obedient," she said, still looking out the window. The small windows positioned high on the dungeon walls were dark. That meant that Kohanah was sitting in the dark. Was the Indian that she had heard praying, still praying?

"Oh?" Richard Henry said, going to her side. "And what have you done?"

His gaze followed the line of her vision. Even in the darkness he, too, could see the dungeon. Again he was reminded of Kohanah and how he had looked at Marilla.

Oh, God, was it the Indian who was to blame for her confusion this night? If so, what *then*? Marilla was old enough to know her mind. If she felt strongly enough about something, it would be almost impossible to dissuade her!

Marilla spun around on a heel and totally, determinedly, faced her father. "Please listen without getting upset," she said, gently placing a hand on his arm. "Please listen and try to understand. You always have in the past. Please do so now, though this time I am asking something quite different from anything I have ever asked of you before."

"Honey, you know that I always listen," Richard Henry said thickly. "Now is no exception. I'm here to listen. Always. That's what fathers are for, you know."

Marilla's lashes momentarily lowered over her eyes, and then she again looked determinedly upward. "Father, I have made daily visits to the dungeon," she said, feeling his arm stiffening against her hand. "I have been going to speak with Kohanah . . . to exchange lessons in languages with each other. I have been taking him food. He is such a special person. He deserves better than what he has gotten at the hands of the white man! Father, if you will recall, being a lieutenant in the cavalry, you fought just as valiantly for what you believed in. The Indians did the same! Only they lost. Must their punishment be so inhumane? So horribly unjust? They deserve at least a decent place to stay while imprisoned!"

She flung a hand in the direction of the window, gesturing toward the dungeon. "That . . . that . . . place is a hellhole. You know that. You've even spoken of such feelings yourself. Surely something can be done! Can't you see that they are given better quarters in which to live? You've mentioned having barracks built. Why not do it now?"

Richard Henry began to speak, but Marilla interrupted, determined to have her complete say before being stopped. She might never be given the same opportunity again. She had gone behind her father's back . . . the first time, ever, for her to do so in such a flagrant way.

"Father, the warfare for the Kiowa was primarily a matter of disposition rather than of survival," she continued, her cheeks glowing from the courage she had found to speak so openly of her intense feelings for the Indians. "And they never understood the grim, unrelenting advance of the United States Cavalry. It was their sense of destiny, courage, and pride that made them continue to fight for their rights. And what did it get them? Prison life that is intolerable, food that is strange, and Kohanah says the inaction of being so confined is even worse than those things!"

Her heart pounding, her knees weak, Marilla suddenly stopped her speech and looked wide-eyed at her father, now awaiting perhaps an explosion. But it was a hurt deep within his blue eyes that made her know that he would not yell or even scold her. His anger with her never came all that easily. She was glad!

"So are you finished?" Richard Henry said in his smooth, easy tone of voice. "Can I have my say now?"

Marilla's lips trembled into a soft laugh, relieved that he was the sort to listen . . . to *care*. Yes, he was a man one could idolize . . . could love with all one's heart. She was so glad that he was her father!

"Yes, I believe I've said almost everything," she said, smiling up at him, yet knowing that she still had to ask for skins and paints for Kohanah. Paints were easily accessible, for her father dabbled in painting himself on days he had time to spend with such a passion.

But acquiring skins might be hard. She wondered if Kohanah might be just as happy with a canvas? Her father had plenty of those in his possession.

"Then I *shall* say my piece," Richard Henry said, touching Marilla's cheek gently, then lowering a kiss to her brow. He went to the window and drew the sheer curtain aside, inhaling the brisk breeze filled with the sweet scent of the sea. "Honey, though you went against my wishes by going to the dungeon to visit the Indian, I can see why you did it. You are a girl with many emotions

. . . with passions. You are not the sort who could sit idly by and see anyone done wrong to. That is good. Such qualities in a woman are to be admired.''

He turned his eyes slowly to her, seeing that she was watching him, seeming to be barely breathing, she was so anxious to hear his reaction to what she had done. "But there's more to this than what you've actually said, isn't there?" he asked, his voice low, yet his words quite pronounced. "You have very special feelings for this one Indian in particular, don't you? Does it even go as far . . . as far . . . as loving him? Have you, in your innocence, allowed that to happen?"

Marilla felt heat rising to her cheeks as she blushed. "Father!" she said, forcing herself to sound shocked. "How could you think such a thing? We . . . we are friends. Only . . . friends . . ."

She could not just yet confess to loving Kohanah. Her father would surely forbid *that*. And Kohanah had not said that he loved her. Telling her that she was beautiful was as far as such truths from him had gone. It was no lie to tell her father that they were not in love. Perhaps Kohanah did not love her at all. Perhaps he was using her, to get what he wanted by complimenting her in such a way. . . .

Marilla's insides grew cold. Oh, Lord, she had never considered the fact that Kohanah might be . . . using her. . . .

"Then that is all that I have to hear," Richard Henry said thickly. He drew Marilla into his arms. "Honey, I have always trusted your judgment." He chuckled low. "Well, maybe not always. The skunk smell still clings to you, you know!"

Marilla was still wondering about Kohanah's true intentions, then scoffed at herself for even thinking such nonsense. Her father's mention of the skunk sank in. She drew quickly away from him, her eyes wide.

Then she laughed, recognizing his way of easing the tension in the room with his subtle joking. "Father, I have scrubbed so often!" she teased back.

Then she eased back into his arms and hugged him, placing her cheek against his powerful chest. "Thank you so much for being so understanding and being the sort of father who listens instead of shouts. I feel as though I can talk to you about anything!''

"But this time it just took a mite longer, huh?" Richard Henry said, caressing her back.

"Well, yes, I guess so," Marilla said, again easing from his arms. "But this time, what I needed to say was much different from anything else I've ever spoken to you about before."

"Well, we will work on that," Richard Henry said, walking back into the kitchen. He began gathering things from the table. "Let's finish this conversation while we do dishes, shall we?"

A kettle of water had been heating on the stove. Marilla grabbed a pot holder and took the kettle from the stove and poured steaming water into a basin. "Then after we finish the dishes you must sample my pie," Marilla said, feeling the bond between father and daughter strengthening now, moment to moment.

"Now, about Kohanah," Richard Henry said, dropping a bar of soap into the water. "What would you like to see done about him and his warriors? You see, I have had my own ideas. Let's work them out together. Perhaps we can come up with some logical answers. . . .''

Marilla looked up at her father, tears silvering the corners of her eyes. He *was* a man of heart. The Kiowa were lucky that he was in charge of their destiny, not someone who hated even the mention of the word *Indian*. . . .

Three

Listening to the incessant pounding of hammers in the distance, each blow causing a deep pride to swell within her heart, Marilla was packing her picnic basket with as many special edibles as possible. Today she was going openly, to join the other women, giving food to the Indians.

It was a special day in many ways. The Indians were putting the finishing touches to their barracks!

For several days now while Marilla's father had been overseeing the Indians building the barracks in which they would be living, he had silently observed Kohanah, making judgments on him. Could he or could he not be trusted with Marilla? She was determined to continue with this friendship that had begun between them.

After seeing how Kohanah worked so diligently, obeying orders, treating Lieutenant Pratt with respect and dignity, Richard Henry had decided that, yes, this was an Indian who understood the white man's rules. Some of those rules governed the ways in which the Indians treated the white *women*.

Kohanah could be trusted. . . .

"Still only in the confines of the fort," Marilla whispered to herself, frowning. "But that is better than noth-

29

ing. Today we will share food from my picnic basket *openly*. We shall celebrate the partial freedom of the Indians, *openly*.''

A smile crinkled her nose as she slipped one orange, then two, into the wicker basket. She viewed the rest of the food arranged neatly at the bottom, and nodded, knowing that this was adequate.

But if only it was a *true* picnic, enjoyed in a carefree way on the beach, alone, not inside the high, threatening walls of a fort, in view of everyone, without privacy.

Perhaps one day . . .

Smoothing a blue-checkered napkin over the food, Marilla carried the basket into her bedroom and stood before the mirror, examining her appearance. Her blue gingham dress made the blue of her eyes more pronounced, the white lace bordering its bodice faintly revealed the upper lobes of her breasts where they lay heaving in her anxiousness of the moments ahead.

Flipping her hair back from her shoulders, she let it tumble in gleaming golden streamers down her perfect back, glad not to have to hide it beneath a dreaded shawl. She placed a hand on her hip, studying her waistline, relieved that the thick gathers of her dress did her no harm there. Her waist still looked as tiny!

Then she viewed her face more closely, touching it here and there, frowning. Would Kohanah see her as beautiful once he viewed her in the brighter light of the outdoors? He had only seen her in the semidarkness of the dungeon. Would he think her skin too pale in comparison with that of the Kiowa maidens he had known back at the reservation? Would he think her eyes too colorless?

So wanting to please him, Marilla bit her lower lip to bloom at least *it* into color.

Taking one last, lingering look at herself, trying to see herself as Kohanah would see her, Marilla felt pleased enough with her appearance. She had dressed in her loveliest dress only a step below those that were silk, and she had brushed her hair until it glistened. He could surely ask for no more than that from the woman who adored him!

The basket hanging heavy at her side, her fingers circled

tightly about its handle, Marilla rushed from the bedroom
through the parlor and to the outdoors where the sky was a
brilliant blue and the air was filled with the pleasant, fresh
aroma of the sea. Gulls wheeled overhead on steady wing,
the sound of the surf was soothingly calm. A storm the
previous night had cooled the temperature; the humidity
had dropped.

"A perfect day!" Marilla sighed, then looked in the far
distance and viewed the log barracks that were nearing
completion, the Indians clamoring around them, putting
the finishing touches to the windows and doors. Even the
roofs had been neatly shaked!

Never loving her father as much as she did now, never
having felt such pride in him before, Marilla reviewed in
her mind how this had all come about as she walked
toward the hum of activity around the Indians' barracks. It
had all begun that night while doing dishes with her father
after having disclosed to him that she had made close
acquaintance with Kohanah.

She and her father had discussed the Indians' plight in
general, not only Kohanah's. Her father had spoken of his
feelings to Marilla, saying that the task at hand at this fort
was going to be that of educating, not punishing. The
Indians had already paid by the loss of their land . . . the
loss of their freedom to hunt for the buffalo!

Lieutenant Richard Pratt would see that the Indians were
moved out of the dungeons and into barracks they would
build themselves. He would put them to work as laborers,
for *pay*. He would enlist the help of the white women to
teach the Indians to read and write English.

Nor would he ask them to forswear their past! He would
not only give Kohanah skins and paints to draw pictures
narrating and explaining Indian life, he would give these
painting tools to all of the Indians who wanted them.

Kohanah had been chosen by his warriors to be the one
who would paint while imprisoned. He was the greatest
artist of them all. His drawings would be valuable!

Marilla had purposely stayed away from Kohanah these
past several days while the barracks were being erected.
She had not wanted to act all that anxious to see him. Her

father might begin to suspect her true feelings for the handsome Indian, and that could prove disastrous. At this moment, he saw her as only wanting to use her teaching skills, to practice on the Indians, before entering into teaching full time once she was back in New York.

It was to Marilla's advantage that her father continue thinking this. One day Kohanah surely would be free. Marilla longed to think of a future with him as a wife, not as a teacher. There was now no doubt in her mind that she loved him, totally!

Feeling eyes on her, following her approach, Marilla found Kohanah amid all of the laborers. His eyes were branding her, silently claiming her as his, and in them Marilla saw that without doubt he approved of her appearance today. And she did his also!

With his fringed buckskin shirt removed, ah, but did not his bare copper shoulders gleam so beautifully? They were rippling with muscles as he resumed hammering. His hair was braided long down his back; the fringed buckskin breeches he wore looked as though they had been poured on him, they were so tight and revealing.

All of this . . . his handsomeness, his virility, his mystique, made Marilla so desire him! Did she even dare approach him to say anything to him? Would he . . . would her *father* realize her true feelings in the way she spoke his name . . . in the way she would look up into his eyes, towered over by his tall height?

"Look grand enough, Marilla?" Richard Henry said, meeting her approach. He wore his usual white shirt with its loose flowing sleeves, denim breeches that fit the shape of his legs, and his holstered pistols. "*We* could even make residence in those barracks and be happy. The Indians did themselves right proud!"

"*You* did yourself right proud," Marilla said, smiling softly up at her father as they stopped to look at the Indian barracks together. "Father, no one else would have been as generous as you. You have to know that these Indians will repay you in kind, by being model prisoners."

"Well, we'll see, won't we?" Richard Henry said, squaring his shoulders. He looked in silence at the Indians, then slowly moved his gaze to Marilla, and to the picnic basket. "I see you were serious. You do intend to pursue your friendship with Kohanah."

His hand moved to a pistol and rested on it. "I hope I am wise in giving permission," he said dryly.

"Father, we've been through all of this before," Marilla fussed, her eyes snapping. "Even you agree that Kohanah is trustworthy . . . worthy of my attentions. He is eager to learn! Let me teach him."

"You will resume teaching Kohanah how to write and read today?" Richard Henry said, eyeing the napkin, wondering what was beneath it besides food. "Perhaps you have a book with you? Or perhaps pencil and paper?"

Nervously avoiding her father's eyes as he focused his full attention on her, Marilla nodded. "I have everything I need," she said, telling a white lie. She did not have to tell him exactly what was inside the basket. If he chose to believe there was a book, a pencil, and paper in it, let him.

Today she wished to do more pleasant things than teach someone to read and write. She just wanted to enjoy being with Kohanah. It would be their first time together without bars separating them!

Richard Henry shrugged casually. He dropped his hand down away from the pistol and kneaded his chin as he studied Kohanah, then Marilla. "Well, I guess there's no talking you out of what you want to do," he said hoarsely. "I shall never be a father who is accused of locking his daughter away to get my way with her. I trust your judgment. Make me proud, Marilla. Make me proud."

While Marilla watched, scarcely breathing, Richard Henry went to Kohanah and the other warriors. She watched eagerly as her father and the Indians exchanged conversation. When Kohanah picked up his shirt from the ground and slipped it over his head and began walking toward her, her knees became weak, her pulse raced. He was coming to her, while the other Indians began going to the women who had arrived with their respective baskets filled with food.

Did Kohanah come to her because he felt that he had been ordered to by the commander of this fort? Or did he actually want to? He was not smiling. He was walking with silent dignity toward her, his moccasin-hushed footsteps as quiet as a panther's. Even when he reached her and stood looking down at her, his eyes of fire still branding her, he did not speak.

Then when he spoke, it was like a voice of thunder, loud and pronounced, while the other Indian captives turned and watched, silent. "*Tsan*," he said. "*Atoya*?"

Not knowing what he had said, only glad that he had finally said *something*, Marilla smiled up at Kohanah. "Did father explain that I had a picnic lunch?" she asked, almost stammering, his nearness was so unnerving to her.

"Picnic? Kohanah does not understand the word 'picnic,' " he said, his voice lowering in pitch.

"Why, no, I should have known that you wouldn't. It is a custom of the white people, not the Kiowa," Marilla said, her fingers trembling, so moved by his eyes, the intensity of them, as he continued to look commandingly down at her. "But you do understand that my father gave me permission to share the food in my basket with you openly, don't you?"

"*Ho*, yes, Kohanah understands that he said that, but Kohanah does not understand why he would be so generous," he said, glancing over at Marilla's father. "Yet your father is like no white soldier in my experience of warring with the whites." He doubled a fist to his chest, resting it just above the heart. "He speaks with kindness from the heart. Kohanah shall always remember this. Always."

"Yes, Father is very kind and generous," Marilla said, looking proudly over at her father. Then she implored Kohanah with her eyes. "You have been painting on the skins that my father gave to you?"

"*Ho*," Kohanah said, nodding. "Many!"

"I would love to see them," Marilla said, her voice showing her anxiousness about everything that Kohanah said. "Will you show them to me? Perhaps when you get settled in your barracks?"

Kohanah frowned down at her. "It is not best," he said, afraid that she would not approve of the paintings. She would be appalled by the drawings of the atrocities of the white men against the Kiowa. This he was drawing so that no Kiowa would ever forget how their lives had been shamed!

"Why not?" Marilla asked, her voice shallow. "What could it hurt?"

"Perhaps one day," he said, choosing to give her hope that she would see them, instead of telling her flatly that she could not. It was best to keep her happy at all times.

Because of her, there was hope. . . .

Marilla eyed him speculatively, then turned with a flip of the skirt of her dress and looked over her shoulder at Kohanah. "Come on," she encouraged sweetly. "Let us sit in the shadow of the wall." She turned, momentarily stopping. "While relaxing and eating, perhaps I can persuade you to show me your paintings one day soon. I would so love to see them!"

Then, rushing onward, glad that he was at her side willingly, she walked with him toward the far fortress wall. But Marilla's insides grew suddenly cold as she felt eyes following her. When she glanced up, she saw that a guard was watching her with keen interest. His green, searching eyes revealed that this was surely not the first time he had watched her! But now it was more open. If he saw her as an Indian-lover, he could think she was fair game!

Jason Roark. Yes, she knew the man. He was among the soldiers who were not married and who hungered for the touch of a woman's flesh. He, along with the rest, had been confined for too long away from the fun offered by city life. Would he chance being shot by this fort's commander by choosing to approach Marilla? Did he believe that she was no longer unapproachable?

Feeling the coldness of his eyes mentally undressing her, Marilla hurried her steps. "I'm starved, Kohanah," she said, trying not to reveal that she was suddenly uncomfortable over this that she was doing because of one man's eyes saying what he did not have to say in words. She hurried to the cool shadow of the wall, the skirt of her dress and the froth of her petticoats bouncing about her ankles. "I shall show you just exactly what a picnic is, Kohanah!"

Marilla chose a spot and spread her linen napkin across the smooth sand. But with Jason Roark on guard duty, pacing the walkway on the high fortress wall, there was to be no privacy. Could there ever be privacy now, with the likes of Jason Roark seemingly awaiting the right moment to accost her? Was this plan to pursue friendship with Kohanah even a threat to Kohanah's life? If he was given cause to protect Marilla against a white man, would anyone understand . . . ? Would Jason Roark provoke trouble purposely to give him an opportunity to kill an Indian?

Not just *any* Indian! *Kohanah*!

A chill rode Marilla's spine, now recalling the times she had sneaked into the dungeon to be with Kohanah. She had always wondered where the guard was, allowing her to move about so easily. Now she recalled just who the guard had been—Jason Roark! He had most surely led her to believe that she was getting by with something when all along it had been he who had allowed it. He had been playing games with her all along. She now wondered when he would collect the debt that he surely thought she owed him. . . .

Would it be soon?

Would Kohanah be the one to suffer for her carelessness . . .?

The thrill of the moment, of this time with Kohanah, was now shadowed with fear *for* him. . . .

Four

࿓

Kohanah stood a few feet away from Marilla. The fortress gates were open, and from this vantage point he could openly view the ocean. Marilla stopped her picnic preparations to watch him, wondering what he was thinking about. Even through his buckskin shirt she could see that his shoulder muscles were tensely corded. His hands were clenched into fists, and his eyes were two points of fire. He most surely was thinking of his imprisonment, hating the white man for it.

"Kohanah?" Marilla said, going to him. She so wanted to take his hand, to let him know that she understood.

But she and Kohanah were not alone. Everything they did was in full view of everyone. Had her father so willingly let Kohanah be with her because he wanted to test the Indian . . . see if the Indian was truly trustworthy? Her father was already talking about going to the Indians' defense, asking that they be released soon. None had caused any problems at the fort. Most had taken their punishment quietly, willingly. If they could be this agreeable while imprisoned, maybe they were ready to accept what life handed them on the reservation!

"Kohanah, you are so quiet," Marilla persisted. Her

hair shimmered in the breeze. She licked her lips, removing the taste of saltwater. "Can't you enjoy yourself? It's been so terrible for you in that filthy, hot dungeon."

"Kohanah wants *total* freedom," he growled. He turned his head in a jerk and eyed her with fire. "My *tsa*, comrades! Inside their hearts they hunger for freedom also! They hunger for the feel of a horse beneath them . . . the great joy of riding a horse!"

Marilla lowered her eyes. "Yes, I know," she murmured. Then she slowly lifted her gaze, to challenge Kohanah's steady, stubborn stare. "In time, you and your *tsa*, comrades, will be free. I assure you of that. My father . . . he is going to see that you get your freedom, as soon as he can make others listen."

Kohanah laughed. "Listen?" he said sarcastically. "When does anyone listen to kind words about the Kiowa? Because no one did, Kohanah is imprisoned!" He flailed a hand in the air. "That is the way it has always been and always will be. There is no hope!"

Marilla grabbed his hand, no longer concerned over who might see her. Kohanah must never lose hope! If he did, his whole race could be endangered! "You must not speak like that," she said dryly. "There is always hope! As long as there are people like my father on this earth, there is hope for *you* and for your *people*, Kohanah."

When Marilla saw Kohanah's eyes soften in mood and take on a look of warm compassion, her insides became awash with a mushiness that was familiar to her of late and was always brought on by Kohanah.

He touched her so deeply with his eyes that she could hardly bear not being able to throw herself into his arms and embrace him. Until today bars had stood in their way. At this moment nothing stood between them but the fear of what might happen if they actually did take comfort in each other's arms.

"*Obaika*—you are always there, encouraging Kohanah. Kohanah thanks you," he said, aching to draw her into his arms, but not daring to do so. He would do nothing to endanger what he had already accomplished by pretending to travel the white man's road, being a model of vigorous, imaginative, and responsible citizenship.

He was going to do far more than disprove the widely held view that the Kiowa could not adapt to change. He would fight to prove that the Kiowa could adapt to change as strenuously as they formerly practiced war.

But they were cooperating intelligently *as Kiowa*, never to be mistaken for a white man's Indian!

"Kohanah, no thanks are needed," Marilla said, then turned and eyed the picnic basket still to be unloaded.

"But perhaps there is one thing you can do as a thank-you gesture," she said, smiling up at him.

"What is that?" Kohanah asked, forking an eyebrow.

"Help me eat the food I've brought for us," Marilla said, easing her hand from his, wishing she could hold on to him forever. "Let us have our picnic before it's time for you to go to your confinement in the barracks."

Kohanah chuckled beneath his breath, his mood lightening, so wanting to enjoy this rare moment with Marilla, the woman who haunted his dreams. She was already a part of him, too closely bonded for him to ever want to let her go.

Yet he knew that when he left this land of imprisonment to go back to the reservation, she could not go with him. She was only a part of his dreams, not a part of his actual future! That could never be. Never!

Casting thoughts of the future aside . . . a future that would not include Marilla . . . Kohanah sat down beside the napkin, which already displayed an arrangement of food. He eyed the cheese, bread, and fruit, not wishing for any of it. Hunger for food was not the cause for the ache gnawing at his insides.

It was for Marilla that he hungered. . . .

"Kohanah, I am so excited to know that you will no longer be staying in that dark, buggy dungeon," Marilla said, arranging food on a plate. She placed it before Kohanah, who was hugging his knees drawn up to his chest. "Tonight you will be sleeping on a bed, with fresh air blowing in from an open window. Your nights won't be as frightful now, will they?"

A thought of the past made Kohanah smile. He lowered his knees and placed the plate of food on his lap. "As a child Kohanah had many fretful nights in the tipi," he said, taking a bite of a peeled banana. He savored the sweetness on his tongue, then swallowed. "I am reminded of one time in particular."

"Tell me about it, Kohanah," Marilla said, arranging her skirt neatly about her; then she also began eating a banana. She was wide-eyed, attentive to what Kohanah had to say. She was oblivious of the cold green eyes watching her every move and of the other women offering their food to the Indians.

For now there was only Kohanah. . . .

"When I was little, my parents would tell me that if I didn't go to sleep they would call the owl to take me away," Kohanah said, looking dreamily into the distance, as though reliving the moment in time that he was talking about. "One night my parents told me to go to sleep, but I didn't. I wanted to stay up with the older people."

He laid the banana aside, chuckling. "My father said, 'All right, I am going to sing an owl song. Just watch through the door and you will see an owl,' " he said, his eyes twinkling. "Kohanah did. As father sang an owl song, I looked through the door. I saw something standing there, something with big eyes."

"Well? Was it an owl?" Marilla asked, laying her banana aside. She clasped her hands anxiously on her lap. "Was it?"

Kohanah laughed deeply, moving to rest himself on his haunches as he looked down at Marilla. "No, I know now that it was not an owl," he said. "It was my *cousin*. He was outside the tipi and heard my parents trying to make me go to sleep. He took some kind of a pan and painted it to look like an owl face. *That* is what I saw in the doorway."

Kohanah nodded slowly. "I did not know *then* that it was my cousin. I went to bed right away." He chuckled. "After that, whenever my father or mother sang that owl song, I went right to bed."

"When did you find out that your cousin had played the

trick on you?'' Marilla asked, laughing softly, thrilled by Kohanah's relaxed nature and openness.

"Many years later,'' Kohanah said. "You see, the Kiowa children were disciplined by frightening them in this manner. The owl is considered an exceedingly dangerous creature. It is said that looking at an owl can cause distortion of facial features and bring illness. Owls are regarded as malevolent ghosts of deceased persons, returning to earth to haunt and torment the living.''

Marilla grimaced. She curled her nose in distaste. "How utterly horrible,'' she gasped.

"But Kohanah now knows that it is only a myth about the owl,'' he said, scoffing. "But you might want to hear a *truth* of our people. The truth of Nuakoiahe, our Great Spirit.''

"I wish to know everything of your lovely people,'' Marilla said, nervously watching the other women disbanding. She had known that this time with Kohanah would be short, but never had she expected it to go so quickly.

"*Nuakoiahe*, meaning 'earth he made it,' is our Great Spirit,'' Kohanah said proudly. "To him is attributed the creation of the earth, its geographic features, and its human, plant, and animal inhabitants. The Creator started everything in the world. Everything belongs to him. When the Kiowa pray, they pray first to *him*. . . .''

Kohanah's words faded. He knew that time was drawing nigh for him to go to his barracks. Though it was good that he had a decent place to go to this night, he hated being there without Marilla!

"*Tsonda*, Kohanah wants to kiss you,'' he blurted, his face a sudden mask of passion. "Kohanah wants to make love to you. It is so hard to be with you and *not* kiss and caress you!''

Marilla's mouth went agape, and her heart skipped a beat; she was taken off guard by his sudden confession. She could feel his gaze move to capture the heaving of her breasts where they lay so snugly at the low-cut bodice of her dress. She could feel the heat of his eyes on her bare flesh as though he were actually touching her. She could see the passion that was engulfing him. She felt so helpless as her own passions became aroused by him.

"Kohanah, please . . ." she whispered, a blush hot on her cheeks. "I can hardly bear my want of you. Please do not make it worse by such confessions of your own! There is nothing we can *do*." She lowered her eyes. "Oh, what *can* we do? I do . . . love . . . you so!"

"Have you been with a man intimately?" Kohanah asked, fighting the urge to lower his lips to her breasts.

Marilla's eyes shot upward, stunned by his question. "Certainly *not*," she gasped, placing a hand to her throat. "I am not a . . . a . . . *whore*, Kohanah."

"Whore?" Kohanah said, forking an eyebrow. "You consider making love whorish?"

"No," Marilla stammered. "Not *exactly* . . ."

"When two are in love, they *make* love," Kohanah said huskily. "At sixteen winters I found ways of lovemaking with a girl of fourteen winters. We made love many times! It is a beautiful experience!"

Jealousy tore at Marilla's insides. She paled. "This girl," she murmured. "She was . . . so . . . young . . ."

"Kiowa girls this age learn the secrets and the art of lovemaking," Kohanah said matter-of-factly. "In your culture you do not do this?"

"Certainly *not*," Marilla said, fidgeting with her dress, a strange ache between her thighs troubling her from the talk of such intimacy.

"This girl," she said cautiously. "Do you love her still?"

"Pale Flower?" Kohanah said, looking debatingly into the sky. Then he looked at Marilla. "No. She is no longer woman enough for Kohanah. Kohanah looks elsewhere!"

"You think that I am woman enough for you?" Marilla tested softly, hardly believing it was *she* being so brazen!

"If Kohanah could possess you, you would be all Kohanah would want for*ever*," he said thickly, then rose quickly to his feet. He looked over his shoulder at the barracks, then at the waning sun. "It is time to go to barracks. Kohanah will paint until darkness falls. This will burn up energies that could be used while making love to *you*."

Marilla moved quickly to her feet, but did not approach Kohanah. She clasped her hands tightly behind her. "I'll see you tomorrow," she murmured. Then she looked at the untouched food, troubled.

Scurrying, she stooped and grabbed a hunk of cheese and a loaf of bread, then rose to her feet and pressed them into Kohanah's hands. "You cannot go hungry, Kohanah. Please take these."

Kohanah looked down at her with passion-heavy eyes, then spun around on a heel and left her. Marilla watched him walk toward the barracks, his proud shoulders squared, his tall, lean figure dignified. There had been many confessions exchanged between them today. It seemed unreal that he could have said such things to her. Although he had not actually said that he loved her, Marilla now knew without a doubt that he did.

Never had she felt so helpless, for she could not be held by him, and, oh, how her arms ached for him!

Frustrated, torn by needs, Marilla fell to her knees and with trembling fingers replaced the picnic foods in her basket. Tears stung the corners of her eyes. She didn't dare look toward the barracks at this moment, or she might do something foolish, like *go* there!

"Oh, stop this, Marilla!" she whispered, fussing to herself.

Half stumbling, she rose to her feet and hurried away, wanting to reach the privacy of her cabin, for she still felt the prying eyes of Jason Roark on her. Had he seen the exchange of lustful glances between her and Kohanah? Did it even matter if he had? Did anything matter if she could never be with Kohanah as she desired at this moment? He might never be hers, and knowing that made an emptiness assail her.

After she reached her cabin, Marilla was too restless to stay there. She felt that she must take a walk and clear her head. She couldn't let her father arrive home and find her in such a dispirited mood! He would damn well know the cause and might forbid her to see Kohanah again!

Grabbing her shawl, aware of the cooler temperature that accompanied dusk, Marilla rushed from the cabin and hurried to the beach. The sun was a red disk on the horizon; vast purple streaks were coloring the sky.

A chill coursed through Marilla as she moved relentlessly onward, yet the seabreeze was invigorating as it caressed her face.

The waves washing up on to the sandy shore were hypnotic in their lacy effervescence. Marilla was drawn to sit down, to watch . . . to think. . . .

A sound behind her made her turn with a start. Stark green eyes staring down at her made her insides go numb. Jason Roark's crooked smile told her that she had made a mistake by walking so far from the fortress alone. Only *he* had seen her leave from his vantage point high on the wall.

Now he had come to demand payment for nothing truly owed him. . . .

Five

❧ ❧

The sunset splashed its brilliant red color onto the face of Jason Roark, making his green eyes take on the look of the devil as he glared down at Marilla. She inched back on the sand, too stunned to rise to her feet. Jason was no longer dressed in his uniform. He wore a cotton shirt that was unbuttoned halfway to his waist, revealing the mat of dark, wiry hair on his chest, and skin-tight breeches, which showed that he was aroused by being near her. His round face, smoothly shaven, was distorted by a large bulbous nose and bushy black eyebrows.

"I saw you come here alone," Jason said, taking a step toward Marilla. "What's the matter? Didn't the Injun want to come with you?"

His mention of Indians shot a warning through Marilla. She had expected him to use her acquaintance with Kohanah to his advantage, but never had she thought that he would be *this* bold. What he had on his mind was obvious. She was stunned that he seemed not to be afraid that Marilla would tell her father. What would she even have *to* tell after the next moments were over with?

Was he going to rape her . . . ?

"You know that the Indians aren't allowed to go beyond

the fortress walls," she said, trying to keep a calmness in her voice. If she pretended that his presence did not alarm her, perhaps that was her best defense against him!

"Perhaps my father should set down the same rules for the *soldiers*," she said defiantly.

She quickly climbed to her feet and squared her shoulders, determined to prove that she was not afraid of him. "I think it would be best for you to go on about your business, Jason," she said, lifting her chin stubbornly, yet clutching the shawl about her shoulders as though it were her lifeline. "I have no desire to be in your company."

"Guess not," Jason chuckled, taking a bold step forward. He kneaded his chin and forked an eyebrow as he let his gaze rove over Marilla. "No, guess not. You savin' yourself for that savage Injun, eh?"

The breeze was getting brisker. Marilla's golden hair was whipping about her shoulders. Jason's coal-black hair was blowing in dark wisps away from his face. Marilla felt the chill of the seabreeze seep through her clothes, causing a sudden chill to grab her.

"Afraid?" Jason said, taking her chill to be a tremor of fear. He was so close now he could touch Marilla. "I ain't going to hurt you. Just going to make you feel *good*."

He grabbed Marilla about the waist and yanked her to him, so close that she could smell the aroma of alcohol and knew that it was the whiskey that he had apparently consumed that was giving him the courage to do what he knew was life-threatening for him. He could be shot, or thrown out of the United States Cavalry, for accosting an officer's daughter!

Turning her face away, Marilla flinched from the foul odor of his breath and the bold clutch of his fingers. "You could never make a woman desire you," she hissed. "You are despicable. You stink as though you had taken a bath in whiskey!"

Jason held Marilla in place with one hand while his other ventured to her breast. "The Injun smells better?" he said, laughing. "All savages I've ever been around smelled like hell."

His hand on her breast, touching it through the thin

material of her dress, caused Marilla to turn her head around with a start, to glare up at him. She fought both his hands, trying to free herself, trying to shove his hand away from her breast. But his hands were too powerful to be moved. He just continued to smile his drunken smile while he had his way with her.

"My father will shoot you if you don't unhand me this minute!" Marilla snapped, now trembling with fear. Her shawl slipped from her shoulders to the sandy beach. "Jason, you are daft to continue with this." She kicked at his legs. "Let go of me! Let go of me this instant!"

Jason lowered his lips to her face and feathered kisses along her cheek. "You ain't going to tell your father nothin'," he said huskily. "Or I'll tell him about all of those times you sneaked in and saw the Injun. I'll tell him you even stole my keys and made love with the savage! You don't want me to do that, do you?"

Marilla's flesh crawled where his lips touched her anew. A bitterness was rising into her throat, sickening her. She shoved with more strength. She still tried to kick him. But her skirt impeded the blows of her feet.

Jason's words stung Marilla's brain. He was going to stretch the truth. He was going to lie about her and Kohanah! But he did not know the bond between daughter and father! He did not know that her father would never take the word of a drunken soldier over that of his daughter!

But how could she convince Jason of that? He would not believe her if she told him that she had already confided in her father about her meetings with Kohanah. This man was beyond coherent thought. The alcohol and his lust were clouding his reasoning.

Her only defense was herself, not the words she might use to frighten him.

"Come on, baby," Jason said, forcing Marilla down onto the sandy beach. "Let's pretend I'm the Injun. Just close your eyes and let my kisses and hands be his. I saw it in your eyes . . . how you hungered to be with him in this way. Just pretend, baby. Just pretend!"

Marilla doubled her fists and pounded on his chest as he moved down to straddle her. She tried to scream, but his lips were too suddenly there, silencing her. His kiss was brutal. His teeth were cutting into her lips. His body was heavy, a knee probing between her thighs.

And then Marilla felt a hand sliding up beneath her dress.

Panic rushed through her like wildfire. This man was not going to waste any time. He was going to rape her.

Gathering all the strength and courage that she could muster up, Marilla shoved at him. She tried to raise her knees to thrust them into his groin, but he had her pinned to the ground, unable to move.

But when he took a respite from kissing her, to enjoy looking down at her for a moment, Marilla knew there was only one thing left to do. She smiled mischievously up at him while her hands swept down to her sides and slowly delved deep within the sand. When she brought them up, they were filled with sand. Then she quickly raised her cupped hands and threw the sand into his eyes.

Jason jerked away from Marilla and jumped to his feet yowling, grabbing at his eyes. Marilla leapt to her feet, fighting the weakness in her knees, and began running. Jason's loud curses faded in the wind behind her the faster she ran.

And then, breathless, she rushed through the wide open gate of the fort, seeing the glow of the candle in the window of her cabin just up ahead, blurred through the tears streaming from her eyes.

Stumbling now, her reserve strength almost used up, Marilla rushed on toward her cabin, the candlelight a beacon, meaning safety.

Then she heard eager footsteps gaining on her from behind. Her insides froze when she heard Jason say her name angrily beneath his breath. If she did not continue running as quickly, he would catch her, and in the darkness would perhaps drag her back out to the beach and possibly even kill her! She was a threat to his future. If she told everything that had happened . . .

"Damn it, Marilla," Jason whispered harshly, as he grabbed her by a wrist and forced her to stop and turn to face him. "I'm sorry! I won't do it again! Don't tell your father! You know what might happen. Please don't tell. I promise never to even get *near* you again."

Marilla panted hard, her breasts heaving. She could hardly find her breath to speak. The tears distorted her vision as she looked at Jason. Her wrists pained her where he held her immobile.

"The likes of you deserve everything you get," she hissed, knowing that she was taking a chance of Jason dragging her away. But hopefully her father could hear the commotion and come to her rescue. . . .

"Marilla? Is that you?"

Marilla sobbed when she heard her father's voice. He *had* heard. He *had* come!

"Father!" she cried, her voice hoarse from the running and the strain of the moment. "Over . . . here, Father!"

The ground became a golden stream of light as the lamp moved closer to Marilla. And then Marilla could make out the handsome features of her father. She was too relieved to see him to even realize that Jason had released his hold on her and was running away, fast disappearing into the gloom of the night.

Marilla ran breathlessly into her father's arms. "Father, it was so . . . so . . . horrible," she sobbed, clinging. "*He* was so horrible."

Richard Henry's insides were cold, feeling the desperation with which Marilla clung to him, hearing it in her voice. He squinted his eyes as he held the candle up, trying to see who was scampering away into the darkness. All that he could make out was a white shirt.

But that was enough to scare the hell out of him . . . afraid that he had let Marilla walk alone on the beach just once too often.

He had seen her go there . . . had even understood why. She had feelings for an Indian that she was struggling with. So was Richard Henry struggling, not to intervene . . . tell her how unwise it was to become enamored of an Indian.

He had found it hard to say, for he was also being drawn into the mystique of Kohanah, sorely liking and admiring him!

Easing Marilla out of his arms, Richard Henry gazed down into her tearful eyes. He moved the candle close to her face, seeing her bruised and bleeding lip. "Damn it," he growled. "Who is responsible for this?"

His free hand wove through Marilla's golden hair, smoothing out the tangles. He glanced down and saw the sand caked to the skirt of her wrinkled dress. "Did the son of a bitch even—"

Marilla wiped her eyes with the back of a hand. "No," she interrupted, not wanting to hear her father say the word "rape." It was bad enough that he was even being put in the position of thinking it! "The man did not have the chance. I . . . I . . . stopped him."

"Marilla, how . . . ? Who . . . ?" Richard Henry said, again raking his eyes over her.

Then he placed his arm about her waist and swept her into the house. "Damn it, Marilla, something has to be done about this. It can't be allowed to happen again. Ever since your mother died, I have feared something like this would happen. You've been left alone too much, to fend for yourself." He shook his head, easing Marilla down into a chair in the parlor. "No. It can't be allowed to happen again."

Marilla's breathing was becoming steadier; her eyes were clearing up. She ran a finger over her aching lip, grimacing with the pain. Watching her father now pacing the room, something told her that the end result of this that had just happened might even be worse than if she had been raped! Was he actually considering sending her away to stay with Aunt Helen in New York? He had spoken of it earlier, but after she had fussed so over not wanting to do it, he had let the subject drop.

But now? Would he force her to go?

Oh, Lord, what about Kohanah? She could not bear to be so far from him!

"Father, what are you thinking?" she blurted, rising to grab his arm. She winced as he stopped and glared down at her. She knew the answer before he actually said it. All of his emotions were in his eyes, telling her how it must be. . . .

"You'll be much better off with Aunt Helen and Uncle Ed," Richard Henry said, placing the palm of his hand on her flushed cheek. "I should have sent you away long ago, honey. The next time a soldier decides to take advantage of you, you just might not be so lucky."

"No!" Marilla softly gasped, shoving his hand away from her face. "You can't mean that. Father, I don't want to go."

He leaned closer to her face. "How did you fight the soldier off?" he said thickly, wanting to persist to show her the truths of the evening . . . that she was too vulnerable. "How did you get away?"

"I threw sand into his eyes," Marilla said, squaring her shoulders proudly. "Father, I told you that I am capable of fending for myself. Did not I just prove it?"

"Can you deny that you were just crying because of the scare the damn soldier gave you?" Richard Henry said in a near shout. "Marilla, you can't close your eyes to the truth."

He would not mention that he also felt it would be best to place many miles between Kohanah and Marilla. Should she stay at the fort, she would grow to hate her father, because he would now forbid her to see the Indian under *any* circumstances. She would not move so freely among *any* of the men. She had budded into a woman, with womanly desires and passions. And she stirred passions in men. That had been demonstrated tonight.

Kohanah had no less passion than the man who had just tried to rape Marilla!

"Do you tear my world apart by ordering me away because I let my fear spill out by way of tears?" Marilla half shouted back. "Do you condemn me because I am a woman, with a woman's weaknesses? When I am angry, hurt, or happy, I cry. Surely you know that, Father."

"Yes, I think I know you almost as well as you know yourself," Richard Henry said, going to Marilla. He drew her into his arms and hugged her to him. "And no, I don't condemn you for crying. It is the reason *for* crying that is why I have decided what must be done. You *must* return to New York. You can finish your schooling there. My tutoring has not been enough for you if you are serious about becoming a teacher."

"Father, I have felt that it was adequate enough," Marilla said, drawing away from him, not feeling like being coddled at this moment. "And, Father, I don't want to be separated from *you*. You plan to stay here for three more years. Such a separation is too long! You will be too alone without me."

"If you remained here with me, I would never relax while not with you," he said, going into the kitchen. He filled the coffeepot with water, added coffee, then placed it on the wood-burning stove. He didn't turn when he heard Marilla come into the room. He scarcely breathed, now knowing the answer he must insist on getting.

His duties awaited him . . . the duties of the commander of this fort!

Spinning around on his heel, he clasped his fingers around Marilla's soft shoulders. "Give me the name of the man who is the cause of such tension between us tonight," he said in a low rumble. "I must go to him. I must find a way to punish him. Then I will send him away, to another fort. I don't want the likes of him under my command."

The leering face of Jason Roark flashed before Marilla's eyes, his wicked smile having been engraved on her consciousness forever. She could taste the ugliness of his kiss. She could feel his hands probing beneath her skirt. . . .

"Marilla!"

Marilla blinked nervously, her father's voice drawing her back to the present. She gulped hard and looked wide-eyed up at him. "Who?" she murmured. "Father, Jason Roark is your man. He was drunk. Where did he get the whiskey?"

"Drunk?" Richard Henry said, raising an eyebrow. "By damn, so *he's* the one who's been stealing whiskey from my supplies. Now I have more than one thing to punish him for."

Swinging away from Marilla, Richard Henry grabbed his holstered pistols from the peg on the wall. He slung the gun belt around his waist and fastened it, then patted the pistols. "I'm going to pistol-whip that son of a bitch until he'll beg for mercy,'' he growled, then rushed from the house, leaving Marilla standing in a strained silence.

Going to the window, she looked toward the Indians' barracks. Through the windows could be seen faint candle-light. Kohanah was spending his first night in a clean, comfortable cell, instead of in the dungeon that reeked of unclean smells.

But if her father had his way, she might never even *see* the inside of the new barracks. More than likely he would put her on a ship at the break of dawn even tomorrow and send her *away*.

"I can't leave without first seeing Kohanah,'' she whispered, her heart racing. "Tonight. I must see him tonight. Once Father is asleep, I shall go the barracks. Somehow I will bargain with the guard to let me in to see Kohanah. Somehow . . .''

Six

The moon was casting slanting streamers of light through Marilla's bedroom window, silvering her bed. But she was not in it. She nervously paced the room, a black velveteen cape drawn snugly about her shoulders.

It seemed to be taking hours for her father to settle in for the night. And until she knew that he was in his room, she could not go to Kohanah. Though there was a chance that she would be caught, it was worth a try, for she had been informed by her father that she would be aboard a ship, returning to New York tomorrow! There had been no arguing her father out of the decision. She had to go. That was that!

She paused to look toward her closed door. She had been watching for the candlelight to fade where it showed beneath the door of the parlor, proving that her father was in his own bedroom with the door closed. Her heartbeats hastened. Finally! The candlelight's glow was gone! Her father was in his own room, more than likely absorbed in a law book. He was already anticipating returning to New York himself to resume his law practice!

"I would gladly change places with him on the ship

tomorrow!" Marilla whispered harshly to herself, moving stealthily toward the door.

Her fingers trembled as she circled them around the doorknob. She cringed when the door creaked as she slowly opened it, her eyes darted to her father's door. Scarcely breathing, she listened for any movements.

But she heard nothing, which had to mean that her father hadn't, either.

Determinedly setting her jaw, Marilla crept across the moon-shadowed parlor, then gripped another doorknob. Her shoulders drew up tightly as she turned the knob, sighing with relief when this door opened much more quietly. Deftly she stepped outside, her heart pounding so hard she felt almost swallowed whole by it.

Squinting her eyes, peering into the darkness, she drew the hood of her cloak up over her head and close around her face. Now the vast space that reached from her cabin to the Indian barracks stretched out before her. It reminded her of battlefields read about in the numerous books that she had devoured to fill the lonely, empty hours of night. In the moonlight, she could be detected so easily!

If only the dark cape would keep her hidden well enough, could obscure anyone's vision of what he was or was not seeing as she dashed across the grounds to the shadows of the barracks.

"I must chance it!" Marilla whispered to herself, mustering up the courage required to continue with her plan. "If not now, *never*."

Clutching at the cape where it was tied at her throat, Marilla began to run, relieved that most lights in the cabins on all sides of her were extinguished. That had to mean that almost everyone was asleep and would not be aware of this flight in the night.

But what of the soldiers? Those on guard? Would they be as lax in their duties this time as they had been when she had fought Jason Roark off in the dark? Or had Jason paid the guard to ensure that there would be no interruptions?

Still running, Marilla glanced up at the high fortress wall. On the walkway a guard had paused to look out to sea, his back to her. She glanced toward the Indian barracks, seeing a guard sitting on a chair, his head bobbing. If she was in luck he would doze off completely. She had a key in her possession that would unlock the door that would lead her into privacy with Kohanah! She had slipped it from her father's key chain while he was taking his evening bath!

Guilt swept through her, making her feel sneaky, yet hadn't her father driven her to this? He had surely known that she would have to see Kohanah for a last time. When she had asked his permission, he had flatly refused her!

"Kohanah would never understand," she whispered. "I cannot bear him doubting my loyalty to him!"

Marilla was at least relieved that Jason Roark was no longer a threat to her. At this very moment he was locked up in the dungeons the Indians had just vacated and was to be shipped off early in the morning to another fort. It was good to know that Marilla would never see his leering face again! Pity those who *would*! One day Jason Roark would come up against a cavalry officer who was not like Richard Henry Pratt, whose heart was made of gold.

Some day *someone* would have cause to shoot Jason, or worse, and he would. . . .

Her footsteps light, Marilla scampered to the back of the Indian barracks and hid in the shadows. She breathed hard; her eyes were wide as she then began to inch along the wall, ducking down whenever she came to a barred window.

Then, finally, she came to the farthest edge of the wall that reached around to the front where the guard was still dozing. Marilla would have to wait until she saw him go into a deep sleep.

She inched her head around the corner of the building and eyed the guard warily. One long, lean leg was stretched out before him, balancing him in his chair as his head bobbed, his shoulders slouched. His arms were folded across his chest, his uniform dark and crisp in the moonlight.

Marilla swallowed hard when the moonlight also revealed the shine of his pistols, thrust into their respective holsters. If he caught her sneaking into or out of the barracks, he could shoot her as an intruder before he even questioned who she *was*.

Yes, she was chancing everything to say good-bye to Kohanah.

Even . . . her life . . .

Her patience running thin, she stepped more boldly into the open. She inched along the wall, watching the guard. Then she smiled widely when she heard the static rumblings of snores and knew that he had finally lost the battle with his drowsiness. He was fast asleep!

Slipping her hand into the pocket of her cape, circling her fingers about the key, Marilla crept on past the guard. Her fingers trembled so violently she could hardly place the key in the keyhole. Steadying the hand with her other one, she finally managed to get the key in place. Slowly she turned it. She grimaced when a loud click proved that the lock was no longer in place.

Taking a slow glance at the guard, Marilla sighed when she discovered that he had not stirred. He was still sleeping as soundly as before. She hoped he would sleep for a lengthy time, for she did not only have to enter the barracks, she had to *leave*!

Gathering the hem of her cape up into her arms, Marilla crept on through the door. When she was inside she carefully closed the door, then turned and eyed the long row of cells. Her heart plummeted. Each cell was separate from the others and the only space available for viewing into them was a small window on each door. How was she to know which cell housed Kohanah? How could she even get inside? Why hadn't she thought to realize that even *they* were locked, as the separate cells had been locked in the dungeon! She needed another key! But she didn't dare risk returning home to get it, then trying to return again, unnoticed!

Feeling as though she had already failed in her plan to see . . . to *be* with Kohanah, Marilla turned and started to leave. But the faint whisper of a voice from somewhere close by made her stop and turn with a start. Though the voice had spoken in a whisper, she recognized it no less! It was Kohanah! Though the narrow corridor in which she stood was dark, Kohanah had surely seen her silhouette move through the door and would know that she was the only woman who would try such a daring stunt as this, to come to the Indian barracks in the night. Only *she* loved an Indian housed *in* the barracks! Only Kohanah knew her Kiowa name, for he had assigned it to her!

"Tsonda?" Kohanah repeated, placing his eyes as close to the small window in his door as possible. "*Manyi*, woman, Kohanah is over here. Follow the sound of my voice!"

Marilla's pulse began to race, her eyes searching as she began to move from door to door. Pity for the imprisoned Indians washed through her, though they were no longer being treating so inhumanely. It was the fact that they were still imprisoned! It made each of them look less a warrior . . . less a *man*.

Yet she knew there was nothing more that she could do for them. As she passed by the doors, making eye contact with some of the warriors, she lowered her lashes in a silent apology.

And then she finally came to the door that she had been searching for. When her eyes and Kohanah's met and held, not even the darkness of the corridor could keep them from exchanging unspoken passions. It was the moonlight flooding in behind Kohanah, into his room, illuminating him, that made her see him so clearly.

And now that she was within touching distance of the man she loved, she knew that he could see her as well.

"*Tsan*, I come," Marilla whispered, reaching a hand to his face, touching its copper smoothness. "But, Kohanah, I can come no farther. I do not have the key. I should have known that I should also look for such a key on my father's chain."

"You have the key that opened the front door?" Kohanah said, relishing the touch of her silken hand.

"Yes, I have that key."

"Then, Tsonda, you have brought the key that fits all the locks in this dwelling. I have observed. I know that is so,'' he said, chuckling. He nodded toward the lock on the door. "Fit it in. Turn it. You will find that you can come easily into my personal dwelling.''

Marilla drew her hand away as though shocked. Her eyes were wide, stunned that one key would fit all locks! She even at this moment had the power to release the Indian prisoners! But if she did, where would they even go? They would be hunted down and shot, or *hanged*.

No. She could not allow that, even if Kohanah suggested it. But he was a smart man. He would not take the chance. He knew that he was in a strange land, too many miles away from his homeland. There would be no true way *to* escape, even if they did leave the fortress walls successfully. Their horses had been destroyed or sold.

On foot, they would get only so far. . . .

Her fingers trembling, Marilla placed the key in the keyhole and turned it with an ease that she did not expect. When the door inched open, the moonlight spilling at her feet like a silver carpet welcoming her into Kohanah's small cell, she laughed softly and hurriedly entered.

"Your father,'' Kohanah said, closing the door behind her. "He does not know you have come? What of the guard? Was he not beside the door?''

"Father is in his room, probably asleep by now,'' Marilla said, slipping the cape from around her shoulders, placing it on a small stool. "The guard outside the door was sound asleep.''

"But both will not sleep forever,'' Kohanah said, lifting his fingers to her hair, twining them through it, marveling anew over how silken it was to his fingers. "If they should awaken before you leave . . . ?''

Marilla placed a hand to his mouth, silencing his words of worry. "If I am caught, that truly does not matter,'' she said, devouring his handsomeness with her eyes. She could not gather enough courage to tell him that this could be their last night together, forever. Once he learned that she was going to New York, he might turn his back on her. If he was loving her only to use her, her usefulness would be running out, tomorrow!

"Oh, Kohanah, is it not grand that we are here together,

totally alone?'' she said anxiously, erasing all thoughts that could ruin this moment with him. She did not risk everything to be here with him, only to ruin it by a few choice words spoken to him. ''It is so wonderful that my father's plans for this building were that each of you Kiowa warriors would have your own space in which to live. You . . . you and *I* have total privacy!''

''Your personality is that of a daring one,'' Kohanah said, chuckling. ''Tsonda, you are like no other woman I have ever known.''

''I'm glad,'' Marilla said, her heart beating soundly as Kohanah looked down at her with passion-filled eyes. ''I want to be the only woman you ever desire!''

''You speak as one who is ready to share intimacies with a man,'' Kohanah said huskily, his hands now lowering, molding her breasts where they lay swollen with need against the cotton bodice of her dress. ''Did you come to let me teach you how a Kiowa makes love? Are you ready for such *kion*?''

''*Kion*?'' Marilla whispered. ''What does that word mean in my English tongue?''

Her face was hot with a blush, now knowing that, yes, Kohanah would believe that she had come to him in the middle of the night for only one reason. To make love! Could . . . she . . . ?

Oh, how she desired it! But he would be the first man. And if she was never to see him again, was it best that her virginity be taken *by* him? What would she tell the man who would eventually become her husband?

Kohanah's hands caressed her breasts, his lips lowered to the cleavage of her low-swept bodice. ''*Kion*?'' he whispered, his breath hot on her flesh. ''Kohanah asks if you are ready for *courting*. Are you . . . ?''

His arms swept around her and drew her against his hard frame of body. He looked down at her, glad to see the need in the depths of her eyes. Even if she did not believe in such courtships, she would with him, for she loved him!

''Tell me, Tsonda, are you ready for my lips and hands to awaken all of your senses into pleasure?'' he asked, smiling down at her. "You came for loving, did you not?"

Marilla wanted to cry out to him, tell him that she had come to say a sad good-bye! She wanted to cling to him now and never let him go! But she did not know how to tell him! Telling him could cause many sadnesses . . . torments. . . .

"Yes, I have come for loving you," she whispered shakily, not even believing that she had said it. But she could not help herself. How could she say no to the man she loved so dearly? His eyes were charged with dark emotion as he looked down at her. His hands were awakening her every nerve ending as they strolled down her back, then around to once again knead her breasts through her dress.

And then he snuggled her even closer and briskly lowered his lips to hers and gave her the kiss that until this moment had been possible only in her midnight dreams. The demand of his lips . . . the heat . . . the passion . . . made her forget the soreness of her lips caused by Jason's brutal kisses. She was only aware of how right she had been to know that kissing Kohanah would be so sweet . . . so *beautiful*!

Marilla trembled as she became further alive beneath his kiss, the pleasure pulsing through her like roses spreading their sweet scent through the air in the early spring.

Almost melting from such wondrous sensations, Marilla twined her arms about Kohanah's neck and sighed when he lifted her fully up into his arms and carried her to his bed, to lay her on it.

Loosening her circled fingers, Marilla let the key fall idly to the floor, making a hollow, clinking sound as it hit, but she did not hear it. All that she was aware of was Kohanah's hands loosening the buttons of her dress . . . of his hands lifting the dress over her head.

And when she was finally nude, lying on the bed in soft pools of moonlight, only then did she stop to think of what was about to happen. Kohanah had slipped his fringed shirt over his head and was now lowering his breeches. In the glow of the moonlight, Marilla could see his powerful man's strength jutting out from his body. And as he knelt down over her, she could feel it as its heat made contact with her bare thigh.

Marilla was ready to protest, fear sweeping through her like torrents of rain drowning her, when his mouth bore down upon hers, hot and demanding, his hands setting her skin on fire as he touched every secret part of her. . . .

She drifted toward him, shaken with desire.

To her now, at this moment, the word "no" did not even exist. . . .

Seven

The sound of the ocean played through the window above
the bed like a soft melody, its softness this night lulling.
Marilla felt as though she were on the sandy beach, the
effervescent silk of the water caressing her flesh as it crept
up onto the shore, then ebbed away slowly . . . slowly
. . . slowly, leaving her body in tune with nature . . . with
the unveiling mysteries of young love. . . .

"Tsonda, Kohanah has always wanted you," Kohanah
said in a husky whisper as he placed his lips to Marilla's
ear. His teeth nibbled on her earlobe, sending currents of
rapture through her. "That you came, that you are in my
arms willingly, proves that you have wanted me as much."

"You knew that I did," Marilla whispered, drawing a
ragged breath when his hand again swept down her body
in hot, possessive touches. "But I never thought it would
be possible." She turned her face away and shut her eyes,
hoping this could also shut out all thoughts of her trusting
father. "I know I should not be here now. I did not come
tonight to . . . to—"

Then she bit her lower lip, silencing her own words.
This was not the time to tell him her true reason for being
there. And feelings of guilt for being there, in such a way,

were also misplaced. Though this was her first time with a man sexually, she would not be ashamed. She loved Kohanah with a fierceness that was almost unbelievable! She was ready to share in the ultimate of pleasures that loving him was giving her.

"You do not finish your words?" Kohanah said, drawing away from her, looking down at her with his dark, stormy eyes. "Were you about to say that you did not come tonight to share in love's experiences?"

Marilla turned her gaze back to him, seeing his flawless features in the glow of the moonlight. His face was dark and finely chiseled as he gazed down at her. The expanse of his sleekly muscled chest lay only a touch from her heaving breasts!

No man could have such a bronzed, handsome face as Kohanah's! And this man was hers? Could it be true? Or was she right to suspect that he could be using her? Tonight he could be using her to the ultimate of extremes, if that was his intention!

"One does not give up her virginity all that easily," Marilla whispered, touching Kohanah's face, savoring its smoothness against the palm of her hand, again forcing herself not to believe that she was being used. "Though you do not think it whorish to give oneself to a man so easily, deep within my heart I feel that . . . that perhaps I am behaving whorishly at this moment. Though I did not come here with intentions of sharing bodies, I *am* here in such a way."

"Why *did* you come?" he asked, his dark eyes imploring her.

"Why?" Marilla said, swallowing hard. "Because I could not stay away!"

She threw her arms about his neck and drew him back down against her. She clung with all of her might, not wanting anything to spoil these precious moments with him. If he questioned her further, she would not be able to let their embraces continue. Flashes of her father's face were still there, troubling her!

"Is it not grand that we are finally able to fully embrace?'' she whispered against his cheek. ''For so long only our hands were allowed to touch. Oh, Kohanah, now we are touching totally! Isn't it wonderful? Please tell me that you love the feel of my body pressed against yours. I so love yours! Never had I thought that any man could stir such delicious feelings inside me. But *you* have. *You* have. . . .''

Her voice trailed off when Kohanah framed her face between his hands and guided her lips to his. Gently he kissed her while one of his knees slowly nudged her legs apart. The touch of his pulsing manhood against her flesh triggered a fire in Marilla. It began at her toes and went in staccato fashion up her body until it lay seething at the innermost part of her brain where she was given the power to enjoy the heady pleasures that were now assailing her! Soon she would be relinquishing her virginity to Kohanah! What intense pleasure would await her *then*?

It was as though Marilla was at the realm of some great discovery! She was breathless with excitement to explore . . . to find . . . to conquer!

''Tsonda, together we will soar, like birds gliding through the sky,'' Kohanah said huskily, his lips brushing against hers as he talked. ''We will mate while in flight!''

''Yes, yes . . .'' Marilla sighed, as his hands lowered to her breasts and began gently kneading them. ''Let us take flight together! Let us become as one!''

She uttered a soft cry of pain when Kohanah plunged his hardness deep within her. But the pain quickly smoothed away and was replaced by sensual pleasure as he began his soft strokes. His lips touched hers wonderingly, and then he kissed her with a heat that reached clean into her soul. She clung to him. She wrapped her legs about him, relishing in his strokes, which were speeding up, moving deeper . . . deeper. . . .

Receiving him with a rhythmic movement all her own, Marilla coiled her fingers into Kohanah's unbraided hair and forced his lips even harder against her own. She wanted to always remember his kiss, how it tasted . . . how it felt! She would carry such remembrances with her

to New York, to fall back on when she was alone, pining
away for him.

But now, with his lips on hers so hard, she felt pain that
reminded her of how her lips had been abused by Jason
Roark! The bruise was not outwardly noticeable, but it lay
there all the same, lying just beneath the surface, a reminder of things *ugly* in life! Had Jason succeeded in
raping her, she could not be here now, with the man she so
desperately loved. She would never have experienced such
bliss within her lover's arms. She would have been scarred
forever, branded by a man she detested!

Kohanah sensed a partial hesitation in Marilla's response
to his kiss and hip movements. He paused, also, looking
down at her with wonder. "Do you not enjoy every moment of our lovemaking?" he asked, smoothing her long,
drifting hair back from her brow.

His gaze absorbed her loveliness, her perfect facial features. He enjoyed the flush of her cheeks, which alone
proved that he was stirring pleasure within her. "Tsonda,
tell me what is lacking and I will make it right."

He kissed the tip of her nose. "Perhaps I do not kiss
you enough?" he whispered, his lips now trailing kisses
along her cheek, down the slope of her chin, and then to
her breasts.

He smiled to himself as he heard her quick intake of
breath as his tongue flicked about one of her nipples.
"Tell me when you have been kissed enough. Then I will
once again resume my strokes within you," he said huskily.

Marilla wanted to cling to him, hold him fast against
her, but his lips were creating such fires along her flesh
that she did not argue when he eased his manhood away
from her. She closed her eyes, trembling with pleasure, as
his lips and tongue continued worshiping her body.

And when she felt his breath hot at the juncture of her
thighs, where only moments ago he had been pleasuring
her so beautifully, her eyes flew open wide and she sucked
in her breath when he took the first taste of her where her
womanhood was throbbing so unmercifully.

The wetness of his tongue, the suction of his lips on her

womanhood, almost drove Marilla wild with rapture. Something at the back of her mind warned her against this way of making love, but the pleasure was so intense, she was beyond coherent thought.

Her head thrashed back and forth. She drew Kohanah's hands up, to mold her breasts. She sighed and sobbed, her whole body flaming with passion. Gently . . . smoothly . . . she felt the pleasure spreading. Warmly . . . hotly . . . and then she experienced a wondrous explosion of feelings that overwhelmed her . . . that dazzled her *senses*! Her whole body was engulfed in this heat. It was like a warm flash of sunshine blossoming within her.

But such wondrous sensations lasted for only a brief moment. Too soon Marilla was floating back down to earth, awakening to reality, and to Kohanah who was now leaning over her, his eyes smiling down at her.

"Your body reacted to *kion*, lovemaking, beautifully," Kohanah said thickly. "Never again will you be the same, Tsonda. Your body will hunger . . . will cry out for more of the same. Kohanah will be here for you! All you need is to come, to ask."

Shame engulfed Marilla for what her body had done as a result of Kohanah's different sort of lovemaking. Never in her wildest dreams had she thought such a thing was possible! Her body had betrayed her! Surely Kohanah could not be happy, for he had not received any pleasure from the way he had made love to her. She had received it alone! How *could* that be right?

"*Aalyi*, I cry," Marilla said, sobbing as she turned her head away. "You must hate me. Why did you cause my body to react so *alone*?"

Kohanah placed his hands to Marilla's cheeks and turned her to face him. He kissed her softly on the lips, then eyed her warmly. "Tsonda, at this moment I am proud of you for two reasons," he said huskily. "First, you show me that you have learned more of my Kiowa language than I thought you had. You know the way to say 'I cry' in Kiowa. That is good! Second, you make me proud because you *let* me make love to you with my lips and mouth. Do you not know that it gives a man pleasure to *give* pleasure? While I was making love to you in such a way, my heart was filled with gladness! Kohanah will always remember the taste . . . the *smell* of you. *Obaika*, you remain forever in my *ten*, heart!''

Marilla hugged his words to her. She flung herself into his arms, a tempest of emotions! Oh, how she loved him. How could she say good-bye to him? He was right to say that she would now always hunger for this that she had discovered tonight. Her body had been awakened to desire . . . to *passion*. At seventeen, she had become a total woman!

But what of the years that lay ahead? To spend them without him? Oh, how could she . . . ?

''It is now your turn for receiving pleasure,'' Marilla whispered, lowering her hand, daring to encircle her fingers around his hardness, which lay so close to the tender flesh of her womanhood.

Still clinging to him, her cheek pressed against his chest, Marilla began to move her hand on him, knowing that what she was doing was right, for Kohanah's body trembled as he voiced a low groan of pleasure.

''You learn quickly more than the language of the Kiowa,'' Kohanah said, her fingers setting his loins on fire. ''You learn the art of lovemaking without even being *taught*. Practiced, you will be like no lover Kohanah has ever before bedded!''

When Kohanah spoke even vaguely of his early trysts with women, it made jealousy tear at Marilla's heart. After tonight, when she was gone, he would have cause to seek love from other women. And he would, as soon as he was free of his imprisonment! Would he, while making love to other women, see *her* in his mind's eye, wanting *her*? Would he be tormented by her absence as she would be by *his*?

Kohanah circled his fingers about her hand and stopped its movements. ''Enough,'' he whispered, gently easing her hand away. ''My body is tormented by need. Kohanah must conquer this need *now*.''

He took her lips savagely with his mouth and when he entered her and again began his eager thrusts within her, Marilla's body trembled, receiving him with total abandon. She clung to him, writhing in response, not recognizing this person she had become. Until tonight she had been somewhere between being a child and a *woman*. After tonight all traces of a child would be banished! Forgotten!

Kohanah drew his lips away and looked down at Marilla. Ah, but she was such a vision, with the moonlight bright in her eyes as she gazed wonderingly up at him. Her eyes seemed to mirror his soul . . . his needs! Could it truly be that she was there, willingly sharing so openly with him? Would she again? How could he live without her now that he had discovered the magic that could be found within her arms?

But he must! Never could she be a part of the Kiowa culture! Never!

Kohanah's steel arms enfolded her again, erasing unhappy thoughts from his mind. This was now. Later would take care of itself. He cradled her close, his body growing feverish with need. "Love me, Tsonda," he groaned in a whisper against her cheek. "Move with me. Let us reach paradise together."

His mouth closed over Marilla's lips, the pulsing crest of his passion near. Kissing her with raging hunger, his hands clasped her buttocks and molded her into the contours of his body. He thrust himself harder within her, his kiss, his body all consuming. . . .

Marilla was breathless with spiraling rapture. Her fingers locked together behind Kohanah's neck, she arched her hips and moved with him, as though practiced. Kohanah's thick, husky groan revealed that he was drawing near that realm of total delight that Marilla had experienced only moments ago.

Even now she was finding a similar passion . . . a similar heat . . . a similar euphoria, but twofold now that her body was joined with Kohanah's, to experience total bliss *together*.

"Kohanah, it is so sweet . . . so marvelous," Marilla

whispered, as he lowered his lips to kiss her breast. A golden web of pleasure was spinning within her, growing larger . . . larger, capturing her, tantalizing her.

And then the web seemingly melted away when she was once again seized by the wonder of blissful madness that accompanied the supreme peak of feelings with Kohanah. Her senses reeled, her body shook and trembled. She cried out against Kohanah's lips as he came to her with a fiery kiss as his body lunged, spilling his warm pool of seed deep within her. . . .

And when Marilla emerged from what she thought surely was how a drunken stupor felt, she blinked her eyes and looked about her, stunned from the experience and the sheer bliss *of* it. Her hands caressed Kohanah's perspiration-laced back as he still lay on her, breathing hard. She kissed his damp cheek, knowing that her feelings for him were forever. How was she to bear not being able to see him again after tonight?

She was not sorry for what they had just shared. It was right! Now when she dreamed of him at night, her dreams could be real, for she knew the true wonders of being with him *totally*!

"I cannot stay much longer," Marilla whispered, her fingers relishing the curves of Kohanah's buttocks, loving the fact that she was with him, nude, and not ashamed. Her hand moved on past his buttocks, around to the feathering of hair at the juncture of his thighs.

She trembled inside when she touched his shrunken manhood, now lying spent against her abdomen. When it quivered against her fingers, Marilla drew her hand back, alarmed.

But Kohanah took her hand and guided it back to him, encouraging her to touch him again. She was astounded by how much larger it was now than moments ago!

"Feel it grow within your hand," Kohanah said huskily. "You give it life again, Tsonda."

Wild sensation began to build inside Marilla again as the heat of his manhood reached into her soul. Its throbbing beckoned to her, arousing her anew. But she knew that this could not continue. She had already spent too much time in such embraces. Should she allow it again, she might never break away.

Her body was alive . . . was hungry for more experiences of the flesh.

"No," she said, drawing her hand away. "I really mustn't."

Kohanah swept his arms about her and drew her up against him, crushing her breasts into his chest. "If you did not have to leave, we could make love all night," he said hoarsely. "We would make continuous love!"

Her face flushed hot, Marilla eased from his arms. "I want to as badly as you," she murmured, looking up into his dark eyes of mystery, hardly believing that she could speak so boldly . . . so openly with him. "If you were only *free*, oh, what a difference that would make!"

Marilla's eyes lowered. "But you are not free," she said in a near whisper. "Neither am *I*, if truths were known. It seems I have no control over my *own* destiny, Kohanah."

Her words struck a chord of danger within Kohanah's heart. He rose up, away from her, and drew her to her feet before him. "What are you saying?" he said thickly. "You speak of destinies. *Yours*. How is it endangered?"

Marilla looked slowly up into his eyes, the moment of truth upon her. It did not seem strange that she was standing unclothed with him. He was now as much a part of her as her own self. In spirit, they were as *one*.

"Oh, how can I tell you?" she said, touching Kohanah's cheek gently. "But I *must*."

"Tell Kohanah *what*?" he said tensely, for he could hear so much in her voice . . . see so much in her *eyes*! "What has happened?"

"It is what *is* to happen that saddens me," Marilla said, then lunged into his arms, hugging him tightly. "Kohanah, my father is sending me away!" she sobbed, clinging. "Tomorrow! Even tomorrow!"

Kohanah's insides grew numbly cold. He stiffened and clasped his fingers to Marilla's shoulders and held her at arm's length away from him. He looked down at her, his eyes two points of fire. "What you say is true?" he growled. "You leave Kohanah? Tomorrow?"

Marilla flinched beneath his fingers digging into her bare flesh. She looked guardedly up at him through tear-filled eyes, not liking his reaction to what she had said. His tenderness seemed to have been banished by truth!

"Kohanah, you're hurting me," she said, her voice quivering. She wiped tears from her eyes with the back of a hand, sighing when his hands dropped away from her.

Kohanah spun around and placed his back to her, torn with feelings. He didn't want to believe she was leaving. Why would she? The selfish part of him wanted her to stay!

He bent and swept Marilla's clothes up from the floor and handed them to her, then drew on his fringed breeches.

"Why does your father see the need to send you away?" he asked, combing his long, lean fingers through his midnight-black hair, which had come unbraided, forcing it to lie back behind his squared shoulders.

Marilla hurriedly dressed, feeling Kohanah's eyes on her, watching her every movement. Was it because he was memorizing her, to remember her after she was gone? Or was it because he was seeing her loss as a threat to him . . . to his *warriors*? Did he truly believe that if she stayed it would be to his advantage?

Oh, had he drawn her into a seduction for all of the wrong reasons . . . ?

If so, she would want to die!

"You do not give Kohanah answers!" he said in a growl. "Why must you leave?"

Marilla buttoned her dress, then slipped her shoes on. She felt trapped. She did not want to tell Kohanah about the near rape, for she did not want him to have *that* to remember about her!

"Father wants me to continue with my schooling in New York," she blurted, grasping on to a truth that made her more comfortable. "I have always wanted to be a teacher. Seems that I will now be given that opportunity. . . ."

The moonlight had shifted its beams and was now silvering canvases of paintings leaning against a wall across the room from Marilla. Her eyes widened and she gasped. Her father had been much more generous to Kohanah than he had admitted to! There were not only buffalo skins on which the paintings had been drawn, but also canvases!

And there were *many*!

It seemed that her father was being more generous to Kohanah than to his daughter!

Turning slowly to Kohanah, she eyed him questioningly. . . .

Eight

❧❧

Kohanah stalked to the paintings and grabbed one and held it beneath the flowering of moonlight. "Now Kohanah understands why your father brings more canvas than buffalo skin to Kohanah," he growled, his gaze burning onto the canvas of brightly painted images. "He does this to lighten the blow of my losing you!"

Marilla looked from the stack of canvases, to Kohanah. Her father had given Kohanah these canvases in time for him to have painted on all of them, proving beyond a doubt that her father been planning her departure long before she had knowledge of it. Had he felt that her feelings for Kohanah were that much of a threat? Were the canvases truly a payoff to Kohanah?

She paled, and her fingers went to her throat. Oh, Lord, her father *had* known of her innermost feelings for Kohanah from the very beginning. Her emotions had been written in her eyes. They had been in her *voice* when she mentioned Kohanah's name! Because she had not been skillful enough to hide her feelings, she was now going to have to give up the man whom she loved more than life itself!

"My father is wise way beyond his years," Marilla said shallowly, casting her eyes downward. "*Far* wiser, it seems, than *I* shall ever be."

"While playing a role of traveling the white man's road, being a model of vigorous responsibility, Kohanah was blinded to truths," he growled, replacing the painting with the others.

He went to the window and grasped hard onto the bars, staring toward the fortress wall and the guard pacing the walkway at the top. "But Kohanah will not be swayed by such truths!" he said dryly. "One must lose in order to *gain*."

Marilla went to his side. She looked up at him, tears near, for his words were so tormented, yet in his face she could still see such strength . . . such a strange calm!

Stifling a sob behind a hand, she saw so much about him that was a reminder of why she loved him. He was tall, lean, but well muscled. He was a young man who showed grace even when he was standing still.

Striking, his features were so very classical!

"When you speak of losing," Marilla said, dropping her hand from her mouth, "do you speak of losing me? Or is it something more, Kohanah?"

"It does not matter," he said, giving her a half-glance. "If you must leave, you must *leave*." He gestured toward the door. "Leave now. It is best that way."

Marilla gasped at his abruptness, at the casual manner in which he was dismissing her. She did not want to go! At least not yet! It was apparent that her father's suspicions were already confirmed. What if he *did* catch her with the man she loved? He surely would not punish Kohanah for something *she* did!

Her gaze went to the canvases leaning against the wall. She had wanted to see the paintings earlier. Now that they were there, so close, surely Kohanah would not deny her the chance. And seeing them would be a way to delay her good-bye just a mite longer!

Her footsteps light, Marilla went and knelt down before the canvases. The moonlight was still illuminating them, even giving them life, it seemed! For never had Marilla seen such true-to-life images. It was as though the figures painted on the canvas should even be breathing, they were so real!

"My word!" she exclaimed, daring to touch the dried oils on the canvas. "Kohanah, I knew that if given a chance, you would do magnificently on canvas! And you *have*."

Then she drew back, stunned when she scooted this painting aside and saw, behind it, the scene depicted on a stretched-out dried buffalo hide. Her face drained of color, her fingers trembled as she shot Kohanah a troubled glance. "Kohanah, tell me that you did not actually witness this," she said, her voice strained. "Tell me that the soldiers did not actually do . . . this . . . to the Kiowa!"

Her eyes moved back to the painting. The gruesome scene revealed an Indian village. Lying on the ground in pools of blood were women and children. Drawn into a circle, on horses, were men in uniform, with rifles in their hands. Kiowa warriors were gagged and tied to the horses, their gaze passive as they looked down at those who had been savagely murdered by the soldiers.

"Not all soldiers are this . . . this . . . vicious," Marilla gasped, in her mind's eye seeing her father, how gentle and handsome he had always looked in his cavalry uniform. "My father, he . . ."

Kohanah moved wolfishly toward Marilla and took the skin and turned its painted side to the wall. He then guided Marilla gently away from the canvases. "You do not want to see the paintings," he said hoarsely. "They speak of many atrocities performed by the white man against the Kiowa."

"You witnessed everything that you painted?" Marilla asked, eyeing the remaining paintings, wondering about them.

Kohanah rearranged the paintings so that the ones he was willing to show Marilla were on the top. He sank onto his haunches and looked at her with a placid expression that did not seem appropriate at such a time as this, but deep within, he was suddenly devoid of feelings.

Without Marilla, so much hope was gone.

"No, Kohanah did not witness all that was painted," he said calmly. "My father and his father before him told many tales of such atrocities as we sat beside the family fire on cold nights of winter. It was then that I learned the future was dim for the Kiowa.''

Kohanah humbly bowed his head. "Kohanah was right!''

Marilla placed her hand to Kohanah's chin and forced his eyes to turn, to meet the compassion in hers. "Surely one day things will turn around for your people," she said softly. "It *must*, Kohanah. It *must*.''

Then she dropped her hands to her lap as she settled down on the floor beside him, her eyes anxiously looking at the paintings. "I have waited so long to see your paintings," she murmured. "Please show them to me now. I promise not to get upset by these others that you show me. I understand that you painted them for a purpose . . . a purpose that you hope will one day profit your people.''

One by one Kohanah showed the paintings to Marilla. They were bright-colored pictures of horses and tipis, showing the Kiowa's fights with the Cheyenne and Osage . . . and with the United States Cavalry.

Some showed the yearly celebration of the great Sun Dance, the coming of the deadly smallpox, cholera, and measles, and the making of a treaty with the white man.

And then Kohanah came to the most recent paintings. . . .

"This painting reveals a white man's guard detachment standing by at Fort Sill, the authorities at Fort Sill, and the defeated Kiowa," Kohanah said, his voice breaking. "The identity of the Kiowa leaders had just been announced. Only the most notorious raiders were named for deportation." Kohanah squared his shoulders proudly. "Kohanah was among these most notorious!''

Marilla swallowed hard, not wanting the word "notorious" defined to her by Kohanah. If she did not know the actual slayings that he had performed, she could envision him as the gentle Indian she had always witnessed him to be while with her! She did not ever want to think of him as a savage . . . killing savagely!

Kohanah cleared his throat, aware of Marilla's strained silence. He could see her tenseness by the way she clasped her hands so tightly together on her lap. Even her knuckles were white. . . .

He moved to another painting. "On this canvas you will see painted a campsite that was made on the way to the railroad that would take the Kiowa to Fort Marion," he said thickly. "The prisoners bathed in the Blue River in Indian Territory. The tents were reserved for the cavalry escort. We warriors were forced to sleep on the bare ground, shackled together with a continuous chain."

Seeing the drawings of the Indians shackled in such a way, their heads bowed to the ground, made a sickness invade Marilla's senses. She was not sure if she wanted to see the rest, but if she did not look at them now, she would never get another chance. And it was best that she understood everything fully, for in her heart, she would always carry the wonders of Kohanah and her love for him with her. *Always*, he would be a part of her life.

Kohanah focused on another painting. He held it squarely beneath the light of the moon. "In this painting you will see an excited crowd that gathered at a railroad station to gawk at the Kiowa warriors," he growled, his eyes becoming filled with fire. "This was a scene repeated in every city along the way." He pointed to the drawings of Indians sitting with blankets drawn over their heads. "Some Kiowa were frightened of riding on a train! Near the journey's end, one chief was shot to death attempting to escape!"

"How horrible," Marilla gasped, then recognized the scene on the next canvas as Kohanah placed it before her eyes. . . .

"This scene was painted of the day after we Kiowa reached this fort," Kohanah said, eyeing Marilla as he spoke. "As you recall, we were all taken to the parapet of this fort, to view the Atlantic Ocean. It was to emphasize just what imprisonment would mean to us! That we would be shut in from all that was beautiful in life!"

He laid this painting aside with all of the rest. "Except that you made this a lie," he said, chuckling low. He drew Marilla into his arms and held her close. "There was you. You are more beautiful than any oceans and plains put together!"

His lips bore down upon hers. He eased her down onto

the floor, his hands eager on her breasts, silently cursing the dress that was a barrier between him and the actual touch of her flesh.

Marilla moaned with ecstasy as she felt her body responding to this wildness transferring from Kohanah to herself. She reached up to his face and touched its softness, drawing his lips more firmly to hers. So much was forgotten while she was being mesmerized by his lips and hands! All uglinesses . . . all sadnesses . . . were banished from her mind.

Then Kohanah jerked himself free and helped Marilla up from the floor. He turned his back to her and went to the window, to again peer into the darkness. Marilla was stunned by his abruptness to turn away from her. She was discovering that he was a man of many moods.

"Kohanah," she murmured, refusing to let him push her aside all that easily. These were their last moments, perhaps forever! She went to him and placed her hand on his arm. "Don't turn away from me. I must leave. Soon!"

"Then why delay it?" he said gruffly, angrily folding his arms across his chest. "You'd best go. Now!"

"Kohanah, please," Marilla pleaded. "If it was possible, I would stay! I would marry you!"

Marilla's insides splashed cold when he turned his head with a jerk and stared icily down at her. She did not want to believe that it was Kohanah looking down at her with such coldness . . . with such detachment! Had their moments together been time spent in mockery?

Marilla placed a hand to her mouth, afraid.

"Kohanah could never marry you should you stay, or should you *and* I become free of all burdens," he said solemnly. "Reservation life is intolerable for Indians. For a white woman used to luxuries it could be the death of her!"

He turned his gaze away, looking gauntly at the paintings. "Anyhow, Kohanah has much to do," he said in a shallow tone, now looking forcefully into Marilla's eyes. "White woman . . . *you* . . . would only be in the way of Kohanah's . . . of all *Kiowa's* destiny."

Stunned numb by his words and their meaning, Marilla

stumbled backwards away from Kohanah. Tears blurred her vision. She choked back a sob as she tore her eyes away from Kohanah and bent to grab her cape. Her eyes searched for the key. Once it was securely within her fingers, she turned and looked at Kohanah, sobbing.

"All along you knew that there was no future for us, yet . . . yet . . . you drew me into a seduction," she softly cried. "Love was not a part of the seduction, was it? Only *lust*!"

She went to Kohanah and beat a fist against his chest. "How could you, Kohanah?" she sobbed. "How could you?"

Kohanah's heart ached, his insides were quivering, so desperately did he want to tell Marilla just how much he loved her and that what he did was only best for her. She would have to forget him! If it meant that she would hate him, then that was the way it had to be! For their futures weren't linked.

Only their hearts . . . only their souls . . .

When Kohanah did not venture to stop her assault on his body, Marilla was quickly sobered. She wiped tears from her cheeks and squared her shoulders determinedly. "I don't believe you, you know," she said, her voice hoarse from crying. "How can I believe that you do not care? I never *shall* believe it! You are not the sort to use a woman in such a way! I know that you aren't."

Flipping her skirt around, she moved to the door. After the cape was secured about her shoulders and the hood was hiding her golden hair beneath it, Marilla walked from Kohanah's cell. She felt as though her insides were being torn apart, and yet she could not help but whisper . . .

"I shall love *you* for*ever*, Kohanah."

Creeping on past all of the other closed doors, Marilla could feel eyes on her, following her. But she did not turn to them. To her, these other Kiowa warriors were an extension of Kohanah, and she did not wish to be hurt any more deeply by letting their eyes condemn her with unspoken words. She was no longer their ally, for she had no power to offer them aid.

She was only a woman whose heart had been severed. . . .

Seeing the closed door that led to the outside, where the guard had been left fast asleep, Marilla had to meet the challenge of getting past him again. If he was awake, or awakened while she was walking past, she had already devised a plan that could surely work. She was only moments away from actually finding out!

The door squeaked as she slowly opened it. The moonlight was a silver sheen on the ground at her feet as she stepped from the barracks. Already she knew that the guard was not asleep, for the chair was no longer occupied!

"What the hell . . . ?"

Marilla's heart plummeted when she heard the man's gasp of wonder at her right side, where he stood in the darkness of the shadows of the barracks.

She turned with a start, the moon on her face like a light, revealing her fully to the guard.

"Marilla? Marilla Pratt?" the guard gasped, stepping into full view. His dark eyes raked over her, then looked at the door that she had not yet had the chance to close. "What the hell are you doin' here in the middle of the night? How in the hell did you get inside the barracks?"

Marilla gaped at him openly, words frozen on her tongue. But as he stepped closer, his hand on his holstered pistol, his eyes accusing her, she knew that she had no time to waste. He needed answers. Now!

"I brought more canvases to Kohanah," she said, valiantly tilting her chin. "My father had promised them. I brought the canvases in place of my father."

Her face burned with a blush, for she knew that she was not being convincing enough.

"Lieutenant Pratt ain't that dumb," the guard said, leaning closer to Marilla's face. "And, hon, I ain't that dumb, either. There's only one reason a woman comes to see a man in the middle of the night." He chuckled low, daring to touch Marilla's cheek. "You've grown to love the savage, huh? Got some to spare for me? Huh?"

Marilla's eyes flared angrily. She slapped the guard's hand away. "I wouldn't get any ideas," she hissed. "And I wouldn't go running to my father, either. You would be in a *peck* of trouble if my father knew that you were sleeping on the job and that I actually was able to slip past you *into* the barracks. My father would make sure you paid dearly for letting this happen.''

''You little whore,'' the guard said, his brow crinkled in a deep frown. ''I wouldn't want to touch the likes of you, *anyhow*. You surely were covorting with the Injun in the dark, in there.''

Guilt . . . shame . . . coursed through Marilla like wildfire. Was she a whore? Oh, Lord, was she nothing less?

Yet she had to defend her virtue! She could not let this soldier whisper about her behind her back once she was back in New York. Such gossip would spread to her father, and it would kill him.

''Whom I love and don't love is none of your business,'' she snapped. She shook her head so violently that the hood of her cape bounced from her head. ''Yes! Love! I said that I *love* Kohanah. Do not dirty this love by calling me whorish! And, sir, do not spread the word around about me and Kohanah once I leave for New York, for my father would not tolerate such talk of his daughter! You will be sorry, sir, if you dare to cross my father's path with such vicious gossip!''

Paling, her knees growing weak from these trying moments, Marilla spun around on a heel and stomped away from the guard. She did not dare look back, for she did not know whether she had made any sense to the guard, or whether he would *tell*. She would live in dread from this moment on, for she had lost so much this night.

Yet it did not seem possible that so much unhappiness had come to her so quickly this night after having experienced such wondrous joy within Kohanah's arms. It was suddenly hard for her to distinguish between what was real . . . and what was fantasy.

But the ache deep within her was real . . . so terribly real . . .

Nine

❧ ❧

Three Years Later
Indian Territory (Oklahoma), May 1878

Ah, Oklahoma! The sun follows a long course in the day
and the sky is immense beyond all comparison. The land
itself ascends *into* the sky. The meadow is bright with
Indian paintbrush, lupine, and wild buckwheat. High in
the branches of a lodgepole pine a male pine grosbeak is
perched, round and rose-colored, its dark, striped wings
invisible in the soft, mottled light. The uppermost branches
of the tree seem very slowly to ride across the blue sky.

Always there are winds. . . .

The chestnut horse blew out a snort as it moved at a
short, choppy trot along a narrow, snakelike path that
mocked being called a road. Marilla clung to the rough-
grained wooden seat of the buckboard wagon on which she
sat beside Charles Agnew, a straight-backed soldier, brac-
ing herself for the possibility that the squeaking wooden
wheels might fall into another dreaded pothole.

The train ride from New York with its crowded seats,

and the black soot from the belching engine blowing in through open windows, had been almost intolerable. But nothing could be as bad, as utterly uncomfortably unbearable, as this buckboard, the only mode of transportation offered at the railhead by a soldier who had come from Fort Cobb to escort Marilla to the house in which she would live, close to the fort and close to the school in which she would be teaching.

Marilla looked across the vastness of the land, at the long yellow grass shining in the bright light, reaching clean away, out of sight. Loneliness seemed to be an aspect of the land. All things on the plains were isolated. There was no confusion of objects before the eyes, but perhaps one hill or one tree. To look upon the landscape with the sun at one's back was to lose all sense of proportion.

Marilla's imagination had seemed to come to life and this, she thought, surely was where Creation had begun!

An eagerness was beginning to swell inside her, for she now knew that she was traveling on reservation land of the Kiowa! Soon she would even see . . . be *with* Kohanah. At last he was free, and she was three years older and her own *person*, free in her own way, to go to him.

But would he even welcome her? He had told her that they could never be together at the reservation. Would he actually forbid it? Even if he saw that she was coming to the reservation in the capacity of a teacher, would he still turn his back on her?

For the past three years Marilla had prepared herself for teaching by attending the most fashionable schools of New York. Now she was ready to put all of her learning to good use.

She would teach the Kiowa children!

Marilla shifted herself so that she was more comfortable on the hard seat. Though she had matured into a woman at the age of seventeen while being held within Kohanah's arms, she now, at the age of twenty, had the appearance of a woman of sophistication in her stylish attire. Her cloak was of a fuchsia coloring, ornamented with a decorative *cordelière*. Her matching bonnet was accentuated with ribbon, bows, and flowers; her gloves were also colorfully fuchsia.

Lovely and golden, her hair was drawn up in a chignon beneath her bonnet. Her pale blue dress beneath the cloak was silk, high-necked, with eyelet lace sewn around the neckline and into the front seam. The point in front and curved side-front seams were boned for stiffness. Her shoes were flat-heeled slippers.

Except for a faint powdering of travel dust on her nose and cheeks, Marilla felt as though she were glowing, her heart was so filled with a love that had been forced to lie dormant within her these past three years. Hopefully she thought she could soon set her pent-up emotions free. She so wanted to be held by Kohanah, be told that he loved her, no matter the color of her skin or the differences in their customs! She had never believed that he had turned her away because he did not love her! No man made love as devotedly as Kohanah had made love to her, if he was not *in* love!

"Won't be long now, ma'am," Charles said, jolting Marilla's mind, reminding her that she was not making this trip alone.

Charles slapped the horse's reins. "If you squint your eyes, in the distance you can see the Indian tipis," he said, giving Marilla a sidewise glance, his brown eyes soft and friendly, his red hair windblown. "But before we get to the tipis, we'll get to the house vacated by the last school-marm. It ain't the best, but decent enough for livin' in."

He frowned. "It'd be best, though, if you had a man to protect you, ma'am," he said thickly. "Out there all alone you'll be at the mercy of the Indians. Most are decent, but you never can tell when one might be a sneaky, low-down—"

The hair bristled at the nape of Marilla's neck. Her eyes snapped angrily. "*Sir*, I've known a few sneaky, low-down *soldiers* in my day," she said dryly, interrupting him. "One in particular, for *sure*."

"Oh?" Charles said, a rusty, bushy eyebrow rising inquisitively. "Back when you were at Fort Marion, in Florida? Before your father left Florida to return to his law practice in New York?"

Marilla's mouth went agape. "How do you know so much about me . . . about my *father*?" she asked shallowly. "Why, Father has only recently returned to New York to resume his law practice. He left Florida after he secured the release of the Kiowa from their imprisonment, enabling them to return to reservation life. Only those in charge at Fort Cobb should know the . . . the full details of my father . . . of *me*, especially since they were the ones I contacted for this teaching position. You, sir, are only a mere enlisted man, not an officer!"

Charles cleared his throat nervously. His eyes wavered as he gave Marilla a slow stare, then averted his gaze straight ahead. "Ma'am, we heard about *you* from a soldier who had been under your father's command at Fort Marion," he mumbled. He gave Marilla another sly glance. "A Jason Roark, ma'am. Do you remember a Jason Roark?"

The name, the remembrance of the crude man, sent a wave of hate throughout Marilla. Her father had merely sent Jason Roark away from Fort Marion. Now she wished that her father had shot the man!

But instead he was in Fort Cobb, close to where Marilla would be living. It was as though she was destined to be subjected to that vile man! She knew Jason well enough to know that he would make life uncomfortable for her. And surely he knew that she was arriving, and in what capacity! She had been the object of conversation, it seemed, among *all* the soldiers.

Her face turned hot with a blush. What had Jason told the soldiers? What lies had he fed them? Had he bragged of conquering her when, in truth, he *hadn't*? Was he going to torment her all over again? If so, what would Kohanah do about it?

Perhaps Kohanah wouldn't even care! She had known that she was taking a chance by coming here . . . a chance that Kohanah would not want her. But now that she had Jason Roark to be on the guard for, wasn't the chance she was taking twofold? One man might want her too much . . . the other not at *all*!

"Ma'am, are you all right?" Charles asked, letting the

reins go limp, to place a gloved finger to her chin to turn her face his way. "Did I say something wrong? Maybe I shouldn't have mentioned Jason Roark."

Firming her jaw, squaring her shoulders, knowing that she must get control of her feelings, Marilla eased Charles's finger away from her face. "Why on earth would you think that saying the man's name would disturb me?" she asked, forcing a smile. "As far as I'm concerned the man simply does not even *exist*. He is a vile man who lies as easily as he breathes."

Marilla looked ahead, her insides suddenly acquiver when she made out the distinct outline of tipis in the distance. There were many three-poled skin tipis spread across the land, their doorways facing east, the direction of the rising sun. One of those tipis belonged to the man she loved!

"No, the name Jason Roark does not disturb me in the least," she said in a low purr. "Nor shall it ever!"

"That's good," Charles said, nodding. "He ain't one of my favorite people. In fact, can't think of one person who likes *or* respects the son of a bitch. He ain't nothin' but trouble. I steer clear of him the best I can. Live longer that way."

Marilla was relieved to know this soldier's reaction to Jason, even more to know that most agreed with him. Her reputation was at stake. She did not wish to wander about Fort Cobb for supplies, with all of the soldiers eyeing her knowingly. If she found that was the way it would be, she would horsewhip Jason Roark herself!

The jerk of the buckboard as the stallion was directed onto an even narrower lane made Marilla grab for the seat with one hand, her bonnet with the other. She looked over her shoulder when she heard her valise and travel trunk clunk loudly as they were tossed about behind her.

Then her eyes were drawn around again when she saw the reason for the turn. At the far end of this narrow lane sat a house, so alone; it was sitting on the plains like a sentinel. The closer she drew to it, the more she could tell about it. It was a house of logs, with white plaster chinking, sitting low on a foundation of bigger logs.

The house was low and drab, its color worn away in wind and rain, the wood burned gray so that the grain showed, the nails turned red with rust. The windowpanes were black and opaque. . . .

"Don't look like much, but comfortable enough for one person to make residence in," Charles said, flicking the reins, hurrying the horse along until the house was reached. He reined in beside a hitching rail and jumped from the seat and went briskly around to offer a hand to Marilla. "Ma'am?"

Marilla scooted from the seat, wincing when she heard a faint ripping noise, realizing the silk of her dress had snagged on splinters of wood from the seat.

But she smiled down at Charles, at least glad to be able to say a good-bye to that dreaded buckboard. "Thank you," she murmured, stepping to the ground.

Looking slowly about her, she could from this vantage point see downhill to a pecan grove, a dense, dark growth along a meandering stream and, beyond, the long sweep of the earth itself, curving out beneath the sky. Great billowing clouds sailing upon the heavens were shadows that moved upon the ground like water, blocking the light. Marilla could feel the motion of the air; she could hear the frogs by the stream. She was in awe of a scissortail as it soared above a tree.

"It's a beautiful land," Marilla sighed, hugging herself. She looked into the distance, searching from Indian tipi to tipi. "The Indians surely had cause to fight for it!"

"Ma'am, I wouldn't so openly voice such an opinion if I were you," Charles said, turning from her, to unload her belongings from the back of the buckboard. "Most still don't like sharin' this land with the Indians. It ain't by choice, believe me. If it wasn't for President Hayes appointing an agent to serve as a liaison with the Indians, making sure they are treated right, there'd be a war for sure again' them. As it is, the agent dispenses provisions, called annuities, evicts trespassers attempting to settle on the reservation, and arranges friendly consultations between Indian tribes and the cavalry. It surely ain't the best of conditions any of us live in here in Indian Territory.

You'll probably leave faster than a cat can swat its paw at a bird!''

"I am not one who gives up all that easily," Marilla said, stubbornly lifting her chin. "I have come to teach. I *shall*."

Flipping the tail of her cloak, dress, and petticoats around, she stepped up on a narrow, creaking porch that fronted the house. The door stood agape. Gingerly she touched it, then stood breathlessly by as it swung slowly open. Cautiously she stepped inside, flinching when a cobweb grazed her cheek, clinging like silken fingers to her flesh.

"Drat!" she whispered, scraping the cobweb away from her face. Her gaze swept on around her. The sun slanting through the window at her side revealed a room with walls studded with wooden pegs, low ceilings with cobwebs spun from side to side, and dust-covered furniture.

Moving across the floor, Marilla looked into another room, grimacing. Two rooms! Two *drab* rooms filled with the most meager of furnishings. In the outer room an ugly iron bed sat against a far wall. Several straight chairs, a table, and a heating stove filled the other spaces.

Afraid to, not wanting to see what the other room had to offer her, Marilla forced her feet to carry her there. This back room was a kitchen with a cooking stove, table and chairs, and shelves built along the walls with odds and ends of dishes and pots and pans arranged across them. Along the wall beside a back door stood a copper bathtub, gleaming as though it had just been freshly scrubbed.

"The bathtub is the only decent thing about this place!" she whispered placing her gloved hands to her cheeks.

But her imagination was already beginning to work overtime. She could dress this house up with flowered wallpaper, fancy curtains, pictures, and bric-a-brac. Bright, braided rugs could cover the planked flooring. Some new dishes and lovely candle holders filled with long white candles could liven up her kitchen table.

"Ain't so pleasant, huh?" Charles asked, kneading his chin as he stepped up beside Marilla, to follow her eyes as she again absorbed the house that would be hers until Lord knew when. She had just grown used to fabulous furnishings, servants, *all* luxuries of the affluent that New York and her father offered her. But to be with Kohanah, she was ready to accept *any* way of life.

Perhaps even life in a *tipi*, should their relationship develop as she so very much desired!

"It will do," Marilla said flatly, untying her bonnet, jerking it from her head. Laying it aside on a table, she began to remove her gloves, a finger at a time, her eyes on the bed. From the way the mattress sagged in the middle, she could tell that it was made of feathers. There was an advantage to that sort of bed. When you slept alone, the feathers hugged you, as though you were being embraced! She hoped she would not be sleeping alone all that long.

If only Kohanah . . .

"Your things are brought in and you seem ready to get yourself fitted in for the night," Charles said, walking toward the front door. "If there's anything you ever need, the fort is only a half-mile to the west."

He swung around on a heel and smiled warmly at Marilla. "Out back you'll find a horse grazing and a buggy. The horse has plenty of hay; the buggy wheels have been oiled. You might want to drop by the fort tomorrow for victuals. There ain't much to cook around here right now." He nodded toward the kitchen. "I brought in some flour and potatoes the other day. That's about all, ma'am." He turned to leave again, then once more spun around. "Oh, and yes, there's coffee." He gestured with a hand toward the kitchen. "I put it on the shelf. You'll smell it if you don't see it. Freshly ground, ma'am. Just for you."

Marilla was finding a sudden liking to this man who spoke gently, who looked as gentle, with his freckled face and red hair. His brown eyes smiled all the time. In them she could see sunshine, they were so warm!

"You have been so kind," she said, going to him, to touch his arm. "I do appreciate it."

Charles lowered his eyes, smiling bashfully. "Ain't much, ma'am," he said, fidgeting with a pistol holstered at his waist. His eyes shot up. "But if you ever need anything, just come and ask for me, personally."

"I will," Marilla said, feeling a sudden urge to hug him, but thinking better of it, for lack of truly knowing him well enough. But he did seem to be the sort one would want for a brother.

She escorted him from the cabin. "Again, thank you," she said, as he climbed onto the buckboard. "You seem to have thought of everything."

"Except for one thing," Charles said hoarsely. "I want to give you some advice . . . warn you to latch the door securely when you settle in. It's best to always play it safe."

"I will," Marilla said, again hugging herself, when realizing just how alone she would be when he rode away. She was one tiny speck out here on this vastness of land. She would be vulnerable to many perils. Her father had argued against her decision to come here, warning her of the dangers.

But in her heart she knew the true danger would be *not* to come. She would lose Kohanah for *sure* if she gave him a chance to find a woman who could fill the empty spaces in his heart. As it was, Kohanah had not been free all that long. After Marilla's father had fought for the Indians' release from Fort Marion and had succeeded, they had been gone from there only a few months! Surely Kohanah had not found a woman in that short length of time! If he truly cared for Marilla, he would not be that eager to take another woman into his heart!

A chill coursed through Marilla as she waved a final good-bye to Charles as he spun the buckboard around and began driving away from her. She watched him until he was only a shadow on the horizon, then turned and went back inside the house, sighing.

Determined to make this work, she removed her cloak, rolled up her sleeves, found a kerosene lantern, and lit it.

Taking it into the kitchen, where the sun was waning at the window, she looked everywhere until she found a water bucket. Thinking that she would have to walk clear to the stream for water, she set the lantern down on the table, grabbed the bucket, and went out the back door. She was surprised to find a well close to where the horse was grazing. She hurried to the well and began to crank a bucket attached to a rope downward, toward the water. When she heard the sound of a horse approaching, she turned with a smile, thinking that Charles was returning with some more of his kind advice.

But the smile froze on her face as her heart skipped a beat within her chest. The outline of the man approaching on a red roan was quite recognizable, for she had carried his image around inside her heart these past three years. How could she not recognize the lithe, powerfully built man with intense eyes and strong, determined face with hard cheekbones and flat planes?

How could she not recognize *Kohanah* . . . ?

"It . . . *is* . . . he . . ." Marilla whispered, letting go of the rope, letting the bucket fall to the depths of the well. She turned and began to run, her feet not moving quickly enough. She could already feel the taste of his kiss on her lips!

"Kohanah!" she cried, waving frantically. "Oh, Kohanah, it is *I*. Darling, it is *I*!"

Ten

❧❧

Marilla's footsteps faltered as alarm set in, touching her with coldness, when Kohanah did not respond to her greeting. Instead his face remained impassive, free of any emotion. The fringes of his doeskin shirt and breeches were all that moved, those only responding to the motion of the wind as his red roan moved steadily onward in a soft trot.

At this closer range, Marilla could see the strained tendons of Kohanah's hands as they gripped the horse's reins. She could see the play of the muscles of his lean thighs beneath his close-fitting breeches. The black hair that was drawn back from his brow into long braids accentuated his copper skin, his intensely dark eyes, and his sculpted features.

In three years he had only changed in that he looked more mature . . . *prouder*. It was as though Marilla's dreams were coming to life. He was actually there, only a hug away.

Except that in her dreams, Kohanah was always as happy to see her, as she was to see *him*. . . .

Kohanah's heart was beating wildly within his chest. He was finding it hard to believe that he was actually seeing

Marilla, instead of fantasizing about her, as he had done so often since their last embrace.

But, *ho*, yes, she was there in a billowing dress, slender, yet fully bosomed. She was as he remembered her, so vibrant, her eyes the color of the sky, so bright, so eager!

His gaze locked on her full, ripe mouth, aching to kiss her, to *taste* her sweetness.

Then he looked beyond the promise of a kiss, to her delicate ivory skin, her face so gentle, her supple body. He longed to uncoil her hair so that it could ripple in golden sprays of sunshine down her perfect back.

Aware of where his thoughts were taking him, not *wanting* them to, Kohanah's fingers coiled more forcefully about the reins, his jaws locked stubbornly, as he reminded himself of his destiny! He was now a proud chief of his band of Kiowa! His purpose in life was to benefit his *people* by all of his thoughts, actions, and deeds. *His* desires of the flesh must not be satisfied wantonly! A white woman was *not* the answer to the problems of the Kiowa, yet it *was* this white woman's father who was responsible for many things good for his people! Did not her father speak for the release of the Kiowa warriors from their imprisonment in Florida, so that they could return to fend for their families? Did not it actually happen because of her father?

Ah, but Kohanah was torn with needs . . . with hopes . . . with desires. If he could but hold Marilla within his arms just one more time, perhaps he would find answers that could benefit him *and* his people. Had not rumors said that she had come to teach the Kiowa children?

Or had she come in that pretense only to pursue *him*? If so, should not he feel honored that she cared enough for him to do this?

Drawing rein beside Marilla, Kohanah looked down upon her with fire in his eyes . . . with a beating heart that he was glad she could not see! His heart would surely betray him so quickly!

"*Tsan*, Kohanah!" Marilla said, weakness surging through her, her love for Kohanah was so overwhelming. "I have come. Do you not care?"

Marilla waited a moment that in truth felt like an eternity, trying to understand this man who had taken her to heaven and back with his hands and lips. How could he be so cold and distant to her now?

Or didn't she already know? Surely he *had* only made love to her to *use* her love and friendship to his advantage while locked away in prison in Florida!

Then a sudden piercing ache tore at her heart when another possibility came to her that she did not want to let take hold. Was he . . . married? Was that why he was treating her so coldly? Did he not have a *need* for her, because he already had a woman to warm his bed?

Marilla bit her lower lip in silent agony, then reached out to him. "*Tsan!*" she repeated more determinedly. "I have come to you! Say that you are glad! If not, I shall *leave*. If I am not wanted . . ."

Not able to find the courage to say anything else, not able to stand there being humiliated beneath the coldness of his eyes, Marilla swung her skirt around and began to run toward the house. She shouldn't have come to Oklahoma! How could she have made such a mistake as this? She *always* thought things out very carefully before entering into *any* decision!

How could *this* decision have been so *wrong*?

Sobs racked her body as she drew her skirts up into her arms so that she could run faster . . . harder! She had to put distance between herself and Kohanah. She could never even think of him again!

Kohanah was stung by Marilla's abrupt exit. One dark wedge of eyebrow lifted; then he thrust his moccasin-clad heels into the flanks of his red roan and rode after Marilla. He had made a mistake by greeting her so silently, so coldly! Seeing her reaction made him know that this was not the way he wanted it to be between them! He could not ignore their shared feelings. He loved her . . . she loved *him*. Somehow it must be made to work between them, for deep down inside him, where his desires were formed, he knew that life had been empty without her. No woman had ever filled the corner of his heart that had been awakened by her sweet kisses and embraces. She was meant to be the one who kindled his desires! Only she!

"*Agantsan*!" Kohanah shouted, his red roan now only a hoofbeat away from Marilla. "Tsonda, wait!"

Kohanah's words reached Marilla like a lifeline, for until he spoke she had felt as though she were sinking into a dark void, a pit that she might not be able to emerge from again. Without Kohanah, life had no meaning! It was as though he had breathed life into her the moment he touched her. Until Kohanah, surely life had had no meaning . . . no direction at all!

Marilla stopped and swung around just as Kohanah reached her and bent from where he sat in his saddle and swept her up onto his lap. Held strongly within his arms, relishing his steel body pressing into hers, Marilla sobbed hungrily as his lips consumed hers with a fierce, possessive heat.

She twined her arms about his neck and gave herself up to the rapture, his kiss banishing all of the doubts from her mind. He did love her. No man who didn't love could kiss so wonderfully . . . so totally.

As Kohanah's powerful hands held Marilla close, as his tongue probed between her lips, a euphoria filled her that was almost more than she could bear. She clung to him, her mind reeling, her body awakening again to needs that, while she was away from Kohanah, the man she adored, had been so long denied.

"My *manyi*," Kohanah said huskily, his lips now only brushing against Marilla's. "My woman, we meet again, always when it is the beginning of the spring moon. You come? You have felt my yearnings for you?"

Marilla threw her head back in a peaceful sigh when Kohanah's lips moved and kissed her delicately tapered throat. "My love, you *are* happy to see me," she said in an almost sob. "Oh, how happy I am! I have yearned so for *you*."

Her breath caught in her throat when Kohanah's hand molded her breast through her dress, eliciting fire there. She did not object when his other hand went to the buttons at the back of her dress and began unbuttoning them. She was no longer aware that they were still on a horse. She felt as though she were floating on a cloud as Kohanah's hand slipped inside her dress and touched her bare flesh, then on around and inside the bodice of her chemise, to fully touch and caress her throbbing breast.

"You were a woman at the age of seventeen winters," Kohanah said, his pulse racing, her silken flesh driving him almost to madness. His fingers kneaded her breast, his thumb circled the stiff peak of the nipple. "You are much more woman at the age of twenty winters. Kohanah wants to touch you all over. Kohanah wants to make love!"

The soft pain between Marilla's thighs was a reminder of what she had shared with Kohanah that night she went to him in the small cell of the Indian barracks. It was something awakening anew, spreading through her, all of her nerve endings responding, like charges of electricity moving from cloud to cloud during a thunderstorm.

"My love, I want you as much," she said, then became lost to him, way beyond coherent thought when once again he kissed her. His fingers dug into the flesh of her breast. She could feel his hunger in the hard, seeking pressure of his lips.

She clung to him, unaware of when the horse had arrived at her house or of when Kohanah had carried her inside and to her bed, or of how or when she had become totally undressed.

She was oblivious of everything but his nude body as it now connected with hers, flesh hot against flesh, lips hot against lips.

When he entered her with one solid thrust and began his eager strokes within her, Marilla lifted her hips in response. She locked her legs about him. Her whole body throbbed and responded with an answering need, floating on ecstatic waves of passion, the joy forbidden her these past three years finally hers to claim, to *savor*.

"Tsonda," Kohanah whispered, trailing kisses from her lips to the peaks of her breasts.

Then he looked down at her, his eyes dark pools of passion. The kerosene lamp that Marilla had placed on the table before she went to draw water from the well flickered

its golden light about the room, moving upon Marilla's
skin as though touching her in a caress. Her long blond
hair had loosened from its bun and now lay upon her
shoulders and against her breasts like a wondrous golden
shawl.

"You are as beautiful . . . as sweet as before," Kohanah
said in a husky whisper. "I love you, Tsonda. I love
you."

Marilla raised a hand to his cheek and stroked it gently.
"I shall always love you," she whispered. "I've loved
you from the very moment I saw you." She twined her
arms about his neck and drew his cheek down next to hers.
"I could not stay away, Kohanah. Please say that it is our
destiny to be together. Please . . . say it. . . ."

Kohanah stiffened within Marilla's arms. He drew
brusquely away and sat on the feather mattress with his
back to her. The word "destiny" had struck a chord of
danger within his heart. How could his destiny include
a white woman? Would not that make him less a man
in his people's eyes? They were bitter against those who
had taken so much from the Kiowa! Could they see beyond
that bitterness when looking upon Marilla? Perhaps they
would remember who her father was and remember also
that he was a white man like no other white man before
them! So was his *daughter* like no other white women!

Marilla's insides splashed cold. She moved to her knees
behind Kohanah, staring blankly at him, wondering why
he had drawn away from her. It was as though he was
playing a game with her. A cruel, even *dangerous* game!
Toying with one's heart was an almost unpardonable sin in
a woman's eyes!

But not wanting to think the worst, the remembrance of
Kohanah's kisses still warm and sweet on her lips, Marilla
embraced him from behind, curling her arms around him.
She pressed her breasts into his back, relishing the touch
of him in even this way.

"Do not turn away from me," she murmured. "Kohanah,
you only moments ago confessed to *loving* me. Do you
love me one minute . . . hate me the *next*? How can that
be? How?"

Placing her cheek on his back, Marilla stifled a sob, but could not stop the flow of tears from her eyes. One by one they wetted his back. . . .

Kohanah flinched when he felt the wetness of Marilla's tears on his back. He did not want to think that he was hurting her so deeply! Her hurt was *his* hurt. How could he allow it to continue?

Looking down, he saw that Marilla's hands were resting on his thighs, so close to where his hardness proved his intense need to be with her. He eyed her hand for a short while longer, then his hardness. With a pounding heart he twined his fingers through hers and guided her hand to his manhood. When her fingers encircled it, obeying his silent command, his breath was momentarily stolen from the burst of pleasure that it gave him.

When Marilla began moving her hand, Kohanah closed his eyes and enjoyed, forgetting everything but this moment of rapture with his woman!

Marilla feathered kisses along Kohanah's back while giving him pleasure with her hand. Words were not important any longer. His actions had told her all that she needed to know. He wanted her. He *loved* her. He was responding to her lovemaking. He was *encouraging* it!

Oh, how it thrilled Marilla to *give* him pleasure. She enjoyed how his hardness trembled within her fingers! She enjoyed the feel of his velvet smoothness and the warmth pulsating from his manhood into her hand, as though she were an extension *of* him, with barriers no longer standing in the way of their love for each other.

Kohanah's heartbeat was wild. His loins ached with need. He eased Marilla's hand away and turned her around so that they were facing each other. Smiling down at her, he placed his hands on her waist and lifted her onto his lap so that her legs were straddling him and the soft mound of hair at the juncture of her thighs was pressed invitingly against his hardness. Softly probing, he found easy entrance inside her and began his thrusts, both his hands cupping a breast.

Marilla's hair bounced on her shoulders as she became quickly breathless with desire. She clasped her fingers around Kohanah's neck and held on to him as she rode him, each of his thrusts seeming to reach clean into her heart.

Closing her eyes, she let the rapture take hold. She moved with him as he momentarily removed his hardness to stretch her out on the bed. His lips then worshiped her body, kissing all of her pleasure points.

Hardly able to bear the waiting any longer, Kohanah entered her again as she nestled close to him. He kissed her with an acute gentleness as the pleasure spiraled and spread . . . spreading . . . spreading.

Then it crested and exploded, their bodies shaking in unison, their gasps blending as though in one voice, one *emotion* of wondrous joy sought and found.

Spent, Kohanah rolled away from Marilla, yet could not keep his hands from her heaving breasts. He shaped them within his palms, kissing one nipple, then the next.

"My *manyi*," he said huskily. "Kohanah's nights will no longer be restless. You have given me peace within my heart . . . within my *soul*. No one but you can give Kohanah such peace. No one . . . but you."

He drew her next to him, holding her close, his breath hot on her cheek. "It is so good to be with you," he whispered. "How I have missed you!"

Marilla was floating with ecstasy. She clung to Kohanah, loving the smell of him . . . a blend of the outdoors and manly muskiness. "You're glad that I came?" she whispered into his ear. "Truly? Are you? You seemed strangely cold when you first saw me."

"Kohanah was battling feelings," he mumbled, his hands now smoothing down her back, across the softness of her buttocks. "Kohanah is now chief. My band of Kiowa are Kohanah's main concern! They still fight for rights stolen by white men!" He drew away from her and looked heavy-lashed into her eyes. "*You* are white, Tsonda. Do you see why I was torn?"

Marilla looked up at him with wide, innocent eyes. "But I was white before, and it did not seem to matter all that much," she murmured. Then a pain of remembrance scorched her heart. Again it was there, as though his kisses and embraces had not erased it from her consciousness at all! Her doubts of why he showed affection for her!

Marilla inched away from him, shoving his hands aside. "Tell me that what I am thinking is wrong," she said hoarsely, tremors suddenly assailing her. "Tell me, Kohanah, that you never made love to me for all the wrong reasons. Tell me again that you love me. Love me for love's sake *alone*."

His brow furrowing, seeing the hurt in her eyes and hearing it in her voice, Kohanah was momentarily taken aback. What was she accusing him of? How could she doubt his love for her after he had just proved it in the way he knew best? He had never loved as fiercely!

He refrained from going to her . . . to embrace her. If she doubted his love now, would she not doubt it forever?

Climbing from the bed, the moonlight slanting in from the window at his feet, the kerosene lamp lighting his face, Kohanah turned his back to Marilla and reached for his fringed breeches. Silently he drew them on, a leg at a time, then tied the buckskin string in front.

Marilla winced as though shot, feeling wounded at the pit of her stomach, which felt so strangely empty. She doubled her hands into two fists and pressed them tightly into the mattress on either side of her as she moved to her knees to watch Kohanah, unbelievingly.

"You don't love me," she said, her voice cracking with emotion. "You use me now as you did before. Why, Kohanah? Why would I benefit you now? Though you are forced to live on a reservation, you are free from the Fort Marion prison. I can no longer plead for your freedom, so why would you use me now? What do you want from me? What!"

Angry fire was rising within Kohanah's eyes. His jaw tightened, his shoulder and arm muscles corded as he doubled his hands into fists at his sides.

"Tsonda, why do you do this?" he growled. "Does not Kohanah have enough to torture his mind and heart without you also adding to this torment? *Obaika*, you remain forever in my heart as the *only* woman to kindle my desires. Why must you doubt me? Why?"

"Because . . . you . . . give me *cause* to," Marilla said in a near whisper, his words of sincere love reaching her heart like a song. "Please, if you *do* totally love me, *please* quit giving me cause to *doubt* such love."

Kohanah frowned. He kneaded his chin contemplatively, somewhere deep inside his heart troubled by remembrances. He *was* recalling when he had loved her and yet had known that a portion of the love was for a set purpose that could benefit his people. Her father *had* been the leader at Fort Marion. Her father *had* had the power to do many things for the Kiowa. When Marilla had been held within Kohanah's arms while in Florida, Kohanah had *known* these things!

He battled his remembrances, sorting them out inside his mind and heart, casting the ugly reasons for loving her aside. This was *now*. She would never know that a part of him ever *did* use their relationship for a purpose other than loving. And he must be sure never to give her cause to doubt him again.

Fiercely, almost savagely, Kohanah drew Marilla back into his arms. His lips bore down upon hers, trying to relay a message he did not wish to speak aloud. He must prove beyond a shadow of a doubt his love to her and he knew the best way to do so.

He would love her with a passion that she never knew existed . . . that she would never *forget*. . . .

Eleven

꒰ঌ ໒꒱

Green eyes squinted over a deck of cards; lips were pursed on a fat cigar, puffing. "Well, what's your pleasure, gents?" Jason Roark asked, holding the cards firmly within the fingers of one hand while drumming the fingers of his other hand nervously on the table. He looked from soldier to soldier. Their gazes were cold as they looked back at him.

He then lowered his eyes to the pile of money that lay in front of him, having been lucky tonight at poker, as he was every night. But tonight his mind wasn't so much on the game of poker as it was on Marilla Pratt. Charles Agnew had met her at the railhead. If everything had gone as planned, she would even now be at the house assigned to the schoolmarm. Way out there, isolated, she would be ripe for picking . . . and he was just the man to do it!

Yet he would have to have eyes in the back of his head at all times if he dared approach her, for Kohanah would most surely be her man again. He was almost surely the reason Marilla had come to Fort Cobb under the pretense of teaching the savages' children.

"Well? Cat got your tongues, or what?" Jason growled, taking the cigar from between his lips, placing it on an ashtray. He began to absently shuffle the cards. "What's it to be?"

Patrick Klein—a young soldier, thin and gaunt, with brown, kinky hair, dressed in coarse, dark breeches and a loose-fitted plaid shirt—eyed Jason warily. He saw him as no less than a son of a bitch, and he wanted like hell to beat him in at least one game of poker tonight.

His gaze swept over Jason, his insides growing cold when he saw Jason's coal-black hair sleeked down against his head with pomade and how his kinky black chest hairs covered his massive shirtless chest. His round face was distorted by a large, bulbous nose, his green eyes held within them a glint quite dangerous and evil. No one at the fort liked Jason Roark. He was loud and boisterous . . . and very opinionated.

But he did know a damn good deal about the game of poker! That was to be admired, if nothing else!

"So you're givin' us a choice now that you've won most of our week's allowance, eh?" Patrick said in his slow Kentucky drawl. He eyed the deck of cards in Jason's hands. He lifted his dark eyes slowly and looked from man to man, the cigar smoke in the soldiers' barracks so thick it was like low-lying fog.

When he saw that no one was ready to speak, to openly challenge Jason Roark, Patrick straightened his shoulders and lifted his chin, eyeing Jason with a set stare. "Five-card stud. Jacks or better to open," he said. He placed two one-dollar bills in the center of the table. "And an ante of two dollars should suffice."

Jason reached for a bottle of whiskey that he had placed on the floor beside his chair. He placed it to his lips and took a quick swallow. Hiccoughing, he put the bottle back on the floor, ignoring the other men at the table, stunned that this little twerp would so openly challenge him. Thus far tonight Patrick had been tight-lipped. Jason had to wonder where he was getting the courage to speak up. But Jason had those sorts to deal with at times. It would be fun toying with the kinky-haired son of a bitch!

"Suits me fine," Jason grumbled, licking his lips of the taste of whiskey, his insides already warmed from having consumed half a bottle tonight. He placed his ante in the middle of the table and waited for the others to follow, then sneered when he looked over at Patrick as he again slowly shuffled the cards. "Yeah. Suits me just fine. If you want to kiss that much money good-bye with one smack, it ain't no problem of mine." He leaned over the table. "Will Mama send you more money to be gambled away, Patrick? Or will Daddy not *allow* it?"

Patrick doubled his hands into tight fists atop the table, his cheeks rosy with anger. "Just deal the damn cards," he drawled. "Seems your mama and daddy didn't teach you good manners *or* breedin'."

Jason's green eyes squinted. He glared over at Patrick, reached for his cigar, and clamped it between his teeth, then began dealing the cards from man to man. "Son, I'm goin' to make you eat those words," he snarled. "When I get done with you, you'll go runnin' back to Kentucky with your tail plumb tucked beneath yore legs!"

When all of the men were holding five cards apiece in their hands, Jason spread his cards out between his fingers, and his insides recoiled. Damn. He hadn't gotten openers! He glanced over at Patrick. Had he . . . ?

"Well?" Jason finally said, looking over at Patrick again, then at each of the other soldiers. Scowling, he placed his cards on the table, face down.

"Check," the soldier at Jason's right side grumbled, slapping his cards face down on the table, looking at the next soldier.

Many grumbles of "check" floated around the table; then all threw their cards onto a pile in the middle of the table and anted again. The cards were dealt a second, then a third time.

Then Jason smiled broadly. He had drawn better than openers. He had drawn four of a kind. He looked the cards over once again, then glanced around the table, his gaze stopping at Patrick. He tensed. Patrick was smiling crookedly, his straight, white teeth gleaming in the soft lamplight. Had he drawn a better hand? Naw. Surely not . . .

Jason glanced back down at his own cards, seeing that he would be drawing into a straight flush. If only he could be dealt an eight of clubs, then he would again be the victor!

"One dollar," Jason grumbled, deciding to bluff the young son of a bitch.

The bet moved around to Patrick. "Okay, I'll call you," he said quietly, his insides glowing, having decided that bluffing was his best way of beating the low-down bastard. He glanced over at Jason and saw his eyebrows tilt with surprise. Patrick wanted to laugh, but instead glanced on around the table to the next soldier who was ready to bet.

Then it was time to discard.

"How many cards, Patrick?" Jason asked smoothly, taking a deep drag from his cigar. He eyed Patrick warily, suspecting a bluff. . . .

Patrick tried to keep a straight face, though he wanted to shout out at Jason Roark that he had him beaten!

"One card'll do," Patrick finally said. "Yep. One'll do."

Jason didn't remove his eyes from Patrick as he dealt out the cards to the rest of the soldiers, then Patrick, and then smiled smugly when he took only one card for himself. He laughed throatily when he saw Patrick's face drain of color. . . .

But footsteps moving into the barracks drew Jason's head quickly around. Suddenly the card game was of no concern to him any longer. His heart skipped a beat when he saw Charles Agnew go to his bunk and stretch out leisurely atop it, fully clothed. If Charles Agnew had returned from his assigned job, that had to mean that Marilla Pratt was only a few heartbeats away. And she would be alone! Surely Kohanah would not know of her arrival this soon.

Glowering, grabbing his cigar from between his lips to crush it out in the ashtray, Jason scooted his chair back and rose quickly to his feet. He had a debt to pay to that wench. Tonight was as good as any to settle the score! He would deal with Kohanah later if he caused him any trouble. A white man's word was law here at Fort Cobb, whether or not Kohanah wanted to accept that truth.

"That's all of the card game for this evenin' as far as

I'm concerned," Jason grumbled, slapping his cards face down on the table. He gathered up the money already won and began walking away toward his bunk. "Patrick, this time you got lucky. You don't have to go against my straight flush! The game's *yours*."

He hurried to his bunk and jerked a shirt on, placed his earnings beneath his mattress, ignoring Patrick's whining objections. He secured his holstered pistols about his waist, gave Charles a quiet stare as he lay there, watching, then spun around on a heel and rushed from the room.

Once outside he swung himself up into the saddle and wheeled his horse around and galloped through the wide open gate of the fort. He leaned low over the horse, anticipating the moments ahead. He would teach that wench to tattle to her father back at Fort Marion. He would finish what he had started, then threaten her with her life should she decide to tattle again. . . .

Charles Agnew scooted from his bunk and grabbed his rifle from beside his bed and walked determinedly from the barracks. Though he had never been one to interfere with anything that Jason Roark did, this time he had no choice *but* to. He knew Jason's destination. Well, it was up to Charles Agnew to stop him!

But first he would tease Jason Roark just a mite. Charles would let Jason get just so close to Marilla's house; *then* he would get the warning of his life.

The fire burned cozily in the fireplace. The copper tub had been brought close beside it and filled with water that had been warmed over the kitchen stove, clear and tempting. Marilla trembled sensually as Kohanah lifted her nude body up into his arms, then lowered her into the water. She eyed him warmly as he stepped totally nude inside the tub and positioned her on his lap, so that her legs were straddling him.

"I feel most wicked," Marilla said, laughing softly. She twined her arms about Kohanah's neck and drew his mouth to her lips. "But, oh, how delicious it is to be here with you in such a way. Kiss me, Kohanah. Hold me and tell me that it is real . . . that we *are* together again." She cast her eyes downward. "Tell me again that you are glad that I am here. I've waited so long. I would die if I had to turn back because you did not want me."

"It pleases me that you are here," Kohanah said huskily. "But you must understand that my people come first. I am now their chief. They depend on me and my ability to make the right decisions *totally*. You must understand this, Tsonda. Perhaps one day you will be the total purpose for Kohanah's existence. Do not be hurt that you are not *now*. The *yapahe*, soldiers, make it hard on my people. They fight against all that is good *for* my people."

"*Nyagyaito*, I hate that you and your people still suffer so at the hands of the soldiers," Marilla murmured, his mouth so close his breath was hot on her lips. She flicked her tongue over his lips teasingly. "But, please, let us not talk about them now. Let there just be us for the moment. Love me again. I so need you, Kohanah. Oh, so much!"

"*Ho*, yes," he whispered. "*Inhogo*, now. *Obaika*, you remain forever inside my heart. Kohanah loves you. Only you."

As his mouth lowered to her lips, he kissed her meltingly, his hands cupping her breasts. His thumbs circled the nipples, causing them to tighten. His tongue speared between her lips and tasted the jasmine sweetness of her mouth.

Marilla eased herself closer to his body by locking her ankles behind him. A rush of pleasure spread throughout her as his hardness probed, then found, its home within the soft confines of her womanhood.

The water splashed against their bodies as Kohanah began his smooth, easy strokes inside her. His lips were now on the hollow of her throat, kissing her there. Slow, yet sure, his hands began to glide over her body, setting small fires along her flesh as he touched each and every secret pleasure spot along their way.

Marilla leaned her head back, her long blond hair clinging to her shoulders and down her back. The light of the kerosene lamp moved upon her skin, seeming to follow the path of Kohanah's hands.

And when Kohanah began to caress her love mound

with his fingers in unison with his thrusts, a soft cry of passion awakened from inside Marilla's throat. She placed a hand to Kohanah's dark, long hair and guided his lips back to her mouth. She cozied her breasts against his powerful chest and kissed him long and hard. Desire was swelling within her. Pleasure was spreading like sunbeams reaching their warming tentacles across a summer sky.

Marilla drew a ragged breath as Kohanah's kiss deepened into something fierce . . . something possessive. She clung about his neck and rode with him, the water slick and warm as it followed their bodies' movements.

Passions were cresting . . . igniting . . . and suddenly it was as though a volcano were erupting as both their bodies quaked with total, consuming pleasure.

Marilla breathed hard as Kohanah raised his lips from her mouth, to lay his head softly against a breast. Her whole body seemed to still be throbbing from the passion momentarily found and spent. She wove her fingers through his perspiration-dampened hair, then kissed his cheek tenderly.

"I love you," she whispered. "Never did I believe one could love as deeply as I love you. Do you know how hard it was these past three years while separated from you? I could hardly bear it, Kohanah! Schooling was all that kept me sane. I buried myself in my studies. Oh, darling, what did you do?"

A tremor went through her body as he lowered his lips to her breast and teased its peak into a renewed tautness. She leaned back and relished the sweetness of his tongue, then his lips, ignoring the fact that he was evading her question. Of course, she knew what he had been doing most of that time! He had been imprisoned at Fort Marion. And now that he was back with his people, he had been busy fighting for their rights!

Yes, it had been a stupid question, one that did not require an answer!

"Seems Kohanah is *panyi*, one alone, in struggles for my band of Kiowa," Kohanah said, drawing away from Marilla. He lifted a bar of perfumed soap from the floor and placed it in the water, getting it wet. Then he began to slide it slowly across Marilla's breasts, then lower, over her abdomen, where the juncture of her thighs revealed the triangle of blond hair, wet and kinky from the water.

"There is so much that is not right," he continued, eyeing her with his dark, fathomless eyes.

"Tell me about it," Marilla said softly, trembling beneath the soft caress of the soap and his hands accompanying it. "I hope that I am able to help in that I am at least going to teach the children of your tribe. Do you recall my teachings to you? Aren't those moments treasured inside your heart?" She placed a hand to the cheek of his strong, handsome face. "They are in *mine*."

"*Ho*, yes," Kohanah said, now smoothing the soap along the calf of one of her legs. "They are treasured within my heart. As will *this* moment be."

"But the problems you face," Marilla murmured. "Tell me. What are they?"

"The sacred Sun Dance is threatened by the soldiers," Kohanah growled, dropping the soap into the water. He placed his hands on Marilla's shoulders. "They do not want us to perform the Sun Dance. So many think it is a supernatural thing that we do and are threatened by it. The Sun Dance, in truth, is an expression of veneration of the sun as the source of life and the promoter of growth and well-being of all living things. It reaffirms tribal unity. The dance is a quest for power, spiritual energy, and insight. The keeper of the Taime, the sacred Sun Dance doll, feels threatened. He fears that the Taime is going to be stolen and destroyed to keep us from the Sun Dance."

His eyes grew darkly fierce. "And the buffalo!" he said between clenched lips. "The buffalo bull in his strength and majesty is regarded as the animal symbol of the sun. In order to consummate the ancient sacrifice, it is required of the Kiowa to impale the head of a buffalo bull upon the medicine pole! How *can* the Kiowa, when buffalo are so few?"

He stepped out of the tub and wiped his skin dry with his buckskin shirt, then slipped into his breeches and dampened shirt. "But tomorrow there is some promise for

my people," he said thickly. "Perhaps the soldiers are
going to give my people a *chance*."

Marilla stepped from the tub and wrapped a robe around
her. She tied it at the waist and stood looking up at
Kohanah. "What do you mean?" she asked softly. "What
happens tomorrow?"

"The early years on the reservation have sorely tested
the Kiowa," he said thickly. "It is hard to accept the
sedentary life that the white man forces upon us. There is
never enough food. The regular rations guaranteed by the
government are often delayed or insufficient. But tomorrow? Hopefully it is a change for the better! The whole
tribe has been given a pass to leave the reservation to hunt
buffalo! It is perhaps a beginning of the white man's
understanding of what the Kiowa is all about!"

Marilla heard the hope in Kohanah's voice . . . could
see it in the depths of his eyes! But something inside her
told her that something was not right here. Was the government playing a dirty trick on the Kiowa? While traveling to Fort Cobb from New York—all the while on the
train, then on the buckboard from the railhead—all that
she had seen of buffalo were the white bleached bones of
those that had died lying across the land. The hunt could
prove to be less than successful.

What, then, would Kohanah think? What would he do?

"Tsonda, would you like to accompany me and my
people on this expedition of the heart?" Kohanah asked
thickly, his eyes warm as he thought of her riding alongside him, as though already his wife! "My people can see
your courage. You will see how *I* feel about not only my
people but also the land! I love the land. I see that it is
beautiful. I delight in it. I am alive *in* it!"

Marilla forced a smile, anxious to do anything with him,
just to be with him. And perhaps she should be with him
when he discovered the deceit. Just possibly she could
ease the pain.

"I would love to go," she said in a rush of words. "I
can go to the schoolhouse later to prepare for my teaching
assignment."

"You will be my *tsa*, partner, as well as my woman."

Kohanah chuckled, drawing her into his arms, snuggling her close. His fingers twined through her hair and urged her lips to his. He gave her a sweet, lingering kiss. . . .

His eyes glinting in the moonlight, Jason Roark dismounted and secured his horse's reins beneath a rock on the ground. He looked straight ahead, seeing the soft lights at Marilla's windows. His loins ached, having waited so long to see her again . . . to touch her . . . to make her *his*. Once she realized that he would kill her if she told anything about him seducing her, she would be a hostage to his needs forevermore! She would not dare cross him, for he would threaten her with Kohanah's life . . . even that of many of his *people*!

No. She would not fight back this time. It would cost her and the savages too much!

Sneering, Jason began running across the land, his shoulders hunched down low. He had thought that he had heard a horse following him a while back and did not want to take a chance that whoever it was would see him sneaking up on the new schoolmarm's cabin. Or was it somebody else with the same thing on his mind? Most men at the fort were woman-hungry!

Yet most would not dare accost the woman who was the daughter of Lieutenant Pratt. Everyone admired the man, even though he was no longer in uniform. . . .

Now at the corner of the house, having seen a horse reined at the front, Jason inched along the wall, anxious to take a peek inside. Though disappointed to know that he was not the first to greet Marilla—he suspected that the one inside was Kohanah, for the saddle on the horse was made of a thick layer of Indian blankets—Jason would just wait his turn! She would be fresh from lovemaking. That would make it easier for the second man to have his fun with her!

"But I hate touchin' the same spot the Injun savage has touched," he grumbled to himself. "Some of his Injun fleas just might rub off onto me!"

Yet wanting her so badly, and wanting to teach her a thing or two at the same time, Jason crept to the window,

now even hoping to get his eyes full of the two in a lovers'
embrace. That would be quite entertaining . . . could even
get him hotter than he already was!

Sneaking a peek through the window, Jason was disappointed when he found both of them fully clothed. Yet his
insides recoiled when he discovered them kissing so tenderly. He could not help but recall how Marilla's lips had
tasted when he had kissed her that one night. The Indian
seemed to be enjoying her just as much! Had he enjoyed
everything else about her earlier? The fact that Marilla was
in a robe led him to believe that he had just missed the
show he had been anxious to see.

Placing a hand on his risen manhood, trying to adjust it
beneath his coarse breeches so that it would lay more
comfortably in place, Jason's breath caught in his throat
when he suddenly felt something cold and hard square in
the middle of his back.

"Now, just you turn around slow and easy," Charles
Agnew whispered, so as not to disturb Marilla and her
companion. He had recognized the horse. There was no
mistaking that it was Kohanah calling on Marilla this
evening. Though Charles questioned her choice of men
callers, it was not his place to ponder over it. Putting the
fear of God into Jason was all that mattered. He couldn't
be allowed to pursue what was most obviously a devilish
goal!

Jason Roark scarcely breathed, the barrel of the rifle still
snugly fitting into his back. "Damn it, how can I turn
around with that thing in my back?" he growled. "And I
recognize the voice. Charles, what in the hell are you
doin' here? Have you come to get a piece of ass also?"

Sparks seemed to fly off inside Charles's head. He
raised the rifle and cracked its butt against Jason's head
just hard enough to stun him. "You bastard," Charles grumbled. "I should've done this long ago. I don't know why I
let the likes of you intimidate me. It took *this* to make me
come to my senses. I knew you'd come out here to assault
Marilla Pratt. I heard the gossip before she arrived. And
damn it all to hell, Jason, that's all it was. Dirty gossip

from your nasty mouth! She's a sweet and pretty thing. How could you even think of harming her?''

Jason lurched with the blow of the rifle. He grabbed at his head and reeled for a moment, then spun around to face Charles. His eyes were wild, his lips agape with wonder. ''You're defendin' a tramp,'' he then snarled. He rubbed his sore head, then nodded toward the window. ''Just take a look inside. The lady, so you call her, is in the arms of a savage Injun! Do you call *that* respectable?''

''I also heard your gossip about her and the Indian.'' Charles shoved the rifle barrel into Jason's ribs. ''I don't understand why she has fallen in love with the Indian, but she *has*. I'm sure that is the reason for her to even come to this godforsaken land. I didn't come to give her my blessing, but I *have* come to protect her from the likes of you.''

''You're a damned idiot,'' Jason argued, wincing when the rifle barrel crushed harder into his ribs. ''Let me go. Let's allow Kohanah to leave; then both of us can take turns with her. You don't know what you're missin'. She's one lively creature in the bed.''

''A voice of experience?'' Charles asked sarcastically.

''Yeah. You might call it that.''

''Jason, no lady would ever let you in her bed unless you forced yourself on her. And the gossip is that she got the better of you and didn't allow it to happen. If it had happened, Jason, Lieutenant Pratt would not have stopped at transferring you to another fort; he would have *hanged* you.''

Charles motioned with the barrel of the rifle. ''Now, get on out of here,'' he growled. ''And, by God, I'm going to be keepin' my eye on you. If you so much as—''

Jason took a bold step forward. He spoke into Charles's face. ''You son of a bitch,'' he hissed. ''If you don't kill me now, you'll regret it later. And you don't have the *guts*. You're all words.'' He pushed the rifle aside. ''And without the gun, you're *nothin'*. You'd better keep an eye on your back is all I can say.''

Charles paled as Jason stomped on past him. He swallowed hard, fear gripping his insides. Then he lifted the rifle and aimed, but his fingers were trembling so violently he could not squeeze the trigger. Or was it because he *was* too cowardly to do what he truly thought was best . . . ?

Lowering the rifle, he turned and eyed the window. Slowly he crept toward it, then looked in wonder at Marilla and Kohanah, who were now sitting on the floor beside the fire, talking. There seemed to be so much between them . . . and more than loving. There seemed to be a mutual respect, a sincere affection. Charles could not help but be drawn into the same feelings. He now knew that he would go to any extreme to help this Indian who had intrigued him from the day he had first met him, and this woman who seemed to be all compassion and heart. . . .

Twelve

❧⟶≈

The early sun was as red as a hunter's moon. It was dawn—cold and clear and deep like water. Marilla rode astride alongside Kohanah as skillfully as any man might do. With each bounce of the horse her long and flowing golden hair trembled on her shoulders and down her back. Her gloved hands held the reins of a chestnut mare. Snugly fitted, her jeans molded her perfect shape. Her fringed buckskin cape fluttered in the wind; her boots were secure in the horse's stirrups.

Gazing into the distance, looking across the land, she saw the low light upon the rolling plains illuminating sweet clover as it took hold of the hills and was bending upon itself to cover and seal the soil. She could feel the motion of the air. She could hear the early morning songs of the birds out of the shadows.

Daring to look at the horses traveling scattered along the land, she saw how the Indian braves were so stiffly erect on their saddles of blankets. They were moving at a short, choppy trot, silence the key to their feelings. Disappointment and hate fused into one emotion on their copper faces, their jaws were set, their eyes were filled with angry fire.

Marilla looked away from them, assailed with regret and remorse for the Kiowa, for they were, moment by moment, discovering that they had been duped again by the white man . . . and surely they were just now understanding why it had been necessary. Because of the loss of the buffalo on this land where they once roamed in great herds, the Kiowa were being shown that they now depended totally on the white man and must conform to this dependency or, as a race, fade away to nothing.

She looked solemnly over at Kohanah. Oh, how brave and courageous he was as he sat so tall on his red roan stallion. Though there was so much written in his bright, deep-set eyes, he looked no less dignified and composed, a chief who was fighting for his people's rights and was feeling the battle lost again.

Marilla swallowed back a lump in her throat, wishing her father could be there to help the Indians again. But he had chosen his law practice over the traumas of being a soldier . . . and Marilla was trying to understand. She did not want to see him as weak, for in her eyes he had always been strong. In *all* ways!

Letting her gaze absorb Kohanah's handsomeness, she saw his long hair drawn close to his scalp, fat having been rubbed into his hair to make it glisten, his long braids wound with strips of colored cloth.

His cheekbones were high, his nose pronounced, his lips seductive. His copper skin glistened as the sun rose higher and higher in the sky.

He was handsome and well muscled, and just being near him made Marilla proud that he had chosen her above all other women he had ever known, to be the one he solely loved!

Kohanah's heart thundered wildly inside him. Once more he had been betrayed by the white man! His fingers fiercely clasped the horse's reins, his knuckles white in his extreme anger. As his people were seeing, they had been set free from the reservation this one day only so that the white man could prove a point. . . . The men with Sharps rifles had done their work well. All that could be found of the buffalo were the bleached bones of the animals gleaming everywhere in the early morning sun. The plains were now empty of the animal needed for the Kiowa's survival!

Conform? How could the Kiowa even *exist*?

Then his gaze sharpened when in the distance he caught the sight of another sort of animal. There was a herd of longhorns grazing where the buffalo had once roamed. The white man's animals were taking the place of the Indians', just as the white man's dwellings were now spread across the land that was once the Kiowa's.

"*Edasemkop*, they stole them from the Kiowa. Now they are nowhere!" Kohanah suddenly shouted, raising a fist into the air. He wheeled his horse around and faced his braves, giving Marilla only a momentary glance. "The buffalo are gone! The *bedalpago*, white people, knew this when they sent us out to hunt for them! We return to the reservation empty-handed, but wiser to the ways of the white men! They cheat! They lie! They *asemtse*—steal!"

Having never before witnessed Kohanah in a rage, Marilla felt her insides turning cold. Would his anger soon be directed also to her, because *she* was white? How could he hate the white man so much and not her? She belonged to the same race that was slowly ridding the land of the Indian!

Marilla's heart bled for Kohanah . . . even for herself. For she was afraid that he would no longer feel free to let himself love her. . . .

"My *yapahes*, warriors," Kohanah said in a softer tone, lowering his fist, spreading his fingers gently on the neck of his red roan. "Though we have been tricked, we have no choice but to return to the reservation. It is now our home. We can no longer fight battles except those of the heart."

Kohanah lowered his eyes to the ground. "Kohanah is *komse*—worn out from burdens of life," he said in a bare whisper, stinging Marilla's heart with the sadness and meaning behind the words. "Let us return home. *Atanta*, I am dissatisfied. *Ho*, I am dissatisfied."

"Kohanah," Marilla said, reaching her hand toward him. "I am sorry. So . . . so sorry."

Kohanah's shoulders were slumped as he rode away

from Marilla, ignoring her. She squirmed uneasily in her saddle when the braves followed his lead, some giving her scornful looks from the corners of their eyes as they passed on by her.

But she would not let this dissuade her from what she knew must be done. She was not going to let Kohanah forget her all that easily just because of the color of her skin. Wheeling her own horse around, she rode at a gallop until she was once again riding alongside Kohanah.

Marilla held her chin firmly high, but hoped that if Kohanah did decide to look her way he would not see the tears silvering the corners of her eyes. He might have lost a battle today, but she would not let his loss be the cause of one of her own. She had waited too long to be with him to give up on him so easily. She would follow him to his dwelling. She would be with him whether or not he invited her. There was too much to lose by not being stubbornly persistent with him at this moment in time.

She could lose *him*, and Kohanah was her breath . . . her heartbeat . . . her *life*.

The sun had moved higher in the sky, brightening everything about Marilla. Under any circumstances other than what seemed a death march back to the reservation, she could have enjoyed the meadows of blue and yellow wildflowers on the slopes, and the still, sunlit plain reaching away out of sight.

Just ahead, a frightened buck was on the run, the white rosette on its rump seeming to hang for the smallest fraction of time at the top of each frantic bound, like a succession of sunbursts against the purple hills.

And then Marilla was following a dirt road alongside Kohanah. Her heart lurched in her throat when she caught sight of a tarantula at the edge of the road. It was larger than she would have ever imagined, dull and dark brown, covered with long, dusty hairs.

Seeing it made shivers ride up and down Marilla's spine, yet there was something innocent . . . something crochety . . . about it as it stopped and then skittered away.

She looked quickly over at Kohanah as he guided his

red roan around the spider so that its hooves would not squash it, seeing his kindness in wanting to spare the spider's life. Perhaps he saw the spider as a symbol of his own race. If one was slain, that brought the race closer and closer to extinction.

Marilla moved her eyes from Kohanah and looked straight ahead. Somehow she had to help him and his people.

But how . . . ? Surely teaching their children would not be enough. . . .

Marilla eased her horse up next to Kohanah's as they now traveled over land that made up the reservation. Buffalo-hide tipis sprawled across the land. Women were cooking meat in copper buckets hanging over outdoor fires, buckets obtained through barter with the Pawnee of the north who had in turn procured them from white traders. Old men sat in the sunshine contemplatively smoking the aromatic mixture of tobacco leaves and bark they called *kinnikinick*, children rushed to the approaching braves, their eyes anxious.

Kohanah lifted his chin high, ignoring the question in the eyes of the young Kiowa, not knowing yet how to explain to them that they would never enjoy the hunt of the buffalo as their elders had. Perhaps they would not even experience the Sun Dance, for without buffalo, there would *be* no Sun Dance!

He had to have time to think . . . to contemplate his next move with the soldiers at Fort Cobb. Out of the corner of his eye he could see several soldiers viewing his return to the reservation. One among them was the hated Jason Roark. He was never to be trusted. If the truth were to be known, he was probably even behind this farce today!

A coldness traveled through Kohanah's veins when he realized that Jason Roark was not watching the Kiowa so much as he was eyeing Marilla! Did the man dare approach her? Did he not know that *Gyaokatema*, Kohanah would cut his throat if he so much as . . . touched . . . her again?

Marilla saw a strange sort of pain in Kohanah's eyes, and then a sudden cold anger. She followed his vision and became engulfed with hate when she saw Jason Roark sitting among several soldiers, his gaze following her, his eyes squinted into a strange sort of smile. It was apparent that he welcomed her arrival to Oklahoma. Just when could she expect him to make his move? Alone in her house, she was vulnerable.

Her hand slipped to the rifle that was in its leather saddle boot at the side of the horse. She now knew she would have to keep it at her bedside at all times. . . .

Kohanah stopped his red roan outside a massive tipi whose hide was greatly decorated with battle pictures ornamented with fine images of fighting men and arms on one side . . . and wide horizontal bands of black and yellow on the other.

Dismounting, Kohanah went to Marilla and placed his hands on her waist. He gently lifted her from her horse, his eyes never leaving her. "Tsonda, soon afternoon turns into night," he said thickly. "You will stay with Kohanah. Tomorrow you return to your home . . . to your way of life."

Marilla smiled up at him. "My way of life?" she said softly. "Darling, do you forget so easily what I have chosen to do with my life? I begin teaching the Kiowa children tomorrow. You see? My life is *your* life. Please accept that what I do is for the good of your people. I want to help in your plight with the white man, if only in a small way. Tell me that you are glad."

Kohanah swept an arm about her waist and led her into his tipi. "Kohanah is glad," he said softly, his eyes commanding as a Kiowa maiden crept from her knees before a fire where a kettle of soup was cooking. He motioned with a flick of the wrist for her to leave, ignoring the questioning in Marilla's eyes as she watched the maiden scamper from the dwelling.

"Sit," Kohanah said, gesturing toward a padding of blankets beside the fire. "Tsonda, the *pia*, fire, will be soon welcomed when the sun loses its heat to the darkness of night. The soup prepared by my cousin will give you strength."

Marilla sighed to herself when she heard that the woman he had just dismissed was his cousin. She settled down on the pallet beside the fire, feeling all mushy warm inside to know that he had not taken a wife in her absence. It was apparent that his love for her had been as strong as her love for him. Oh, that in time they could relax with that love, and share it forever!

But now too much was troubling Kohanah. She must be there, just for comforting, if that was all he asked of her. She tensed when he began to move briskly about the tipi, picking up objects, slinging them about. . . .

"*Aalyi*, I cry inside!" Kohanah said dejectedly, tossing several spoons across the tipi. "The spoons were made of the horns of the buffalo!" He picked up several other objects and threw them angrily. "Water is transported in the paunch from the buffalo!"

He went to the fire and settled down onto his haunches before it, hanging his head into his hands. "So much depended on the buffalo," he groaned. "Why? Why did the white man have to take even this from the Kiowa? How can the Sun Dance be performed without the buffalo? How?"

Marilla crept to Kohanah. She moved to her knees and slid around in front of him, then eased his hands from his face. She cupped his face in her palms and gently kissed him. "Kohanah, I am so sorry," she whispered. "I wish there was something I could do for you to ease your torment. All that I have to offer you at this moment is my love. Will you let me love you? Your torment will be eased, if only for a little while."

Her lips brushed against his, her hands went to his shirt, her fingers slid up beneath it, to touch the wondrous marvel of his powerful chest. "Let us make love, Kohanah," she whispered. "Let us make love *now*."

Kohanah eased her hand from beneath his shirt and rose to his feet, placing his back to her. "It is not the time for Kohanah to be weak," he growled, doubling his hands into fists at his sides. "It is time for Kohanah to be *strong*."

His words stung Marilla. She leapt to her feet and went to him and stepped in the line of his vision. "Kohanah, are you saying that loving me makes you look weak?" she asked shakily. "How can you mean that? Is it because I am . . . white? Do you prefer a Kiowa maiden? If so, why did you not marry one in my absence? Why did you come to me last night . . . make love to me? Why did you even ask me into your dwelling now?"

She took his hands and held them tightly. "Tell me, Kohanah, why you did not choose a Kiowa maiden in my absence?" she said dryly. "Did thinking of me make you look weak in your eyes? If so, why did you not marry one of your own skin coloring to make you look strong?"

Kohanah slipped his hands from hers and drew her within his arms. "Do not doubt my love for you, ever," he said hoarsely. "It is just the times that make me behave as I behave. It is no easier for me now that I am out of prison than when I was behind locked doors. The doors still remain locked. But it is wrong for Kohanah to put such a burden on you. It is not your problem. Only Kohanah's. Only Kohanah's."

Tears silvered Marilla's eyes. She twined her arms about his powerful chest. "My darling, your problems are also mine," she softly cried. "When I fell in love with you in Florida, it was then that I chose to *make* your problems mine. Please do not turn your back on me now. We have shared so much together already. Do you not recall the night I came to you in the barracks? I gave of myself wholly to you . . . the first man ever. It was a wonderful night of awakenings. Awaken me again, Kohanah. Awaken me *now*."

Kohanah coiled his fingers through Marilla's hair, savoring the softness against his coarse fingertips, and drew her face upward so that their lips could meet. His insides trembled in ecstasy as Marilla's mouth parted and their tongues met in a love dance. With his free hand he began removing her blouse, his fingers trembling as he was finally able to fully cup a breast. His thumb and forefinger teased its nipple into a stiff peak, evoking a quivering sigh from deep inside Marilla.

The joy caused by Kohanah's hand and lips made Marilla feel as though she were melting. She smoothed her fingers up beneath his shirt and marveled anew over the strength of his hairless chest. As he was doing with her nipples, she drew one of his between her fingers and gently pinched it into a stiff peak, then began scooting his shirt up. Kohanah leaned away from her and let her draw his fringed shirt over his head. He stood back and let her continue undressing him until he was standing beautifully nude beside the dancing flames of the fire, his body golden in the reflections.

"Now it is my turn," Marilla said, smiling seductively up at him. "Watch me, Kohanah. I shall remove each piece of my clothing slowly . . . meditatively. The moments we are together like this must be treasured, never hurried."

Marilla tossed her blouse aside. "Thank you for wanting me," she whispered. "You will see that what we are about to share *will* help lift the burdens from inside your heart. It's like magic, my love, when we are together. Do you not see this also? Do you not already feel it?"

"*Ho*, Tsonda," Kohanah said huskily. "Now is forever when I am with you. *Kion*, lovemaking, becomes magic only with you. You are not like the land and the buffalo! No white man can ever take you from me. You are mine, forever."

For a brief moment Jason Roark's ugly face flashed before Marilla's eyes, and she recalled how he had been watching from afar. He had seen her enter Kohanah's dwelling. He was surely watching . . . even now. . . .

"No. No one." Marilla sighed, tossing the last of her clothing aside. She bent and removed her boots, then went to Kohanah and fit her body into his, relishing the touch of his muscled form against her flesh. Boldly, she placed her fingers on his buttocks and pressed him closer, feeling the outline of his risen manhood against her abdomen, taking her breath away with its pulsing strength.

"Love me?" she whispered, looking up at him, her hair spiraling in golden wisps across her shoulders and down her back. "Love me now?"

Kohanah placed his hands on her shoulders and began lowering her downward, his eyes feasting on her loveliness . . . on her perfectly rounded breasts with dark nipples stiffly peaked at the end of each, at her tiny waist that led his eyes downward to curving hips, then around to where golden hair lay in a perfect triangle at the juncture of her thighs.

As he lowered her onto the pallet of furs and blankets, Kohanah smoothed his hand across her breasts, over her belly, and then between her legs. His fingers searched and found the pulsing bud of her womanhood and began to stroke her while his lips crushed hers in a fiery, passionate kiss.

Marilla laced her arms about his neck and clung to him, her pulse racing as his fingers continued to catapult her into another world that knew only wondrous feelings of rapture. As his fingers stroked and his kiss strengthened, she became mindless.

Not able to take much more, Marilla moved a hand to his and urged it away from her, then placed her hands on his hips and guided his hardness inside her. Sighing, she placed her legs about him and locked them together at the ankles. Pleasure spread through her body as he began his easy strokes within her. She had wanted him to awaken her again. Oh, how he had the skills to do so! All of her nerve endings tingled with the wondrous feelings that he was arousing inside her. Those feelings were building . . . building . . . building. . . .

Marilla drew a ragged breath when Kohanah's lips set her mouth free, now to consume the nipple of her breast. His teeth nipped and teased her, his hands now exploring her body, taking in the roundness of her, stroking . . . setting her more and more aflame with desire.

Her fingers splayed against his chest, Marilla looked up into dark, smoldering eyes as Kohanah looked down at her, softly smiling.

"You wanted to make love," Kohanah said huskily. "Tsonda, Kohanah will love you until the heavens become speckled with stars. Will that be enough?"

"Never," Marilla said, her eyes sparkling like the stars Kohanah was speaking of. "Don't you know that I shall never get enough of you?"

She kissed first one of his cheeks, then the other, then kissed his eyelashes, closed over his eyes. "You are my

only reason for living, my love,'' she purred. ''You are
my existence. Love me fiercely, Kohanah. Make my whole
body quake with the loving!''

Kohanah buried his face next to her neck and moved
within her with faster, quick, sure movements. He knew
that the stars were not in the sky, but he could not hold
back any longer. He had to have fulfillment now. He had
to give Marilla fulfillment!

His lean, sinewy hips moved. He groaned against her
soft skin. His fingers dug into her buttocks, lifting her
higher. It was as though he reached clean into her soul
with his hardness. Her warmth, encircling his manhood,
clinging to it like a silken hand, made him grow almost
shaken with desire.

''My love,'' Kohanah whispered, the wonders of sharing with her filling him with intense pleasure, sweeping
through him like wind currents gone crazed across the
plains!

Marilla clung to him. Her fingernails dug into the flesh
of his shoulders, her breath was coming in slow rasps as
she felt the pleasure spiraling through her in great splashes
of rapture. She closed her eyes and enjoyed. . . .

Fulfilled, Kohanah drew away from Marilla. He kissed
her cheek softly, then rose to his feet while she watched
him. She turned over and lay on her stomach, propping her
chin up with her hands, too content, for she knew that it
was only for the moment. Too much was unsettled for
Kohanah, yet could it ever be any different? There was not
much of a chance that life would ever get easier for the
Kiowa, or *any* Indian, for that matter. Too much had been
undone in their normal ways of lives. Kohanah had been
sent to prison for rebelling against these changes once. She
could not let herself think that it might happen again. . . .

''What are you doing?'' Marilla asked, as Kohanah
went to a tattered buffalo hide and began easing it aside.
''What have you got hidden there?''

She scooted to a sitting position, and her eyes grew
wide as she watched Kohanah's paintings slowly being
uncovered . . . the paintings that he had so skillfully created on canvas while he was imprisoned. Strange how she

could have forgotten about them! They had been so important to him then. They seemed to be as important to him *now*.

"Your . . . paintings . . ." she said in a mere whisper. Drawing a blanket about her, she went to Kohanah and took a closer look, seeing so much about them that she recognized. "Oh, Kohanah, they are as beautiful as I remembered them."

While the fire danced on the bright colors of the paintings, Kohanah turned and faced Marilla. "These paintings are my only hope," he said thickly. "Soon the white father in Washington, President Hayes, will come to barter for my paintings. Perhaps this will guarantee the Kiowa some of the things that are now being denied us. We shall see."

"President Hayes?" Marilla gasped. "He's coming here?"

"*Ho*, he is," Kohanah said, his eyes gleaming. . . .

Thirteen

❦ ❧

The morning sun crept through the smoke hole of the tipi, shining in Marilla's eyes, awakening her. At first startled by her surroundings, having forgotten that she had slept with Kohanah for a full night, the very first time in her life, Marilla jerked up into a sitting position, scattering a blanket away from her. Warm, knowing hands on a breast made her turn her eyes to Kohanah who lay beside her, smiling.

"*Eonti*, I like awakening with you in my dwelling," Kohanah said deeply. "*Gyapa-ingua*, dawn, is much more pleasant with you at my side. It makes Kohanah see the newborn day with more promise."

Warmed all over by his touch, Marilla curled down into Kohanah's arms, blissful. "My darling, I could be here upon awakening every morning if you would just say the word," she whispered, tracing his perfect lips with her forefinger.

She jerked her hand away when she saw Kohanah's lips form a pout. "But, of course, I know that the time is not right," she reassured him. "I am sorry to have even suggested it. Your people come first. Truly I understand that and I am honestly trying not to be jealous."

128

She crept fully into his arms and placed a cheek against his bare chest. "But it is so hard," she sighed. "I want you all to myself. It is the woman in me that wants this. And when a woman has to share a man, she cannot help but be jealous of those with whom she shares."

Kohanah twined his fingers through Marilla's hair. "My woman, you need not ever be jealous of anyone," he said huskily. "Though my heart bleeds for my people and I do everything to make things right for them, my feelings for you are quite separate and *special*. In time, surely we will have the right to be totally together. It is our destiny, Tsonda. Ours alone. Just practice patience."

A sullen thumping of a drum that had just begun in the distance outside the tipi drew Marilla around. Her eyebrows forked. "What is that?" she gasped. "It . . . it sounds so sad."

Kohanah began to quickly dress. "The drum warns my people to rise from their beds, to prepare for their journey into Fort Cobb. It is the day for my people to go to the fort and line up for rations," he grumbled. "It is Kohanah's duty to supervise . . . see that no one is cheated. It is enough that we were cheated yesterday of the buffalo. Today no one will be taken advantage of."

"Rations?" Marilla said, hurriedly dressing, in an attempt to keep up with Kohanah. "I know of no such practice."

"It is done monthly," Kohanah said, uncoiling his hair, to add bear grease to it, then braid it again with colorful cloths woven into it. "It makes my people look like beggars, but they must take the handouts or else come close to starving."

He turned and looked down at Marilla, his dark eyes tormented. "This is what has come of the life of the Kiowa," he said blandly. "My imprisonment did not help our cause. Will anything, ever?"

He cast a sidewise glance at the paintings. "Only in my paintings do I see some hope," he said softly. "When white chief President Hayes comes and makes his offer, I shall make my counteroffer. It is known that President

Hayes champions many moral causes. We shall see if the gossip about this great man is true!''

Straightening her hair, combing her fingers through it to rid it of its witch's tangles, Marilla once more went and looked down at the paintings. "How did the President hear of your.paintings?'' she asked softly, turning to glance at Kohanah. "Is he actually interested in purchasing them?''

"*Ho*, he has sent word of such intentions,'' Kohanah said, slipping into his colorfully beaded moccasins. "It was through a cunning scheme of mine that he learned of the paintings, for I had heard of his love of artwork.'' Kohanah chuckled beneath his breath . . . his eyes twinkled. "There is much about my artwork that will interest him.''

Marilla turned puzzled eyes fully to him. "Kohanah, what aren't you telling me?'' she asked, going to him, to take one of his hands fondly in hers. "What about your paintings will interest him so?''

Kohanah eased away from her and went and picked up a painting that had been done on a buffalo skin and held it in the light of the morning sun that was spiraling down from the smoke hole in the peak of the tipi. "Look at the painting,'' he said dryly. "What do *you* see?''

Marilla did not have to look long to understand what his point was. He was holding up the painting that portrayed the worst of the atrocities of the United States Cavalry against the Indians. If such a painting became famous, shown in all the museums of the country, everyone would know about the wrongs that had been done to the Indians.

"Yes, I see,'' she murmured. "But why would the President want the paintings?''

Kohanah placed the colorful skin gingerly back in place with the other skins and canvases and folded the buffalo-skin cover back over them protectively. "He will want the paintings to *hide* them,'' he said, laughing throatily. "He will make sure no one else ever sees them.''

Marilla's eyes brightened; then she frowned. "But, Kohanah, why would you want this to happen?'' she asked, looking from Kohanah to the covered paintings.

"You are proud of what you have painted. Why would you want them to be hidden forever?"

Placing his hands on Marilla's shoulders, Kohanah looked down at her determinedly. "To bargain with the white chief President for my people's rights, Kohanah would part with all his paintings," he growled. His eyes grew darker in intensity. "Now do you understand?"

A coldness seemed to be grabbing Marilla's insides . . . yes, understanding so much, yet afraid of the knowing. "Yes, I . . . think I do," she stammered. "But what if you are wrong? What if President Hayes takes the paintings and never gives you anything in return?"

"He will not get the paintings until I have his word . . . his promise," Kohanah said flatly. "Isn't the white chief's word as good as the promise of another sunrise?"

Marilla flinched somewhat with those words. Though President Rutherford Hayes was a good-natured man, one who enjoyed books and artwork more than politics and who was respected for his sincerity and honesty, there could be a side of him that wanted to protect his constituents, the same as Kohanah wanted to protect his people. Most men in politics were capable of doing anything to make themselves look better in the limelight. Surely President Hayes was no different.

Yet just perhaps he could be trusted. Marilla's father knew Lucy, the President's wife, and knew the President, through *her*. They had met in college, for President Hayes's wife was the first President's wife to have a college degree. Marilla's father had nothing but kind words to say about both the President and his wife! If Kohanah did not get along well enough with the President, just perhaps *she* could go to him, plead the cause of the Kiowa after informing the President of just who her father was. . . .

Smiling sheepishly up at Kohanah, Marilla stepped up on tiptoe and kissed him. "Things will work out," she said, a promise on her lips, though she would not tell him that she had ways that he did not know about to possibly make things right for him. "You'll see. Things *will* work out."

"It is time to go," Kohanah said, framing her face

between his hands. "Today you wished to begin teaching the Kiowa children. That must be delayed until tomorrow. Will you ride to the fort with us? Or do you wish to distance yourself from us when in the presence of so many white men?"

Marilla felt the color draining from her face. She gasped. "How could you think such a thing?" she defended hotly. "Kohanah, never think such a thing of me again. I could never be ashamed of my feelings for you *or* your people."

Placing an arm about Marilla's waist, Kohanah swept her out into the morning sunlight. Marilla looked across the land, past the tipis. The sun seemed at home in the plains where the long yellow grass shone in the shimmering new light. Birds were singing out of the shadows . . . grasshoppers were just beginning to fill the air.

Then Marilla's eyes were drawn elsewhere, to an aging man who was standing in the center of the village, his hair long, wiry, and gray, hanging way down his back along his fringed buckskin outfit, his hands trembling as he peered toward the rising sun.

"That is Old Man Nervous, so named because of the trembling of his hands," Kohanah said softly. "He is the keeper of the calendar. Each morning he stands on that exact spot of ground near the center of the village and watches to see where the sun appears on the skyline, then records his findings on skins. By means of this solar calendar does he know and announce to our people when it is time to plant, to harvest, to perform this or that ceremony."

Kohanah turned dark eyes down to Marilla. "The old man gazing each morning after the ranging sun represents the epitome of that real harmony between man and the land that signifies the Indian's world," he said thickly. "This is something that can never be taken from my people."

One by one the Kiowa left their tipis and mounted their horses. Marilla was helped onto her horse by Kohanah's strong arms, not even thinking about the hunger pangs gnawing at the pit of her stomach. It seemed that everything in her life this day would have to be delayed, for it was important to see just how the Kiowa were treated on what was called "ration day."

Pressing her heels into the flanks of her mare, she rode away alongside Kohanah, feeling as though she truly belonged. . . .

Though Marilla had been brought up living at one fort or another after her father had joined the United States Cavalry, Fort Cobb was not the same as those of her past. There was something cold and uncaring about it, but she understood why she was feeling this detachment. Standing with Kohanah, she was getting a full view of just what ration day was . . . and what it meant to the Kiowa, Comanche, and Apache who seemed to have equal roles in the handouts from those at the fort.

As she stood in line with Kohanah, Marilla's heart bled for him, for he seemed misplaced . . . as though he did not belong.

Yet he had not lost his grace . . . his poise.

He was doing what had to be done to survive. . . .

The building was long and gloomy, the windows high on the walls casting only faint light through their grime. Two soldiers stood at the head of a massive table where supplies were separated and handed to each member of the tribes as they passed by. Marilla's gaze met and held Jason Roark's. He *would* have been the one to have asked to be assigned the task of giving handouts to the Indians. He would enjoy seeing them belittled.

Or had he asked for this assignment because he knew that she would be there with Kohanah? Had he seen that she had spent the night with Kohanah? Was she going to have to be on guard, forever, against that evil man?

When his pale eyes squinted and his face twisted into a knowing smile, everything within Marilla turned cold.

But a strong arm suddenly about her waist made her remember all that was good in life. Kohanah. He would never let Jason Roark harm her.

Yet how could Kohanah keep him from it? Kohanah would be going his own way most of the time . . . she *hers*. . . .

Marilla's gaze went to the other soldier. She smiled

sweetly at him, recalling just how cordial he had been when he drove her from the railhead to her home. Charles Agnew. He was kind. It was evident in the way he handed out the supplies to the people, always with a smile and kind word. . . .

Marilla's gaze was drawn elsewhere . . . to an elderly Kiowa woman who appeared to be nothing less than one hundred years of age. As she stepped up to the counter and held out her arms for her supplies, Marilla marveled at her. Her body was twisted and her face was deeply lined with age. Her thin white hair was held in place by a cap of black netting, though she wore braids as well. She had but one eye, and was dressed in the manner of the Kiowa matron . . . in a dark, full-cut dress that reached nearly to her ankles, with full, flowing sleeves and a wide apronlike sash.

Behind her was a man of equal age, it seemed, one who was being treated with awe and respect by the Kiowa who stood in line with him. Marilla turned questioning eyes to Kohanah.

"Who are they?" she whispered.

"That is Kaguat Pa, Bud Moon, the keeper of the Taime, and his wife Little Bud Moon," Kohanah said, squaring his shoulders with pride. "Bud Moon protects the Taime, the sacred medicine idol, the Sun Dance doll of the Kiowa, a vital element in the Sun Dance ritual. Without this idol the dance cannot be performed, and the dance *must* be performed to reaffirm our tribal unity!"

Marilla nodded slowly. "How can he be protecting the Taime now? He is away from his tipi," she murmured.

"Even the keeper of the Taime must come to the white man's fort on ration day," Kohanah growled. "His survival depends on the white man's offerings also."

Marilla grew silent and watched the performance between the Indians and the two soldiers handing out supplies. Each member of the family had a ticket, which they handed to the soldier; then they were issued clothes and food. What disturbed Marilla the most was that the Indians were not asked which size they needed for clothing or shoes; they had to take what was given to them. Then they went around the large room trading things back and forth, to find the right size.

Marilla paled when something caught her eye from across the room. Standing in the shadows was an elderly Indian who had just been given a pair of breeches. He was cutting the breeches off at the thighs. He put on the two legs and threw the rest away, then put his breechcloth on around his waist. He then cut off the heels of a pair of shoes that had been given to him, mumbling that heels were no good to him; moccasins, the traditional footwear of the Indian, were flat.

The other rations handed out to the people were bacon and rice and dried fruit. Some of this was thrown away by the Indians. They said the bacon came from way off east, where there were big fat water snakes. They said if they ate the rice it would give them worms!

Marilla was glad when Kohanah stepped up and accepted his rations and was able to leave the dreaded building that disgraced the Indians, for nothing that had been given to them had amounted to much worth. And Marilla was glad to be away from the watchful eye of Jason Roark. Even Kohanah had become aware of the evil man's heated stares. . . .

The sun was slanting in the afternoon sky when the ration ordeal was finally over, and Marilla rode silently alongside Kohanah who was seeing to her safe arrival back to her own home. After being a part of the Indians' affairs the entire day, it didn't seem right that she should separate herself from their way of life for even a moment. She did not want the chance to forget what she had witnessed today. It was important that she always remember the plight of the Kiowa, to understand why Kohanah would delay his proposal of marriage to her. She understood the importance of his being alone in his leadership of his people. He had much to tend to. She would only be in the way!

Shadows were becoming long now; there was a deep blush on the sky, and the wide open plains seemed to glow with the setting sun. At this time of day there was a deep silence. Nothing moved. Everything seemed to have stopped so that the sun might take leave of the land.

And then there was a piercing call of a bobwhite. The whole world seemed startled by it!

Marilla looked over at Kohanah, unnerved by his silence. He had surely not heard the bobwhite. Did he even see the wonders of the setting sun? Was he aware that he had arrived at her house? Never had she seen him look so withdrawn, so unaware. . . .

Then Kohanah suddenly dismounted and went to Marilla and lifted her from her mare. While he held her fully within his arms, his lips met hers in a quivering, soft kiss; his hands clasped her possessively close to his muscled chest.

"Tsonda, the day was so long," Kohanah said huskily, carrying her on into her house. "If not for you, the hardships of ration day would have been almost too much for Kohanah to bear! My people! They suffer so!"

Marilla touched his face gently. "Yes, I know," she murmured. "I saw. I *felt* their sadness and embarrassment. I am so sorry, Kohanah. But it seems I have a need much too often to tell you that, don't I? My darling, I doubt if things can ever be easier for you. I feel so helpless."

"Kohanah fights for the right to perform the Sun Dance," he said thickly, placing Marilla on the floor beside the glowing logs on the fire. "If Kohanah wins that battle, then perhaps the others will come easier. The Sun Dance will make my people stronger! Faith will once again be in their hearts . . . in their eyes!"

"Can the soldiers prevent your Sun Dance?" Marilla asked, placing a teakettle on the wood-burning stove, preparing water for tea. Tea was good for the soul. She would try anything to get the bitter taste from her mouth that being at ration day with the Indians had caused.

Again Jason Roark's face flashed before her eyes. Oh, how he had enjoyed humiliating the Indians—especially Kohanah!

"*Ho*, yes, they can," Kohanah said, drawing Marilla up next to him. His dark eyes studied her; he was again taken by her loveliness. She had grown into a woman these past three years. He could not wait until he would never have to say good-bye to her again. To have her in the mornings when he first awakened would surely make the burdens of life much easier for him to bear.

But not yet. In time . . .

"But I have told you this," he said darkly, swinging away from Marilla. "Who is to know to what length they will go to prevent the Sun Dance from being performed? This sort of promise, also, I will get from white chief President Hayes! He must give his promise that no one can interfere with what must be done for my people! The dance must be performed!"·

Marilla turned Kohanah to face her. She snuggled into his embrace. "Kohanah, let us talk of no more problems tonight," she sighed. "Let us take from each other. Let us make love. For so long we could not. Now we have the freedom to. There is no one to stand in the way of our precious moments together."

She placed her hands on his cheeks and drew his lips downward. "Kiss me, Kohanah," she whispered. "Touch me all over. I'm yours. I'm . . . yours. . . ."

Her words faded as Kohanah's mouth teasingly brushed against her lips while his hands were busy disrobing her. Marilla's heartbeat was going wild as his fingers grazed against her breasts and then swept lower, to caress her where she was already unmercifully throbbing.

When he drew her against his steel-hard body and she could feel the outline of his manhood pressing against his deerskin clothes, she placed a hand on him there and gently squeezed. She smiled to herself when Kohanah uttered a guttural moan, then swept her up into his arms and carried her to her bed.

As she slipped her boots off, she watched Kohanah remove his clothes, his dark eyes smoldering with passion as he looked at her from head to toe.

And then he was sharing the bed with her, his hands moving over her, touching her familiarly, lifting her up on a wave of desire. He sought her mouth with a wildness and kissed her hard and long.

When he entered her and began his steady thrusts within

her, she trembled sensuously, arched, and cried out against his lips, while clinging to him about his neck.

As Kohanah rode her, his hands cupped and kneaded Marilla's breasts, his tongue probed between her lips and tasted of her sweetness again. Searing flames scorched Kohanah's insides. He could feel the wondrous pressure building, threatening to explode. . . .

Marilla was becoming breathless with rapture as she opened herself more widely to his thrusts. She was feeling the curl of pleasure unleashing, spreading . . . growing hotter . . . melting, it seemed, everything within her into a delicious, spiraling sensation.

And then it was too soon over, and they lay spent in one another's arms. Marilla was the first to stir as her stomach rumbled unmercifully. "Kohanah, I'm starving," she said, suddenly moving to a sitting position. "Do you realize we did not eat this entire day?"

"Food was not important then; it is not important now," Kohanah said, his body still tingling from the aftermath of loving Marilla. "You are all Kohanah needs now to feed hunger!"

"But the body must be fed, also," Marilla giggled. The whistling of the teakettle drew her from the bed. She threw on a robe and slipped into house slippers and rushed into the kitchen.

While she was placing cheeses and fruit on a tray on the table, she was unaware of Kohanah staring from the bedroom window at a lone rider looking down from a rise in the land. His eyes narrowed. He knew Jason Roark, even from this distance. Kohanah would soon have a lesson to teach that man, yet it must be something skillfully, quietly done, for Kohanah's remembrance of prison was too keenly etched onto his brain. He did not want to go to prison again for the likes of Jason Roark!

Then Kohanah's eyebrows forked. There was another man on the horizon! He also knew him! It was Charles Agnew, and it seemed these two men were having words! Did both of these men have their hearts set on making Marilla theirs? It would be easy to rid the earth of one soldier, but . . . two?

Grumbling, he began to pull on his clothes. . . .

"So what do I now call you, Charles?" Jason growled, spitting across his shoulder. "My assigned nursemaid? Do you figure you've a right to tag along with me everywhere I go?"

Charles sidled his horse closer to Jason's. The saddle leather groaned as he leaned his face square into Jason's. "You know damn well it ain't you I'm bein' a nursemaid to," he grumbled. "I warned you once not to get near that new schoolmarm and I meant it."

Jason leaned into Charles's face. "And I told you you'd best keep your distance from me," he threatened. "Or you won't live long enough to get a fair touch of that lady. That's what this is all about, ain't it? You want a piece of her, too, don't you?"

Charles grabbed Jason by the collar and yanked hard. "Jason, for a long time you had me scared to even get near you," he said dryly. "Even last night you put quite a fear in me. But I won't let you intimidate me any longer. You listen to *me*. Don't go near that lady, for that's what she is, Jason. A *lady*."

Jason chuckled, then slapped Charles's hand away. He straightened his shirt collar and glanced down at Marilla's house. "You call her a lady?" he grumbled. "Why, I bet she's even now in bed with that savage. She's an Injun-lover, Charles. That sort ain't of no 'count, except to use and have fun with!"

Jason kneaded his chin contemplatively. "I bet she even approves of the damn Sun Dance," he spat angrily. "She'd be the sort to believe in such superstitious hogwash. Well, I've something to say about that. The Taime? Just what if it disappeared?"

Charles studied Kohanah's horse, and then the house. "Jason, don't you see yet just how wrong you are about so many things?" he said blandly. "Kohanah ain't just any Injun. He's special. Marilla wouldn't love anyone unless they were special! And you'd best forget about the Taime. No Indian would allow you to get within spittin' range of that sacred doll."

He wheeled his horse around, envisioning Marilla's sweet, innocent loveliness, wishing that he had met her before she met Kohanah. He would have given her such a loving!

Jason thrust his heels into the flanks of his horse and rode up beside Charles. "Now, Charles," he said icily. "I think this is the last time I will put up with any of your snoopin' around seein' to what I'm doin'. If you know what's best for you, you'll find another interest to busy yourself with." He slapped a knife sheathed at his waist. "This weapon here? It makes no noise whatsoever when it slips into the flesh of a person's back. . . ."

Charles swallowed hard and paled, then rode on away, somehow knowing that Jason did not make such threats lightly. . . .

Fourteen

❧❧

The sun was just spreading its orange feelers along the horizon when Marilla drove her buggy into the Indian village. She slapped the horse's reins, determined that today she would begin teaching at the crude log schoolhouse that had been erected by the soldiers at the far edge of the village, providing her with no more than was absolutely necessary to give the "savages," as the Indians were labeled by so many of the soldiers, the beginnings of an education. Most feared that once the Indians were developed and cultivated mentally, when they grew up to be adults they would be more apt to catch the soldiers in their acts of deceit against them.

But an education—though a mock education the soldiers expected it to be—had been a part of the agreement with the Indians when they had been placed on the reservation.

Marilla was going to prove that she could do more than give them a mockery of an education. She would teach the children—even the grown-ups if they chose to come and sit in on the classes—everything that she had been taught in her own classrooms! The Kiowa would soon be able to read and write, even to use mathematical equations. . . .

Attired in a prim and proper pale yellow cotton dress, its

high neckline trimmed in a fine white lace, its skirt fully
gathered and worn over a lace-trimmed petticoat, Marilla
felt that she looked the role of a schoolmarm. She even
had a yellow satin bow in her hair, drawing it in a mass
back from her ears and brow. Her hair hung like golden
spun silk down her straight back, her blue eyes sparkled as
she searched for and found Kohanah's tipi in the early
morning light. She could envision him sleeping beside a
glowing fire, his skin so bronzed . . . his body so
muscled. . . .

Then she drew her horse's reins tight, causing the buggy
to weave dangerously into a sudden stop when her eyes
were drawn elsewhere, to another tipi. The color drained
from her face and she felt a sick feeling grab her insides
when she saw Little Bud Moon, the elderly wife of Kaguat
Pa, Bud Moon, the keeper of the Taime, lying halfway
out of her tipi, clutching her aged fingers lifelessly to the
ground. Blood shone viciously red on her face and . . . her
. . . scalp was missing!

Placing a gloved hand to her mouth, willing herself not
to retch, Marilla was momentarily stunned, so much that
her eyes were riveted in place, the sight of the dear old
lady magnifying tenfold in her eyes as she continued to
look at her lifeless form.

Then Marilla's senses returned and she became rational
as she suddenly realized that if Little Bud Moon had been
viciously murdered, surely Bud Moon had not been spared!
As man and wife, they shared the same dwelling and he
most surely was dead, lying somewhere within his tipi
close to his wife.

"Kohanah," Marilla whispered, feeling cold all over
from her discovery. "He must be told!"

Shivers raced up and down her spine as she jumped
from her buggy and ran, stumbling, toward Kohanah's
tipi. "Oh, Lord, Kohanah," she whispered. "How I hate
to tell you! You already have enough troubling your heart!"
She swallowed hard. "Who is responsible? Who would
do such a thing? And why . . . ?"

Throwing aside the entrance flap to Kohanah's tipi,
Marilla rushed on inside. She stopped and placed her

hands to her mouth as tears streamed from her eyes when she saw Kohanah still sleeping so peacefully beside his banked fire, a blanket only partially hiding his nudity beneath it. His eyes were so peacefully closed . . . his breathing so even. In a matter of moments all of this would change. Marilla would give him news that would shatter any sort of trust that he had left in him.

Falling to her knees beside Kohanah, Marilla pressed her hands softly to his cheeks. She leaned over and kissed him on the lips, tears salty as they coursed from her eyes down to her mouth. When Kohanah's eyes fluttered open and he saw her there, there was not so much surprise in them to see her as there was a total loving.

"Tsonda, you came to me in a dream only moments ago," he said huskily, taking her hands, drawing her down beside him. "You are here now, in real life. Did my dream beckon you here?"

His eyebrows furrowed into a sudden frown and he released her when he looked closer at her and saw her tears, and then the total sadness in her eyes. He leaned up on an elbow as Marilla scooted up into a sitting position, rubbing her eyes free of tears.

"Why do you cry?" Kohanah asked harshly, placing a hand on her chin, drawing her face close so that he could study her. "You have come to teach Kiowa children this morning. Does this make you sad?"

Marilla's heart was aching, the remembrance of Little Bud Moon almost too much to bear. She blinked her eyes nervously and swallowed back another lump in her throat, then took Kohanah's hand and held it tightly. "Kohanah, I have terrible news," she said, her voice weak. "As I was riding through your village, I . . . I saw . . ."

Kohanah rose from his pallet of furs and blankets and drew Marilla up before him. He clasped his fingers to her shoulders. "Tell me," he said hoarsely. "*Inhogo*, now! What did you see? What has made tears silver your *doba*, face?"

Marilla's eyes were cast downward. She cringed at what his reaction would be. But the longer she waited to tell him, the more apt someone else, perhaps even an innocent child, would be to find Little Bud Moon. And perhaps the keeper of the Taime would still be alive?

"It is Little Bud Moon," she blurted, jerking her head up, to look squarely into Kohanah's troubled eyes. "She has been murdered! I saw her only moments ago. She lies partway out of her tipi!"

She swallowed hard, finding it almost impossible to tell Kohanah the rest. But she had to!

"She has not only been murdered, but scalped!" she said, flinching when Kohanah stepped back away from her, shock registering on his handsome face.

Marilla took several steps back as Kohanah drew on a brief loincloth and rushed from the tipi, not having said anything, his feelings having been revealed enough in the pain in his eyes.

Getting the courage to follow him, suspecting that she was just about to witness something even more horrible if she followed Kohanah into the keeper of the Taime's dwelling, she knew that she must go with Kohanah, for he would need support as never before. She wanted to be the one whom he would reach out for, for the comforting . . . for the encouraging. . . .

Lifting the hem of her dress into her arms, Marilla rushed from Kohanah's tipi and followed him, his long and hurried strides much too much for her to keep up with. She faltered somewhat when she again caught sight of the dead elderly woman, yet drew courage from loving Kohanah to continue with what must be done. She stood over Kohanah as he dropped to a knee beside Little Bud Moon, looking at her dejectedly, then stepped over her and went on into her tipi.

Marilla hesitated a moment, then cringed when she heard a loud wail of grief coming from inside the tipi. She now knew beyond a doubt that Kohanah had found another needless death and had finally shown his feelings other than in the haunted depths of his dark eyes. His wail reached clean into Marilla's heart. She rushed inside the tipi, knowing that Kohanah would need her. Then she covered her mouth with a hand and turned her eyes away, for Bud Moon had been as viciously murdered as Little Bud Moon, and his scalp had also been removed.

"*Aalyi*! *Aalyi*!" Kohanah said, kneeling down beside Little Bud Moon, rocking back and forth, his eyes turned heavenward. He chanted in Kiowa for a while, then looked down at Bud Moon.

"In death his face is that of a child," he whispered, then covered Bud Moon's body with a blanket.

Bolting to his feet, Kohanah began searching frantically through the Taime keeper's belongings. Marilla watched, silent. Then, as Kohanah became almost frenzied in his search she went to him and placed a hand on his arm, to momentarily stop him.

"What are you looking for?" she asked, trembling.

"The keeper of the Taime would only be murdered for one reason!" Kohanah half shouted, flailing a hand in the air. "Someone has stolen the Taime! Did I not tell you that the soldiers would do anything to keep the Kiowa from performing the Sun Dance?"

Marilla looked up at him, her eyes innocently wide. "But both were scalped," she managed to say in a voice hardly louder than a whisper. "Surely no soldier would do that."

"Only one who wanted to make it look as though a savage Indian had done it!" he said, contempt thick in his voice. "No Kiowa, and no other Indian of any other tribe, would kill and scalp to steal the Taime. It is sacred in the eyes of all my people!"

Marilla eased her hand from Kohanah's arm. She stiffened her back and squared her shoulders, clasping her hands tightly behind her. "Tell me what the Taime looks like and I shall help you look for it," she offered. "Perhaps whoever came to steal it didn't find it."

"*Ho*, yes, you can help in my search," Kohanah said, kneading his brow nervously. His eyes moved from place to place in the tipi, from bundles of clothes that had been ransacked, to pots and pans that had been thrown about. Blood had sprayed along the buffalo hide of the tipi, making mocking designs that resembled petals of roses.

"The Taime is a small image less than two feet in

length," Kohanah explained softly, now directing his eyes downward, looking into the soft blue of Marilla's. "It represents a human figure dressed in a robe of white feathers, with a headdress consisting of a single upright feather and pendants of ermine skin. Numerous strands of blue beads hang around its neck, and painted upon the face, breast, and back are designs symbolic of the sun and moon. The image itself is of dark green stone."

He paused and stepped away from Marilla, his eyes again scanning the interior of the tipi. "It is preserved in a rawhide box," he continued softly. "It is never under any circumstances exposed to view except at the annual Sun Dance, when it is fastened to a short upright stick planted within the medicine lodge, near the western side."

Kohanah again began to desperately search, Marilla looking through the ancient Indians' belongings on the opposite side of the tipi from Kohanah. But it did not take long to know that their search was in vain. The murderer had gotten what he came for. The Taime was gone!

Marilla watched as Kohanah carried Little Bud Moon into the tipi and covered her beneath a blanket beside her husband. Again he offered some chants, intermixed with tormented wails, then rose to his feet and guided Marilla from the dwelling.

"I must inform my people of the murders and thievery, and then I must ride to the fort to tell the soldiers what has happened," Kohanah growled. "The one responsible must be made to step forward! He must return the Taime to the Kiowa, then *die*!"

"I shall go with you to the fort," Marilla said softly, already knowing which soldier she would go to for help: Charles Agnew. He had shown that he had feelings for the Kiowa. He would help to find the one responsible for this ghastly action!

Then her insides grew numbly cold with the remembrance of another soldier. Could Jason Roark be this heartless . . . this evil . . . ?

Riding into the fort in her buggy, Kohanah and his many braves riding in front of her, Marilla became quickly puzzled at the activity that buzzed around her. Some soldiers were cleaning up the fort grounds, others were repairing some of the old buildings and the corrals that housed the horses. It was the activity that she had grown accustomed to seeing in the forts just prior to a dignitary's arrival. Would this cloud the issue that Kohanah was coming here to argue over? Would anyone even concern himself with the murder of two Indians or the stolen Taime?

Looking guardedly at Kohanah's proud bare back and muscled shoulders as he rode on his red roan, wearing only a loincloth and moccasins, she knew that surely he would stop at nothing to find the one responsible for the sadness now engulfing his village. If the soldiers refused to help him, what then?

Eagerly, Marilla averted her attention back to the soldiers. If she could just find Charles Agnew! Perhaps he would accompany Kohanah into the general's office. Perhaps he would help argue the case of the Kiowa. He did seem the sort to be moved by such tragedies that had occurred.

But Marilla frowned disconsolately when she saw no signs of Charles anywhere . . . still only the hustle and bustle of those who were readying the fort . . . but for *what*?

When Kohanah reined in his horse before the main headquarters, an oblong log cabin with the American flag fluttering high in the wind over it, Marilla guided her horse to draw her buggy close by. Quickly climbing from it she went to walk with Kohanah. She held her chin boldly high, no matter that all activity seemed to have stopped in the courtyard. All eyes were now on her and the Indians, who did not wait to be announced to General Stanton, the one in charge of this fort, but instead walked on in and now stood before the powerful man's desk, staring determinedly down at him.

"What is the meaning of this rude interruption?" General Stanton growled, his dark eyes narrowing as he rose slowly up from his desk. His blue uniform was pressed to perfection; his face was freshly shaved except for the tiny strip of mustache that curved above his thick lips. His dark hair had been groomed neatly to hang just above his collar line, his fingernails had been freshly manicured, shining beneath the soft rays of a kerosene lamp on the desk.

Several guards clamored into the room and fell into place about the silent, glowering Indians. Again Marilla scanned their faces, hopefully searching for Charles Agnew. Instead, she found a face of her nightmares. Jason Roark. No other time than now could he be as ugly, as threatening, with his round face distorted by his large bulbous nose, his bushy black eyebrows and long, sleekeddown, coal-black hair.

Oh, how had fate been so unkind to her that he would be there instead of at another fort? If only her father were in charge here! He would banish the man from the face of the earth this time!

Jason's cold, glaring green eyes unnerved Marilla as he challenged her set stare. She started to draw her eyes around but stopped and shivered when a slow smile, as though mocking her for something, raised his lips into a crooked curve upward. What was on his mind? Was he mentally undressing her, or was he thinking about a triumph? Had he murdered the two elderly Indians? Had he stolen the Taime? If so, how could she ever prove it?

Kohanah's deep, resonant voice, filled with command, yet a cutting sadness, drew Marilla's attention back to the general, whose eyes were burning with impatience. . . .

"Violence was performed against my people last night," Kohanah said with a cold smoothness. "Two of my people were killed." He doubled a fist at his side; his jaw became set. "Our Taime was stolen. You are the leader. You must find and punish the one responsible. You must return the Taime to the Kiowa!"

General Stanton leaned his weight against his desk and bent closer to Kohanah's face. "You do not order me around, Indian," he spat. "*I* make the decisions here."

Kohanah's heart began to beat soundly inside him, so much that he could hear its pounding within his ears, as though war drums were throbbing in a steady rhythm. He had to collect himself, not show his anger, for it would not benefit him or his people. "It was a soldier who killed two innocent Kiowa," he said smoothly, his shoulders squared, his gaze flat. "You find. *We* punish. That is not asking too much. Anyone who steals and murders must be dealt with. If you do not wish to deal with him the white man's way, it would pleasure me to deal with him in the ways of the Kiowa."

General Stanton cleared his throat and straightened his back. He walked from behind his desk and looked from a window, clasping his hands tightly behind him. "You say it was a soldier," he said blandly. He swung around and faced Kohanah. "Do you have proof of that statement?"

Kohanah was not to be dissuaded by his demeanor. He stood proudly erect, his eyes never leaving the general. "No proof," he said flatly. "But it is fact that only a soldier would kill such a beloved man as Kaguat Pa and his wife. They held a high position among the Kiowa. The Taime was protected by them!"

Kohanah's eyes faltered for the first time. "But now they are gone and also the Taime," he said, his voice quivering.

"The Taime," General Stanton said, flailing a hand in the air, exasperated. "The idol used for witchcraft in your Indian community has been discussed until I am blue in the face."

He went and stood directly before Kohanah, his eyes gleaming. "Kohanah, do you witch?" he asked, smiling slowly. "You know that to put such faith in an idol makes you guilty of witching . . . of believing in supernatural powers."

General Stanton stepped back away from Kohanah when Kohanah refused to answer him. Slowly he looked from soldier to soldier. "Anyone here see anything strange sitting around, like a Sun Doll?" He chuckled. Then he grew pale when all of the Kiowa took one step closer, Kohanah in the lead.

Turning his gaze to Marilla, General Stanton frowned. "And what, may I ask, are *you* doing here with these Indians?" he asked shallowly.

"Thank you for even asking," Marilla said sarcastically, lifting her chin stubbornly. "General Stanton, you make me ashamed to have ever had any association with the United States Cavalry. My father would pale if he saw your attitude today toward the Kiowa. They have come to ask your help and you do nothing but mock them! That is most deplorable! If my father were here—"

"But your father isn't here and he is not, nor will he ever be, in charge here," General Stanton said, his face growing red with anger. "It is well known how he protected, even aided, the Indians at Fort Marion. But this is not Fort Marion and *I* am in charge."

He threw his hands up in despair and went and sat back down in his chair behind his desk. "I am weary of hearing about this Taime and Sun Dance business," he said, hanging his head within his hands. "And today is the worst day of all to discuss anything except the arrival of our President."

Marilla's heart skipped a beat; her mouth dropped open. She looked over at Kohanah, then back at the general. "President Hayes is arriving today?" she gasped, taking a step closer to the desk. "Why wasn't I informed? Why weren't the Kiowa? This is something everyone should know. Kohanah has had personal contact with the President. Surely you know why the President is coming here. Didn't you want Kohanah to have the chance to prepare for his arrival in a special way, the way your soldiers are so obviously doing? Aren't you *ever* fair, General Stanton, in anything you do?"

Swinging her skirt around, Marilla stomped from the room, followed by Kohanah and his braves. Once outside, Marilla took a deep breath and turned her eyes slowly to Kohanah. "I'm so sorry," she murmured. "Nothing seems to have worked out for you."

Then a slow smile sparkled her eyes. "But, Kohanah, the President is truly coming," she said softly. "Surely he will help you in all ways. He is a kind man. When you tell him of the murders and of the stolen Taime, *he* will listen."

Kohanah's eyes were two points of fire. He nodded slowly. "*Ho*, he will listen," he said icily. "He will listen well!"

Marilla's insides quivered strangely when she heard the

coldness of Kohanah's words, even saw the hate deeply
within his eyes. Had General Stanton seen enough of the
same not to let the President have an actual audience with
Kohanah?

If Kohanah was denied even this, what *would* he do? He
surely could take only so much more; then he would rebel
again. Another prison term could kill him. . . .

While Kohanah prepared for the arrival of the President,
delaying the burial rites for the two slain Kiowa until after
the President's departure, Marilla was on her way home,
to get dressed in a more appropriate gown in which to
meet President Hayes. She was anxious to meet him, also,
for perhaps she could use some of her own persuasion for
Kohanah's benefit.

But what if he didn't remember her *or* her father? It had
been some time since Lucy Hayes had attended college
with Marilla's father. . . .

Worrying about the President arriving before she returned to the reservation, Marilla flipped the reins of her
horse, scurrying the buggy along the snakelike dirt road,
lined on one side by tall willows, a meandering creek on
the other.

Then something along the banks of the creek drew
Marilla's attention. She paled when she looked closer and
saw that it was a man partially immersed in the water,
only his head and shoulders exposed.

Fear entered her heart as she drew her reins taut and
stopped the horse. Lifting the skirt of her dress she jumped
from the carriage and ran to the man, then took a staggering
step backwards when she recognized the face turned side-
ways, with soft brown eyes staring blankly toward her.

"No!" Marilla whispered, stifling a gasp behind her
hand. "Please, God, no. Not Charles Agnew!"

Falling to her knees, Marilla winced when she touched
his face, its coldness seeping into her fingers. Tears flooded
her eyes as she grabbed Charles under the arms and tried
to drag him from the water. But his clothes were too
water-logged. She couldn't budge him. Her gaze went to

the blood-soaked shirt, and she could tell that he had been knifed in the back. . . .

Trembling, Marilla hung her head into her hands. "Who could have done this?" she sobbed. "Why. . . ?"

Tired from cleaning and sprucing up the fort for the President's arrival, Jason Roark lay on his bunk in his cabin, smiling crookedly. His hand slipped down beneath his bed and touched a rawhide box. He would look at the Sun Doll again later. Right now he had another chore that needed to be done.

Stretching his arms above his head, yawning lazily, he rose from the bed and picked up a sheathed knife from his table. Drawing the knife from its sheath, he frowned when he saw the telltale remains of dried blood. He had to rid himself of all evidence. Now!

Going to the window, he recalled the well at Marilla's house. Today when everyone was absorbed in the President's visit, he would take the knife there and dispose of it.

Then very soon, *she* was the next thing on his agenda. . . .

Fifteen

❧ ❧

The flames in the firepit rolled across logs like streaks of orange velvet. There was a moment of strain upon President Hayes's first arrival in Kohanah's tipi, but after the introductions, everyone seemed compatible enough for the upcoming talk of paintings and everything else that was troubling Kohanah's mind.

Marilla sat beside Kohanah, her low-swept dress of white silk organdy and trimming of lace making her radiantly shine in her petite loveliness. Her golden hair hung long and loose across her shoulders and down her back. A cameo necklace lay at her throat, meeting the beginnings of the cleavage of her high, rounded breasts.

She sat straight-backed on her pallet of furs, her blue eyes sparkling as she found it amusing how the President was studying her, trying to connect her name with one that he remembered out of his past.

Only a few knew of President Hayes's absentmindedness, his tendency to forget names.

But he rarely forgot a face. . . .

Then her face shadowed with a frown when she let her thoughts drift back to Charles Agnew and how she had found him. She had not told anyone yet, for fear that perhaps Kohanah or one of his braves would be accused of the murder. It had been done with a knife.

But Marilla almost knew for sure that Jason Roark was responsible, for only he seemed to be the cause of chaos when he was anywhere near.

Yet why *would* he kill Charles? Had Charles possibly seen Jason in the act of murder and thievery in the Kiowa village? Was Charles killed to silence him?

Marilla had decided to inform Kohanah of Charles Agnew's death, then General Stanton, after the President left. By then, she hoped, everything in life would look much more cheerful. If only the President would listen to Kohanah . . . help him in his efforts to make things right for his people. And the one responsible for the murder of two innocent Kiowa should be found and properly punished!

Slowly turning her eyes to Kohanah, Marilla felt her heart blossom into a renewed love for him. He was dressed handsomely in his buckskin jacket that was fringed on the sleeves and across the shoulders, and his leggings that fit tightly were also fringed down both sides of the legs.

In his braids he had woven the beautiful fur of the otter. His dark eyes were proud and sure; his strong face with its hard cheekbones was determined.

He was lighting a long-stemmed pipe festooned with the scarlet feathers of the woodpecker.

Her gaze moved slowly back to President Hayes. She felt honored to be in his presence, for any reason. He had come into the tipi without any accompanying soldiers or guards, showing his trust in the Kiowa. He was dressed well in a gray suit and matching satin ascot with a diamond stickpin shining among its folds. He had gray hair, a mustache, a neatly trimmed beard, and a long, smooth nose on a slim face that was barely wrinkled. His eyes were brown and very friendly.

Taking one last puff on the pipe, Kohanah handed it to the President. "Share with me the pleasures of the *satop*, pipe, which has always represented peace," he said smoothly, glad when the President curled his long, lean fingers about the stem of the pipe and placed it to his lips and drew smoke into his mouth. "Welcome to Kohanah's *do-giagya-guat*, tipi with battle pictures drawn onto it. It is good that you have come. My invitation to you came from my *ten*, heart."

President Hayes took another long draw from the pipe, then handed it back to Kohanah. "It is my pleasure to be here, Kohanah," he said, his dark eyes warm. He sat on a rich pallet of furs, across the fire from Kohanah and Marilla, his legs crossed. He placed his hands on his knees.

"You are a chief admired by those of us in Washington," President Hayes continued. "We all appreciate your cooperation in trying to make your people understand life on the reservation. Without your leadership, I fear much chaos would break out. You are a man of great knowledge and fortitude. These are traits most admired in a man."

Kohanah placed the pipe aside and folded his strong arms across his chest. He did not thank the President for his praise, for it was only words. Kohanah needed more than mere words of praise this day. He needed reassurances, cooperation, on the President's part!

"There is much my people still do not understand," Kohanah said dryly. "Perhaps they never will. For you see, the Kiowa culture is withering and dying like grass that is burned, hurried by the prairie wind. There has now come a day of destiny when, in every direction as far as the eye can see, carrion lies on the land. The bleached bones of the buffalo lie scattered everywhere! The buffalo was, and forever will be, the animal representation of the sun, the essential and sacrificial victim of the Sun Dance. The wild herds are destroyed. So is the will of my people almost destroyed. There is nothing to sustain them in spirit."

Kohanah's eyes grew fierce with anger as he glared at the President. "There have been two recent deaths in my village!" he said hotly. "The keeper of the Taime and his wife were slain. The precious Taime was stolen! I ask you to help find the one responsible and see that the Taime is returned to my people. It is *pai-aganti*, the time of hot weather soon, the time to begin making plans for the Sun Dance. But without the sacred Sun Dance doll no dance can be performed.'' His eyes lowered sadly. ''Without *buffalo*, no dance can be performed. My people are sad. They now have neither!''

President Hayes cleared his throat nervously. ''I am sorry for your misfortune,'' he said blandly. ''But I am not the one to speak to. There are those at the fort whom you must go to. General Stanton is in charge. It is his duty to speak and act in my behalf in such matters as these.''

He let his gaze move to the canvases that were lined up against the far wall for viewing. ''I have come to speak of the paintings, Kohanah,'' he said, finding this a much more comfortable topic of conversation. ''As you know, I would like to add some of your priceless artworks to my personal collection. Would you care to show them to me, one by one, and explain what each depicts?''

Kohanah doubled a fist at his side, now seeing that the President was going to ignore everything but the paintings. His gut twisted with the knowing, hatred for the white man swelling inside him anew.

But he had expected this response from the President and had schemed throughout the restless night of no sleep, planning how he would handle this sort of disappointment. He would toy with this man who was the speaker for the whole white nation. In the end, the President would know who was in control!

''Will you bring the canvases over closer to me, so that I may view them one by one?'' President Hayes commented, drawing a pair of spectacles from his inside coat pocket.

While Kohanah rose to his feet and strode tight-limbed toward his paintings, President Hayes turned his attention back to Marilla. With his spectacles on the bridge of his nose, he peered more closely at Marilla. ''Young lady, please correct me if I am wrong, but haven't we met before?'' he asked, looking her up and down. ''There is so much familiar about you. And am I right in assuming you are here because you have only recently arrived to be the teacher of the Indian children? This is why you saw fit to sit in on this meeting? You felt that you could help in some way since you are so knowledgable in both languages?''

Marilla had lost her luster, it seemed, for she was

feeling Kohanah's disappointment. She had expected more
from a man whose reputation was one of kindness and
understanding. "You are right in your one assumption,
Mr. President," she said, her voice cool. "You do know
me through your acquaintance with my father. Some say
that we resemble each other in our facial features. Lieutenant Richard Pratt is my father. Before he joined the United
States Cavalry, he attended college with your wife, Lucy.
You have been with him many times, before you were
President, and since."

Forcing a sweet smile, Marilla looked more attentive,
remembering her scheme to get in the good graces of the
President, hoping her persuasion could help Kohanah, if
even in a small way. "How *is* Lucy?" she asked softly,
blinking her thick eyelashes at the President. "How are
your *children*?"

President Hayes relaxed, glad to have something other
than Indian matters to discuss, yet nervously watching
Kohanah separate one painting from the other, as though
pondering which one he would show first. "Lucy and the
children are fine," he said thickly. "They enjoyed Easter
at the White House, with so many children scampering
around on the lawn, looking for eggs."

He placed a hand on a knee and leaned his full weight
against it, bringing his face closer to Marilla's. "My wife
enjoyed the Easter egg hunt so much with the children this
year she has something quite special planned for next
year," he said, chuckling.

"And what might that be, sir?" Marilla asked, attentive
as she could stand to be.

"It is Lucy's notion that there should be something
other than having the children just hunt for the eggs," the
President said, his eyes twinkling. "There will be an egg
rolling contest. My children and others whom we will
invite will participate. Do you find that a fascinating plan,
Miss Pratt?"

Marilla found it hard not to tell him that she found it a
ghastly time to discuss Easter egg rolling contests, when
the lives and the customs of the Kiowa hung in balance.

But she was here to charm. She must remember that!

"Why, sir, I do believe that will become quite an accepted custom, and perhaps be carried on through the future of all other Easter egg hunts on the grounds of the White House," she purred.

Then she recalled the President's fondness for reading. "Sir, have you yet read the novel *Ben Hur*?" she asked softly. "General Lew Wallace has won nationwide acclaim for this novel."

"Yes. Quite a fascinating book," the President nodded. He again cleared his throat nervously, knowing when he was being charmed. But for what purpose? No matter. He would reciprocate with his own unadulterated charm, as well!

"Miss Pratt," he said, clicking his false teeth. "I have an interesting tale to tell, since you are so educated. Just recently Thomas Edison visited the White House to demonstrate his favorite invention, the phonograph. He hopes this form of entertainment will one day be in everyone's parlor. It is unique, to say the least!"

Marilla forked an eyebrow questioningly. "What is a phono . . . ?" she began, but stopped when Kohanah made his appearance at her side, holding one of his most beloved paintings in the light of the fire. She admired it anew . . . the painting that showed the yearly celebration of the great Sun Dance. The bright colors seemed to make the painting come to life. Anyone would seek this painting for his collection! Most surely the President!

President Hayes readjusted his spectacles on his nose and squinted his dark eyes as he began to study the painting. Marilla held her breath, wondering what he would offer Kohanah for what she saw to be a masterpiece. When he discovered that it was not money that Kohanah was after, what then would the President's reaction be?

In a sense, Kohanah was going to suggest *blackmail*. . . .

President Hayes rose to his feet and kneaded his chin contemplatively as he studied the painting more closely. A look of sincere admiration danced in his eyes and caused his cheeks to blossom into a soft pink flush of excitement, for he saw the worth of the painting, as so many before him had seen it.

"I see," the President said softly. "To be admired, for sure, Kohanah."

Eagerly his gaze swept to the other paintings, and he did not wait for Kohanah to bring them to him. He went to them, and with smooth-tipped fingers he moved one painting closer to his eyes, and then another, until he had observed them all with intense interest.

After viewing the last one, he turned on a heel and faced Kohanah. "I cannot take them all off your hands," he said suavely. "But there are some I will gladly pay a large sum for. If you don't mind, I would like to point them out to you."

Marilla looked anxiously at Kohanah, knowing exactly what to expect next. She rose to her feet and watched the transaction, clasping her hands nervously behind her. . . .

"*Ho*, yes, point them out," Kohanah said flatly. "Then Kohanah will see if the price is high enough, for all paintings are valuable not only to me but also to my people. There is a deep meaning painted onto each canvas. Each painting tells bits and pieces of the Kiowa history."

Deftly, with an air of caution, President Hayes stepped away from those paintings done on canvas, to the one in particular done on a buffalo skin. The skin was curled and dried at the edges with age, yet the drawing was still as bright in color and as descriptive in design as the day it had been painted while Kohanah was in his jail cell, before the canvases had been given to him by Marilla's father, on which to do his drawings.

This painting in particular represented the worst of the United States Cavalry atrocities against the Kiowa. Blood was the main element painted on the buffalo skin. Its dominant color, scarlet, represented all wrongs done against *all* Indians.

Kiowa, Comanche . . . Apache . . .

"This painting is the most powerful of all," President Hayes said hoarsely, pushing his spectacles more snugly onto his nose. "It is not done on canvas. That is why it is unique. That will make it valuable, as I see it."

Kohanah's eyes narrowed and his nose flared with anger. He had known exactly which painting would be chosen first by the President. He had been right. The President wanted this painting to take and hide away, so that no one could ever see how the Kiowa had been treated when the settlers came swarming onto the land like unwanted ants!

Stalking over to the painting, Kohanah drew it up and held it before him, staring boldly into the President's eyes. "It can be yours, if . . ."

The President's eyebrows forked, and he took a step back. "If . . . ?" he repeated. "You say *if* . . . ? Why do you hesitate in selling it to me? Is it because I have not yet stated a price? You must know that I am willing to pay you more money than you have ever seen in your lifetime, Kohanah."

President Hayes withdrew a great leather wallet from his inside coat pocket, but was stunned when Kohanah set his portrait aside and placed his hand on the President's, easing the wallet back into his pocket.

"No. No money," Kohanah said flatly. "Money is not what Kohanah wants for his paintings."

President Hayes paled as he slipped his hand down away from his wallet. "Why did you invite me here to purchase your paintings when it is evident you are not willing to take money for them? And it is obvious that you would not *give* them away. What is it you want, young man?"

"White chief, Kohanah would part with them all for a price," Kohanah said, gesturing toward his precious paintings with the swing of a hand. "I will state my price. You pay. You get the *paintings*."

Marilla looked from Kohanah to President Hayes, almost numb from wondering what was going to happen next and who would win in this battle of wits.

From the reaction of the President, she was afraid that, again, Kohanah would be the loser. . . .

President Hayes glanced over at Marilla, then back to Kohanah. "I would like to hear what the price is," he said blandly, removing his spectacles from his nose with a jerk. "Speak up, young man. What is it you want?"

Kohanah lifted his chin boldly and folded his arms across his chest. "Kohanah asks for rights for his people. The one who murdered the keeper of the Taime and his wife and who stole the Taime must be found and dealt with properly. You must deliver the Taime safely back into my hands. You must give us your permission to perform the Sun Dance once the Taime *is* returned to us."

Kohanah paused, as though weighing his next words. "You must deliver to my people at least one buffalo, for without it, we cannot perform the ritual of the Sun Dance!" he said, no emotion in his voice.

President Hayes's mouth went dry, his face paled. Then he narrowed his eyes. This had gotten way out of hand. He wanted some of Kohanah's paintings to add to his priceless collection of artwork in the White House, and he wanted others to burn because they displayed the atrocities of the white man against the Indians.

He knew very well that he could not take the paintings by force, for the news would spread that he was taking advantage of Indians who were now living in peace. He was always thinking of what he might do to look best in the American public's eyes . . . wanting always to be remembered as a favorite President.

But never had he considered that the transaction with Kohanah might come to this. He was astounded by the Indian's ease at negotiating blackmail with him!

"Young man, I fear that this discussion has come to an end," President Hayes said, turning on a heel, walking toward the entrance flap, slipping his spectacles into his coat pocket. He paused and bowed to Marilla. "Good day, Miss Pratt. Whenever you speak with your father, please give him my regards. Tell him an open invitation to the White House is always his. I am sure Lucy would enjoy seeing him again, also."

His eyes wavered. "And, Miss Pratt, should you ever come to Washington, do not hesitate to come and visit with my wife and me, also," he said, then left the tipi in short, angry strides.

Marilla was almost struck numb by the President's abruptness with Kohanah and his decision to leave so quickly without further negotiations, whatsoever, with him. She looked over at Kohanah whose eyes showed an intense pain in their depths, the sort of pain that she had become familiar with when they first met in Florida.

Would it ever end . . . ?

Stifling a sob of distress from behind a hand, Marilla went to Kohanah. She looked adoringly up at him, willing him to look down at her. And when he would not, she thrust herself into his arms and hugged him to her. "Darling, do not despair," she murmured. "Other opportunities will arise. Somehow. They *must*."

"He is not a wise man," Kohanah growled, then eased his arms around Marilla and buried his nose in the jasmine scent of her hair. "Tsonda, do not *you* despair so. It was a ploy used by Kohanah that did not work. There *will* be other ways to win with your people. But for now, there is the way of the *Kiowa*. My braves and I will have to find the man responsible for the deaths of our beloved friends. My braves and I will find the Taime. We *will* perform the Sun Dance, even if we have to use only the *skin* of the buffalo to make the ritual valid in my people's eyes."

"You remain courageous at all times," Marilla sighed; then remembrances of Charles Agnew flashed into her mind's eye. She drew quickly away from Kohanah and placed her hands on his cheeks and raised his head upward, so that their gazes could meet and hold.

"My love, there is something that I must tell you," she blurted. "On my way home today I came across a body. Kohanah, someone killed Charles Agnew! His body lies even now only half immersed in water. I could not move him. He was too heavy. And I did not want to go to the soldiers at the fort to report the death because I was afraid that they might blame the Kiowa! *And* the President was due to arrive. I did not want to tell anyone because of *him*. That could have clouded his visit. Already there had been two deaths unaccounted for."

"The kind white man," Kohanah said, grimacing at the thought of losing one of his allies. "That is bad. But who *would* kill him? Why?"

"There is only one man that enters my mind who might do this," Marilla said, swinging away from Kohanah, settling down in front of the fire. Though the fire was hugging her with its warmth, a chill coursed through her when she thought of Jason Roark. "Jason Roark. But why would he?" She combed her fingers through her hair. "Perhaps it was some personal vendetta."

Kohanah sank to his haunches beside Marilla. His eyes turned golden in the fire's glow as he peered into the dancing flames. "Or perhaps it is because Charles Agnew was a friend to the Kiowa," he growled.

"Though we both suspect Jason Roark of many things, you must be careful, Kohanah, when you begin your search for the man responsible for all that has happened here recently," Marilla warned. "I would not be so hasty to go right to Jason Roark. He may have a scheme to trap you somehow, to make you look bad to the authorities."

Kohanah nodded. "It is Kohanah's plan to begin search-ing elsewhere to throw Jason off the track," he said, chuckling. "And then Kohanah will go in for the kill!"

Marilla went to her knees before Kohanah, blocking his view of the fire. She placed her arms about his neck and her lips close to his. "Oh, darling, you must be careful," she said softly. "I would die if you were imprisoned again. If you are not careful how you handle this situation, you might not even be imprisoned. You might be hanged or shot!" She lunged into his arms. "Oh, please . . . please be careful."

Kohanah ran his fingers through her hair and kissed her lightly on the lips, then held her away from him. "Kohanah knows ways of eluding the white man now as never be-fore," he said stiffly. "Do not worry about me. I move about in the night like a panther."

He looked at the entrance flap. "Now that the business with the white father of Washington is over, other business must be taken care of," he said solemnly. "There are two burials awaiting my people."

Marilla's eyes wavered. "Kohanah, what about Charles Agnew?" she murmured. "I can't just leave his body lying there, unattended."

"Tomorrow. Tomorrow Kohanah will help you with the body," he said blandly. "You can then take it to the soldiers at the fort and explain where you found it. They must start their investigation to find the one responsible.''

''But what if they believe *you* did it?''

''Charles Agnew was a friend to the Kiowa. No one will suspect the Kiowa.''

''I hope you are right,'' Marilla sighed. She rose to her feet, aching from the tension experienced the last several days. ''Tomorrow. Will you begin your search for the killer and thief?''

''*Ho*, yes. Tomorrow . . .''

The word ''tomorrow'' seemed a threat to Marilla and Kohanah's happiness, somehow. Marilla eased into Kohanah's arms and hugged him, then fled from the tipi, knowing that he would not want her around when he performed the sacred burial rites of his two beloved Kiowa.

But, hopefully, in the future, he would welcome her at his side, at all times. She, wanted, oh, so much, to be his wife, to share every breathing moment with him.

And she would. In time, she would. She would not give him up so easily for *any* cause. Sooner or later he would know of her determination to have him, totally. . . .

Boarding her buggy, Marilla looked toward a cloud of dust on the horizon. It was the procession of soldiers accompanying President Hayes back to the fort.

A strange sort of sadness assailed her. . . .

Sixteen

❧∼≥

Marilla stood before General Stanton's desk, unnerved by
how he still thumbed through papers instead of becoming
attentive to her after she had just delivered the body of
Charles Agnew to him. She didn't know if he was ignoring
her because he needed time to gather his wits or because
he was going to show her just who was in charge. He
seemed to be gaining force in his dislike for her. Just
because her father had been the sort of soldier everyone
liked and admired, General Stanton appeared to be taking
his jealousy of Marilla's father out on *her*.

Or was it something else . . . ?

Slapping her butter-soft leather gloves against the palm
of her hand, her pale blue cotton dress with eyelet trim and
a froth of lace edging her petticoat at her ankles, Marilla
felt her patience growing thin. She was being insulted,
yet she had been taught at a very young age to respect her
elders, so she continued to stand in silence, staring down
at the middle-aged man in his freshly laundered uniform,
with his hair sleeked down to his head.

Emitting a nervous sigh, Marilla flinched when doing so
drew General Stanton's dark eyes upward. His finely manicured nails shone beneath the glow of the kerosene lamp

165

on his desk. His aroma was that of one who had just shaved.

"Miss Pratt, will you please repeat to me just how and where you found Charles Agnew's body?" he asked, shoving his stack of papers aside. He placed his fingertips together before him, leaning his elbows on his desk. "Will you also explain just how you managed to get his body in your buggy?" His eyes raked over her. "A tiny thing like you wouldn't be able to drag a man's dead body, *much* less *lift* it."

"Do I detect a lack of grief for the man?" Marilla said, her voice quivering. "Sir, you didn't even flinch when I came to you with the news that Charles Agnew was dead. Wasn't his sort valuable enough to you? He was one of the nicest, *fairest* gentlemen I have met in uniform."

She lowered her eyes, so wanting to say that in a way, Charles Agnew reminded her of her father, when her father was young and ambitious. There was no doubt that her father would have admired Charles Agnew . . . would have possibly helped him along in rank much more quickly than others of Charles's age.

General Stanton rose from his chair and stepped around his desk, to stand close to Marilla. "You are evading the issue here," he growled. "I need information. It seems only you are available to give me such information. Or do I have to call Kohanah in, to question *him?* Surely he is the one who assisted you in loading Charles into your buggy. Or have you made acquaintance with others besides the Indian and his braves?"

Marilla paled at the thought of Kohanah being drawn into this affair. It had been enough to have worried the long night through that Kohanah might even be accused of the murder. Wasn't it always easier to blame an Indian for murder, instead of a soldier?

"Sir, I have already told you exactly how I found Charles and where," Marilla said dryly, tilting her chin stubbornly. "Now as I see it, it is up to you to find the guilty party. It seems there is one among you who did not appreciate having someone as gentlemanly in your group of soldiers. Look for the one who is way less than a gentleman and I am sure you will find your murderer.''

"And just whom might you be referring to?" General Stanton said, sarcasm thick in his voice, his fingers busy twisting the end of his thin black mustache. "But, of course, I can wager a guess. You are referring to Jason Roark, are you not?"

Marilla took a shaky step back, stunned by the general's insinuation, without his even saying the words. She saw it in his eyes . . . the knowing. He had heard the gossip spread by Jason Roark. Did the general actually believe that she had been intimate with Jason in Florida? It seemed that Jason would always be a thorn in her side!

"And would you find it so hard to believe that a man like Jason Roark could be capable of murder?" she hissed, placing one hand on her hip, her gloves dangling from the other. "I suspect that he is guilty of three murders in one night. Now what do you have to say to *that?*"

General Stanton strolled casually back to his chair and eased into it. He took a half-smoked cigar from an ashtray and relit it, smoke like a screen hiding his face as he eagerly puffed.

"Now I would say that you have plenty of reason to accuse the man of murder," he said dryly, peering at Marilla through the cloud of smoke, his eyes dancing. "Ma'am, it doesn't take a genius to figure out what you would like to see happen to Jason. Hanging the man would put an end to a lot of hardships for you, wouldn't it?"

Angrily, Marilla began slipping her gloves on, smoothing them on, a finger at a time. "I see that I am wasting my time here," she said sourly. "I have done what must be done. I have brought Charles here, so that his body can be delivered to his family for burial. I have told you all the details of where and how I found him. I have even told you who I truly believe is responsible. Now I shall take my leave!"

"Marilla, before you leave, I have something besides Charles Agnew's death to speak to you about," General Stanton growled, jerking his cigar from his mouth. His eyes glared as he looked up at her. "It seems that you, being the daughter of Lieutenant Pratt, could have prevented the breakdown of relationships between President Hayes and Kohanah yesterday! Do you realize the humiliation I felt when the President left the fort without even a civil good-bye to me after he was insulted by Kohanah? A great dinner had been planned. My position in the army would have been helped if the President and I could have spent time together, discussing politics and the future of this country.''

He slammed a fist on the top of his desk. "How could you have allowed it to happen, Marilla? So much depended on the President having a pleasant meeting with Kohanah," he said, in an almost whine. "Now I won't ever get the chance to meet the President again, much less get an invitation to visit him at the White House.''

Marilla's eyes widened, her cheeks became flushed. Now she understood so much that inflamed her senses. She placed her hands on General Stanton's desk and leaned down into his face. "So that is what this is all about," she said hotly. "Sir, you are not upset at all about Charles Agnew's death. You truly do not even care who did the ghastly deed! You are too concerned over your own secret desires of being in the political ring once you leave the army!''

She straightened her back, quickly forgetting her earlier thoughts of being respectful to him, not only because he was her elder but because he held quite a prestigious position in the army, which she had always respected.

"Sir, I am glad that Kohanah saw fit to stand behind his beliefs, no matter if it did cause some embarrassing moments for the President *and* you," she said determinedly. "I would have not persuaded Kohanah to do anything differently, for I understand his plight. I have from the very first moment I saw him. I shall always work *for* him. *Never* against him!''

She turned to walk angrily away but was stopped by the cold and calculating words of the general.

"Well, Miss Pratt, it seems that I must send my men to arrest Kohanah for the murder of Charles Agnew," General Stanton said, crushing his cigar into the ashtray.

Everything within Marilla turned numbly cold at his words. She turned slowly to face the general, then walked back to his desk. "Sir, that would be a waste of your soldiers' time," she said in a low hiss, even ready to *lie* for the man she loved . . . even ready to be ostracized *for* loving him!

"General Stanton," she said smoothly. "It seems that Kohanah has an alibi for that entire night when Charles was murdered. Sir, *I* was with Kohanah. The . . . entire . . . night!"

Her pulse racing, knowing that she had just told a lie that would possibly stain her reputation for the rest of her life, that she wantonly slept with a man before she was wed to him, Marilla stood her ground and stared boldly down at the general. And she also knew that it was not that she had slept with a man before marriage . . . it was that the man was an Indian! The gossip-mongers would have fun with this!

But she would not let knowing this dissuade her from protecting the man she loved. And she would soon be Kohanah's wife! That would make all wrongs right in everyone's eyes, would it not . . . ?

Or could anyone ever understand or give her a blessing when she married a Kiowa chief?

She only hoped that her father would. His blessing truly mattered to her!

"Seems you are ready to defend the Indian at all costs," General Stanton said, clearing his throat nervously, staring disbelievingly up at her. "But as long as you stand behind this story, it seems my hands are tied. Kohanah will not be arrested."

He rose slowly to his feet and met Marilla's challenging stare. "But, young lady, I will give you fair warning," he said icily. "You had best warn your Indian companion to stay out of my way. Practicing blackmail on the President is one matter. But fooling with me is *another!*"

With a flip of the skirt of her dress, Marilla turned and rushed from the room. Once outside, she leaned against the wall of the building, drained. Yet she had to go to Kohanah and warn him to be careful. She now understood that General Stanton was dangerous and had revenge on his mind as far as Kohanah was concerned.

Though Kohanah was sending out silent warring parties in the area, to search for the party guilty of the present crime against the Kiowa people, he had planned to stay behind, to wait for her. He had suspected trouble for her once she arrived at the fort with the body.

"I must go to him," Marilla whispered, hurrying on to her buggy. "He must be warned! He must!"

Kohanah was sitting beside the fire in his tipi, his eyes tormented as he gazed down into the flames. The burial rites were completed and his two beloved Kiowa had been laid to rest. His silent warring party had left only moments ago to begin their investigation into the murders and theft. He would join them as soon as Marilla returned and he knew that she was safe.

Though he had told Marilla many times that his people came first with him, in his heart she was of prime importance. Without her, so much would be futile. He did not know how he had existed without her these past three years. That she had come on her own to be with him made his love for her twofold!

Hearing the arrival of her buggy outside his dwelling, Kohanah rose to his feet and met Marilla as she lifted the entrance flap and stepped inside. He placed his hands on her shoulders and looked down into the soft blue of her eyes, then drew her within his arms when he saw how troubled she was. It was there in the depths of her eyes and in the way she stared up at him, drawn in expression. Her time with the soldiers at the fort had not been easy for her. She should not have had to go there alone!

But Kohanah had not been free to go and speak in her behalf, or his *own*. The man in command at the fort more than once had shown his dislike for Kohanah. It was because Kohanah was a strong leader! Kohanah appeared to be a constant *threat* to General Stanton.

"Hold me, Kohanah," Marilla murmured, clinging to him. "I so fear for you. General Stanton was even ready to arrest you, except that I gave him cause not to."

Kohanah eased her from his arms and held her away from him. He looked down at her, puzzled. "Why would he threaten to arrest me?" he asked thickly. "What do you mean you gave him cause not to?"

Marilla swallowed hard, her eyes riveted in place as Kohanah stared down at her, awaiting an answer. "He was ready to accuse you of murdering Charles Agnew," she said in a rush of words. "But I told him that you had an alibi. You could not have done it."

"Alibi? What alibi did you speak of?"

"That I was with you that entire night, Kohanah. I lied. I told the general that we were together. All night."

Kohanah dropped his hands away from her, stunned. "You told this white man that you, a white woman, spent the full night with Kohanah, a Kiowa?" he gasped.

His dark eyes softened in mood. He swept Marilla back into his arms. "You love me this much that you would let the world know that you would sleep with me?" he said thickly. "That you even slept with me, a Kiowa? Marilla, Tsonda, my love."

His lips bore down upon hers. He kissed her with impassioned heat, his hands molding a breast with one hand, while with the other he was lowering her to his pallet of furs beside the fire.

Marilla's head was spinning with the wonders of his kiss, the sweet bliss claiming her as his hands busied at undressing her, her breasts drawing within their flesh the heat of the flames in the fire pit. And then her breath caught in her throat when Kohanah cupped both her breasts and kneaded them feverishly.

But remembrances of why she had come in haste to him from the fort made her senses return. She moved her lips from his and looked up at him, sensuously trembling when she saw how he looked down at her so passionately. She hated to spoil the minute.

Yet she dared not wait to warn him about the general's threat. Perhaps Kohanah would have to go to his men, warn *them*. She did not want to be responsible for anything that might happen due to her being so lax in telling him.

"Kohanah," she said, framing his face between her

trembling hands. "Perhaps this isn't the time for making love. General Stanton made a threat against you. He is going to be waiting for you to make a wrong move; then he will do everything within his power to place you in prison again. Even your warriors' lives are in danger. Perhaps you should go to them. Warn them to be careful during their investigation. General Stanton is quite upset over the President's hasty departure after the President got so upset with you."

"This sort of threat is not a new thing for the Kiowa to cope with," Kohanah said angrily. "The Kiowa have learned to look over their shoulder when they ride the plains. It is not easy *being* Kiowa. But you know that."

"Kohanah, I know that you could be in danger if you aren't careful while trying to find the one responsible for the death of the keeper of the Taime and his wife, and for the thievery of the Taime," Marilla softly argued. "Promise that you will be careful?"

Kohanah swept Marilla's dress on down, away from her, then slipped her shoes off, his eyes filled with warmth watching her. "No more talk is needed, Tsonda," he said huskily. "Loving you is what Kohanah needs at this time. Only loving."

"But I had planned to go to the schoolhouse as soon as I warned you about General Stanton," Marilla sighed, her fingers now working with Kohanah's clothes, drawing his fringed shirt over his head. "I must make preparations to begin teaching. It seems that everything keeps getting in my way. Do you ever think I will actually be a teacher to your people? Do you?"

"You have already been beneficial to my people in so many ways," Kohanah said, brushing a kiss across her lips. He stood and lowered his leggings, removed his moccasins, then leaned down over her, nude. He placed his hands on either side of her and let his lips taste and tease her pleasure points. "Do not worry so, about so many things. Just enjoy, Tsonda. Just enjoy."

"Is that a command, my chief?" Marilla asked, her voice foreign to her in its huskiness. "What if I refuse?"

Kohanah chuckled low. His eyes gleamed as he looked

down at her. "Do you obey orders all that easily?" he asked, forking an eyebrow. "From what I have observed, you do as you please. Always!"

"With you, it will always be different," Marilla sighed, Kohanah's fingers kneading her between the thighs, where she throbbed with need of him. "How could I not always want to do what you want of me? You are so gentle. You are so sweet. I do love you so."

"As do I love you," Kohanah said, then eased his hardness toward her beckoning triangle. "Let us savor this moment together. Soon I will join my warriors. My search for the guilty party will be intense. But, Tsonda, it will be done with caution. Kohanah does not want to worry you needlessly!"

"Nor I you," Marilla whispered. Her eyes closed with rapture when he entered her with one eager thrust. As his strokes within her began, she twined her arms about his neck and drew his lips back down, to kiss her. She clung to him and moved and rocked with him, their bodies in tune, in the same old rhythm known to man since the beginning of time.

But their love seemed special . . . unique.

Marilla was experiencing desire as she had never known it before as her body was growing more feverish with each of his thrusts within her. And then he moved slowly with acute deliberation, teasing her into a near madness, then again hurried, carrying her along on ecstatic waves of pleasure that spread through her, until all other sensations but those he was evoking inside her were blotted out.

Kohanah's fingers went to her breasts and tweaked her dark nipples to hardness. She placed her hands on his buttocks and pressed him closer, shaken with desire as his lovemaking became more intense.

And then his lips went to her breast. Marilla held her head back and sighed when his tongue flicked about the nipple of one breast, his hand cupping the other. Her body was turning to liquid under his masterful hands and lips. She let the euphoria take hold and welcomed him as he made the sudden last plunge that carried him along with her on the cloud of pleasure that swept through them, equally . . .

When it was over and they lay in a sensuous embrace, breathing hard, Marilla once again was catapulted into the real world of worry and doubt. She stroked Kohanah's perspiration-laced brow, her mind wandering to another man, wondering just where he might be and what his next move would be.

She knew almost beyond a doubt that Jason Roark was responsible for everything that was going wrong that had any connection with her life.

She closed her eyes hard, not wanting to see Jason Roark in her mind's eye again. He haunted her thoughts now, more oft than not. . . .

Jason Roark sat on horseback on a knoll, overlooking the Indian village. He had seen Marilla enter Kohanah's tipi. He was now waiting for her to leave, to follow her. But he would have to make sure Kohanah did not catch him. It was already evident that Kohanah's warriors were searching for a murderer and thief. Jason did not want to hand himself over to the Indians on a silver platter!

Narrowing his eyes, Jason leaned forward in his saddle when he saw Marilla leave Kohanah's tipi and board her buggy, then saw Kohanah leave, to travel in the opposite direction.

Jason's lips lifted into a smug smile when he watched Marilla travel across the village, then go into the school building, isolated on the far edge of the village. He was going to have the opportunity to get what he had come for. Her! For Kohanah was not going to be near, to catch him in the act! Nor would any other Kiowa. Most of the warriors were gone from the village.

"Little Miss Priss, ol' Jason Roark is just about ready to teach you a thing or two about life," he chuckled, thrusting his heels into the flanks of his horse. . . .

Seventeen

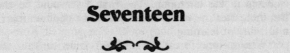

The afternoon was quickly fading into night. The one room schoolhouse was dark and dreary, but smelled wonderfully of freshly hewn logs. Marilla stood at the front of the room, looking at the rows of roughly crafted benches on which her Indian students would be sitting. A wood-burning stove stood at the far end of the room with a pile of wood stacked beside it.

Then she turned and went to her desk, on which she had placed her teaching tools, books, and writing paper. She would ask Kohanah to spread the word tomorrow that the children could come to school. There had already been too many delays. . . .

The squeaking of the door at the far end of the room beside the stove made Marilla turn with a start. She squinted her eyes, trying to make out the person standing in the dark shadows. But she wasn't able to tell who it was, except that it was a man.

"Who's there?" she asked, having only moments ago decided that she had done all that could be done here. She had scrubbed the benches, desk, and floor. With night falling so quickly on the plain, the rest of the preparations would wait until morning, just prior to the arrival of the

students in the afternoon. The first day would be short.
But thereafter she would see to it that the children received
a full day of learning.

"Who's come to call? It ain't no damn student, that's
for sure," Jason Roark chuckled, stepping into the light,
holding a cocked pistol in his right hand. "Now, easy like,
Marilla. And don't scream. My finger is already too heavy
on the trigger of my pistol. Just move over here real slow
like. You and I are goin' to leave without no one noticin'."

Marilla took a shaky breath. Her back stiffened, realizing just how alone she was. Jason Roark was surely going
to take her to his cabin, which he had built away from the
fort barracks, for privacy when he wanted it. No matter
what she did or said, she had no choice but to do what
Jason Roark ordered.

Marilla's only hope was Kohanah. In a matter of time,
he was planning to let Jason believe that he had gotten
away with everything, when in truth, it was Kohanah's
plan to abduct Jason and draw answers from him. He
would demand the return of the Taime, which would be
the proof that was needed to point an accusing finger at
Jason Roark!

"Jason, how do you think you will get away with this?"
Marilla said, her voice drawn. "You are already under
suspicion for too many things. If I come up missing, you
will be the first person accused of my abduction."

"Don't you see?" Jason said, chuckling. "I ain't got
nothin' to lose if what you say is true. *And* I believe that
because suspicions have already been aroused about me,
everyone will believe that I wouldn't try something again
so soon."

He motioned with the muzzle of his pistol. "Move," he
growled. "I've been waitin' too long already, Marilla.
Three long years I've been thinkin' about you. But never
in a *million* years did I believe I would get a chance to
finish what I started in Florida. You walked right into my
hands when you chose to come to be with your savage
Injun lover."

"You've hated Kohanah from the moment he arrived at
Fort Marion. But Kohanah hates you as much, and he will

kill you for what you are doing here," Marilla hissed, moving slowly toward Jason. "I wish my father had ordered his men to execute you, instead of sending you off to another fort, to wreak your own sort of havoc. But he let the kind side of him rule the moment. If he only knew the true sort that you were, he would have hanged you!"

"Well, your father didn't hang me and as for Kohanah . . . he doesn't dare try anything with me," Jason said, laughing throatily. "He's already got a taste of what prison life is. He wouldn't do anything to put himself back behind bars. His people would suffer with his loss. So you'll soon see that if he has choices, he will choose his people's welfare over yours!"

Jason's words stung Marilla's heart. Doubts assailed her, and she even began feeling guilty for wanting Kohanah to come to her rescue, for he *would* be endangering himself and the welfare of his people. It would be her fault if something happened to him, for she should have been more careful than to let Jason Roark have the opportunity to abduct her.

She should have expected it and had a pistol close by, ready. . . .

Marilla flinched when Jason grabbed her by the arm with his free hand, while thrusting the muzzle of his pistol into her ribs with the other. "Outside," he said in a low growl. "Just you climb into your buggy nice and easy. Look natural. Drive to your cabin."

Marilla's hair flipped about her face as she was shoved outside into the darkness. She gave Jason a puzzled look from across her shoulder. "My cabin?" she gasped. "I'm to go there?"

"You heard right."

"But, Jason, I don't understand. I would think you would want me to go anywhere *but* there with you."

"You think I'm stupid or something?" Jason drawled, looking from side to side, glad that no one was in viewing range. "You are to go there and leave your buggy and horse so as to draw suspicion away from you not being there, then go from there with me to an abandoned shack I've already got set up for your arrival."

"But everyone will see you with me, Jason."

"No one will pay any attention to a soldier riding escort with you to your cabin, now, will they? No one but Kohanah would have cause to question this, and he's gone, ain't he? He's out lookin' for the one responsible for the two savages' deaths. I'd have thought he'd have looked for me long ago. Guess I fooled him, huh?"

Marilla paled. She turned with a start and faced Jason. "You *did* kill the two Kiowa, didn't you?" she said dryly. "You even killed Charles Agnew, didn't you? Why, Jason? Why?"

"I didn't confess to any of that," Jason said, his pale eyes narrowing threateningly. "Now, you just do as you're told, do you hear? Get aboard your buggy. Drive away from the Indian village. Look natural. I'll be right behind you. Though no one will be able to tell, I'll have a pistol aimed at your pretty back."

Fear was mounting inside Marilla. It seemed that Jason had everything figured out . . . calculatingly planned. It wasn't that far to her cabin, so the chances that anyone would even notice that a soldier was riding with her were slim.

But . . . what of Kohanah? Just how far had he ridden? Would he see? Or would he sense that she was in danger? They seemed so attuned to each other in feelings and thought!

She did not know whether to want Kohanah to come to her rescue or not. She wanted nothing to happen to him. If necessary, she would even die to protect him. Her love for him ran that deep. She knew that.

At this moment, she . . . knew . . . that. . . .

Her knees weak, her face pale, Marilla went to her buggy and climbed aboard, out of the corner of her eye watching Jason as he swung himself up into his army saddle. Though she did not wish to believe it, he *did* look natural enough as he sat there, ready to escort her home. Most would think it was at her own request, since there had been three brutal murders in such a short time.

Wouldn't it be natural for the army to want to protect her, though she knew that they couldn't care less about her? General Stanton had only his own welfare on his mind, and *she* had done nothing to help him in the eyes of the President, so she did not expect to get help from him!

Slapping the reins, urging her horse away from the rustic school building, Marilla rode with square shoulders and watchful eye as Jason traveled along only a few feet behind her buggy.

The village was now behind her, a snakelike dirt road lay ahead, reaching out across the land. A thick stand of cottonwoods hovered beside a meandering creek on one side of the road. . . . The moon was silvering the trees. An owl broke the eerie silence, momentarily startling Marilla.

Sighing, she snapped the reins against the horse again, full of dread of what the next few hours would bring her. Since her arrival in Oklahoma, it had been one traumatic moment after another. She had planned for . . . oh, something so very different. She had only wanted peaceful moments within Kohanah's arms. She had wanted to see the eager, beautiful eyes of the children looking up at her in the schoolhouse. She had wanted to plan a marriage with the man she loved. . . .

But now perhaps none of that would ever happen. And all because of Jason Roark!

Clouds scudded across the dark sky, the moon behind them. Kohanah had ordered his warriors to stay hidden while he ran across the stretch of land that reached to Jason Roark's cabin. His face shadowed with a frown when he drew closer to Jason's cabin. There was golden lamplight in the windows, but Jason's horse was not reined at the hitching rail at the side of the house. Did that mean that Jason had left only momentarily? Or had Jason left the lamp burning to throw off suspicion? Was he up to no good again? Kohanah's warriors had found out that Jason wasn't on duty at the fort tonight, nor was he at the soldiers' barracks!

So where was he?

Determined to search Jason's house for any sign of the Taime, Kohanah crept on to it. Stealthily he moved along the side of the house until he reached a window. Slowly, yet deliberately, he peeked inside, scarcely able to see anything through the grime.

But he could see enough to know that he had been right . . . that Jason wasn't there. He swung away from the window and rushed inside.

His eyes narrowed and he recoiled when he saw the filth that lay about the cabin. Clothes, papers, and unwashed dishes and pans were strewn about. A fire burned low on the grate of the fireplace; a teakettle had boiled dry in the hot coals.

Then Kohanah looked toward the bed. Its sheets and blankets were yellowed with age and filth, and in disarray. The feather mattress showed the imprint of Jason's body, the neck of a whiskey bottle was peeking from beneath the pillow.

With a growl, Kohanah proceeded with the task he had come here to accomplish—to find proof of Jason's guilt!

Going to the bed, Kohanah tossed the pillow aside, then threw the whiskey bottle across the room, where it crashed onto the floor, breaking. The aroma of whiskey filled the room, glass shattered in splinters across the barren floor.

Kohanah yanked the mattress from the bed, then turned the bed over, looking beneath it. But he found nothing.

After searching the cabin with his eyes, he went to the cabinets in the kitchen and emptied them of everything, still finding nothing.

"He has hidden it well!" Kohanah grumbled, doubling his fists at his sides.

Then in his mind's eye he remembered Marilla. Jason wasn't here, nor was the Taime. Could he have gone to harm Marilla . . . ? Wasn't she possibly behind Jason's reasons for everything that he did? Kohanah was recalling Marilla's tale of what Jason had attempted with her in Florida!

"Kohanah has been foolish!" he said thickly, setting his jaw hard. "Marilla should never have been left alone! What if . . . ?"

Spinning around on a moccasin-clad heel, Kohanah ran from the cabin, across the straight stretch of land in the

flood of moonlight as it crept from behind the clouds, and
to his horse.

"Come!" he ordered his warriors. "We have come to
the wrong place tonight! We must go to my woman! I fear
that wherever she is, Jason Roark will be found also!"

Momentarily pausing, Kohanah looked into the darkness
of the heavens. Marilla would not have stayed at the
schoolhouse after dark. She should be home!

Thrusting his heels into the flanks of his red roan,
Kohanah thundered away, his warriors close behind him.
When he reached Marilla's house, he breathed more eas-
ily, for her horse and buggy were there.

But his heart skipped a beat when he didn't see smoke
spiraling from her chimney or lamplight golden in the
windows. It was not the time of night that she would
already be in bed. She should, in truth, be preparing her
food for her evening meal!

Dismounting, he ran to her cabin and threw aside the
door. His gut twisted, his fear mounted, for she was not
there.

Hanging his head in his hands, emitting a half sob,
Kohanah felt as though he had betrayed the woman he
loved. If anything happened to her. . . .

Rushing back outside, Kohanah used his skills as a
tracker. He studied the fresh horse tracks that had recently
led away from Marilla's cabin. One set was more promi-
nent than the others. That surely was Jason's and it also
meant that Marilla had not been on a horse of her own.
She was riding with Jason Roark.

His eyes brimming with hate, Kohanah shouted out
orders to his men. They followed along behind him as the
moonlight gave him the steady view of the hoofprints he
was following. They led him in the opposite direction from
the fort.

Soon hope rose within him, for he was recalling an
abandoned cabin far back from the road, which he had
discovered one day while roaming the land. It did seem
that the tracks were leading him there.

No longer did Kohanah take the time to study the tracks.

He raised a fist into the air and gave orders to his warriors to follow him with haste!

Marilla's life lay in balance!

Marilla squirmed against the bonds at her wrists and ankles where she lay on a bed that reeked of body odors. She gave Jason a sour stare above the gag that had rendered her voiceless, watching him pour another shot of whiskey into a glass. After building a fire in the fireplace, he had brought in a bottle of whiskey from his saddle and was now sitting at a rickety table, slowly emptying one glass after another, eyeing Marilla amusedly. Perhaps he was drinking whiskey to give him courage to continue with his plans for her, or he was just toying with her, making her squirm while awaiting her fate with him.

If it was the latter, it was working, for Marilla was dying a slow death inside, not holding out any hope now that anyone would find and rescue her. She had been taken far from the road, to a cabin that surely no one even remembered having been built there. It was obvious that the cabin had been inhabited recently only by raccoons and skunks! Their waste lay along the shabby, curled boards that made up the flooring of the cabin. The aroma of aging wood and mildew stung Marilla's flaring nostrils.

"You don't look so smug and righteous now, Marilla," Jason said, letting a hiccup roll from deep inside him. "I've taken you down a notch or two, haven't I?"

He glowered at her, his uniform a mockery, it seemed, since Marilla had been raised by a man in uniform, a man whose heart was golden and whose morals were always above reproach.

"When I get through with you, there won't be nothin' left to even spit on!" he threatened darkly.

He leaned back in his chair and began slowly unbuttoning his shirt. "First I get my enjoys with you, and then . . . who knows?" he said, laughing throatily. "One thing for sure, I beat Charles Agnew to you. Seems he didn't know the best way to approach you. He wasn't the sort to take anyone by force. He didn't even know how to watch out for himself, much less figure out how to woo a lady."

Marilla's insides splashed cold with the mention of Charles. Was Jason implying what she thought he was implying? Was he close to admitting what she had suspected all along?

She tried to scoot back on the bed as Jason sauntered toward her, the twisted, wiry dark hairs on his chest so in contrast to Kohanah's chest, which was void of any traces of hair.

But she couldn't move. Jason had wrapped a rope around the mattress *and* Marilla, securing her in place. She recoiled when Jason knelt down beside the bed and jerked the gag from her mouth, his lips pursed for a kiss.

"No! Don't!" Marilla said, shuddering when his lips drew closer, the aroma of alcohol overpowering. "Jason, you can't get away with any of this. You will be caught."

She closed her eyes when recalling how she had found Charles, then forced herself to find the courage to question Jason, since he had taken it upon himself to bring Charles into the conversation. Jason seemed drunk enough now to give her some answers . . . answers that could hang him, *if* she could get loose and prove what had happened here.

It would be her word against Jason's, and she knew that General Stanton wouldn't listen to her. If he wouldn't, then *who?* She couldn't drag Kohanah into this. She just couldn't!

"Though you got away with killing Charles Agnew, you won't get away with raping and then murdering *me*," she managed to say before his lips bore down upon hers in a fiery, wet kiss.

His teeth cut into her lips as he ravaged them with his mouth. She cried out with pain against his lips, then shuddered with distaste when she felt one of Jason's hands slowly creep up inside her dress, moving along her leg, then her inner thigh.

Marilla managed to toss her head aside, then screamed, startling Jason away from her and back to his feet. He towered over her, reeling in his drunken stupor, a puzzled expression pinching his face. His bulbous nose was red, his eyes bloodshot.

"Now what'd you go and do that for?" he asked thickly. "You scared the livin' hell outta me."

"I can't stand to have you touch me," Marilla hissed, raising her head up from the bed, staring hotly up at him. "How could I, after you killed two innocent Indians and then Charles Agnew. Where's the Taime, Jason? Did you bring it out here and hide it, just the same as you are hiding me away?"

Her eyes darted about the dingy room. "Where is it, Jason? I know it's here," she stormed.

Jason lumbered back to the table. He lifted the whiskey bottle to his lips and took several deep swallows, then slammed it back down on the table and turned and glared at Marilla.

"I see no reason not to admit to what I did," he said, chuckling. "For, you see, I plan to throw you in the same hole as I threw my knife—the murder weapon, you would call it. When they find you at the foot of your well, you won't be anything but bones."

"My well . . . ?" Marilla said, paling.

She slowly laid her head back down on the bed, feeling suddenly empty. Now that she absolutely *knew* that he was the guilty party, it did not give her any feeling of victory for having drawn the answers from him, for she apparently was not going to be able to use the information *against* him.

She would be dead!

"But, of course, that isn't where I hid the Taime," he bragged, going across the room to kneel to the floor. Grunting and groaning, he worked on a loose board in the floor. "Seems I had a better place for the Injun's stupid sun idol. But I ain't had the time yet to take a good look at it. You just might as well look at it *with* me, don't you think? It's a fascinatin' thing, to say the least. A lot of hogwash superstition involved with it, but interestin' all the same."

Marilla strained to see what he was doing, stunned that he was actually volunteering to show her the Taime. He was not in the least apprehensive about having stolen it or having killed two innocent people to *get* it. She held her head up, silently watching him tear the board away. . . .

"I showed Kohanah up for the weak bastard that he is," Jason said thickly. "Now neither he nor his people can perform the witch dance."

He turned his cool green eyes to Marilla. "And I showed him, by taking *you* away from him."

He frowned deeply. "That savage Injun is nothin' but a pack of trouble. Always has been. Always will be. Takin' the doll away takes his *power* away. His people will lose confidence *and* respect for him. Takin' you away from him will make him feel defeated in every way!"

"One day you will pay for all your evil ways," Marilla hissed, jolting with alarm when the board splintered in two as Jason gave it one more yank.

Then her eyes were drawn quickly elsewhere. There was a movement at the window. Her breath was stolen away when she caught a quick glimpse of Kohanah, as his dark eyes peered in at her.

Marilla was torn with feelings. She wanted to feel relief that Kohanah had searched for her and found her, yet a part of her feared what he had to do to save her.

If Kohanah killed a white man, he was . . . the same as dead himself. . . .

She held her breath, awaiting Kohanah's arrival in the room. . . .

Eighteen

✧～✧

When the door burst open, Marilla winced. Even though she had expected Kohanah to enter the cabin at any moment, his abruptness in doing so startled her. Her eyes moved with him as he raced across the room and grabbed Jason by the collar before Jason had the chance to draw his pistol. The rawhide box in which lay the Taime dropped clumsily from Jason's fingers as he looked wildly at Kohanah, his face draining of color.

"You!" Jason said in a throaty gurgle. "How did you find this cabin?"

Kohanah tightened his hold on Jason's collar, bodily lifting him up from the floor. He held Jason close to his face. "Do you forget that *savages* know the art of tracking so well?" he asked mockingly.

His gaze moved momentarily to Marilla. "You dare touch my woman?"

His gaze shifted to the floor, seeing the rawhide Taime box. "You dare steal the Taime?"

Kohanah threw Jason across the room, where Jason hit the wall with a loud thud. "You dare kill two of my people?" he stormed, drawing a knife from a sheath at his waist.

186

Going to kneel over Jason, Kohanah placed the knife at his throat. "Death could come so easy for you," he said, his teeth clenched. "The knife is silent but quite deadly."

Kohanah grabbed Jason's dark hair with his free hand. "You scalp my people. Perhaps Kohanah should scalp *you*," he said in a low, threatening hiss.

Marilla had been watching, stunned speechless, but now the true threat was sinking in to her consciousness. If Kohanah killed Jason, *he* would be killed. Even if Kohanah *didn't* kill Jason, only threatened him, Kohanah would be imprisoned, because Jason would live to tell of the threat. It seemed that Kohanah would be the loser no matter what he did. Marilla felt more helpless because of this than by still being held in bondage on the bed.

"Kohanah," she pleaded. "Don't kill him. Please. You must think of yourself . . . of what will happen to you *and* to your people."

Kohanah lifted Jason up from the floor with one hand, while holding the knife at his throat with the other. "Walk with me to the bed," he ordered flatly. "Release Marilla; then take her place on the bed."

A nervous drool was rolling from the corner of Jason's mouth. His eyes were pools of fearful tears. He scarcely breathed as he walked along with Kohanah to the bed, the tip of the knife just barely breaking the flesh at his throat. He could feel warm trickles of blood emerging from the slight wound.

"Don't kill me," he sobbed. "Kohanah, I'll do anything you ask of me. Just . . . don't . . . kill me."

"Death would be too swift . . . too merciful, for the likes of you," Kohanah said harshly. "Kohanah has other plans. Imagination is needed when dealing with evil men like you."

Jason looked guardedly over at Kohanah, fear tightening about his heart. "What do you intend to do?" he asked, his voice cracking with fear.

"You'll see," Kohanah chuckled. He lowered his knife and gave Jason a shove toward the bed. "Release my woman. Quickly."

Nodding anxiously, wanting to please, hoping that if he

cooperated he might be spared, Jason leaned over the bed
and began working with the ropes at Marilla's wrists.
When she emitted a cry of pain as his fumblings tightened
rather than loosened the ropes, he gave Kohanah a fearful
look, expecting to be hit.

He sighed with relief when Kohanah only stood watch-
ing, his arms folded angrily across his bare, massive chest.
Perhaps Kohanah was not going to be that savage to him
after all. All Jason wanted to do was get out of this alive.
Then he would go to the fort and voice complaints against
Kohanah! It would be easy to convince everyone that
Kohanah was at fault here, that Jason Roark was innocent
of wrongdoing! And Marilla's word would mean nothing
any longer. She was almost surely being looked upon as an
Injun-lover, someone not even worth wasting time on!

Marilla jerked her wrists free as the ropes finally fell
away. She rubbed their rawness as she waited for the ropes
to be untied at her ankles. And when the rope that had
been holding her to the bed was finally untied, she moved
shakily to her feet on the opposite side of the bed from
Jason, and stood for a moment, trying to get her balance.
The ropes had cut off her circulation, rendering her weak
and dizzy. . . .

Kohanah went to Marilla and placed an arm about her
waist, drawing her into his embrace. "Tsonda, you are all
right?" he asked softly, keeping his eye on Jason. "He did
not harm you?"

"No," Marilla murmured. "But only because he did
not have time to. He was too busy drinking his whiskey,
drawing courage from it for whatever he had in mind for
me."

She turned and snuggled against Kohanah. "Oh, Kohanah,
thank you for coming . . . but what is to become of you
because you *have?*"

"Kohanah does what must be done," he said blandly.
His gaze once more moved to the Taime box. "This man's
guilt lies not only in the fact that he abducted you, but also
in his possession of the Taime."

His eyes softened. "It is good that the Taime will once

again be in the possession of my people. A new keeper of the Taime must be appointed. Soon!''

Kohanah eased Marilla away from him and went to stand over Jason, who was now on the bed, trembling. ''Tsonda, come and tie the evil man's hands and ankles,'' he said softly. ''I shall give you the honor of doing this. It is a way to repay him for having done it to you.''

With only a moment of hesitation, not wanting to get near the man, Marilla went back to the bed and began tying the ropes around Jason's wrists, then went to his ankles and also bound them.

She stood back and watched Kohanah leave the cabin and return just as quickly, carrying a leather saddlebag. Her eyes widened when she watched him remove a smaller leather pouch from the saddlebag.

''Kohanah has ways to make white man suffer,'' he said darkly. ''It will be in ways not visible to the eye of those watching. But within the evil man's eyes, *much* will be seen!''

''What are you going to do?'' Marilla asked, her back stiff, unable to cast worries of Kohanah from her mind. If Jason Roark managed to get free and went to the fort and told about Kohanah, the Kiowa chief's freedom would be gone.

Perhaps even his life.

Yet there was a faint ray of hope within Marilla's heart. If Jason went to the authorities about what had happened here in this abandoned cabin, wouldn't he also have to explain why he was there? Couldn't Marilla point an accusing finger to him at last?

But would General Stanton believe her? Or would he pretend he didn't, just because he had reason to dislike her?

''Get me the bottle of whiskey from the table,'' Kohanah said, interrupting Marilla's troubled thoughts. ''Bring it to me, Tsonda.''

Marilla looked at him questioningly. ''The whiskey?'' she asked shallowly. ''You want me to bring you the bottle of whiskey? Why?''

Kohanah turned to her and frowned. ''You will soon

see," he grumbled. He nodded toward the bottle. "Get it. Bring it to me."

Marilla's weak legs carried her to the table. She winced when the aroma of the whiskey floated upward into her nostrils as she picked it up and carried it to Kohanah. She didn't question him further, for he seemed too absorbed in what he was doing to even answer.

But she could not help but be more and more puzzled, for Kohanah was sprinkling some sort of white powdery substance from the leather pouch into the bottle of whiskey.

Jason's pulse began to race. He worked anxiously with his bound wrists, trying to get free, only managing to make his flesh raw and almost bleeding where Marilla had tied them much tighter than was required to render him helpless.

"Kohanah, have mercy," Jason begged, watching Kohanah shaking the whiskey, mixing the powdery substance with the alcohol. He had heard about the hallucinogenic cactus, the peyote, and suspected that the powdery substance Kohanah had just added to the whiskey was crushed, dried peyote and was going to be forced upon him. He had heard of the hallucinations that had been the result of the hellish peyote. Sometimes one's mind would never regain its normal functional activity!

Mixed with whiskey, the peyote could even be deadly!

"Did Little Bud Moon and Bud Moon beg for mercy before you scalped then stabbed them to death?" Kohanah asked smoothly, his eyes lit with angry fire. "Did you laugh at them while they begged? Did you abuse the Taime? You will be cursed forever if you did."

"I should've known never to fool with that thing," Jason sobbed, his eyes wild. "But what you just said proves that witchcraft is involved in the use of the Sun Doll. It was my right to steal it from you . . . to keep you from using it. You surely would have placed a curse on everyone at the fort had you performed the ritual that has supernatural overtones!"

"The Taime is not used in such a negative way, *ever*," Kohanah said, his voice devoid of emotion. "It is for the blessing of my people *only*. If you were not so ignorant, you would have known that. But now it is too late for this knowledge to benefit you. White man with a black heart, you are just about to go on an adventure of the mind that you will never forget.''

Kohanah moved to the bed and stood over Jason. "That is, if your mind has the ability to remember anything after the peyote simmers your brain like the sun splashes its fiery rays on the grasses of the plains during the heated months of summer,'' he threatened. ''Your brain will be reduced to ashes, just like the dusty fragments of the peyote that I mixed with the firewater.''

''Tsonda, come and hold Jason Roark's head still while I pour the liquid down his throat,'' Kohanah said, nodding to Marilla. ''Then you will watch with me while demons are set free inside the evil one's brain!''

Her every nerve ending tight, her breath coming in short rasps, afraid of what she was about to witness in the next few moments, yet knowing that Jason Roark deserved everything and even more than Kohanah had planned for him, Marilla went to the bed. She flinched and shuddered as she placed her hands on either side of Jason's face, his eyes pleading up at her.

''You can't let him do this!'' Jason said in an almost strangled slur. ''Marilla, I'm sorry for all the trouble I've caused you. Please . . . please accept my apologies and stop Kohanah. I'd rather die than be put through the torture of the peyote! I may survive, but as a vegetable . . . not *human*.''

''Do you think apologies will bring the two innocent Kiowa back to life?'' Marilla asked, her voice quivering. ''Will it bring Charles Agnew back to life? No. It's too late for apologies *or* begging, Jason. I only hope that your hallucinations will bring you face to face with the devil.''

Jason tried to fight off her hands by trying to move his head. But Marilla was finding a reserve of strength that she had never known before as she held him in place. But she couldn't watch as Kohanah started pouring the liquid mixture into Jason's mouth. His throat was going into spasms. He was gagging and struggling to breathe. He was coughing and spewing spittle from the corners of his mouth.

"It is done," Kohanah said, stepping back away from Jason, smiling smugly down at him. He tossed the empty bottle across the room, shattering it in pieces against the wall, and across the floor. "Tell me what you are seeing, white man. Do you enjoy the pictures that are already being painted inside your brain?"

An earsplitting scream was cause for Marilla to jerk her head back around, to look down at Jason. She took an unsteady step back. Her insides grew clammy with a strange coldness when she saw Jason's face contort into frenzied agony and his eyes grow glassy as he stared into space.

"Lord . . ." Marilla whispered as Jason's whole body started convulsing, twisting, and straining against the mattress. Bloody drool rolled from the corners of his mouth as he screamed over and over again, his eyes now bulging with hidden pain.

And when Marilla could hardly stand to watch any longer and had turned to walk away, Kohanah grabbed her hand and drew her back to his side. "It is important that you watch everything, to always remember how the Kiowa punishes those who are evil," he said dryly. "If you are to become part of the Kiowa culture, you must learn to accept everything *about* the Kiowa. Even that which is ugly in your innocent, lovely eyes."

"Kohanah, I'm not sure if—"

"You watch. It is necessary."

"But, Kohanah, it is so . . . so . . . inhumane."

"Murder is inhumane. This is tame, compared to murder."

"But I don't care to watch."

"You must."

"I shall try."

"There is even more, Tsonda. Kohanah has one more task to perform to help increase the peyote's effects on Jason Roark's body."

Marilla was dumbstruck when Kohanah went to Jason and lowered his breeches to his knees, exposing his manhood, which was just now showing a sign of slow arousal. Gasping, blushing, Marilla turned away, but when Kohanah's hands were on her cheeks, encouraging her to witness that which he did, she held her shoulders straight, lifted her chin stubbornly, and forced herself to watch.

Kohanah took a length of rope and tied it at the base of Jason's swollen member. He then picked up his saddlebag and removed another leather pouch of powdered peyote and sprinkled it on Jason's private parts.

Jason's loud howls pierced the air, causing chills to crawl along Marilla's flesh. Embarrassed and filled with a strange sense of foreboding, she jerked her eyes away again, closing them. She placed her hands over her ears, trying to drown out the terrible sounds of pain.

For the first time ever, she was having doubts about loving everything about Kohanah. At this moment he was so cold and calculating . . . perhaps could even be described as savage, as most white people called all Indians. It would be hard for her to accept this side of him. He had forced her to watch for his own reasons, but to her, these reasons were all wrong. It would take forever for her to erase Jason's cries of anguish from her mind. She would forever recall the horrible sight of Jason and how the peyote had affected him.

Though he deserved the worst of punishments, this seemed *too* inhumane, for even *him*.

Lifting the hem of her dress up into her arms, Marilla broke into a mad run and left the cabin. Her gaze captured the silhouettes of many Kiowa warriors on their horses against the backdrop of night, patiently waiting for Kohanah to leave the cabin.

Sobbing, ignoring their presence, Marilla ran on past them, then stumbled and fell in a heap on the ground, sobbing. Even here she could hear the deafening screams . . . the pleading. Would Jason continue on into the night? Or would he finally lapse into a drug-induced coma and *die?*

Should she even care?

A warm hand on her shoulder made Marilla jump with a start. She looked slowly up and found the moonlight illuminating the face of the man she loved—oh, Lord, would always love, no matter what she had just witnessed him so callously doing! In his heart, he was doing what was right, in the way he knew best.

If she had been forced to witness a scalping, would that have been any easier for her? Jason had scalped two innocent Kiowa! She must remember that! He had not only scalped, but *killed* as well.

"*Tsan*, I come, to you with an open heart, Tsonda," Kohanah said thickly. "Do not turn away from me. You must prove to me that you understand what I do for my people. So much depends on your understanding."

Marilla swallowed back a lump in her throat and nodded. "Yes, I know," she murmured. "I know."

"Kohanah will return you to your dwelling," he said, leaning to place his hands on her waist, urging her to her feet. "Kohanah will stay with you until you are feeling better about things."

Marilla looked nervously toward the house, hearing the welcome silence. Then she questioned Kohanah with her eyes. "Jason Roark is so quiet," she murmured. "Why is he?"

"His brain is still fighting the peyote, but his voice has been silenced," Kohanah said flatly. "A gag has been placed about his mouth. He can no longer cry out. He will have to lie there and accept what fate hands him, silently and alone!"

A shudder coursed through Marilla; then she smiled weakly as Kohanah swept her fully up into his arms and began carrying her toward his horse. She placed her cheek against his bare chest and twined her arms about his neck, wanting to block out everything in life but him.

At this moment, things were too clear . . . too deeply imbedded inside her mind, for her to let go.

Yet, when she looked up into Kohanah's strong face, his lips sculpted sensitively, his eyes as dark as the night, she knew that she had to let go, for *him*. She had to be there *for* him, always a support in anything that he might be forced to do in his search for ways to make things right for his people!

Hopefully, one day they would also be *her* people. . . .

When Kohanah lifted her onto his horse, Marilla enjoyed what was now the melancholy stillness of night. If she didn't look back toward the cabin, she perhaps could forget what had happened, for the night was beautiful with the clouds blown away and the moonlight silvering everything within reach with its light.

Suddenly a liquid note of a whippoorwill drifted across the land, beautiful in its innocence. Marilla snuggled against Kohanah, feeling like an extension of that innocence, tainted only somewhat by her experiences this night.

Clinging to Kohanah, sitting on his lap as he rode away from the dark and dreary cabin, Marilla enjoyed this moment of peace with the man she loved. She did not want to think about what the future held for him.

Once Jason Roark's torture was discovered, what then . . . ?

Jason lay in a stupor. He was just beginning to separate reality from hallucinations as the effects of the peyote slowly began to wear off.

Sharp pains shot through his loins as he fought against the arousal that the peyote was stirring within him. The pain was constant! It was nagging! Only a woman could ease such pain. And there was no woman. Marilla had escaped. Perhaps even if he had a chance to be with a woman again, he would not be capable of performing as a man. What had Kohanah done to his private parts? In Jason's drugged stupor, he could only feel pressure and burning where he so unmercifully throbbed for release. He could hardly stand it!

Fighting against the bonds at his wrists, Jason cried softly, determined that he would get free, somehow.

He had a debt to pay and he would.

Somehow he would. . . .

Nineteen

જજ

If not for Kohanah holding her within his gentle arms, Marilla would have felt like a part of a nightmare. Now in her cabin, a fire burning cozily in the fireplace, she wanted to shake off all feelings of foreboding, yet it was hard not to be overwhelmed when remembrances of how Jason had been tortured entered her mind. She had to keep reminding herself that he deserved no mercy at all and that the punishment Kohanah had handed down to him was right, that it should be acceptable in her eyes and heart!

But it was hard to accept, since she had been born of a man who had always sought the most merciful means of punishments for those who had wronged him. With Kohanah she now understood that things would always be different. She would have to learn to adapt, or give him up.

And never could she walk away from him.

Never.

He was her every heartbeat. . . .

"You no longer tremble," Kohanah said, easing Marilla from his arms so that his eyes could study her. "Is it because of the fire Kohanah built for you, or is it because you have finally found some sort of peace within my arms?"

He placed a hand on her cheek and let a thumb caress her beneath her chin. "Kohanah loves you so much," he said thickly, knowing the dangers of staying with her after having just bound and tortured a soldier.

Yet he had to stay with Marilla, through the night if necessary, for he had to dispel her misgivings about him. If he lost her now, he could not bear it. He had already lost too much in life.

"Never do I want to see you suffer in any way. Watching Jason Roark take his punishment caused you to suffer. Kohanah is sorry," he said, his voice deep, yet soft.

"Oh, Kohanah," Marilla sighed, leaning her face into his hand, relishing his gentleness, the touch of his hand against her flesh. "Do not apologize for something that you had to do. *I* apologize for causing you to be uncomfortable over my inability to understand your methods of punishing Jason. I will try to be more understanding in the future."

She flung herself back into his arms and pressed her cheek hard against his bare chest. "I promise you that I will try to be more understanding," she murmured. "You have enough on your mind troubling you. You should not have to include me in your worries. I have come to Oklahoma to give you my support. Totally. This one time it seems that I forgot. You had to force me to observe Jason's punishment. That was wrong. I should have watched it willingly."

"One must learn by observing," Kohanah said, then drew away from her and picked up the rawhide Taime box, silently studying it. It did not appear to be harmed in any way.

But if Kohanah hadn't arrived when he did, Jason Roark would have opened the box and defiled, possibly destroyed, the Taime!

"The Taime," Marilla said, moving to Kohanah's side, looking down at the closed box. "Is it all right, Kohanah? May I see it?"

Kohanah placed the box on the table beside Marilla's bed and looked at her with a dark frown. "It is all right," he said dryly. "I checked it before placing it in my saddlebag." His eyes wavered. "But, Tsonda, I cannot show it to you. Only *I* am allowed to gaze upon it, because I am chief and it is my duty to see that it is not harmed."

"Why can't I see it?" Marilla asked, lifting an eyebrow quizzically. "What is it about the Taime that creates so much . . . so much interest? Jason Roark even risked his life to gain possession of it."

"Jason Roark only wanted possession of the Taime to cause pain to the Kiowa," Kohanah said sourly. "And if Jason viewed it, he is now cursed. Death will come to him soon. If not tonight, soon. You cannot look upon it, either, for as I have told you before, it is not meant for the Taime to be viewed, except during the celebration of the Sun Dance."

He framed her face between his hands. "Tsonda, this is just another thing that you will have to accept about my culture," he said softly. "You will view the Taime and witness its wonders on the day of the Sun Dance. You will find that it was something worth waiting for."

"I eagerly await that moment," Marilla sighed, smiling up at him. "Not only for a selfish reason, to just view it, but because when the time comes that it is possible *to* view it, that will mean that everything has fallen in place for you, Kohanah, so that the Sun Dance is possible."

Suddenly so tired, so drained, Marilla slipped from Kohanah's arms and sat down on the bed. She hung her head in her hands. "Kohanah, I feel I must go to bed," she said, the strain evident in her weak voice. She raised her eyes to gaze upon his handsomeness. "Please go on. It is not necessary for you to stay. I'll be fine."

Kohanah fell to one knee and placed his hands on Marilla's shoulders. He slowly eased her down onto the mattress, then drew her hair from beneath her head, so that it lay in a soft, glimmering mass about her face. "Kohanah will stay," he said flatly, determined not to leave her alone just yet. Her mind would not rest this quickly after being traumatized. He wanted to be there for her, to demonstrate his full love and devotion to her. His warriors had been instructed to return to the village, keep watch there for any unusual military activity. . . .

"You truly don't have to," Marilla softly argued. "You have to return the Taime to your people. A new keeper of the Taime must be appointed."

"Tomorrow," Kohanah said dryly. "The hour of the night is not right to bring my people to council. Tomorrow, Tsonda. When the sun rises midway in the sky, a new keeper will be appointed."

He pulled a blanket up over her, then caressed her brow with the palm of a hand. "Sleep, my lovely one," he said softly. "Sleep."

Sighing, feeling a great calm filling her while Kohanah's hand softly gentled her, Marilla's dark lashes drooped over her cheeks as she shut her eyes. When Kohanah's lips brushed her throat in a sweet kiss, she opened her eyes and smiled up at him, then reached for him and drew him down beside her.

"I'm glad you've chosen to stay," she murmured, cozying up to his side. "How do you always know what is best for me, Kohanah?"

"That is because you are mine," he said, chuckling low. "Destiny has brought us together. Destiny makes us become as one in thought and deed. Tsonda, do you not see this as I do?"

"*Ho,* yes," Marilla whispered, once again closing her eyes. "Oh, yes, my love. I see this and so much, much more."

Kohanah drew her closer, hearing her even breathing, an indication that she was nearing sleep. He placed his lips to her throat once again and breathed in the sweet scent of her. . . .

The sun slanted through the grime-covered windows of the cabin in which Jason Roark lay, his lips parched and his wrists burning and raw from working so hard at trying to get himself free of his bonds. He was one of the lucky ones. He had regained his full faculties after a night of hallucinations and pain tearing at his loins.

Even now Jason's loins were on fire, yet his manhood had lost its swollen tightness as soon as the effects of the peyote had worn off.

Again he had to wonder if he would ever have the ability to make love to a woman! If not, Kohanah would be to blame, for even *that*. That, perhaps, had been the worst humiliation of his life . . . when he had lain helpless, his manhood throbbing with need, yet being denied it, while Kohanah and Marilla had watched.

"Kohanah is going to pay," Jason snarled. But how? He was beginning to doubt that he would ever get free, to go to the fort to tell what Kohanah had done to him.

His face grew red with a blush, knowing that he could never tell everything that had happened. Would they at the fort even believe him, for there were no signs of visible torture! They might just believe that he was accusing Kohanah of ugly deeds only because of Jason's obvious dislike of the Indians, especially Kohanah.

"I must manage to get them to listen . . . to go and arrest him!" Jason growled, struggling even more determinedly with the ropes at his wrists.

The sun settled into the broken fragments of the whiskey bottle beneath the window, across the room from where Jason lay. He blinked his eyes nervously when reflections from the glass danced in his eyes. This drew his attention to the glass and to its sharp, jagged edges. His lips curled into a smile. If he could get to the glass, he could free himself!

A frown quickly replaced his smile, for he knew how hard it would be to get to the glass. With the rope tied so securely around his private parts, each move of his body would be sheer torture! But to get himself free there, he first had to release his wrists!

Taking a deep breath, building his courage, he eyed the floor, then the edge of the bed. Grimacing, he rolled his body over and eased his feet to the floor, his bound ankles rendering him almost completely helpless. Pain shot through his loins, into his groin, and to his brain, causing him to scream.

Sweat poured profusely from his brow as he let his body ease to the floor, so that he could scoot an inch at a time toward the glass. When he finally reached it and posi-

tioned himself over one of the sharpest edges, he cried out
as the glass cut not only the rope but also his wrists.

Tears streamed down his cheeks as he began moving the
rope back and forth across the jagged edges. He worked
feverishly until he felt the first jerk of his wrist, which
meant that the rope was finally coming uncorded. In only a
matter of moments he would be free. He *would* be able to
get to the fort. Kohanah's imprisonment was a reality.
Soon . . . soon . . .

A tongue brushing her lips lightly drew Marilla from a
restful sleep. An incredible sweetness swept through her
when she opened her eyes and looked up at Kohanah as he
leaned over her, his eyes sheened with desire.

"Tsonda, you rested well?" Kohanah asked, twining
his fingers through her hair, lifting it from her neck. His
lips brushed her throat.

Marilla's breath quickened with yearning, his hard body
against hers causing a warmth to blossom inside her.
"Yes, I rested quite well," she murmured. "And what a
delicious way to awaken. Oh, Kohanah, I do love you
so."

Her whole body quivered when he tantalized her closed
lips with his tongue, his hands unfastening her dress.
"Kohanah has been watching you for some time," he said
huskily. "You are as beautiful in your sleep as you are
awake. But seeing you . . . being with you . . . makes
Kohanah want you. Kohanah wants you . . . now."

Her breasts exposed, the dress along with her under-
things now being lowered past her thighs, Marilla looked
adoringly up into Kohanah's dark, passion-heavy eyes.
"But, Kohanah, this is the tomorrow you spoke of last
night," she murmured. "You have duties. And what if
Jason Roark managed to get free? You did not kill him. He
will be free to go to the fort and lodge complaints against
you!"

As she splayed her fingers against his magnificent bare
chest, Marilla's face lost its luster in the depths of a frown.
"Kohanah, should you have to go back to prison, I don't
think I could stand it," she said, an incredible sweetness

sweeping through her as Kohanah's hands cupped her breasts, and he lowered his lips to first one nipple, then the other, flicking his tongue sensuously about them.

"The name Jason Roark poisons the very air it is breathed on," Kohanah growled, drawing momentarily away from Marilla. "Let us not speak of him. Kohanah was not free to murder him. Only by way of torture could the evil man be dealt with. If he was murdered by me or my warriors, all of my people would have had to pay. It is most certainly not a pleasant thought to think that if he regains his full faculties he will go to General Stanton and point an accusing finger at me, but it cannot be helped. Hopefully, the white man in charge at the fort will see the truth behind the lies!"

He stood and lowered his fringed breeches and leggings. "If Kohanah goes to prison, Kohanah find a way to be set free again," he said matter-of-factly. "I did what had to be done in the only way it could be done. For now, that is."

"For . . . now?" Marilla asked, her voice shallow. "Then you do have plans to do worse to the man later?"

"If this one time does not put enough fear into the evil man's mind and heart, yes, something else is planned for him," Kohanah said, climbing onto the bed. He moved over Marilla and parted her thighs, the fires of his passion kindling into heated flames. "But let us not dwell on such as that now. Let us make love. Then I must return to my people. Decisions have to be made. I am the one who makes them!"

Kohanah's lips met Marilla's in a tender kiss as he buried himself deep inside her. He kissed her hungrily, his thrusts slow and easy. Their embrace was long and sweet; his hands savored the touch of her soft flesh as they searched and found her most sensitive pleasure points. He smiled to himself when she moaned throatily against his lips, hungrily arching up to meet his strokes within her.

Marilla clung and rocked with Kohanah, the press of his lips so warm . . . so soft . . . so soothing. Her senses were beginning to swim, filled with wondrous joy that she had been given another opportunity to be with the man she loved in such a way. Every day carried risks. At any given moment everything could be changed. The nightmare that she had experienced the previous evening was nothing in comparison with how it *could* be.

But she would take things one day at a time. . . .

Kohanah's fingers dug into Marilla's buttocks and lifted her closer as he sank himself deeper into her, taking from her all the sweetness that she was willing to part with. This moment was . . . forever. . . .

Marilla was never shocked by the intensity of her feelings for Kohanah, for she had loved him from the very first moment she saw him. Even then she had known that to be with him, totally, would be sheer heaven on earth. He was a combination of many things to her . . . velvet one moment, steel the next!

She could never want another man. There was only Kohanah and the magic he wove around her. His hands and lips were the moon, the stars, the *universe*. He was the creator of so many wondrous things to Marilla. There was such a great peace . . . such a great comfort in his lovemaking. It was slow, yet very . . . very . . . gratifying. . . .

Kohanah's passion and desire matched Marilla's. As she began to climb higher, reaching for her peak of passion, he felt the melting sensations spreading within him. He felt giddy. He felt so at peace with the world! If there was only Marilla, how wonderful life would be!

Marilla's entire body throbbed with building desire. She twined her arms about Kohanah's neck and locked her ankles about his waist, drawing him closer. His hands were stroking her breasts. His kiss was now just a soft brush of his lips. . . .

The moment of mindlessness was suddenly upon Marilla when the pleasure spread and touched her all over. She emitted a sob of joy against Kohanah's shoulder just as his body stiffened and then made the last maddening plunge as his pleasure was also reached and enjoyed.

Still tingling all over with the aftermath of rapture's glory, Marilla clung to Kohanah, his brow wet on her shoulder as he rested his head there. "My darling, you always know so much about how to make me enjoy lovemaking," she whispered, running her hands down his muscled back, savoring the pure touch of him. "How I missed you these past three years. They were the longest years of my life."

"The future is what is important," Kohanah said dryly, leaning up away from her. "The past has created the present and the present is not good. The future must be guaranteed to be better. For everyone!"

Marilla saw his urgency in dressing and understood that they would be saying a quick farewell. Wanting to accompany him to his village, get involved in teaching while he did his duties as chief, *and* wanting to be near in case the soldiers came for him, Marilla rushed from the bed, chose a dress from her trunk, and shook the wrinkles from it. Slipping it over her head, she paused and listened, fear entering her heart when she heard the approach of several horses.

Before she could fasten her dress, before Kohanah could step into his moccasins, the door of Marilla's cabin burst open and several soldiers entered the room, pistols drawn.

Paling, her fingers dropping away from the hooks at the back of her dress, Marilla took a wide step and stood protectively in front of Kohanah. Her insides rippled cold when she saw Jason Roark move into the cabin, his hand resting on a saber at his right side. There were no signs on him anywhere of his moments of torture the previous night, except in his eyes. It was as though Marilla were reliving the entire evening in the depths of his cool green eyes. Never had she seen such a deeply imbedded hatred as now.

But she would not let him intimidate her. It was now her word and Kohanah's against Jason's. Very soon Marilla would know just how much General Stanton hated her *and* Kohanah!

"What is the meaning of this?" Marilla said angrily. She squared her shoulders proudly and placed her hands on her hips. "Though the cabin in which I now make residence belongs to the army, it is mine for the duration of my stay as a teacher. You have no right whatsoever to burst in, for *whatever* reason."

"Lady, we have every reason in the world to be here," a soldier said, his rugged face wrinkling into a frown. He nodded toward two other soldiers who shoved Marilla aside and grabbed Kohanah by his arms. "Kohanah is under arrest." His eyes moved boldly over her. He smirked. "As for you, General Stanton will deal with the likes of you, personally."

A heated blush rose from Marilla's neck upward, coloring her face. Her eyes wavered, seeing the knowing in the eyes of all the soldiers. If they had burst into her cabin only moments ago, they would have found. . . .

Moving her gaze slowly to Jason, Marilla felt the pit of her stomach churning. What she now saw in his eyes was lust intermixed with seething hatred for her. With Kohanah imprisoned, she would be fair game for him.

Well, she would let neither happen! She would go to Washington, if necessary, to talk to President Hayes in person. She had to make all things right with him, for he was the voice of authority at this, and every fort in America.

Her gaze moved to the Taime box, glad that so far no one's attention had been drawn to it. It was her duty now to return it to Kohanah's people. Though Kohanah would not be there to do it, the keeper of the Taime still must be chosen.

In her mind's eye she was seeing the vulnerability of Kohanah's paintings. She would go and rescue them. She would keep them in her possession until he was free.

Her heart tearing, she looked at Kohanah. Oh, God, what if he was imprisoned this time, forever? What if they killed him before she got a chance to go to the President and plead his case? If only her father were in charge at Fort Cobb!

Her eyes brightened. If President Hayes would not help Kohanah, just perhaps her father could! He could use his skills as an *attorney* this time to assist Kohanah, not as a soldier in command!

Twenty

～～

Filled with so many emotions even too hard to define, Marilla walked around inside Kohanah's tipi, feeling his presence in everything she looked at and touched. It did not seem possible that he had been placed behind bars at the fort, yet she and Kohanah had known the chances of it happening again.

But having anticipated it did not make the reality of it any easier to accept or cope with. And she did not have time to deliberate silently over what had happened, or how. She had to get her chores completed in the Indian village, then go to the railhead and board a train for Washington. Though President Hayes had not cooperated with Kohanah in her presence, perhaps if she spoke to him alone, he would listen to reason.

Injustice was being done here. President Hayes was not a man to tolerate injustice.

"And perhaps Lucy can help in the persuasion," she whispered. "If only father could meet me in Washington. His old friendship ties with Lucy could be of some help. . . ."

Her eyes widened. Why hadn't she thought of that before? She could wire her father! Surely he could find time to help in Kohanah's cause again! He could meet her in Washington and talk with the President and his wife, *with* Marilla!

Just this tiny ray of hope was cause for Marilla to move about the tipi more anxiously. She took all of Kohanah's paintings and placed them carefully in the back of her buggy and covered them with blankets. Having worried about a soldier maybe seeing her with the paintings, and not thinking the blankets would suffice for disguising them, she had brought some sacks of flour and potatoes and other household staples to place around the covered paintings, so that it would look as though she had been to the general store for supplies, nothing more.

Going back into the tipi, Marilla looked sadly about her, at Kohanah's warring paraphernalia . . . his bows and arrows, his fancily carved spears, and a rifle. Her gaze fell upon one of his fringed outfits, heavily adorned with colorful beads in many assortments of designs sewn onto the deerskin fabrics. His chieftain's headdress, which displayed many lovely feathers, had been laid out at the far end of the tipi on a cushion of furs, as though having been done so meditatively.

Then Marilla's gaze went to the blankets and furs placed by the cold ashes in the fire pit. She stifled a sob behind her hand when in these she still saw the imprint of Kohanah's body, as though he had just risen from a peaceful night of sleep.

"Oh, Kohanah, I must help you," she whispered harshly. "I *must!*"

With a swish of skirt and petticoat, Marilla turned and fled from the tipi, not stopping to look at the wonderful designs painted on the outside, not wanting to again be caught up in missing Kohanah. She had one more duty to perform for Kohanah; then she would be on her way to Washington. If only she could be in time. What would General Stanton's plans be for Kohanah? Kohanah had not committed murder, so surely his sentence would not be all that severe. Kohanah had rescued her from Jason Roark and he had taken his stolen Taime, to return to his people! The resulting torture had been for both those things *and* the fact that Jason was guilty of killing two Kiowa *and* Charles Agnew.

"But Jason failed to tell the full truth to General Stanton," Marilla stewed, climbing aboard her buggy, flicking the reins. "He only told him what would benefit *him*. Anything to get Kohanah arrested, and to leave me vulnerable for another possible rape attempt!"

Her jaw set firmly. She had one more place to stop after delivering the Taime to what she thought might be the rightful hands. She would go and reveal *her* truths to General Stanton, whether or not he would believe her. Her only worry was that in doing so she might draw attention to her buggy and the paintings! She hoped she had hidden them well enough. . . .

She drove her buggy to the center of the village where a tipi of a smaller size than Kohanah's stood, but nothing less than impressive with its colorful designs painted on the buckskin hide covering. Marilla hoped that she had chosen the right one in which to entrust the beloved Taime until Kohanah was free to choose himself. She had heard how proudly Kohanah had spoken of Old Man Nervous, the keeper of the calendar. He was almost in equal standing in the village to their shaman.

Yes, he was surely the one. . . .

Climbing from the buggy, going to the back where she had hidden the rawhide Taime box, Marilla lifted it carefully and walked determinedly toward the entrance flap of Old Man Nervous's tipi. Before she had to announce her presence there, Old Man Nervous stepped from the tipi, his faded eyes filled with questioning.

Marilla smiled warmly down at his slight figure, moved by the graceful lines of his aged face. As before, his gray and wiry hair hung long and loose down his back, way past his waist. He was dressed in a loose sort of buckskin robe, embellished with colorful beads in the design of the sun, stars, and moon. His hand trembled as he raised it in greeting to Marilla, then lowered shakily when he saw the Taime box held gently within her hands.

"Old Man Nervous, as you surely know by now, Kohanah has been taken by the soldiers to jail," Marilla said dryly, hating to even say the words. She held the box out before her. "Kohanah was taken prisoner before he had a chance to bring the Taime back to his people and appoint a new keeper of the Taime. Kohanah had brought the Taime to my cabin before bringing it on to your village. The soldiers did not see it when they came and took Kohanah into custody."

She gestured again with the box. "Please take it and care for it," she murmured. "I know of no one else whom Kohanah would trust as much. When he is released, he will come to you and then do what must be done with it. For now, please guard the Taime as though you were the keeper."

Old Man Nervous's hands trembled as he took the box within them. He nodded, his eyes clouded with tears. "You are good woman," he said in a deep, resonant voice. "Our people will always remember your kindness. Thank you."

Marilla started to say something but stopped when she heard the sound of approaching horses. She glanced quickly over her shoulder and froze inside when she saw many soldiers weaving their horses around the scattered tipis, their focus apparently on her.

Looking back anxiously at Old Man Nervous and then the Taime, Marilla placed a hand on his arm and began walking him back inside his tipi. "None of the soldiers must know that you have the Taime," she said in a harsh whisper. "Hide it, Old Man Nervous! Hide it well!"

She stepped back outside the tipi and held her chin up stubbornly as the soldiers wheeled their horses to a stop only a few yards away from her. When two soldiers dismounted and came and stood before her, their faces shrouded with frowns, fear suddenly grabbed at her heart. What if something had happened to Kohanah? Was that why they were there? Had he tried to escape and been shot in the attempt?

"Ma'am, your presence is requested by General Stanton," one of the soldiers finally said. "If you would be so kind as to let us accompany you there . . ."

Marilla eyed first one soldier and then another, then

scowled up at the soldier who had given her the order.
"Does this have to do with Kohanah?" she asked guardedly. "Is he . . . all right?"

"He's behind bars where he belongs, if that's what you
mean, ma'am," the soldier said in a low, mocking drawl.

"It's an insult that he's in jail and you know it,"
Marilla snapped, her anger now replacing her fear for
Kohanah. She flipped her skirt around as she stomped to
her carriage. "And I have much to say to General Stanton
about that matter." She glanced over her shoulder at Old
Man Nervous's tipi, glad that he had not left his tipi so
that he would become involved in the soldiers' interference.

"I wouldn't be too hasty with words with the general,"
the soldier said, hurrying his steps so that he could assist
Marilla up into her carriage. "I think he has much to say
to you, though."

Marilla stiffened when the soldier placed his hand on
her elbow, hoping that he would not eye the back of her
buggy very closely. She *had* to keep possession of
Kohanah's paintings. They were all that was left of
Kohanah's that could be used for bargaining. If the soldiers got hold of them, the end was the same as met!

Slapping the soldier's hand away, Marilla glared up at
him. "Sir, I do not need your assistance," she hissed.
"Please leave me to myself. I can board my buggy without
assistance. Surely you can mount your horse as skillfully?
If so, I suggest you do it."

She smiled to herself when she saw an irritated frustra-
tion enter the soldier's dark eyes. He ran a finger nervously around the collar of his uniform, glancing across
his shoulder at the other gawking soldiers, then stormed to
his horse and swung himself up into his saddle.

Sighing with relief, Marilla lifted the hem of her dress
with one hand and pulled herself up into the buggy with
the other. Smoothing gloves onto her hands a finger at a
time, she watched the soldiers slowly begin to disband. All
except for the one soldier who watched her irritably from
his army saddle.

Grabbing her reins, Marilla flicked them against the
horse and then followed alongside the soldier, wishing that

he would travel in front of her. She would worry the entire journey to the fort about him wondering about her loaded buggy. If he should ask to see, what could she do? How could she keep him from discovering the precious paintings?

Riding on through the village, Marilla became aware of eyes following her from the doorways of many tipis. The dogs had scattered, the children had been whisked into their dwellings, no old men sat leisurely smoking their pipes. It was as though the village had become imprisoned when Kohanah was locked away.

Or worse yet, it seemed that the village had lost its life . . . its reason for living.

Sad. Marilla rode on to the fort, anger mounting with each spin of the buggy's wheels. . . .

Once the fort was reached and the buggy was drawn up in front of the general's cabin, Marilla could not show her hesitancy at leaving the buggy and its precious cargo. She hoped she could say what had to be said to the general quickly, and he could say what had to be said to her even more quickly.

But something else was plaguing her—the need to see Kohanah before she left for Washington. She had to see if he was all right, and she wanted to tell him what she was going to do. She had so much more to tell him.

The welfare of the paintings . . . the Taime . . .

Saying a silent prayer that the paintings would be safe where they were so carefully hidden, Marilla marched into the general's office, her hair and skirt flying in her haste. She went directly to his desk and leaned down into the general's face, her palms flat on his desk.

"You are a most despicable man," she hissed. "You know you are wrong in jailing Kohanah. The guilty party runs around loose, laughing at you and your mistake. Doesn't that matter to you at all? Where are your scruples, General? How did you acquire this position, anyhow? Surely you paid your way, for never have I, in my many years of associations with the cavalry, met such an unscrupulous man."

Seeing his irritation in the squint of his dark eyes and in

the way he grabbed up a cigar and clamped it between his pursed lips and began puffing hard on it, Marilla eased off. She straightened her shoulders and clasped her fingers together behind her.

"Are you finished?" General Stanton asked, jerking the cigar from between his lips. One eyebrow forked as he stared up at her, not offering her a chair, nor offering to rise from his in a polite gesture.

"Never could I say enough to let you know how I feel about this intolerable situation at Fort Cobb," Marilla said calmly. "If my father were only—"

Stanton shoved the cigar back between his lips and glowered up at Marilla. "Your father isn't nor shall ever again be in charge of a regiment *or* fort," he growled, his cigar hanging stiffly from the corner of his mouth. "So you are wasting time in bringing his name into the conversation."

He smiled crookedly up at her. He raked his eyes over her, then challenged her with a set stare. "Young lady, when you were hired to come to this area, it was only to teach the Indian children, in an effort to educate them in the ways of the white man," he said coldly. "You weren't hired to come and work against us. Now that we have proof of your feelings for . . . your allegiance *to* . . . the damn Indian chief, it is my duty to inform you that your services are no longer needed here. Pack your bags and leave. Immediately."

He nodded toward the soldier who had accompanied her to the fort. "John will see you safely to the railhead," he said dryly.

Marilla blanched. She teetered as though she had been slapped in the face. It was one thing to be dismissed from a teaching position that she had not yet even begun, but it was the reason behind it. Where did it state in the laws of the land that the army would have the right to choose her friends if she was under their employ? It was undemocratic, to say the least.

And to be accompanied to the railhead? How could she load the paintings onto the train without the soldier seeing them?

She couldn't leave them in the village. The soldiers could search every tipi whenever they chose to. Nothing was safe there. Nothing!

Then anger seethed inside her, burning her to the core, it seemed, when she thought of Jason Roark going free. He was the cause of all of this! If not for him, the agitation against the Taime would not have even begun among the soldiers. If not for him, so many things would not have happened! It was her duty to try to prove his guilt!

Her eyes opened wide when she now recalled his confessions to her while he gloated over her bound body. The murder weapon! He had told her that he had thrown it into the well behind her cabin! He had intended to kill and throw *her* in there, also.

Marilla's nostrils flared angrily as she regained her composure and took a step closer to the desk. She doubled her hands into tight fists at her sides. "General Stanton, I don't give a damn what you think about me, and I don't want to care that you have fired me from my position, but I can't just stand here and let you do this to me," she said between clenched teeth. "Nor can I let you condemn Kohanah for that of which he is innocent! I warned you earlier about Jason Roark. Now let me tell you a few more things about him that I hope will open your eyes!"

Knowing the chances were slim that Stanton would believe her because of his dislike *for* her, and knowing that if he did believe her, he would not admit to it, Marilla told him about Jason's abduction of her and of his plans *for* her. . . .

"And the knife that killed three innocent people?" she continued. "If you would only take the time, you would find the knife at the bottom of the well behind the cabin you assigned me for my short stay here. If not for Kohanah, I would be in that well now, also. It was to be my grave. Jason Roark planned it that way."

She loosened her fingers and sighed. "I can tell you exactly how to find the cabin where Jason took me after he abducted me from the schoolhouse," she said more softly. "You will find ropes on the bed that held me captive!"

General Stanton frowned up at Marilla. He took the

cigar from his mouth and placed it in an ashtray. Rising
from his chair, he went to a window and stared from it.
"Those ropes were used to hold Jason Roark on the bed
while Kohanah tortured him," he said blandly.

He swung around and frowned at Marilla. "Didn't the
savage know that Jason could escape and come to tell
about his abduction by the crazy Indian?"

He scratched his brow idly. "What puzzles me is why
Kohanah didn't kill Jason. He *knew* Jason *would* tell about
what Kohanah did to him. If anything doesn't make sense
here, that doesn't."

Marilla saw a faint glimmer of hope as she saw General
Stanton pondering over the truths. She went to him and
spoke up into his face. "Sir," she said, forcing politeness.
"You have got to know that Kohanah had only one re-
course to get the Taime returned to his people and to save
me from rape and eventual murder. But he knew that he
had to stop at murder. His people depend on him. Totally.
Inside his heart he had hoped that the truth would surface
about Jason and that what Kohanah did *to* Jason would be
seen as fair in the eyes of the white man."

She grabbed him by the arm, her eyes wild. "You must
free Kohanah and place Jason in jail," she pleaded. "Let
me remain here with the Kiowa, to teach them." Her
upper lip stiffened as she dropped her hand away from him.
"I swear, General Stanton, I will stop at nothing to see
that the right thing is done here. Nothing!"

Stanton's mind was swirling with all the information
that had been given to him. Damn, how he hated that
Jason Roark! This would be a good opportunity to get him
out of his hair! But then he would lose the opportunity to
teach Kohanah a lesson in obedience! It was evident that
he had to choose between the two men. And if he must, it
would be a step backwards if he released Kohanah again!
Kohanah was a troublemaker! He needed to be taught a
lesson, if only for a little while.

He kneaded his chin. Yes. That was the answer. He
would bide his time while Kohanah was in jail, yet something told him that the damn well had to be drained so that

if there *was* a knife, the evidence would be there whenever the time was ripe to arrest Jason Roark.

But he would not confide any of this to Marilla Pratt. There was something about her that made him sweat. She seemed to have powers of persuasion that he had never seen in a lady before. She was just as dangerous as Kohanah! It was imperative that he force her to leave!

"My mind is made up," he said, slowly turning to challenge Marilla with a set stare. "You are to leave the reservation. Kohanah will remain in jail." He smiled smugly down at her. "Now, Miss Pratt, just you go ahead and make threats, for I am one who is never swayed by expressions of intentions to do harm." He flicked his wrist in a gesture of dismissal. "I am tired of this conversation. Please take your leave."

Marilla stood her ground. She folded her arms across her chest stubbornly. "You will be sorry," she hissed. Then she gave the waiting soldier a glance over her shoulder, again worrying about the paintings. "But if you insist that I leave, I shall." She again challenged him with her eyes. "But only on two conditions, without me causing one hell of a stir in this fort."

General Stanton sighed heavily. He raked his fingers nervously through his hair. "What is it?" he said, sinking back down into his chair. "At this point I think I may grant any wish to you, just to get you out of here."

"Good," Marilla snapped. "First, I do not want to be accompanied to the railhead like some spineless ninny. I want to travel there on my own. I promise that I will leave your horse and buggy in a safe place. Let a soldier come for it later. I have had enough of soldiers for a while."

Her eyes wavered and she swallowed hard. "Secondly," she murmured. "I wish to see Kohanah. I must see if he is all right. I must have an opportunity to bid him farewell."

She pleaded with her eyes. "Surely that isn't asking too much of you," she said softly. "Take me to Kohanah. Let me say good-bye."

Stanton picked up his cigar and clamped it between his teeth and glared up at Marilla. "He means that much to you?" he said hoarsely.

Marilla tilted her chin stubbornly. "He means everything to me," she said dryly. "Everything."

General Stanton stared up at her for a moment, his eyes studying her intensely. Then he nodded toward John. "Help Miss Pratt onto her buggy; then accompany her to the jail," he said softly. "Open the door for her and then leave her and the savage in peace for a few moments. Do you hear?"

Disbelief that the general was at all agreeable made Marilla momentarily in awe of his changeable personality. Then she turned and left the cabin, not thinking that, though General Stanton had given her permission to see Kohanah, he had done nothing else that deserved a thank-you.

As she boarded her buggy, Marilla's pulse raced. She would soon be with Kohanah again, if only for a moment. This was the tomorrow he had spoken of . . . a tomorrow that had taken so much from him, his people, and *her*. . . .

Jason Roark stood in the shadows of the fort wall, observing all that was happening. He was in wonder of Marilla heading toward the jail. If General Stanton was as angry as he should be with her, surely he wouldn't be allowing her to see Kohanah! Had she told him everything? Had she remembered to tell him about his confession of where he had hidden the knife? Had the general listened or did he still condemn Kohanah for all the wrong reasons, which, in turn, were the right ones for Jason?

Placing a hand on his holstered pistol, he knew what his next move must be. He must be sure to keep watch on that damn well, or retrieve the knife himself. Such evidence could get him a noose around his neck. He had hoped for more from General Stanton.

He had hoped that General Stanton's hate for the Indian and his dislike for Marilla would make Jason Roark come out of this, whitewashed with innocence. . . .

General Stanton paced the floor, Marilla's words about Jason troubling him. The knife. The damn knife. It must be retrieved now, or if Jason did throw it in the well, *he* might retrieve it *himself!* He had to know that Marilla had disclosed the truth about the knife, having only told her at the time about where he had hidden it because he had planned to also kill her! The knife was the proof that General Stanton would eventually need to hang the damn son of a bitch Jason Roark. Kohanah was trouble, but Jason Roark was second in line! He was not only a troublemaker but also stupid, for having come to tell of his experiences with Kohanah. Only a man who hated Kohanah so much could put his own life in jeopardy!

Going to the door, Stanton motioned for a soldier to come into his office. He explained the problem and had the soldier vow an oath of silence. He instructed him that as soon as Marilla was gone from the cabin and was on her way to the railhead, it was up to this soldier and several others who were also trustworthy to go to the well and look for the knife.

If it was found, the soldiers were to bring it to him. . . .

Twenty-One

As she was waiting for the door to be opened that led into the cells, Marilla was struck with remembrances of another time, another place. Was it truly three years ago when she had visited Kohanah in the dungeon at Fort Marion? At the time she had not known that her initial visits with Kohanah had begun a lifetime of caring for him and of fighting for his rights.

It wasn't a nostalgic remembrance so much as a sad one, his now having been arrested again slowly eating away at her insides, like a festering sore.

The door swung wide open, revealing a long line of cells on either side of a long, shadowed corridor. All of the cells were empty except one. Marilla's heart broke when she saw Kohanah's handsomeness silhouetted against the wall of his cell by the sunlight filtering through the outside bars behind him.

"Take your time, ma'am," the soldier said, his voice thick with mockery. "Seems this may be the last time you'll see your Injun friend."

Kohanah turned his head with a start when the door clanked open at the far end of the corridor, revealing the golden streamers of Marilla's hair against the gray back-

218

ground of the drab setting. He went to the bars and clasped his fingers around them, peering intensely toward her, having feared for her safety after being forced to leave her in the cabin when he was arrested.

But it seemed that she was all right, and he was in awe that she was actually there! Had General Stanton softened his policy? Was he beginning to see the wrong in this that he had done? It didn't seem likely that Jason Roark could fool anyone for long, especially anyone with a good measure of intelligence.

If not for General Stanton's stubborn prejudice against Indians, he could be regarded as an intelligent man. . . .

Ignoring the sarcastic soldier, Marilla swept down the corridor, forcing herself not to cry when she reached Kohanah and saw how helpless he looked standing behind bars again. Her gaze moved over him, naked except for his loincloth, revealing his copper body of sinew and muscle.

Raising her eyes, Marilla felt her insides warmed with love as she looked upon his strong, determined face and hard, high cheekbones, and lips that could send her into a world of wondrous delight. His eyes were darker with the intensity of his emotional state. His shoulder muscles were corded as his fingers held on to the accursed bars.

"Tsonda, you have come," Kohanah said thickly. "How is that you were given permission to? Are you all right?"

Seeing his long, lean fingers so close, Marilla could not help but wrap her own about them, the touch of his flesh against hers sending the usual sweet rapture through her.

"Kohanah, I have so much to tell you," she murmured, almost choking with pent-up feelings for him. "But first let me say that I am all right, although I cannot say that I have been treated any more fairly than you." She lowered her lashes, then again looked up at him. "Darling, General Stanton has relieved me of my teaching duties. I no longer have the privilege of teaching your Kiowa children. He is . . . sending me away."

Her fingers clasped harder onto his. "Oh, Kohanah, I'm not sure I can bear it," she said in a half-sob. "If I leave you behind, what can I even venture to guess may happen to you? What if they decide to ship you away to another fort where I won't be able to find you? What if they choose . . . a noose as punishment?''

Kohanah eased one hand free. He reached through the bars and cupped her delicate chin within the strength of his callused hand. ''Tsonda, you have already given me enough quiet and comfort to last a lifetime,'' he said huskily. ''Do not worry so about my welfare.'' Anger flared in his eyes. ''This General Stanton. He punishes Kohanah in many ways. To order you to leave is perhaps the worst punishment of all!''

''Don't you get so upset,'' Marilla said, taking his hand from her chin, twining her fingers through his, relishing these last moments with him before having to once again say a sad farewell. ''While I am gone, keep in your mind all that is good that I plan to do for you.''

''Good? What do you speak of? Will it endanger you?'' Kohanah growled, leaning his head down, speaking into Marilla's face. ''Kohanah won't allow you to endanger yourself in any way. Kohanah will forbid it!''

''No, Kohanah, it is wrong to even think of forbidding me to do anything,'' Marilla said, pleading with her eyes. ''Trust me. I know what I'm doing.''

A twinkle entered her eyes and a smile softened her expression. ''Wait until I tell you what I have already done,'' she said. She paused and looked over her shoulder to make sure they were alone . . . alone enough for her to reveal many truths to him. She was anxious to see Kohanah's reaction to things that she had taken upon herself to do. Things for him and his people!

''What have you done?'' Kohanah asked, forking an eyebrow inquisitively.

Marilla looked up at him anxiously. ''Kohanah, I took the Taime to Old Man Nervous,'' she said in a near whisper. ''He is going to keep it in his protection until you are released. I have taken your paintings from your dwelling and plan to keep them safely with me until you are released. I could not leave either of these things lying around for the soldiers to confiscate. Do you approve? Did I do the right thing? I pray that I did.''

Kohanah was rendered speechless for a moment, having

never thought his woman could be this in tune to what needed to be done for him and his people. It was not because he had taught her! She did everything from the heart!

From the very first she had picked up on his feelings, his wants and needs, his customs.

He had chosen wisely when he singled her out to be his!

Kohanah placed a doubled fist to his chest, over his heart. "I am touched," he said thickly. "My heart is filled with such love for you . . . such *pride*. How can Kohanah ever thank you for being so much *to* Kohanah?"

Tears silvered Marilla's cheeks; she was unable to hold them back any longer. She eased her hands through the spaces between the bars and framed his face within them. She drew his lips down, close to hers, their breaths mingling. "My darling, no thanks are ever needed," she whispered. "Only your love. My devotion to you is forever."

Their lips met in a sweet kiss, lingering, Kohanah's hands at her waist, drawing her closer to the bars, yet aching inside that he could not fit her completely into his contours so that they would blend as one being again, for what if they could never be together again? Though they were devoted and filled with love for one another, that did not guarantee a future of being together. So much depended on General Stanton's decisions, and as far as Kohanah could see, this man was almost as stubborn as he himself was!

Trembling, Marilla moved her lips away. "Kohanah, I haven't told you everything," she murmured. "I plan to leave today, to board a train for Washington. I'm going to wire my father from the railhead and ask him to join me in Washington. Together we will plead your case again with the President. Let us hope that a decision can be reached to release you before General Stanton reaches his own decision on how to deal with you."

A mischievous sort of glint entered Marilla's eyes. "There is one faint ray of hope on the horizon," she said, laughing beneath her breath. "Jason Roark. I may have just given cause for a noose to be slipped around his neck. If the general even half believes what I said about where he can find the knife—Jason's murder weapon—in the well behind my cabin, Jason Roark's meanness will be ended and you will be set free.''

"If General Stanton hates Kohanah so much, nothing will sway his decision about what is to be done to me," Kohanah said in a low growl. "Yet I will not lose hope, Tsonda. Never do I lose hope. My people await my return."

"And so shall *I* return," Marilla said determinedly. "As soon as I settle things in Washington, I shall return to you. Nothing can keep me away. General Stanton doesn't have the right to order me around. He'll soon find that out, also. When my father returns with me to speak in my behalf *and* yours, General Stanton will learn quite quickly that he was wrong to treat you and me so unjustly!"

"Your father will come here?" Kohanah asked, his eyes wide, filled with wonder. "He, the man with the big heart, will come here?"

"If it is necessary for him to speak to General Stanton in your behalf, he will come," Marilla reassured him. "But I hope that only a wire will be required to ensure your freedom. The President has only to give the order and it will be done."

Kohanah turned abruptly away from her and began to pace. "Again he will ask for my paintings," he growled. "But he cannot have them. They are all I have for bargaining! The Sun Dance must be performed. The Kiowa must have permission to perform it in peace. Somehow a single buffalo must be found *for* the Sun Dance. The President could assure me at least one buffalo!"

"Don't worry about your paintings," Marilla murmured. "They will be in my possession. No one will have the opportunity to get them. And I will not give them to the President. You have my word on that." She swallowed hard. "But I don't know about the other things that you need. Except to say that you have my assurance that I will do everything within my power to persuade the President to grant you *everything* that you have requested."

Kohanah stopped his pacing and went to stand before Marilla. Moving a hand through the small spaces between the bars, he twined his fingers through her hair and drew her face to his. "Tsonda, my love travels with you," he said thickly. "Go in peace."

Their lips met in a tender kiss, a kiss of promise and everlasting love. Marilla hugged his words to her. She breathed in the familiar scent of him, to take with her on the long journey of hope. . . .

Having retrieved her belongings from the cabin, Marilla was now at the railhead loading them onto the train. She watched Kohanah's paintings being placed on the seat next to her, having paid for two seats instead of one. Whenever a blanket slipped and disclosed a painting, she would hurriedly put it back in place.

Breathing uneasily, Marilla settled down into the seat, guardedly watching for any signs of soldiers. But there were none. General Stanton had at least kept his word on this. She had been able to go to the railhead alone. Her next stop was Washington.

Smiling to herself, she let herself see her father in her mind's eye. He had never let her down yet. She could expect him to meet her in Washington. It would be so grand to see him again . . . to be hugged by his long, lean arms. . . .

Jason Roark rode hard toward Marilla's cabin, having to follow the least traveled roads, fearing he would be seen. Until he got the murder weapon back in his possession he was the same as dead. He regretted having absorbed himself in the consumption of alcohol instead of taking care of Marilla quickly. If she were dead, none would be the wiser about what he was guilty of. The fact that General Stanton might choose to believe her, might even set Kohanah free, surprised him all to hell! He had thought that he was safe, that Stanton's hate for Kohanah and his displeasure with Marilla would make him overlook anything that she would have to say in her and Kohanah's behalf!

But it seemed that General Stanton wasn't as corrupt as Jason had first thought! And if General Stanton chose to fully pursue the investigation into the murder of Charles

Agnew and the two damn Indians, Jason Roark would, indeed, be the loser!

Knowing that he was close to Marilla's cabin, Jason directed his horse so that he would be arriving from the back. Leaning low over the thick mane, he thrust the heels of his army boots into his horse's flanks, then wheeled his steed to a sudden halt when he saw not only the cabin but also several soldiers surrounding it.

His heart seeming to have dropped to his feet, Jason quickly dismounted and tethered his horse to a low limb of a tree and went closer to the cabin on foot. Dropping to his stomach, lying on a slight rise, he looked down at the soldiers who were busy at the well. He now knew that General Stanton had listened to Marilla and was ready to use whatever proof he could find!

Then his lips lifted into a slow, smug smile. There was only one hope left. Perhaps Stanton had listened to Marilla's tale about the knife, but had not believed that she knew of it because Jason had told her. Perhaps the general thought that it belonged, instead, to *Kohanah!* Perhaps it would be used as evidence against Kohanah!

But until Jason knew for sure exactly in which way the guilt would be shifted, he would have to lie low! He would have to go into hiding! Yet, wouldn't his absence from the fort be all the proof that General Stanton would need, to know who was the guilty party?

Jason no longer felt so smug. He went back to his horse and rode away, his hate for Kohanah and Marilla and *all* Indians stinging his insides as never before. . . .

The room was of a rich decor. The massive desk sitting before a wide spread of windows was made of oak, the bookcases filled with expensive law books, the floor covered by a thick Oriental carpet. Richard Pratt rose from behind his desk and took the wire that he had just received to the window and reread it, then stared down from his office on the tenth floor of the building on Madison Avenue to the horse-drawn carriages on the busy streets.

"Marilla, oh, Marilla," he whispered, troubled. He raked his fingers nervously through his dark hair, the gray at his temples making him look more distinguished now in his expensive suit than when he wore a uniform of the United States Cavalry. "Will it ever end?"

His blue eyes wavered at the thought of when she had met Kohanah and how so quickly she had been caught up in the intrigue of him. So had Richard, but not as intensely. It had been easy to fight for Kohanah's rights because of his likable nature. And it seemed that the need had arisen again!

"And I must," he whispered, returning to his desk, easing back down into his plush leather chair. "If not for Kohanah, for *Marilla*."

He began gathering papers and placed them in a leather satchel. Yes, he would go to Washington. For his daughter, he would do anything. . . .

Twenty-Two

꧁ ꧂

Nervous, Marilla stood beside her father, awaiting the arrival of President Hayes in the East Room of the White House. When she had met with her father at the hotel on Pennsylvania Avenue only moments ago, she had been warmed all over by his affectionate hug and by the fact that he cared enough for her *and* for Kohanah to drop everything in New York and meet with her and the President in Washington.

Her gaze swept over her father . . . seeing him as nothing less than handsome in his brown velvet coat lavishly embellished with gold threads around the cuffs and down the front, his white shirt with ruffles and fancy stitchery, and his breeches of dark charcoal-colored broadcloth.

His blue eyes showed his anxiousness to see Lucy Hayes again, perhaps even more than the President. Their friendship, which had begun in college, seemed to be an enduring one.

Marilla felt spruced up enough in her dress of blue satin trimmed with gold lace down the front of the low-swept bodice, her hair luxuriantly coiled atop her head in an elaborate chignon, held in place with a slide that displayed tiny sparkling diamonds, with only a trace of tight ringlets framing her face.

Shifting her eyes, she looked around the room, seeing the expensive taste of the President and Lucy Hayes. Oriental rugs graced the wide floor; the imported furniture was formal, upholstered in plush. A great sweep of gold satin drapes had been drawn back from the windows. A formidable partner's desk of Irish design stood in front of a window, a hurricane lamp of fabulous design on one end, a scattering of books and ledgers on the other. Two leather Hepplewhite armchairs flanked a tall standing lamp, with a velveteen sofa opposite them, to form a comfortable corner, where a great fire blazed on the hearth of a fireplace.

Then Marilla's eyes were drawn to the paneled walls. Her pulse raced when she saw the elaborate, rare paintings that hung along the entire wall. Would Kohanah's eventually join them? Or if the President ever acquired any of Kohanah's paintings, would he destroy Kohanah's precious artwork, to keep the world from knowing the truths *of* the Kiowa?

Kohanah's paintings lay hidden beneath a layer of blankets in Marilla's hotel room. Hopefully they would be in Kohanah's possession once again soon. So much depended on her ease with the President today . . . and on *his*. Surely a decent, civil debate could be held.

But if President Hayes recalled with distaste his anger at Kohanah and his disappointment *with* him, perhaps all was already lost, and the journey to Washington futile. . . .

A shuffling of feet behind her drew Marilla around. Her back stiffened and her insides grew tight as she watched President Hayes come into the room. His dark eyes were warm, his gray hair, beard, and mustache neatly groomed, his dark blue coat with buff lapels accentuated by his crisp ruffled shirt and buff breeches.

"How nice it is to see you again, Marilla," President Hayes said, going to her, kissing the back of her hand while she smiled dutifully up at him.

He then went to Richard and shook his hand and slapped his shoulder fondly. "How long has it been, Richard? Lucy is going to be upset that she wasn't here to see you."

He chuckled beneath his breath. "She's out on one of her crusades. She's enjoying the life of a President's wife. It's given her an excuse to voice her opinion about a lot of things. It doesn't matter that she's a mother of eight. She seems to be the sort who can do it all. Lucy enjoys the life of a President's wife much more than I enjoy being President."

When hearing that he would not be meeting with Lucy to rehash old times, disappointment showed in Richard's eyes, but then he thought that perhaps it was best that Lucy wasn't there after all. The trip to Washington had been for business, not for leisure. And had he gotten together with Lucy, so much besides business would have been discussed. Now only matters of importance would be exchanged with the President.

"That's too bad," Richard said, clearing his throat nervously, looking over at Marilla, who was showing her uneasiness in the way she was clasping her hands so tightly behind her. "But there will be another time for chatting with Lucy. Old friends have a way of getting together, you know."

President Hayes stroked his beard and forked an eyebrow, looking from Marilla to Richard, then once again at Marilla. "What brings you here on this fine day in May?" he asked thickly. "Or need I ask? Marilla, I saw your devotion to the Indians. Do you bring this devotion even to Washington for discussion?"

Marilla smiled nervously up at the President. "So much was said when you were at the Kiowa village," she murmured. "But so much has happened since that must be told. The plight of the Kiowa is not an easy one. Surely you can sympathize with them, though you and Kohanah did not see eye to eye on matters of importance *to* the Kiowa. Perhaps I can persuade you to listen and reevaluate your judgments. Perhaps you will see why swift decisions must be made in favor *of* the Kiowa."

A frown creased President Hayes's brow. He studied Marilla silently for a moment, then gestured with a hand toward the seating arrangement in front of the fire. "Tea should arrive soon," he said blandly. "Let's enjoy it by the fire while we talk."

He gave Richard a half-smile. "I must apologize for not having wine to offer you and Marilla," he said, taking Marilla by an elbow, guiding her to the sofa. "Lucy refuses to have alcoholic beverages of any sort in the White House." He stepped away from Marilla as she eased down onto the sofa. "Some call her Lemonade Lucy because of her refusal to serve alcohol to her guests. The name is less than flattering, I must say."

"Yes, an unkind reference to a very gracious lady," Richard said, settling down onto one of the Hepplewhite armchairs while the President sat down in the other. "But knowing Lucy, she wouldn't be as offended by the nickname as she would be amused. She has a wonderful sense of humor."

"Yes, a gift from God, since she has so many children to give her headaches," President Hayes said, chuckling. He lost his smile as he focused on Marilla, recalling exactly why she was there. "And now, young lady, I think it's time for you to speak your piece. But first let me say I admire your devotion to the Indians. Kohanah must feel very fortunate to have you in his corner, so to say."

Marilla arranged the skirt of her dress neatly about her, her delicate cheekbones blooming with color, her skin gleaming like rich, warm satin beneath the soft glow of the fire on the hearth. She glanced over at her father, then looked determinedly at the President.

"My dedication to the Indians was learned from my father," she said softly. "As you know, he was responsible for the Indians being set free from Fort Marion in Florida. He was responsible for many kindnesses to the Indians while they were incarcerated there, and he is here today to speak in their behalf again, if it becomes necessary for him to do so."

A male servant attired in a long-tailed coat came into the large room, carrying a pot of tea and three dainty china teacups and saucers on a tray. He poured tea into the cups, offered them to each individual, then left the room.

"When Marilla wired me, telling me of the injustice

being done to the Kiowa at Fort Cobb, I saw that I had no choice but to come and meet with you and Marilla, not only to speak in the Kiowa's behalf but also to give my daughter moral support," Richard said, steadying the cup and saucer on his lap. "You are a fair man. This was proved when you refused to give special favors to party politicians, even though your fellow Republicans became bitter toward you because of your decision not to."

"Yes, there still is bitterness toward me." President Hayes sighed, sipping on his tea. "But enough talk about that. Marilla, tell me everything that has happened. Perhaps I can do something about it."

Marilla looked past him, over his shoulder, at the portraits hanging on the walls. She was reminded all over again how the President had refused to talk reason with Kohanah when Kohanah had refused to sell him his paintings. Was the conversation even now going to lead to Kohanah's paintings? Was the President going to ask for them again? If he knew that she had them in her possession, how would he react *then?*

Marilla took a slow sip of tea, focusing her attention back on the President, then set her teacup and saucer on a table. She straightened her back and placed her hands on her lap, challenging the President with a set stare.

"You know that prior to your visit to the Kiowa village, tragedies had occurred," she said softly. She went into detail to rehash her discovery of the murder of the Taime keeper's wife, which led to the discovery of the murder of even the Taime keeper.

She now revealed the discovery of Charles Agnew's body.

She told the President the horrible truth of Jason Roark's abduction of her and the discovery that he had the Taime in his possession, which proved that he had been the one who killed *for* it. She told the President of Jason's confession of where he had thrown the murder weapon . . . the knife that had killed all three people in question, two Kiowa, one white.

She regretted having to tell what Kohanah had done to Jason, which, in turn had caused his imprisonment.

"So you see, Mr. President, Jason Roark is running around free and Kohanah is imprisoned," Marilla said anxiously. "Because Kohanah is an Indian, and because General Stanton does not want to give in one inch to an Indian, he has closed his eyes to the truth. Kohanah should be free. Jason Roark should have a noose around his neck, or perhaps even worse done to him! Can't you do something about this?"

President Hayes rose from his chair and began to pace, combing his fingers meditatively through his beard. "Kohanah can cause many sorts of feelings within a man when one is forced to come face to face with him in a disagreement," he said smoothly. "I know. Kohanah made the worst surface in me. He as much as blackmailed me, you know. And no man sits still for blackmail."

Marilla's skirt whirled around her delicate ankles as she rose quickly from the sofa, to go to the President, to grab his arm. She flinched when she realized that she had caused him to stop pacing by her bold attempt to get his full attention. Then she stubbornly lifted her chin.

"All arguments have already been spoken in defense of Kohanah and the Kiowa," she said softly. "You know them all. I have come to plead for his release and for Jason Roark to be dealt with as any man who is guilty should be dealt with."

She glanced over at her father who was seemingly enjoying this all, sitting back in his chair, his eyes gleaming merrily. He nodded toward her and winked to show his silent approval of how she was handling things. He was glad that he had come, not to argue for his daughter's cause, but to watch her in action and to admire her. She could be an attorney. She knew all the right moves and words to use, that was for sure!

Feeling the President's dark, friendly eyes on her, Marilla turned her gaze back to him. "And not only have I come to request that you see that justice is done for Kohanah," she said dryly. "I also hope that you will give your full approval for the Sun Dance to be performed by the Kiowa. There have been enough problems causing the delay. Why, there aren't even any buffalo for miles around for the

Kiowa to *use* during their sacred ritual. Perhaps you could also—''

President Hayes laughed suddenly . . . a deep, friendly laugh as he placed his hands on Marilla's shoulders, causing her words to fade away to nothing. ''Young lady, enough! Enough!'' he said, smiling down at her. ''I understand exactly what you're asking of me. And perhaps I can make arrangements to see that wrongs are made right at Fort Cobb. Perhaps a buffalo can even be sent to your Kohanah for use in the Sun Dance, to which I most heartily give my blessing.''

Surprising Marilla, he drew her within his powerful arms and hugged her. ''My dear, you are a woman of heart,'' he said softly. ''And since my meeting with Kohanah I have had time to think over everything that happened between him and me and I have decided that I have nothing but respect and admiration for that man. But . . .''

Marilla's insides froze when he used the word ''but'' and eased her from his arms, to look directly down into her eyes. ''But what . . . ?'' she said demurely.

''It is imperative that I have one of Kohanah's paintings in particular, to keep others from viewing it in the future,'' he said thickly. ''I do not wish to see old grudges renewed now that peace has been established between the whites and the Indians. If you could just convince Kohanah that it is best that I have that painting, you would make this President one happy, relieved man.''

''The painting that you speak of . . . it's the one done on hide, the one that depicts the atrocities performed against the Indians by the cavalry?'' Marilla asked, stiffening. ''You don't want anyone realizing by viewing this painting that the Indians were wronged?''

''Exactly.''

''But, sir, I would rather not interfere in such matters.''

''You are here now, interfering.''

Marilla paled. ''I wouldn't call this interfering,'' she said softly, lowering her eyes. ''I have come here to *help*. That is all.''

President Hayes nodded silently. He took Marilla by the elbow and gently guided her back to the sofa. ''Marilla,'' he said, easing back down onto his chair opposite her. "I am not the sort to use blackmail when talking over agreements. So you must understand that I do not require the painting to carry through with the promises that I have already made you. Just do what you can when you get back to the reservation. Talk with Kohanah. Tell him of the importance of my having the painting. It is for both his people *and* mine that I have the painting, to keep others from having it in the future. Peace is the true issue here, is it not?"

"Yes, sir," Marilla said, relieved that the President was not going to use the painting as blackmail, as Kohanah had done. Being the kindhearted man that he was, he was going to make everything right for Kohanah, regardless. He had believed her, totally. He needed no more proof than her word, and perhaps the fact that her father was a man trusted by everyone!

Then her eyes wavered as she remembered that she had not thought to tell the President of her unfair dismissal from the school. In a rush, she even confessed that to him, squirming uneasily in her chair when, for the first time this afternoon, she saw a heated anger flash in his eyes.

"It seems that I have much to say in my wire to General Stanton," President Hayes said sourly. "That man gives me cause not to like him every time I hear of him. My dear, you will be reinstated in your teaching position at the Indian village."

He rose from the chair and went to his desk and wrote something on his letterhead stationery, then folded it and brought it back to Marilla. "Upon your return to Oklahoma, give this to General Stanton," he said softly, placing the letter in Marilla's hand. "Along with the wire that I plan to send him, this will make him understand just exactly what I expect of him." He laughed softly. "I don't believe you will be having trouble with him again. Nor will Kohanah."

"Thank you," Marilla said, her hands trembling, so taken was she by the President's kindness. "You are so very, very kind."

President Hayes settled back down in his chair and

focused his attention on Richard. "So tell me, Richard, how's your law practice coming along in New York?" he asked casually. "I miss my law practice quite often. But I doubt if I shall ever get back to it. I've lots on my mind that needs doing once I leave the White House behind."

"Perhaps you'll change your mind," Richard said, laughing gruffly. "Lord, Mr. President, you were one of the best attorneys around before you left to fight in the war. Everyone remembers how you won statewide attention as a criminal lawyer in Cincinnati. Your defense arguments in two widely publicized murder trials saved your clients from receiving the death penalty."

President Hayes gazed into the flames of the fire, his mind recalling exactly how the fight had been won in the courtroom. "Ah, but those were the good old days," he said quietly.

Then he turned his eyes back to Richard, looking from him to Marilla. "Lucy should be home by evening," he said, casting thoughts of the past aside. "You must stay for dinner. The children are always glad to have a new face at the table. And afterward? You are invited to join in with the family to gather for music and singing."

He leaned forward and smiled from Marilla to Richard. "Now, I won't take no for an answer," he said, chuckling low. "But first, let me send that wire to General Stanton so that Marilla can relax and join the singing." He rose quickly to his feet and went to his desk and sat down and began composing the wire.

Marilla was touched, so very, very touched, by the President's sincere kindness, yet singing and merriment were the last things on her mind. What if the wire got to Oklahoma too late? What if General Stanton had already handed out his punishment to Kohanah?

The next several days would be long for Marilla. Her every heartbeat would count out the moments until she could be with Kohanah again, to see that he was totally safe. . . .

Twenty-Three

❧❧

The journey from the railhead to Fort Cobb was a strained one for Marilla as she sat square-shouldered and tense beside a soldier. The ensuing buggy ride was clumsy and hot as the vehicle rolled across the land. Adjusting her bonnet, then smoothing the skirt of her finely printed, fully gathered cotton dress about her legs, she was recalling the one other time she had arrived in Oklahoma, and the man who had been waiting at the railhead to pick her up. Charles Agnew. It did not seem possible even yet that such a kind man had been murdered so needlessly. She did not even know exactly why Jason Roark had killed him. And it seemed that she never *would* know, except that somehow Charles had gotten in Jason's way.

Looking across the land, golden with sunshine, so flat that she could see for countless miles, the clouds skipping across the sky like white puffs of cotton, she became caught up in thoughts. President Hayes had apparently sent the wire to reinstate her in her teaching position, for she had been met by one of General Stanton's soldiers. He had been ordered to take her to Stanton, to meet with him to confirm the reversed decision.

She had to wonder if the President also had sent word

that Jason Roark must be captured and dealt with properly. Would Kohanah truly be eventually free? The President had promised, oh, so many things.

But how long would it take for it all to come about so that Kohanah might live at least a semblance of a normal life with his people? Would he *ever* be able to?

Casting all doubts from her mind, Marilla smiled to herself. Even a buffalo had been promised Kohanah. The Sun Dance would be performed. But when? So much depended on just how soon General Stanton would set Kohanah free!

Her heart aching, Marilla could hardly wait to go and see Kohanah in his jail cell. She had so much to tell him. He would be so glad to hear! Perhaps he would even be set free in her presence? The letter from the President not only gave orders to reinstate Marilla to her teaching position, confirming the wire that had been sent to Stanton, but also to set Kohanah free.

Giving the soldier a sidewise look, Marilla was tempted to ask him so many things, yet he was not at all like Charles Agnew. In his neat blue uniform, he was stiff and quiet, his eyes peering straight ahead. He had only barely spoken a good day to her when he met her at the railhead to assist her into the buggy.

Looking away from him, pained by so many remembrances, Marilla was at least glad that she had placed the paintings under the protection of her father. Until she knew that Kohanah was safe and well and released from his imprisonment, it was best that the paintings be as far away from Fort Cobb as possible. There could be hardly any place as far away as New York!

She hoped Kohanah would understand and accept this decision. . . .

The fort walls now in sight, Marilla squirmed uneasily on the seat. She clutched her purse, within it the letter that could make her life, and Kohanah's, better. She watched the fort drawing closer and closer. . . .

When she was finally standing before General Stanton's desk, waiting for him to read the letter from the President, she looked anxiously across his shoulder and out the window, at the jail. She had wanted to go to Kohanah at once, but had known that she must first deal with General Stanton, to make sure that he understood how things were to be. Once he read the letter from the President, then she would go to Kohanah. She wondered if he had been told of her planned arrival. Had he even seen her arrival from the window of his cell?

A low sort of grumble drew Marilla's eyes back to Stanton. She looked down at him as he was refolding the letter, his eyes dark with humiliation and anger. Slowly he lifted his head to gaze up at her.

"You continue to be a thorn in my side and yet I must be forced to tolerate you?" he said, slapping the letter down on his desk. He grabbed a half-smoked cigar from an ashtray and thrust it between his pursed lips, then lit it.

After taking several long draws from the cigar, he jerked it from his mouth. He rose from his chair and went around to glare down at Marilla, standing so close she could feel his breath on her face. "How dare you go to the President and stir up more trouble for me," he said dryly. "My future is bleak, to say the least, because of you. I shall never advance higher than where I am now. I shall always be forced to deal with Indians and . . . and . . . the likes of you. I'm sure you will be happy to hear that I've asked to be assigned to another post. I've had enough of Kohanah and his people."

He leaned closer. "And *you*. You and your Indian lover have won, you know. But we'll see just how long you'll last living the life of a lowly Indian, won't we?"

Chuckling, he made a turn and went to sit back down behind his desk. "You are dismissed, Miss Pratt," he growled. "The school is yours. The whole damn Indian village is yours."

An evil grin flashed across his face as he gazed contemptuously up at her. "Perhaps in time you'll even have a brood of your own Injuns to teach at the damn schoolhouse you are eager to teach in."

Getting more humiliated by the moment by his manner toward her, Marilla's face grew hot with an angry flush. "You are the poorest excuse for an army officer I have ever come face to face with," she said icily. "No matter what post you are assigned to, things will never be better for you, for your contemptible character won't allow it. I wish for nothing but the worst for you, *sir*."

She again looked past his shoulder at the jail. "And thank you for dismissing me, *sir*," she hissed. "I have better things to do. I'm going to go to Kohanah and spread the news that you will be releasing him soon."

She moved her eyes back to the general. They were flashing as she looked down at him. "You *will* be releasing him soon, won't you?" she hissed. "The President's orders will be followed quickly, won't they? If not, I may have another journey to make to Washington, but not before I wire him and tell him of your insolence."

General Stanton smashed his cigar out in an ashtray, then leaned back in his chair and folded his arms across his chest. He smiled strangely up at Marilla. "Why not take a stroll to the jail and just see how Kohanah has been dealt with?" he said, his lips quivering into an evil, tormenting smile. "Miss Pratt, go on. Go on and see. Then we'll see what you have to say to the President."

An icy sort of chill crawled across Marilla's flesh. Her eyes wavered as she took a step back, stunned by what he had said. His words were threatening, as though she was too late! Had the President's wire arrived too late for Kohanah? Was she soon to discover that he had just been shot, or *hanged?*

With a flurry of skirt and petticoat, Marilla ran out of the office. She was breathless as she reached the locked door of the jail. Almost clawing the soldier who was standing guard, she looked wildly up into his pitiless gray eyes. "Unlock the door," she said in a rush of words. "Now!" she said in an almost scream. "Damn it, unlock the door now!"

"Open it for her, Toby," General Stanton said smoothly, walking up to Marilla, amused by her desperate state. "Let her go in. This could be a bit amusing."

Marilla's eyes narrowed angrily as she turned around in a jerk and glared at Stanton. "So help me, if you've harmed Kohanah, you'll pay," she hissed, then swung back around and breathlessly waited for the door to be unlocked.

When it opened wide, giving her full access to enter, Marilla's knees grew weak as she moved cautiously across the threshold, afraid of what she would find. The long hallway that led past the long line of cells was dark. Only faint ripples of light filtered through the windows of the cells. Recalling exactly which one had housed Kohanah, Marilla hurried on toward it, then grew numb inside when she found that it was vacant.

Placing a hand to her mouth, she stifled a gasp behind it. Tears silvered her eyes, then her cheeks, as she moved on to the cell and clasped her hands around the bars. "Oh, Kohanah," she whispered. "Where are you? What have they done to you? If you were free, the general would have surely told me so. This means that you must be—"

"No, he's not dead," Stanton chuckled behind her. "He's as free as you are, Marilla. I just thought I'd have a little fun with you by not telling you right away. It was nice to see you tormented for even a moment, since you've caused so much torment for me."

His eyes wavered. "Seems the murder weapon was found in your well, just as you said," he said blandly. "I came to the conclusion that you wouldn't have told me it was there if it was Kohanah's. It had to be Jason's. So we've got all of our soldiers on the lookout for him, for it seems he's taken to hiding these days."

He clasped his hands tightly behind him and squared his shoulders. "Seems your trip to Washington was a waste of time, for I set Kohanah free way before receiving the President's wire," he bragged.

Marilla's insides grew numbly cold. Slowly her fingers left the bars. Slowly she turned and faced Stanton, fighting the urge to slap him, for causing her even a moment of grief over having thought that Kohanah was dead. She wiped a tear from her cheek.

"You are cruel . . . evil . . . deranged!" she whispered harshly, then stomped away from him.

Taking the horse and buggy that had brought her from

the railhead, she drove away from the fort. She snapped
the reins against the horse, riding hard along the winding,
snakelike road that had been burned into the ground by the
horses and the sun, angry tears again stinging her cheeks.

The whipping wind jerked her bonnet from her head.
The satin bow beneath her chin came untied, sending the
bonnet flying in the air behind her. Her loosened and
flowing golden hair fluttered and shimmered about her
face, along her shoulders, and down her back. She was
finding it hard to get over the anger and humiliation caused
by the general, yet the part of her that, oh, so dearly loved
Kohanah was telling her that she should be happy! Kohanah
was free! No matter how, Kohanah was free! And she
would be with him *soon*. There was so much to say to him
. . . so much to *share*.

The scattering of tipis ahead made Marilla's pulse race.
Squinting her eyes, she sorted through them and found
Kohanah's. She could see smoke spiraling lazily from the
smoke hole and knew that he must be there, or not so far
away that he would not return soon, to discover her there.
But she would hope and pray that he was there so that she
would not have to wait another moment to touch him, to
kiss him, to see for herself that he hadn't been harmed
while in the custody of the deranged General Stanton.

A lone horseman in the distance, standing on a slight
butte overlooking the Indian village, caught Marilla's attention. A thrilling sort of sensation swept through her,
beginning at her toes, settling inside her pounding heart.
She would have known Kohanah anywhere. It was *his*
handsomeness silhouetted against the blue sky of May. It
was as though he was in some sort of deep thought,
meditating, or pondering over the fate of his people.

Snapping the reins, guiding the buggy away from the
dusty road, Marilla headed toward Kohanah. When his
head turned and he saw her heading toward him, he blinked
his eyes nervously, making sure she wasn't an apparition,
then thrust his heels into the flanks of his horse and rode
toward her.

Meeting him halfway, Marilla jumped from the buggy
just as Kohanah swung himself out of his saddle. As they

embraced, Kohanah's lips bore down upon Marilla's, kissing her long and sweet, her pliant body leaning into his, silently beckoning.

Leaning away from her, framing her face between his hands, Kohanah looked down at her, absorbing her nearness. "You have returned," he said thickly. "Kohanah thought he had lost you forever!"

He jerked away from her and went to the buggy and searched it, then turned around, frowning at Marilla, folding his arms across his massive bare chest.

"Never do you have to worry about losing me!" Marilla said firmly. "How could you doubt me so much? I would never part from you but for only a short while. Kohanah, you are my life . . . my *soul*. My every heartbeat is *yours*. I thought I had proved this to you. Over and *over* again."

"Kohanah has reason to doubt anyone whose skin is white," he growled. "Even you, Tsonda."

Marilla was taken aback by such a confession. She thought that she had gained so much trust from him, but now she discovered that she hadn't. What was she to think? To do? Wouldn't he ever feel free to trust even her?

Shaking herself out of her stunned state, knowing that Kohanah had gone through so much at the hands of the white man, she refrained from confronting him with how he so little trusted her. In his eyes, trust was to be earned. Though she thought she had earned his trust, in his eyes she had not.

Well, she would not stop now. She would fight to the bitter end until he could see how wrong he was *not* to trust her.

"I have so much to tell you," she said, beaming up at him with smiling eyes, forcing herself, yes, to forget his hurtful words! "Let us go to your tipi. Let me tell you so much that will make your heart sing!"

Kohanah's hands went to her shoulders. His fingers dug into her flesh, hurting her. She paled as he glared down at her. "Tsonda, my trust in you is lacking totally," he said stiffly, glancing over his shoulder at the buggy.

Marilla paled, puzzled by how he had gotten so cold toward her after searching the buggy. "Kohanah, what's the matter?'' she asked shallowly. ''Why are you behaving like this?''

''*Manyi*, you return, but not Kohanah's *paintings*,'' Kohanah said, his lower lip thrust out in an angry pout. ''You took them away but did not bring them back. Why is that?''

A wondrous sort of relief flooded Marilla's senses, now understanding all of Kohanah's reservations about her today. He surely thought that she had appropriated the paintings and was not going to give them back to him! He could not know that they were in New York, safely in her father's possession.

A burst of joy caused her to wriggle from his grasp. She then flung herself into his arms. ''Oh, Kohanah, there for a moment I thought you didn't trust me at all,'' she said, hugging him tightly to her. ''But now I understand! I totally understand. It's because of the paintings!''

She realized that he did not return the affection. He was standing stiffly, ignoring her show of love and devotion to him.

Shakily, she stepped back away from him. Her eyes wavered as she looked up at him, his face dark with a frown. ''Darling, do not fret so over your precious paintings,'' she said softly. ''They are safe. I did not bring them back with me because I did not know that you had been freed from your imprisonment. I could not risk having them confiscated by General Stanton, now, could I? My father has them with him in New York. Kohanah, they could be no safer than with him. You know that. All we need to do is wire him. He said that he would deliver them to you, personally. He is anxious to see you again. He admires you so, Kohanah. Surely you know that.''

Kohanah's eyes softened, his tight jaw loosened, his heartbeat was consuming him. He looked at Marilla as though he were seeing her that first time three years ago. She was as lovely . . . as desirable . . . as sincere, as then. His heart pained him for having doubted her and for knowing that he had caused her pain, for revealing his doubt!

Swiftly drawing her into his arms, he hugged her, breathing in the sweet scent of her as he leaned his nose into the depths of her golden hair. "Tsonda," he whispered, his breath hot on her ear. "My *manyi*, woman, let's go home. Words are not enough to express my feelings for you at this moment. Let's . . . go home."

Tears burned at the corners of Marilla's eyes; she was so happy, so filled with a sweet passion for the man she loved. And he had asked her to go home with him, as though she *belonged* there . . . as though she were a part of that home. She must make it true! She must persuade him to marry her, to prove so much to so many!

Especially to herself. Only by marrying her would Kohanah prove his devotion . . . his commitment *to* her. She had already proved hers to him. . . .

Wrapping her arms about his neck, Marilla snuggled against Kohanah as he carried her to her buggy and placed her gently on the seat. While he attached his horse to the buggy, she watched his movements, his litheness. Wearing only a loincloth, he looked savage and wild. A thrill coursed through her, loving him so much, having never feared that wild side of him.

She adored him, so adored him. . . .

Twenty-Four

❦

Kohanah carried Marilla into his tipi, then stood her before him. His eyes warm and passion-filled, he watched her as she unsnapped her dress and eased it slowly from her shoulders, revealing her heaving bosom. Held captive by his gaze, Marilla lowered her dress on down away from her and stepped out of it, then removed her lacy petticoat and silken undergarments. She was under his spell. Everything that she had to tell him would wait. It seemed that he wanted her more than anything else at this moment.

This gave her hope . . . hope that perhaps she was more important to him than he had ever voiced aloud. Always before it had been his people who came first. Of course, they surely still did. Only now, during this precious moment of togetherness, *she* was of prime importance in his heart, mind, and soul.

She would savor this, keep it close to her heart. . . .

Now only a nude silken body standing before Kohanah, she trembled and sucked in her breath when he reached for her and his palms moved seductively over her. Her body was yearning for him. She was hungering to be kissed . . . to be taken to paradise with him again. It seemed like so long ago since they had been together in such a way. That they were *now* seemed to be a miracle, after all that had happened.

Sometimes small miracles *did* happen, to fulfill destiny's biddings!

Kohanah's fingers ran down Marilla's body, caressing her, making her shiver. His fingers moved purposefully slowly, taunting her . . . teasing her . . . stroking her fiery flesh. Marilla's sensations were searing. She closed her eyes and moaned sensually when she felt his hands being replaced by the feather-light touches of his lips.

First he kissed the softness of her neck as she held her head back so that her hair tumbled long and free down her back. He kissed her with a soft brush of a kiss on her lips. Then she felt the gentle nip of his lips on her breast while his tongue flicked and tasted of the budding globe, swelling with arousing sensations.

And then with exquisite tenderness he fell to one knee before her, his lips drugging her while his hands parted her slim white thighs and he found her pulsing love mound and caressed it with his tongue, then suckled on it, like a baby feeding from a mother's breast.

Her heartbeats almost consuming her, his loving her this way sheer torture to her brain, causing her to soar with pleasure, Marilla twined her fingers through his hair and sighed shakily. When a soft explosion flooded her senses with delight, and her body trembled, she let the ecstasy take hold of her, only coming back to reality when Kohanah eased her down onto a pallet of furs beside the fire pit.

The fire was now only a few sparkling embers, casting off a bare amount of golden light onto Kohanah's handsome coppery face. As he gazed down at her, his dark eyes were fathomless, his body hard upon hers as he mounted her. Somewhere between sending her into a plateau of wondrous feelings and bringing her back down to earth, he had removed his loincloth and she could feel his hardness probing between her thighs, where she still throbbed from his skill at making her body become so foreign to her.

She drifted toward him and laced her arms about his neck, intoxicated by his nearness. She trembled with readiness as he drove swiftly into her, causing her to arch upward and cry out as their bodies began to move in rapture's rhythm. Her body, pliant and willing, absorbed the bold thrusting, his body hardening and tightening with his each and every stroke within her.

Clinging to his sinewed shoulders, feeling his flat belly against hers, their bodies straining together hungrily, Marilla sank into a chasm of desire when his lips bore down upon hers, claiming her mouth, his kiss hot and demanding. With quiet, eager fingers he found her breasts and kneaded them, causing the nipples to tighten against the coarseness of his flesh.

Marilla's hands could not keep still. She wanted to touch him all over. The hours and days away from him only made her want of him become more intense. She felt as though she could never get enough of him . . . a hunger that needed to be continually fed, it seemed.

Her fingers trembled as they traveled over the wide expanse of his hairless, copper chest, over his flat, firm stomach, across his narrow hips. Then she let them stray lower, to get a brief touch of his manhood each time he left her with his in and out thrusts.

She coiled her fingers through his pubic hair, then circled her hands on around and splayed them onto his hard, muscled buttocks. She rode with him. She sighed. She parted her lips and let his tongue enter her mouth and probe.

As he grew feverish, his body plunging more determinedly into hers, Marilla strove to take a deep breath when his lips lowered to press into the passion-swollen lobe of her breast. She could feel his pleasure blending with hers. In a matter of moments, they would be catapulted together into another world . . . perhaps even another time.

Who was to say where one's soul traveled at that moment of wondrous bliss sought and found within the arms of the one you loved . . . ? Marilla had felt separated from herself each time she had experienced the ultimate of pleasure with Kohanah.

So who *could* say . . . ?

Kohanah's body hardened and tightened, awaiting that surge of passion so familiar to him while within the arms of his *manyi*. He tasted of the sweetness of her breast, his fingers exploring her silken flesh, never getting enough of her softness . . . that which could only be compared to what a cloud must feel like.

At this moment he felt as if he were riding on a cloud, soaring . . . climbing higher into the heavens, the wonders of his woman limitless!

Ho, yes, she was his woman. This time when she was gone from him he had realized more than ever the importance of having her with him. He could not exist without her. He was only half a man without her.

"Become my wife," Kohanah whispered into her ear, pausing in his strokes. "Tsonda, become my wife soon?"

Marilla's eyes opened quickly. She gazed up at Kohanah in wonder, the question coming so abruptly . . . at such a time as this. But did it not seem appropriate? They were proving their total devotion to each other in a way that only two people in love knew how. And he was proving to her just how important she was to him!

Oh, how long she had waited for this!

Ever since Florida, she had waited. . . .

Smoothing a dark strand of hair back from Kohanah's sweating brow, Marilla smiled up at him, tears sparkling in the corners of her eyes. "Yes, Kohanah," she murmured. "We should be married. *Soon*."

She cast her eyes downward, then slowly looked back up at him. "But, Kohanah, can we wait long enough for father to come from New York to be with us?" she said softly. "He would want to be a part of the wedding ceremony. In the white man's culture, the father gives his daughter away. My father would be so proud to give me away to you."

Kohanah brushed a gentle kiss across Marilla's lips. "Kohanah can wait *if* your father can arrive *soon*," he said huskily. "You will ask him to come *soon*?"

"*Ho*, yes," Marilla whispered, trembling with ecstasy. "Soon. I shall wire him even today. My father will be so pleased, Kohanah. So . . . pleased."

She cupped his cheek in the palm of her hand. "Oh, Kohanah, *I* am so pleased," she sighed. "Even today I was thinking that it would be so wonderful if . . . if we could be wed. It means so much to me that you asked me. It *proves* so much to me."

Kohanah kissed the sweet softness of her neck. "You have proved so much to *me*," he said huskily. "It was time for Kohanah to make a commitment . . . a total commitment to you. It is done. Now life will be easier."

He drew a fraction away from her and looked down into her eyes. "It will be easier, Tsonda, because nothing will separate us again," he said determinedly. "Once we are man and wife, everything will fall into place. You will see."

"I hope so," Marilla whispered. Drawing his lips to hers, she softly kissed him. "Oh, how I hope so."

Fragments of what she had been anxious to tell him . . . about the buffalo, about the permission to perform the Sun Dance without fear of confrontation from the soldiers . . . bubbled inside her brain, then faded away to the far recesses when Kohanah began his wondrous strokes inside her again.

She clung to him, his lips once again drugging her as he kissed her with fire. The explosion of rapture came in what seemed a burst of sunshine spreading its melting warmth throughout her. She trembled and arched, crying out softly against Kohanah's lips as she felt his body harden, then quiver in passion's grip along with her . . . the release so gratifying, so joyous.

It was so beautiful . . . so right. . . .

Embracing, wishing the moment would never end, Marilla kissed Kohanah's perspiration-laced brow, then sighed as he rolled away from her and then drew her next to him, holding her gently within his muscled arms. "My *manyi*," he whispered, still reeling from the pleasure he had found within her arms. "My *manyi*."

Now down from her cloud of rapture, Marilla knew that it was time to share so much with Kohanah other than passionate embraces and kisses. She moved to her knees and straddled him as he lay on his back. She leaned down over him, letting her breasts dangle against his chest, her hands on his cheeks, directing his eyes up, to look into hers.

"Kohanah, wait until you hear all of the good news that I have brought to you," she said, smiling down at him. "You will be so glad . . . so happy!"

"That you are here makes me happy," Kohanah said, placing his hands over hers, drawing them to his chest, holding them. "At this moment, nothing could take the place of the happiness I feel for being with you and for knowing that it is time for you to become my wife and that you accepted. Tsonda, you jest when you say you have more good news for this Kiowa."

"If I told you that the President has given you permission to perform the Sun Dance without interference from the soldiers, would that not make you just as happy?" Marilla teased, watching his expression change to that of wonder. "If I told you that the President said he would somehow manage to ship a buffalo bull to you for use *in* the Sun Dance, would that not make you just as happy?"

Kohanah's face became suddenly shadowed with a frown. He eased Marilla away from him and rose to his feet. In one jerk he had his loincloth on. He moved to his haunches before the fire pit and began to stir the dying embers with a stick.

Marilla's insides grew cold when she saw his withdrawn attitude and heard his silence. He should be ecstatic, yet he seemed less than glad over what had been revealed to him.

Why? Oh, why would he not be happy over the good news?

Slipping into her petticoat, Marilla went to Kohanah and knelt beside him. She pleaded up at him with her eyes. "Kohanah, what's wrong?" she said dryly. "What did I say that disturbs you? I thought I had brought you nothing but wonderful news. What don't you agree with?"

Kohanah weighed his thoughts carefully, again finding himself not trusting the white man. So often they spoke with a forked tongue. This man who was called President of the white man surely would not change his attitude this quickly. It did not fit the scheme of things in the place called Washington!

"You will see that neither of these promises will be kept," he finally said in a low growl, slowly turning his gaze to Marilla. "He will again ask first for Kohanah's paintings. Did he not demand them when you were there, bargaining with him? Tell me, Tsonda, that he did not ask for my paintings, then Kohanah just might believe that there is a grain of truth in what he has promised!"

A warning shot through Marilla, recalling the President's interest in the one painting. Should she tell Kohanah? Yes, she must, to make him know that the painting was requested but had not been a part of the bargain!

"Your paintings were discussed," Marilla said, placing her hands nervously on her lap. "But believe me, Kohanah, the President does not require them to do as he promised."

She cleared her throat and momentarily lowered her eyes, hoping that she could make him understand exactly what the President had said, and why. . . .

"Darling," she blurted, quickly raising her eyes, seeing that he was watching her carefully. "The President did not demand anything. But he *did* request that you consider selling him one of your paintings. It was only a request, Kohanah."

"The one on buffalo hide?" Kohanah said blandly. "It is the one he wanted when he was here."

"There is a reason for that," Marilla said, guarding her words. "I believe you already know what that reason is. The painting shows atrocities against the Kiowa at the hands of the soldiers. The President doesn't want anyone in the future to see the painting . . . to use it to stir up trouble between the Kiowa and the white community. Kohanah, I see the reasoning behind this. Surely you do, also. And if the President is so kind to do so much for you, surely you can consider doing this one thing for him."

"I haven't seen anything yet that he has done for Kohanah!" he growled, flailing a hand in the air, frustrated.

"Kohanah, though you were set free by General Stanton, the President did not know that and had me hand-

deliver a letter to Stanton ordering him to release you!''
she said anxiously. "I saw the letter. I read it. He did
order your release. Is that not proof that he has only
kindness in his heart for you?"

"He only wants the painting," Kohanah said dryly.
"That is his only reason for displaying friendship to a
Kiowa chief! Nothing more."

His eyes grew cold and dispassionate. "Do not say any
more to me about this," he said, his voice devoid of
emotion. "This is not the time. Marilla, time will tell
whether or not what you say and think is true. Until then,
let us not talk of it anymore."

Marilla leaned over him and moved into his arms. She
placed her cheek against his chest, hearing the nervous
beating of his heart. "Oh, Kohanah, I am so sorry that I
have said anything that made you unhappy," she murmured. "I truly thought that I had brought good tidings
. . . not bad. Forgive me?"

Slowly Kohanah twined his arms about her waist, then
lowered her back down onto the pallet of furs. "Forgive?"
he said huskily. "There is nothing to forgive. Again you
thought you were helping Kohanah. Again Kohanah disap-
points you by being cold and distant. Kohanah is sorry. Do
you forgive Kohanah?"

Marilla traced the sensual outline of his lips, knowing
that it did not matter how he felt about the President at this
moment, for very soon he would discover that he was
wrong and would admire President Hayes just as much as
she had learned to.

Until then, though, she would try her hardest to make
Kohanah happy with life. She would love him so much
that he would not have time to ponder his losses and
sadnesses! She would draw all unhappiness from him with
the power of her kisses and embraces!

"Forgive?" she whispered, brushing his lips with a soft
kiss. "Darling, I will always grant you forgiveness for
anything . . . anything. Please love me again. Let us
forget that apologies were even required between us today.
Just love me."

Kohanah slipped her petticoat down over her hips. His

fingers enwrapped her breasts, his lips on fire with her kiss. . . .

Jason Roark lay upon the ground on the slight rise that overlooked the Kiowa village. He had seen Marilla's arrival. He had known that if he waited long enough she would return to Kohanah.

But now he would have to bide his time until she was alone.

Or, better yet, perhaps there were ways to disillusion Kohanah about life again . . . disillusion him about Marilla.

But what could he do to torment the man . . . torment him enough to give up and send Marilla away forever?

Looking cautiously from side to side, always on the watch for the soldiers who he knew were scouring the land for him, he decided it was best to go back into hiding.

But the damn cave that he had found was getting more cramped each day, having to share it with his damn horse and any other critter that managed to crawl into it.

He shivered when he thought of the many long, fuzzy-legged tarantulas that he had killed. If one ever managed to get on him, he would more than likely have a heart attack from fright!

Going to his horse, he swung himself up into the saddle. Riding low, he slapped the reins against his horse and sank his heels into its flanks, living for the day when he would get his vengeance.

First Kohanah, then Marilla.

Or should it be first Marilla, then Kohanah . . . ?

A crooked smile creased his dust-laden, whiskered face. . . .

Twenty-Five

❧ ❦

A drum made of a heavy iron kettle, half filled with water, with a piece of cooked buckskin stretched across the top and tightly tied in place, beat in a steady rhythm outside Kohanah's tipi. Within the tipi a marriage between Kohanah and Marilla was being blessed and celebrated. . . .

Dressed in a fine buckskin dress, decorated with elk's teeth and beadwork, her hair worn in two long braids down her back, Marilla sat proudly beside Kohanah, already his bride, but there were rituals that had to be performed now, and later, to confirm the joining of hearts and hands.

Marilla looked across the blazing fire at her father who had arrived safely with Kohanah's paintings. In his blue eyes she could see traces of tears. She knew that the tears were from happiness, for he had given her and Kohanah his blessing as soon as the wedding ceremony was over.

It had taken two weeks for Marilla's father to set things right in his law office before getting away to come to the wedding. In those two weeks a new keeper of the Taime had been appointed and Marilla had begun teaching the Indian children, but not without Kiowa braves guarding her from somewhere close by at all times. Word had been received that Jason Roark had been seen in the area. She hoped and prayed that the soldiers would find him soon, so that she would not have to be always accompanied by Kiowa braves wherever she went.

Thus far Jason Roark had even eluded the Kiowa. But it was as though he was always somewhere close by, watching, yet not close enough to be seen or tracked. He was probably viewing the excitement in the village this day, hating Kohanah even more for having won Marilla!

Marilla glanced over at Kohanah, so proud of finally having won *him* for *herself*. This day he looked the epitome of handsomeness, stealing Marilla's heart away anew. She absorbed him fully with her eyes, her heart racing, so joyous over being his wife.

Fat had been rubbed into his dark hair. Then his hair had been wound into long, thick braids wrapped in otter skin, his fancy headdress of many colorful feathers then slipped into place on his head. His dark, deep-set eyes were bright and proud. He looked dignified in his fringed shirt, leggings, and moccasins.

Holding his chin firmly high, his arms folded across his chest, Kohanah looked straight ahead, over the heads of his people who were sitting around the fire, waiting for the celebration to continue in his tipi. It was his and Marilla's hour, but his people's, also, for their chief had chosen a woman . . . a woman who had already demonstrated to the Kiowa her commitment *to* them.

It did not matter at all that her skin was white, her hair golden, her eyes blue. . . .

Knowing this touched Marilla, deeply.

Marilla turned her attention from Kohanah to look elsewhere, wanting to learn from this day all that she could, so that in the future she would know how to behave at other weddings and ceremonies.

An old woman was tending to the food cooking over the fire, while another elderly woman prepared food that did not have to be cooked. There was to be a feast following a brief ceremony under the direction of the shaman of the village.

Marilla had been told earlier about the food that was to

be served so that what she was observing wasn't all that
new to her. She had been taught by one of these elderly
women that the meat of a cow had been sliced thin and
hung up to dry in the sun. That way it had been preserved
for the winter and then put into a bag made of hide. The
bones of the cow had been broken up and boiled to get the
grease out. This grease had been put into a bag made of a
cow's udder, which had a buckskin drawstring.

The meat from the animal had been cooked and dried.
The large intestines had been stuffed with a long piece of
raw meat, the whole thing then boiled, ready for eating.

Wild grapes had been gathered in the fall, boiled, and
mixed with a little flour and made into balls. They had
been put into a skin bag. A berry called "rock sour" had
been dried and preserved.

Marilla had been taught that dried meat and fruit were
served at every meal. She looked down at the prairie
chicken eggs being prepared on a wooden platter today,
already boiled hard. A rabbit was roasting on the coals in
the firepit. Over the fire was corn, boiling together with
tongue.

A favorite food of the Kiowa was now also being placed
on wooden platters. It consisted of ground meat and mar-
row mixed with sugar.

One thing in particular that Marilla recalled was that the
Kiowa, who had a lot of pounded meat, were considered
well off. . . .

The shaman, elderly and thin, his face marred by pock-
marks and dark circles beneath his eyes, his hair wiry and
long hanging across his thin, bent shoulders, stood up in
the tipi and worked his way to the fire. He held four cow
hoof rattles in his hands. After holding them down close to
the fire until they began to smoke, he motioned for four
young braves to step forth.

One by one he handed the boys the rattles, then sent
them away again, so that they were standing behind the
circle of guests in Kohanah's tipi, all of whom were
elderly, because respect was paid to the aged . . . age
being a sign of experience and wisdom to the Kiowa.

The younger generation of Kiowa were seated outside

the tipi, except for the four young men who had just begun to sing and chant to the accompaniment of their shaking rattles and the drum that beat at a steadier pace outside the dwelling.

The shaman, noted for his curative abilities and skill in clairvoyant forecasting of events, who enjoyed the acclaim and patronage of his fellow tribesmen, began praying to Nuakoiahe, the One Who Made the Earth. He prayed that Kohanah and Marilla would be happy and would be blessed with many children. He prayed that Kohanah and his woman would receive comfort and the power and love of the Great Spirit!

When the shaman ceased speaking and sat down behind Kohanah, the other Kiowa joined in with singing and chanting, while the old woman in charge of cooking began dipping food out with a buffalo horn spoon into bowls made of turtle shells. These fowls were offered to those who had been invited to sit inside the tipi with the new bride and bridegroom. Bowls of ordinary wood filled with food were taken to those who sat outside.

And then the feast began with a more relaxed atmosphere. Marilla ate heartily. She was gloriously happy, yet she dreaded the ritual that awaited her . . . one that she would share with Kohanah. It was not the ordinary custom of the Kiowa during the wedding celebration, but one that Kohanah had requested of her, personally.

Marilla could not help but believe that he was testing her, to see if she would accept all the ways of the Kiowa.

Yet maybe not. It did not seem right that he would marry her and *then* test her!

Darkness had fallen over the land like a soft black velveteen cloak. While torches made of bundles of grass burned into the early evening hours close beside a stream, Marilla walked alongside Kohanah, carrying bark from a cottonwood tree. This bark was carried inside a small framework of bent willow twigs, covered over thickly with blankets.

"Place the bark in the center of the dwelling, but make sure it does not fall into the pit dug in the ground,"

Kohanah said thickly while carrying rocks. "On this bark
I shall place the rocks."

Marilla did as she was told, not wanting to make any
mistakes. Though Kohanah had already accepted her as
she was, it was best to impress him with what she could
be.

After the rocks were placed on the cottonwood bark and
the bark was lit with one of the torches, Kohanah stirred
the rocks around inside the flaming bark, heating them. He
then carried in a pile of dried horse manure and let it begin
also burning.

"It is time to undress," Kohanah softly commanded.
"Kohanah will undress you . . . you will undress Kohanah."

Trembling, looking down at the layer of willow twigs
spread out on the floor, on which they would lie, then
looking at the cottonwood bark burning so close beside it,
Marilla worried about fire consuming the small cubicle
with her and Kohanah in it!

But the purpose of this ritual was to steam their bodies,
to cleanse them of all impurities, so that the wedding night
would begin their life together with absolute purity. Marilla
had to assume that Kohanah knew enough about the steaming ritual to keep them safe, as they were supposed to be
pure once the ceremony was completed.

Letting herself forget everything but that which Kohanah
demanded of her, Marilla looked up into his dark eyes as
he drew the buckskin dress over her head, leaving her
quickly nude.

In turn, she undressed him. Seeing him so tall, lithe,
and powerfully built awakened all the desires anew inside
her. It would be hard to lie next to him nude and not crawl
into his arms to make love with him. She would have to
will herself not to reach out and touch him. As far as she
knew, loving him would come later, after this final ritual
was completed.

"Lie down, Tsonda," Kohanah said softly.

Silently obeying, Marilla moved to her knees onto the
willow branches, then stretched out beside the blazing
fire, feeling the intensity of the heat that had penetrated the
scattering of rocks. She watched as Kohanah left the tiny

dwelling, then returned with a container of water, lodging it in the pit that was encircled by the fire.

With a stick, Kohanah pushed several of the red-hot rocks into the container of water, then stirred the fire about it, making the flames grow higher. He left and returned again with another container of water and used a buffalo horn to dip water and pour it on the remaining hot rocks in the pit.

Marilla began sweating. She wiped perspiration from beneath her nose and across her brow. She welcomed Kohanah at her side, seeing his body slick and glistening with perspiration.

Her heart began to pound the hotter she got. She began to squirm in her uneasiness, then melted inside when Kohanah began gliding his fingers over her in a light caress.

Though uncomfortable and tortured by the heat that was enveloping her, Marilla could not deny the wondrous feelings that Kohanah was awakening inside her as his fingers continued to touch and torment the most vulnerable points of pleasure on her body.

When he began to caress her love mound, she tried not to squirm, knowing that was surely what was expected of her. She bit her lower lip, willing herself not to cry out when she felt the pressure building inside her . . . like something uncoiling, the rapture spreading like wildfire.

And then Kohanah's hands moved away from her. He stood up and beckoned to her with an outstretched hand. "Come. It is time to leave steaming behind," he said huskily. "It is now time to bathe. After bathing we will make love. The Great Spirit has blessed our union. Everything between us will forever be good!"

Taking his hand, Marilla rose to her feet. When they stepped from the small dwelling, the light from the torches revealed just how red Kohanah's body had become from the sweltering heat.

She glanced down at her own body, gasping when she saw that she looked as though she had been boiled alive!

She welcomed the water as Kohanah led her into the stream. Enclosed in the dense overhanging growth of the banks, the current was slow and the water seemed to be standing still. But it was cold!

Though its cooling effect was for a moment a shock to her system, Marilla's body quickly adjusted to the temperature change. She splashed all of the perspiration off her body, then once again became catapulted into a world of bliss and joy when Kohanah moved to stand behind her, pressing his body to hers. She could feel the readiness of his manhood, hard and probing between her thighs. She quivered with passion as his hands crept around and cupped both of her breasts, his thumbs circling her nipples, causing them to harden against them.

"Kohanah, should we . . . here . . . ?" she whispered, looking cautiously around her. "What if someone is watching?" Though it was dark and the village was nowhere close by, she could never forget Jason Roark. He could be watching even *now*!

"Complete privacy is ours," Kohanah said huskily, moving around, before her. He lifted her up into his arms and began carrying her from the water. "My braves are posted. They will not allow anyone near us. It is time for us. Only us."

"Do your braves always follow your commands so dutifully?" Marilla asked as Kohanah eased her to the ground beside the water.

"All of my people are dutiful," Kohanah said, positioning himself over her. He touched the core of her womanhood with his ready hardness and began to softly probe. "My *manyi*, woman, even you?"

Marilla opened her legs, surrendering her all to him. She gasped and closed her eyes in pleasure as he entered her in one maddening thrust. "Yes, even I," she whispered, twining her arms about his neck, her legs about his waist.

Caught up in sheer rapture, Marilla began to ride with Kohanah, arching to meet his every thrust. It was hard for her to believe that from this night forth they would be together, sharing rapture's dream every waking hour of their life!

How wonderful it would be to awaken with Kohanah's

kisses and embraces! Marilla would close each day with his lovemaking!

Could it truly be real? She had waited so long.

Could . . . it truly be real . . . ?

Kohanah's thick, husky groan, mingled with Marilla's soft cry of passion, showed her just how real it was. His lips came to hers in a meltingly hot kiss as their bodies tangled upon the thick cushion of grass along the ground. His buttocks moved rhythmically, his hands fired her as they moved across her willing, pliant body.

Kohanah's fingers then moved to her shoulders and bit into her flesh. His kisses bruised her lips while wild ripples of desire spread and swelled, blotting out all sensations other than this warmth tingling throughout her.

Passions crested, then exploded. Bodies quaked and shook, then became still, perspiration once again shining on their bodies.

Marilla lay beneath Kohanah, breathing hard, spent. Yet as always before, she could not keep her hands still. She smoothed them over him, feeling him, relishing in his closeness.

Her husband! He was . . . her husband! It was a fantasy come true for her. Never did she want anything to get in the way of their happiness again. Never!

Kohanah rolled away from her, his chest heaving. He took Marilla's hand and placed it above his heart. "Do you see what you do to me, Tsonda?" he said, chuckling low. "You make me defenseless against my enemies! My heart has been weakened by your lovemaking!"

Marilla felt the throbbing of his heart and then, when he released her hand, scooted over to him and snuggled next to him, fitting her body into the curve of his. She felt more content now than ever in her life.

But his mention of the word "enemy" was cause for her to be catapulted once more into the real world.

"Darling, I don't like to think that you have any enemies," she murmured, looking up at him, the light from the torches playing along the sculpted lines of his face. "Now that General Stanton is gone, perhaps things will be much easier for you and your people. The new commander at Fort Cobb has a reputation of being more understanding.''

Kohanah snuggled her closer. "I hope you are right," he said in a low growl. "For tomorrow Kohanah and his braves will test that theory!''

Marilla's insides splashed cold. She eased away from Kohanah and moved to her knees. She looked down at him, her eyes wavering. "Darling, what do you mean?'' she asked softly. "What are you and your braves planning to do tomorrow?''

"It is time for the Sun Dance. It cannot be delayed for much longer," he said softly. "The President you spoke so fondly of has not sent the buffalo bull he promised. Kohanah must leave the reservation and search again for a buffalo for the Sun Dance ritual! If soldiers try to interfere, Kohanah will have to retaliate.''

Marilla tensed, hearing the venom in his voice. "Please don't do anything hasty," she pleaded, taking his hands, clasping them hard. "Give it a while longer. Shipping a buffalo to you is not all that simple, Kohanah. I am even surprised the President saw fit to! But he did promise and he is a man of his word!''

Kohanah moved to his feet, looking into the heavens at the milky streak of stars overhead. "Time does not wait for the Kiowa's need of the Sun Dance," he growled. "Kohanah will do what must be done *now*." He turned his eyes to Marilla. "Say no more, Tsonda. The hunt begins at dawn tomorrow!''

Marilla flinched beneath his commanding tone and then, not wanting this to spoil their wedding day and night, crept to her feet and went to Kohanah to slip into his arms. She melted into him as he hugged her.

"Kohanah, I understand," she murmured. "I will say no more. Please don't *you* object when I tell you that I am going to accompany you on this mission. I must, for if not, I would die a million deaths inside while awaiting your return.''

Kohanah placed his nose within the golden tendrils of her hair. "If you wish, you are welcome," he whispered. "It is good that you want to be at my side, even during time of sorrow, for sorrow *will* be the emotion I carry with me while searching for buffalo. If none is found . . .''

Marilla felt his pain, but held within her heart the hope that the President would get the promised buffalo bull to Kohanah before trouble arose between Kohanah and the new commander at Fort Cobb.

But it was obvious no buffalo would arrive before Kohanah's planned departure. The sunrise would come way before the next train from Washington. . . .

Twenty-Six

❧❧❧

The rising sun was sending its gilding rays over the land, giving life and light. Marilla's wedding gift from Kohanah, a cream-colored palomino, was moving at a short, choppy trot through the village alongside Kohanah's red roan. A silent figure standing beside an outdoor fire next to a fancily painted tipi drew Marilla's attention. An elderly and lean Kiowa warrior, with long gray braids and with zigzags of paint across his wrinkled face, was impressive in his age and bearing.

Seeing how his outspread arms were raised toward the heavens, praying aloud to the rising sun, a shiver coursed along Marilla's flesh. The elderly man's voice was loud and penetrating, traveling from the village, on across the land, along the rolling grasses. He was an arrowmaker for the village, performing his early morning ritual.

As Marilla rode on past him, she glanced over her shoulder and watched as the arrowmaker sat down beside his outdoor fire. His bent and knotted fingers began his dedicated daily chore of making arrows . . . old men being the best arrowmakers, for they could bring time and patience to their craft.

Marilla had been told that throughout the history of the

Kiowa, fighters and hunters had always been willing to
pay a high price for arrows that were made well. If an
arrow *was* well made, it would have tooth marks upon it,
having been straightened with the arrowmaker's teeth, the
arrow then drawn to the bow to see if it was straight.

As she rode on past the Indian and through the village,
traveling away from it, Marilla was caught up in the
mystique of all that she was learning about Kohanah and
his people. Just prior to their leaving his tipi, she had
silently witnessed *him* praying to a sacred fetish that he
had referred to as a "worship," a "medicine bundle."

Wanting her to understand everything about him, Kohanah
had explained softly to her that his medicine bundle had
been passed down in his family from generation to generation. It was a small bundle covered with leather on the
outside. Inside were small bits of cloth and leather and
pictographic representations of the myths of the origin of
the Kiowa.

Treating the bundle with awe and reverence, Kohanah
had then prayed over it, taking a piece of cloth and covering the bundle as he prayed, not praying to the bundle
itself, but to the power.

Marilla had knelt at Kohanah's side, trying to learn how
to participate in even this custom, touched deeply by the
reverence Kohanah had paid to the bundle, as he had
prayed softly for the power to find a buffalo today . . . and
for the safekeeping of his people, while he searched for
one. . . .

Loving the sheer adventure of being with Kohanah and
his braves this morning, the real lure of it, forcing from
her mind the dangers of the Kiowa traveling from the
reservation without permission from those in charge at Fort
Cobb, Marilla rode astride the beautiful palomino, once
again wearing the delicately soft buckskin dress that Kohanah
had given her to wear while she was a part of his village
and people.

High moccasins rose past her ankles, touching her skin
like soft butterflies' wings. Her hair was braided long and
golden down her back, a headband kept the hair at her
brow in place.

If not for her pale white skin, she even felt Kiowa this day!

Within her heart, she *was* becoming Kiowa, and she was proud!

Looking at the Kiowa braves on their steeds, Marilla was touched by how they were all so tall, straight, relaxed, and graceful with their classical features. Confidence was etched in the depths of their eyes and the set of their jaws, although each and every one of them knew that there was little to be confident or hopeful about.

As she slowly moved her gaze to Kohanah, Marilla's heart cried out to him, for if he did not find a buffalo today, what would he do? She silently prayed that President Hayes would keep his word! But *quickly*!

Kohanah wore the same determined look on his face, his long braids, tightened jaw, and bright deep-set eyes so very entirely dignified and imposing!

His attire was his usual buckskin outfit, but today he held a spear in his left hand, one that he had said was deadly and efficient. He had taken great care in its manufacture, especially in the shaping of the flint point, which was an extraordinary thing. A large flake, or chip, had been removed from its face, a groove that extended from the base nearly to the tip. Several hundred pounds of pressure, expertly applied, had been required to make the grooves.

The spear was beautiful as well as functional. Many of the minute chips along the edge of the weapon served no purpose but that of aesthetic satisfaction!

Riding with the skill of a man, the saddle leather groaning beneath her, the bridle bit rattling, Marilla focused her attention and eyes back on the terrain, ignoring the nervous snort of the palomino as she pressed her heels into its flanks, to keep up with Kohanah whose steed had ventured on just slightly ahead of her. Kohanah had told her that his horse was fast and easy riding and was afraid of nothing. When it was turned upon an enemy, it charged in a straight line and struck at full speed. Kohanah would have no need to even have a hand upon the rein. . . .

*   *   *

Kohanah rode tall in his saddle, seeing how the spring morning was so deep and beautiful, reminiscent of mornings long ago when he was a child accompanying his father on the buffalo hunt. Except for the lack of sightings of buffalo in every direction, it was now as it had been then. The whole face of the country was covered with a luxuriant growth of grass, giving a peculiar pleasure in its deep and soft greens, with occasional clusters of timber in a deeper green.

For only a brief moment Kohanah allowed feelings of melancholia to sweep over him, letting him remember one morning in particular of his childhood. . . .

Kohanah and his father and the accompanying Kiowa warriors had been riding along the edge of a small herd of buffalo. It was in the spring and many of the cows had newborn calves. Nearby, a calf was lying in the tall grass, red-orange in color, delicately beautiful with new life.

Kohanah had broken away from the warrior hunters to go to the calf, to gaze upon its innocent loveliness, when suddenly the mother buffalo was there with her great dark head low, and fearful looking. When she charged at Kohanah, he had fled for safety on his pony, for he had not been with the warriors that morning in the capacity of a hunter himself, but as one who would observe how it was done. Small boys were expected *not* to kill animals! They practiced with blunt arrows by shooting at birds, this considered a way for them to achieve marksmanship.

It had saddened Kohanah when his father had come to his rescue and had killed the mother buffalo, leaving the calf orphaned. That evening he could not enjoy feasting on the mother *or* the calf, for *both* had been taken in the buffalo hunt that day. . . .

At this moment, a buffalo of any size would be a welcome sight to Kohanah! The buffalo was the animal representation of the sun, the essential and sacrificial victim of the Sun Dance. In order to consummate the ancient sacrifice, the head of a buffalo bull should be impaled upon the medicine pole!

But across the land there were no buffalo grazing or wandering, only the bleached remains rotting in the wind, rain, and sun! There was such a stillness! It seemed to touch Kohanah all over with silent, clutching fingers, mocking even the reason he had been born to be a part of this earth . . .

A full day of travel without sighting even one buffalo was now behind the Kiowa travelers. Darkness had fallen. Stars pulsated overhead. Small campfires dotted the land where the Kiowa warriors had spread out, to keep vigil late into the night for signs of a lone buffalo. Marilla sat lazily beside Kohanah, her stomach full of roasted rabbit.

Loosening her braids, letting her hair tumble in a golden sheen about her shoulders, Marilla looked over at Kohanah, troubled. He had said scarcely a word since they had left the village. Though he had wanted her to accompany him on this venture, it was as though she were not there at all.

But she understood. Surely Kohanah's heart was bleeding, now knowing that once again the buffalo hunt had been in vain. Tomorrow would be no different from today. They would be heading back to the village, empty-handed! The wives and children would see that once again the hunters had not achieved their goal, and the braves would be shamed of their lack of prowess.

Knowing not what to do, whether to break the silence between her and the man she adored, or whether to reach out and touch him, to lend him her comfort, Marilla rose to her feet and spread a blanket. Though it was required for the men to stay awake, she did not see how she could. Her eyes burned with the need for sleep. Her whole body ached from the long hours in the saddle! Another day ahead of her of all of the same made her cringe!

Yet she wanted to look strong and willing in Kohanah's eyes. So much depended on her show of abilities during these early days of their marriage. For so long he had shunned the mention of marriage. She had to prove that he had been wrong to do this.

At all costs, she must prove her worth *to* him, totally!

Kohanah gazed over at Marilla as she stretched out on the blanket facing the fire, still fully clothed, looking the obedient squaw, except for her beautiful golden hair. The dancing light of the fire was casting weaving shadows on her gentle face and wide blue eyes. Her hair was soft and shining, her body supple and slender.

Marilla's full, ripe mouth tempted Kohanah, who knew that to kiss her lips would give him at least a moment's peace.

But he had to practice restraint and forget hungers of the flesh. This was a time set aside for his people, and Marilla was there only to learn *of* his people. . . .

Feeling Kohanah's eyes on her, Marilla smiled over at him. "My husband, do I show my lazy side to you?" she dared to ask, loving the sound of the words "my husband" on her lips. They belonged there, and would be, forever.

Kohanah stiffened, so wanting to lie down beside her, to draw her into his arms. He picked up a twig and began snapping it into minute pieces, forcing himself to stare into the fire instead of at Marilla.

"It is good that you are resting," he said blandly. "Tomorrow is another long day. We travel far to return to our village."

A frown creased Kohanah's brow. When his eyes wavered, something grabbed at Marilla's heart, for rarely had she seen his eyes show anything but strength.

This alone spoke of his sadness . . . his emptiness!

"It is good that summer comes soon," Kohanah said, trying not to think of the Sun Dance that should be performed just prior to summer. "The Kiowa are summer people. In the winter, they abide the cold and keep to themselves. But when seasons turn and land becomes warm and vital, they cannot hold still. An old love of roaming returns to them!"

Marilla moved to a sitting position. She clutched her arms about her legs, drawing her knees up before her. She was glad that Kohanah had chosen to talk, even though she knew that it was forced, to lighten the moment for her.

"I, too, have always loved summertime," she murmured. "Summers in New York were wonderful. The river beckoned, always! I knew where all of the beaches were. As a child I spent much time swimming."

"As a child, Kohanah spent much time in the water,

also," Kohanah said, once again catapulted back in time, at this moment, absorbing the memory into his heart and soul like some delicious sweet morsel to be tasted and relished. "My friends and I learned the skills of swimming together, alone. Those days when life was simple and free, I learned so many things of the land!"

Kohanah looked over his shoulder, where the sky and earth met as one in darkness. "The earth is the Kiowa's mother, the sky our father," he said thickly. "The Kiowa have always lived on the land. He has always taken his living from it. But he never destroyed it."

He turned his eyes back to the fire and tossed the broken twigs into it. "Kohanah loves the land," he said solemnly. "Kohanah sees that it is beautiful. But the land is quiet now. There are no more buffalo to sustain it in spirit, as it is the same for my people!"

Stifling a sob behind a hand, Marilla went to her knees before Kohanah. She cupped his face between her hands and lowered her lips to his. She brushed his mouth with a kiss.

"My darling, though this is a time of suffering and despair for you and your people, it surely will get better," she tried to reassure him. "It must!"

Taking her hands, lowering them from his face, Kohanah led Marilla back down onto the blanket and covered her up with another. "My woman, rest," he said softly. "You must have strength to continue with our journey tomorrow."

He bent down and kissed her, then went and again sat beside the fire, contemplating what tomorrow would bring to him and his people, and now to his *wife*. Marilla was his responsibility now, and from the bottom of his heart he knew that he did not have much to offer her.

Only love. At least he had enough of that to sustain her for a lifetime of embraces. . . .

Having been lulled to sleep by his weariness, Kohanah felt his heart quicken him back awake when from somewhere close by in the darkness he heard a blowing, a rumble of breath deeper than the wind. His pulse raced. He had heard the same exact sound many times while on the hunt for buffalo! Praying to the Great Spirit that he was awake and not in a dream wishing this to happen, Kohanah reached his hand shakily toward his spear.

Scarcely breathing he circled his fingers about the shaft and crept to his feet, careful not to arouse Marilla. This was his moment of victory! He was the Lord of the universe. For him the universe was especially *this* moment. For him the moment was an *element* . . . like the *air*! The vastness of the nearing victory was by and large his whole context.

For him there was no possibility of existence elsewhere. There was only *now* . . . this moment. . . .

Another rumble and blowing from the nearby animal told Kohanah which way to go. Moving stealthily through the night, his spear at his side, his eyes were lit with fire as he scanned the land for the animal.

And then there it was. On the skyline! The massive head of a long-horned bison, then the hump, and then the whole beast, huge and black against the sky, standing to a height of seven feet at the hump, with horns that extended six feet across the shaggy crown.

For a moment the beast stood poised there; then it lumbered obliquely down the bank to the nearby creek.

Kohanah took on a crouching position in the darkness, scarcely visible. He moved not a muscle. Only the wind lifted his braids and then laid them back along his neck. The beast was now only a few steps upwind. There were no signs of what was about to happen. The beast meandered. Kohanah was frozen in repose.

Then the scene exploded. In one and the same instant Kohanah sprang to his feet and bolted forward, his arm cocked, the spear held high. The huge animal lunged in panic, bellowing, its whole weight thrown violently into the bank, its hooves churning and chipping earth into the air, its eyes gone wide, wild, and white.

There was a moment in which the animal's awful frenzied motion was wasted and it was mired and helpless in its fear. Kohanah hurled the spear with his whole strength and the point was driven into the deep, vital flesh.

The animal in its agony, staggered and crashed to the ground, dead.

A strange sort of light emerged on the horizon as the sunrise shadowed the land with orange splashes. His heart pounding inside him, Kohanah stepped closer to the beast, now able to see it for what it was.

Paling, his knees weakening, feeling as though he were being stabbed in the heart by a hundred knives, Kohanah faltered.

A loud cry of rage and surprise split the air when he discovered that he had not killed a buffalo at all, but instead, one of the longhorn cows that now grazed on land once occupied by buffalo! He had wanted a buffalo bull so badly that his eyes had fooled him. His heart and his mind had played tricks on him when he saw the beast in the darkness of night! While once again becoming the hunter of long ago when he had freely hunted and killed many buffalo, he had let himself be guided into the foolish notion that this animal was a buffalo.

Everything that he thought he had seen, he had only imagined! Only the animal dead at his feet was real.

Nothing more!

Marilla awakened with a start when she heard the piercing, heart-wrenching cry. She looked about wildly, not seeing Kohanah beside the fire, close to her. Stumbling to her feet, she looked across the land, the sunrise illuminating everything within viewing range, shading it orange.

And then she saw Kohanah. He was standing with his shoulders stooped, his head bent into his hands. A sob tore from deep within Marilla when from this range she could see an animal lying at Kohanah's feet and saw that it was not a buffalo. It was a longhorn cow. Had Kohanah thought, in the darkness of night, that he had slain a buffalo? If he had slain the cow knowingly, he would not be sad over it. The truth of what had happened was clear in his reaction to the animal at his feet!

Fearing his reaction if she went to him and let him know that she was aware of his mistake, Marilla settled back down beside the simmering campfire and softly wept. . . .

Twenty-Seven

❧❧

The sun was creeping low toward the horizon, a whippoorwill sang its plaintive melody somewhere in the distance. Marilla looked over at Kohanah and saw that he still rode proudly tall on his red roan, though in only a matter of moments he was going to have to reveal to his people that again his hunt for a buffalo had been in vain. Oh, if only they would understand that he was not at fault . . . that just because he was their leader he could not perform miracles.

Slowly turning her head, looking straight ahead, weary from the long ride, Marilla clung to her palomino's reins. The Kiowa village was in view, smoke spiraling from the smokeholes of the tipis so peacefully, as though everything in the world was right.

Marilla's eyebrows forked. Everything was the same as when they had left, except that against the darkening sky there was a pulsating orange reflection. This sort of light in the sky could only be made by an outdoor fire, and such a fire was only lit when there was cause for celebration.

Her heart aching, Marilla could only believe that the fire had been lit by the Kiowa people to celebrate the return of the hunters, with faith that they would be returning with a buffalo bull. Such a reception would make Kohanah's disappointing news twice as painful to his people. He would feel ashamed that he had not been able to do that which had caused his people to plan a celebration! Without the buffalo bull, he might be scorned, looked upon as one who was no longer worthy of being chief!

Suddenly the world came alive with men, women, and children running from the village, toward the returning hunters. Hands waving, there were cries of joy and shouts of jubilation. Marilla tensed as once again she looked at Kohanah, fearing his reaction. . . .

Head held high, eyes straight ahead, Kohanah directed his braves, with Marilla at his side, on through the throng of those greeting them so eagerly. He did not flinch when small children ran alongside his steed, clamoring, grabbing at him, shouting happily at him, some even chanting. Too soon disappointment would rob them of their smiles and laughter! Kohanah could hardly bear to tell them the news, and so he avoided it as long as he could.

As he rode on into the village, the sky now dark overhead, the outdoor fire lighting the area like daylight, Kohanah's eyes wavered when at the farthest outer edge of the village he saw many new cows fenced in with those already owned by the Kiowa. His heart skipped a beat when among those cows he saw something else quite distinct silhouetted against the dark heavens, and this time, it was real, not a delusion!

"A buffalo bull," Kohanah whispered harshly to himself, his eyes brightening. "The white chief kept his word! And not only did he send a buffalo . . . he has given my people more cows as well!"

Kohanah's whispering drew Marilla's eyes to him. When she saw the light in his eyes, she followed his gaze and became warm all over inside when she saw the gifts that President Hayes had generously sent. No matter what the reason was behind the President's generosity, whether it was because he hoped that Kohanah would reciprocate by giving him the paintings he desired, or because he saw the plight *of* the Kiowa and did this from the bottom of his heart, it truly did not matter. That Kohanah's people had finally been treated fairly was the true cause for celebration here!

Children coming and grabbing at Marilla's dress, laughing and singing, made her laugh softly. When she dismounted along with Kohanah before his tipi, she almost went off balance as the children clung to her. She looked over at Kohanah. It was the same for him. Children were clinging and singing, looking adoringly up at him.

But Kohanah was not smiling. His eyes still looked troubled as his people came milling around him.

Then it dawned on Marilla why he appeared so troubled. Though the Kiowa did have a buffalo bull with which to celebrate the Sun Dance, Kohanah had not been the one to bring it to them.

It had been a white man's gift to the Kiowa . . . not a gift from their *chief*.

Easing the children away from her, Marilla went to Kohanah and locked an arm through his. "Darling, be happy," she softly encouraged. "Your people will have the opportunity to perform the Sun Dance. This is what is important now, not who gave them the buffalo bull for the celebration."

Kohanah glanced down at Marilla, seeing her as such a pillar of strength in his eyes. A smile quivered on his lips as he nodded. "*Ho*, yes," he murmured. "You are right. But tomorrow we will celebrate. Tonight we rest. It has been a tiring, disappointing journey, one that has made my heart heavy with sadness."

Placing an arm about Marilla's waist, he held his chin high with dignity and led her into his tipi, leaving his people behind to celebrate alone in their own way. Anticipating their return, members of his village had built a fire in his dwelling and had set a kettle of food over it, to slowly simmer. The fragrance of rabbit stew cooking was pleasant. The lazy reflections of the fire lighting the room a soft gold made Marilla close her eyes, yawn, and stretch.

Gentle lips kissing her sweetly made Marilla's insides grow mushy with rapture. Her breath was stolen when Kohanah slipped a hand inside her dress, smoothing its way upward, parting her thighs. His fingers began to caress her, causing the core of her womanhood to harden against them. A sensual throbbing made her head begin to reel.

With much practice now, Marilla moved a hand to Kohanah's hardness and caressed him through the softness of his buckskin trousers, feeling him growing harder against her hand. She moved her hand in a slow motion over him, savoring the feel of his largeness. When it twitched, she knew that she should cease her arousing manipulations, for he was nearing the point of climbing that pinnacle of ultimate pleasure without her.

While the Kiowa sang and chanted around the large outdoor fire, Marilla was lowered to the pallet of furs beside the fire. She lay there watching as Kohanah slipped off his clothes, revealing his beautiful, aroused copper body to her.

She sighed with ecstasy when he knelt over her and began disrobing her, kissing her all the while across her breasts, down over her flat tummy, then flicking his tongue upon the point of her complete arousal.

His tongue was soft, wet, and wonderful when he bent down and flicked it over the moistness at the juncture of her thighs, causing her to become almost mindless with pleasure.

And then his lips went to her breast, while his hands continued what his tongue had begun, caressing . . . caressing. . . .

"You are my soul," Kohanah said huskily, looking down at Marilla with eyes dark with passion. "Being with you, loving you, gives me such inner peace."

"You have chosen to be with me tonight instead of with your people," Marilla said softly, cupping his cheek within the palm of her hand. "Will they understand? Don't you hear? The drums and rattles are accompanying your people while they sing and celebrate. Should you not be with them?"

Shyly Marilla lowered her thick lashes over her eyes. "Kohanah, you even said that tonight was for resting," she teased.

"Make love, *then* rest," Kohanah said, chuckling low, brushing soft kisses along Marilla's delicate, tapered neck, then the hollow of her throat. "While we were on the hunt, lovemaking had to be denied us. Two days and one night without loving you is too long! Tsonda, we will make up for those moments missed *now*. My people do not question anything that I do. If Kohanah wishes privacy, it is given. So shall it be the same for you, *manyi*, my woman.''

Having bathed in a stream early in the morning before anyone could see them, even then resisting the urge to embrace and kiss, Marilla could still smell the sweet scent of the outdoors on Kohanah's body as she kissed his shoulder, then licked his flesh, as though he were some ripe, delicious fruit.

Her eyes squinted mischievously as she urged Kohanah away from her and directed him to stretch out on his back on the pallet while she knelt over him. "Let me love you in a way that you enjoy so much," she whispered, running her fingernails teasingly along his distended staff. "My darling, just close your eyes and enjoy. Let all of your troubles fade away. Your mind will become filled with ecstasy, my love. Just let it happen.''

Kohanah's breath and heartbeat quickened when Marilla worked her way down his body, kissing and licking all the way. When her mouth reached his throbbing hardness and her tongue began loving him in the way forbidden to some who frowned upon it as sinful, he twined his fingers through her long and flowing hair and drew her lips even closer.

Guiding her head in the movements he desired most, Kohanah closed his eyes and enjoyed the moment, *ho*, yes, forgetting everything but the golden spirals of pleasure spreading through him. His woman was skilled in many ways. He had been foolish not to take her as a wife earlier. She knew everything about him. What pleasured him. What saddened him.

She was wise in, oh, so many ways. . . .

Just reaching that brink where he would be beyond that point where he could give Marilla pleasure in return, Kohanah gently pushed Marilla's head away. Placing his hands on her waist he lifted her up, then turned with her and placed her back on the pallet of furs.

Moving downward, he splayed his fingers against her flat tummy, lowered his mouth to her triangle of soft hair, then pleasured her in the same way she had just pleasured him. His tongue flicked, tasting her sweetness. Marilla tossed her head back and forth. She moaned softly as she felt the pleasure grabbing her all over, threatening to spill over inside her. . . .

But just as she reached that point, Kohanah straddled her and entered her in one quick thrust and began his continued strokes within her.

His mouth came down upon hers, their tastes mingling in a fiery kiss. His hands cupped and kneaded her breasts, the nipples hardening against his palms. Her body arched, meeting his every thrust with one of her own. She wrapped her legs about his waist, drawing him closer . . . closer . . . closer. . . .

Her hands clutched the sinews of his shoulders. Her lips trembled against his, feeling the rapture rising. When he stiffened and momentarily slowed his strokes, she knew that she could relax and let the feelings of pleasure overwhelm her, for he was also ready to meet her on that ultimate plateau of bliss.

Kohanah's pulse was racing. He clung to Marilla, the ultimate peak of sensation once again within reach. He took one deep, long breath, pausing his body's movements, then made a last maddening plunge within her and let the explosion of ecstasy claim him, so intense this time that it could almost have been described as painful!

His hardness reaching clean into her soul, it seemed, Marilla cried out softly, her entire being throbbing with release. But even when it was over and they were left breathless and spent, their bodies strained hungrily together, their lips on fire with renewed kisses. . . .

"Kohanah cannot get enough of you tonight," he whispered huskily against her parted lips. "It is so good to have you with me . . . to know that as long as we have breath and life you will be here with me."

"Yes, forever, Kohanah," Marilla whispered, running her hands over his corded shoulders and then lower, to his hard buttocks. "Nothing will ever part us again. Nothing. From today forth, everything will be right for us."

She paused for a moment and leaned her ear in the

direction of the closed entrance flap. "Listen to your people. They are so happy. Tell me that you are as happy and that you have forgotten how you happen to have the buffalo. It should be enough that you have it. From the very first moment I met you, you have talked about the Sun Dance and about its wonders. Tomorrow I shall see exactly why!"

"*Ho*, yes, it is *pai-aganti*," Kohanah said, rolling away from her. He rose to a sitting position, staring down into the flames of the fire. "We met at this exact time of year those many years ago, Tsonda. From that moment on, you have filled my life with sunshine." He slowly turned his eyes to her and smiled softly. "Tomorrow Kohanah fills your life with sunshine and so much, much *more*. *Ho*, yes, you will see the wonders of the Taime *and* the Sun Dance."

Marilla drew a soft bear pelt about her shoulders and moved to a sitting position beside Kohanah. "I am so happy that President Hayes kept his promise to you," she sighed. "I must send a wire tomorrow and thank him for both you *and* me."

She glanced over at him. "Of course . . . after the Sun Dance, darling," she blurted. "The Sun Dance comes first. I can hardly wait."

Kohanah rose to his feet and drew on a loincloth, then strolled over to the canvases that were stacked against the wall. "Kohanah thanks the white chief in his own way," he said, lifting one canvas, then another, studying them, recalling the exact moment each of them was painted.

Some were painted while he stood, sweating, in the dungeon at Fort Marion, his heart heavy with burdens, his mind burning with hate! Others were painted after he had been moved from the dungeon into the barracks, when life was easier. Some were painted after Kohanah had known the wonders of Marilla's body joined with his . . . intertwined as though they were one body, one heartbeat, one soul. Those paintings were the most colorful, matching his feelings of happiness in loving the young woman who had given him more than he had ever expected from someone of a different skin coloring. She had given her all then, and now.

"Kohanah gives the white chief whatever paintings he desires," he said thickly. "When you send your wire to him, to give him your thanks, tell him Kohanah will thank him in *that* way."

Kohanah's eyelids were heavy over his dark eyes as he turned on a heel and gazed down at Marilla. "Tsonda, I would like to take him the paintings, to hand them to him personally," he said hoarsely. "It is my desire to travel with you, to do this, personally. Tell the white chief President that Kohanah *will* arrive with the paintings, himself!"

Marilla was momentarily at a loss for words. Kohanah's decision to travel to Washington with her was so sudden, so unexpected. He had been on a train only once and that had been under deplorable circumstances. He had never seen the wonders of a large city! Excitement over this chance to share such experiences with the man she loved caused Marilla to fly to her feet. The bear pelt fell away from her as she rushed to Kohanah and lunged into his arms.

"Kohanah, how wonderful that would be," she said, hugging him to her. "I'm so glad you want to do this. Oh, so glad."

Kohanah ran his hands down the sensual curves of her body, then held her partially away from him so that his lips could once again taste of her sweetness. Picking her up in his arms, he carried her back to the pallet and placed her there.

Easing his loincloth down from his body, he nudged her thighs apart and slipped his renewed hardness back inside her and began stroking within her. His teeth nibbled at the hardened peak of her breast, his fingers were digging into her buttocks, lifting her higher . . . higher . . . higher. . . .

The outdoor fire in the village had burned low and was now only flickering orange embers. Everything was quiet. Not a sound could be heard anywhere throughout the Kiowa village; the celebration was over until the sunrise of the next morning. Then it would begin again, and would last into the wee hours of the night. Much food would be consumed. There would be singing and dancing. There would be much romancing beneath the light of the silvery moon!

Jason Roark lay close to the earth, his horse tied to a tree close behind him. His green eyes scrutinized the Indian village, and he smiled crookedly when once again he looked at the buffalo bull standing so quietly among the herd of cows. He had seen the procession from the rail-head when the cows and lone buffalo had been unloaded from a boxcar.

It hadn't taken much common sense to figure out why just one buffalo would be delivered to this land, now void of such an animal. Only one group of people had been hunting a buffalo.

The Kiowa!

"Well, they ain't goin' to have one for long," Jason said beneath his breath, chuckling. "Ol' Jason here is goin' to make quick work of that animal. Won't Kohanah get the surprise of his life tomorrow? Won't his damned savage people? I'd love to be there watchin', but I don't dare give that a try. I'm even takin' a chance comin' here tonight."

But taking chances was nothing new to Jason. He had lived on the edge of chance all of his life. That was how he had gained his reputation as a gambler!

It seemed that he was just about ready to take the gamble of his life. If one savage Injun caught him stealing the buffalo, *his* head would be used as a sacrifice to the sun god tomorrow, not the damn buffalo's!

A rope in his left hand, a revolver in his right, Jason moved to his feet and began running stealthily over the darkened land, keeping watch in all directions for any sign of movement. As far as he could tell there were no guards anywhere in sight.

"Seems the Kiowa have become lax in judgment," Jason gloated to himself. "They think they're safe on this reservation. Even their cattle and prized buffalo!"

Squinting his eyes, stepping cautiously closer to the corral made of cottonwood timbers, Jason focused his full attention on the buffalo bull. If that damn thing bellowed, he'd be in a lot of trouble. He would have to rope the bull easy like and lead him out of the corral without annoying him.

Now inside the corral and standing beside the buffalo, the bull's dark, lazy eyes studying Jason questioningly, Jason eased the rope about its neck and gave it a jerk, surprised that the buffalo was so willing to be led away. It seemed sluggish. Perhaps the long train ride had taken a lot of spirit out of him! That was in Jason's favor!

Closing the gate to the corral, Jason led the buffalo through the village, up a slight rise, and to his horse. Tying the rope that held the buffalo into his horse's reins, Jason swung himself up into the saddle and rode silently away, leading the buffalo behind him.

He kept himself low over his horse, his eyes still guardedly watching. He finally felt safe when he was back at his hideout of scooped-out land where an underground cave led to a creek. He secured his horse and the buffalo, then jerked a knife from a sheath at his waist.

His eyes gleaming, he raised the knife and took several plunges into the side of the buffalo. Its bellow of pain echoed from the cave and across the land, momentarily frightening Jason into believing that perhaps it would even be heard as far away as the Indian village!

But relaxing, the buffalo now dead at his feet, Jason fell to his knees and began carving the buffalo up, dismembering it.

Snickering, he removed the head and went to the creek and tossed it in, watching it sink and settle into the muddy mire at the bottom.

Then walking back to the buffalo bull, he continued stripping it of its flesh, down to the bone.

Bloody and reeking of death, Jason wiped his knife clean on his breeches, then began loading the buffalo's bones into a leather bag. Securing the filled bag to the side of his horse, Jason had one more thing to do, again hoping that he wouldn't be caught. . . .

Smiling wickedly, he swung himself up into his saddle and rode from the cave, across the land, toward the Kiowa village.

"I'll return everything but the head," he said, laughing

throatily. "The damn savages got no use for anything but the damn head. . . ."

Marilla squirmed and turned in her sleep, slowly awakening. As she reached out beside her, everything within her melted sensually when she felt Kohanah's nude body so close, so handsome and peaceful in sleep. Snuggling closer to him, fitting her body to his, Marilla felt herself beginning to slowly drift back to sleep.

But a harsh cry, a bloodcurdling scream of horror, drew her quickly awake and to a sitting position, her eyes wide and wild as Kohanah flew to his feet to grab his rifle for protection.

"What was that?" Marilla asked, tugging her buckskin dress over her head while Kohanah slipped his loincloth up over his hips, his hand still clutching his rifle.

"You stay here," Kohanah flatly ordered, his eyes dark and troubled as he looked down at her. "There is trouble in my village. You stay here. Be safe!"

"Kohanah, I will only be safe at your side," Marilla softly argued, moving to him, stubbornly standing beside him. "And I want to see what is the cause for such cries just as badly as you!"

Slipping an arm protectively around Marilla's waist, Kohanah led her from the tipi, then stumbled on something just outside the dwelling as he looked questioningly into the wild eyes of one of his braves.

"Kohanah! Lord, look!" Marilla gasped, looking down to see what she had stumbled over, almost causing her to fall.

A shiver coursed across her flesh and the hair at the nape of her neck stood on end when she saw the bloody bones spread out along the land, just outside Kohanah's tipi. A sick feeling began to plague her, as she wondered who had placed these here, and *why*.

Kohanah's eyes lowered. His eyebrows forked, then he once again looked up at his brave. . . .

"The—the buffalo," the brave stammered. "It is gone! This must be what is left of it! Someone who did not want us to perform the Sun Dance did this, Kohanah. That is shown to be true, because all bones of the animal are here except its *head*."

Marilla's heart ached . . . cried out for Kohanah. She bit her lower lip to keep from crying, her mind recalling the one man who would commit a fiendish act such as this.

Jason Roark!

Kohanah's spine stiffened and his heart felt weak as he realized the significance of the stolen and slain animal. Again his people would be denied the Sun Dance! The man responsible would have to be found and dealt with! And he would not let this stop the Sun Dance. Too much had gotten in the way, for too long. If a buffalo skin had to be used to make the sacrifice, then it would be done. Kohanah had many buffalo skins!

Moving to his knees, his eyes two points of fire as he studied the footprints that led to and away from his dwelling, Kohanah nodded. "We will follow, then *kill*," he growled, doubling his hands angrily into fists.

Determinedly, Marilla went into the tipi and grabbed one of Kohanah's rifles. When he came inside she stood with her shoulders squared stubbornly. "I shall help you track down the man," she said. "I want to see him get what he deserves."

Kohanah went to her, pride swelling inside him. "Tsonda, you deserve to accompany Kohanah and warriors," he said thickly. "But you must know . . . the man who did this will not be killed as quickly as a rifle releases its ball. Kohanah has other plans for him. He will die, but very . . . very slowly. There is a way the Kiowa is familiar with."

He grabbed up a leather bag and opened its drawstrings. Thrusting his fingers inside, he dipped them in bright red paint. He drew several stripes across the bridge of his nose and cheeks, then motioned for Marilla to sit down beside him.

While he painted her face, she waited and watched, her heart beating wildly . . . anxiously. . . .

Twenty-Eight

~~~

Beyond the wind the silence was acute. Shadows of morning were withdrawing like smoke.

With her hair in long braids down her back, Marilla rode beside Kohanah, two scouts riding on ahead, following tracks that Marilla *knew* without a doubt were Jason's!

Then suddenly Kohanah wheeled his horse away from the others and rode toward the ravine at his right side. Fear of being without him caused Marilla to follow him, wondering what was drawing him away from his braves.

Feeling suddenly, strangely queasy, something unusual for Marilla, she bobbed in the saddle as her palomino carried her down a steep incline, to the small, narrow, steep-sided valley.

She forgot her passing brief feeling of queasiness, and her eyes widened in horror when she saw that the earth was crawling with spiders. They were great tarantulas swarming over the land near the water, their silky webs woven over little wells in the ground.

These tarantulas were even larger than others that she had seen since she had arrived in Oklahoma. Their bodies were at least two inches long, their leg-spread seven inches.

They were larger than she would have ever even imagined, dull and dark brown, covered with long, dusty hair.

There was something crochety, yet dangerous, about them . . . the way they stopped, then angled away, climbing over one another clumsily if one got in the way of the other.

Seeing them made Marilla's flesh crawl, but she drew her palomino to a halt when Kohanah stopped his red roan only a few feet away from her. She gagged when he went to the spiders carrying a large buckskin bag and spread it open on the ground, urging the spiders inside by guiding them with a stick.

"Kohanah, what are you doing?" Marilla asked, her voice quivering. "Why do you want those spiders?"

Kohanah turned to her, smiling smugly. "Soon you will see," he said, again focusing on the work at hand.

One by one the spiders scurried into the dark confines of the bag, as though they were going into one of their dark wells dug into the ground.

When Kohanah had the bag filled and the drawstring closed, he went back to his horse and slung the pouch over his saddle, securing it with the end of the drawstring.

Swinging himself back into his saddle, he nodded to Marilla. "Come. We will once again join my braves," he said flatly. "We can't be far from the evil man's hideout. He is not a clever man. He did not cover his tracks. He would not think to travel far from our village. He forgets the cunning ways of the Kiowa."

Wheeling her horse around, Marilla once again rode alongside Kohanah, occasionally glancing at the bag in which crawled surely a hundred spiders. She was just beginning to guess how they were going to be used. Somehow Kohanah was going to use them in his punishment of Jason Roark.

Another brief feeling of nausea claimed Marilla, so much that she teetered in the saddle, but again was given cause to forget about it when a Kiowa brave came thundering on his horse toward her and Kohanah.

Stopping at Kohanah's side, the brave pointed across the land. "The tracks lead to the cave found by some of our hunters a winter ago," he said, breathless. His eyes went to the heavens, following slow spirals of smoke reaching upward. "The thief did not think to worry about building a fire. Even it leads us to him!"

Kohanah grabbed his rifle from its leather sheath. "We will surprise the man," he growled. "Order the braves to dismount, except for a few. Those few will take chase if he tries to escape."

Her heart beating wildly, Marilla wondered what she should do under these circumstances. The only thing that she could think of was to stay with Kohanah. Follow his every move . . .

Dismounting, Marilla hurried to Kohanah's side as he dismounted. She led her horse behind her, following Kohanah's lead. They walked stealthily toward the entrance to the cave, her nose catching the very identifiable scent of buffalo cooking over a fire. Jason had stolen the buffalo from the Kiowa. He was having a feast with the Kiowa's buffalo. Surely he was too distracted to know that anyone was approaching him. . . .

Suddenly a horse sprang from the cave opening. Jason Roark was bent low over the saddle, riding for all he was worth, trying to escape. In a flash, Kohanah was back in his saddle and giving chase. He had no need to slap his reins or goad his horse with his heels thrust into its flanks. The horse knew what was expected of him. He was charging in a straight line toward Jason.

But Kohanah could not wait for his steed to catch up with Jason's horse. Kohanah had his own way of doing things when he was impatient.

Holding on to his reins with his right hand, he lifted his rifle with the other and aimed. His finger searched for and found the trigger and slowly but determinedly pulled it.

Lowering the rifle, Kohanah smiled smugly as the ball hit the target, shooting the horse out from under Jason. When it fell, it pinned Jason's leg to the ground.

When the first Kiowa brave rode up and tried to hit Jason with his gun butt, he managed to duck under part of the horse. But when Kohanah reached him and quickly dismounted, Jason began to cry and beg for mercy. There was no denying the anger seething deeply within Kohanah's dark, fathomless eyes. Jason could recall the other sort of punishment that Kohanah had handed out to him.

This time it would be no less primitive . . . no more merciful!

Kohanah grabbed Jason by an arm while several of his braves rolled the horse away from him, leaving Jason free. Taking him by the throat, Kohanah glowered into his face. "You will die this time," he hissed, laughing when Jason's eyes bulged out as·Kohanah's hands tightened about his throat.

"But not now. Not this simply," Kohanah said, dropping Jason back to the ground. "You will die slowly."

Jason tried to crawl away, but was stopped when Kohanah grabbed him by the waistband of his breeches and drew him back to lie at his feet. "What are you going to do with me?" he pleaded. "Please let me go. I'll never interfere in your life again."

Jason's eyes moved to Marilla. "Marilla, you can't let the Injuns do this to me," he said, sobbing. "You're civilized, not savage. Tell Kohanah to let me go. I'll leave Oklahoma. None of you'll ever see me again. I give you . . . my word."

Marilla challenged Jason with an angry, set stare, in her mind's eye recalling Charles Agnew, the innocent keeper of the Taime, and his gentle wife, and the most recent atrocity committed by Jason Roark. She could still smell the bloody remains of the buffalo as the bones lay spread across the land in front of Kohanah's tipi. She could see the blood of the buffalo on Jason's *clothes*!

President Hayes's kindness had been abused, as had the Kiowa. Jason Roark deserved whatever sort of punishment Kohanah had planned for him, and she knew without asking that it had to do with the horrible tarantulas.

Marilla stubbornly folded her arms across her chest, not even bothering to give Jason an answer. Her gaze shifted to several Kiowa who were busy digging a narrow, deep hole in the ground with their hatchets. Her insides grew cold. Did Kohanah plan to bury him alive? If so, why was the hole deep and narrow? Was Jason going to be buried standing up? And what did Kohanah plan to do with the spiders?

Suddenly she felt an uneasiness about being an observer, yet her hatred of Jason made her stand firm in her decision to stay there.

Kohanah held Jason down on the ground by pressing his foot into his stomach. When Jason squirmed and tried to take hold of Kohanah's leg, Kohanah pushed his foot harder into his stomach.

Marilla stood by silently watching. The hole was now large enough for a body, and she was not at all surprised when Kohanah kicked Jason into the hole, feet first. Jason's wails and screams echoed across the land, yet were heard by no one except those who were watching him and who were throwing dirt down around his body. The hole was only deep enough for his body, not his head.

Shivers ran across Marilla's flesh when she suddenly realized exactly what Jason's fate was going to be: He was going to be buried up to his chin.

And the spiders . . . ?

She took a step backward when the last of the dirt was tossed into the hole around Jason's body and Kohanah stepped up to Jason and opened the buckskin bag and began sprinkling the tarantulas on Jason's head. Marilla swallowed hard when she heard Jason gurgle with fear, unable to cry out any longer, fear having stolen away his ability to speak.

"You chose an isolated place for your hideout," Kohanah said, smiling smugly down at Jason. "No one will find you for days. The spiders will have fun with you, and then the sun will do the rest."

Jason looked wildly up at Kohanah. A spider crawled across his lips as he finally managed to speak, if only in a whisper. "The dirt," he gasped. "It's crushing in on my chest. The spiders! They're . . . biting . . . me. It stings terribly. I'm in pain. Horrible pain!"

"The bite of the tarantula secretes a poison that is quite painful, but is considered no more dangerous than that of other spiders," Kohanah said, pushing some of the straying spiders back onto Jason's face with the toe of his moccasin. "You will not die from the bites, but you will suffer endlessly from the pain now, and later, when the wounds will fester into welts in the sun. You will slowly die from lack of water and nourishment."

"Please . . ." Jason pleaded, his voice barely a whisper, his green eyes pooled with tears. "I'm sorry for all I've done to cause you pain. Please let me go. Please!"

Kohanah turned on a heel and walked solemnly back to his horse, nodding to Marilla. "It is time to return home now," he said dryly. "There is much to say to my people. They must know that the person responsible for so much of their sadnesses will bother them no more. They must know that tomorrow the Sun Dance will be performed, but without the buffalo bull as planned."

Marilla went to Kohanah and placed a hand on his arm. "But how, Kohanah?" she asked, shutting her ears to Jason's continued pleadings. "There is no buffalo."

"The ceremony will be performed with the skin of a buffalo," Kohanah said in a low growl. "My people must learn to adapt to changes. The lack of buffalo roaming the land forces many changes on my people."

Marilla leaned up and hugged Kohanah, then turned to go to her palomino, when suddenly another bout of queasy weakness claimed her insides, but this time much worse than the last. She grabbed at her stomach when she felt the sudden urge to retch.

As the bitterness rose up into her throat, she swallowed it back, coughing. Kohanah went to her and clasped his hands onto her shoulders.

"Tsonda, what is it?" he asked, his voice troubled. "You are suddenly so pale. Was today's experience too much for you?"

The urge to retch still strong at the base of her throat, Marilla lowered her head into her hands. "I feel so ill," she murmured. She tensed when once again Jason's voice reached her, its pleading tone making her aware of just what was going to happen to him. Though he deserved it, she did not want to be a witness to it any longer.

Yet, could she ride the palomino? She felt so strangely

light-headed, something quite new to her. Though petite, she was normally a very strong, capable person.

There could be only one reason for this change in her. Perhaps . . . ?

"No, I don't believe I'm ill because of what happened here today," she finally answered, swallowing hard again. "But please, let us get away from this place. I feel the need to lie down. To rest."

Kohanah helped her to her palomino and eased her into the saddle. When he felt that she was secure enough, he hurried to his own horse and swung himself into the saddle, then moved his horse so that it was close beside hers as they began riding away. Jason's voice faded in the wind the farther they traveled.

Then again Marilla grabbed at her throat, feeling the urge to retch once more plaguing her.

"Kohanah, I must stop," she said thickly. Her eyes searched for and found the stream they had not been so far from since they had left Jason behind. "Perhaps if I splash some water on my face I might feel better."

Kohanah inched his horse closer and grabbed Marilla about the waist, bringing her onto his lap on his horse. Holding her securely and gently in place, he rode to the stream and stopped beneath a heavy shading of cotton-wood trees.

Lifting Marilla from the horse he carried her to the bank of the stream and set her down on a soft bed of grass. Lowering his hands into the water, he brought her a drink, then wiped her brow with the cool palms of his hands.

"You are better?" he asked hoarsely. "Tsonda, it is because Kohanah let you be witness to ways you are not accustomed to? You should not have seen Jason Roark buried in such a way. You should not have seen the spiders being set free upon his face. It was a mistake that Kohanah will not make again."

Marilla leaned up on an elbow and reached out to touch Kohanah's soft, smooth cheek. "It was I who asked to join in the expedition," she murmured. "You are not to blame." Her face became rosy with a blush as she cast her eyes momentarily downward, then looked slowly back up at him. "Kohanah, I think the sickness that I am feeling is for an entirely different reason than what you are thinking."

Kohanah arched an eyebrow. "What are you speaking about?" he asked softly. "Why are you ill? What has made you sick?"

Marilla lay down on the ground on her back and took Kohanah's hands in hers. Her eyes filling with tears of joy, she moved his hands to her stomach and rested them there.

"Soon, my love, you may be feeling movement where your hands are now resting," she said in an almost whisper. "Kohanah, the chances are good that I am with child. It's been just long enough since my return to you for me to have become pregnant. My darling, my queasy stomach is perhaps because of my pregnancy. I have missed my monthly weeps this month. I *could* be with child. My darling, *your* child."

Kohanah was speechless, perhaps for the first time in his life, so taken by the news that he could not find the words to express his happiness. He looked down at Marilla with wide, grateful eyes, seeing her as awesome in her loveliness, even more beautiful now than the first time he had seen her.

Why hadn't he noticed this change earlier? She was radiant in her loveliness, as though something within her was making her glow.

And it was because she was carrying his child?

It had to be true! The Great Spirit owed him a blessing after having failed Kohanah in his prayers so often of late. A child could make so many things right for him. A son to carry on in his likeness when he was no longer of this earth! Who could ask for more than that?

"Tsonda," Kohanah said, drawing her up into his arms, snuggling her close. "Nothing could make me happier. Your words are a gift that forever I shall repay you for. You will be treated so gently, you will never have to ask for a thing."

Marilla clung to him. "Kohanah, all I want is to be with you and to see you happy," she whispered, thrilled to know that her suspicions were making Kohanah so happy.

Oh, Lord, what if she was wrong? What if she wasn't
with child? What *if* seeing Jason treated so inhumanely had
caused her sudden sick feeling? Today *was* the first time
she had felt nauseated since she realized that she had not
had her monthly weeps. She had not even thought to
wonder about why she hadn't, because she had been so
tied up in giving support to Kohanah in every way that she
could.

If she wasn't carrying Kohanah's child, it would be
another disappointment that he would be forced to deal
with.

Life was one disappointment after another for him.

Could he bear another . . . ?

Now she wished that she had kept her suspicions to
herself. But the words had come out so easily, as though it
was a baby inside her, already speaking its mind aloud,
like its mother who had been outspoken since she was old
enough to talk.

"Do you feel like traveling now?" Kohanah asked,
looking over his shoulder at his waiting braves. "It would
be best to get you to my dwelling. Many squaws could see
to you . . . make you comfortable."

Marilla picked herself up from the ground. "Kohanah,
I'm not helpless," she said, laughing softly. She cleared
her throat nervously, swallowing the bitterness that had
been left there by her sudden sick spell. She placed her
hands on the small of her back and stretched. "I'm just
fine. I'm fit as a fiddle to ride my horse back to the
village, and when I get there I can see to myself."

She went to Kohanah and stood on tiptoe and kissed his
brow. "That is, until you return to our tipi," she whispered. "Then, my darling, I will be glad to let you take
over. No one can give me peace of mind like you. Darling, let's go. I'm fine."

Kohanah picked her up in his arms and carried her to
her palomino and fitted her into her saddle. He looked at
her with pride in his eyes as he handed her her reins, then
went and swung himself up into his own saddle and rode
away beside her.

Marilla's eyes pooled with proud tears, yet fear was

eating away at her heart. She must be with child. She *must*! She could not give Kohanah a reason to be disappointed again, especially not with *her*. One disappointment did seem to lead to another. She could not stand it if he ever decided not to want her as his wife!

Focusing her eyes on the loveliness of the land around her, forcing herself not to worry about the question of her pregnancy, she admired the still, sunlit plain reaching out of sight, as though seeing it for the first time.

The meadow was bright, yet not to be trusted, for at times the plains were bright and calm and quiet; at other times they were black with the sudden violence of weather.

It was now noon on the plain . . . bees were swarming. . . .

Twenty-Nine

❧~❧

Shadows of night were just fading away. The sun was revealing its spokes of reddish orange on the horizon as it began to slowly rise in the sky. This year Marilla was an observer of the preparations for the Sun Dance ceremony. Next year, when she was more familiar with the customs and rites of Kohanah's people, she would be a vital part *of* the ceremony.

In Kohanah's absence, not knowing where he had drifted off to, Marilla had positioned herself beside the outdoor communal fire, watching the building excitement all around her.

She didn't feel misplaced, just enthralled. . . .

In the center of the village the dance structure had been erected. It was circular in form, its entrance facing the east, with a central post to symbolize a source of spiritual and mystical power, the *sun*.

The central post was ornamented near the ground with the robes of very old, almost withered away, buffalo calves, their heads up, as if in the act of climbing it. Each of the cottonwood branches above the fork was ornamented with more buffalo robes, with the addition of shawls, calico, and scarves, and covered at the top with black muslin.

Attached to the fork was a bundle of cottonwood and willow limbs, firmly bound together and covered with a buffalo robe, with head and horns, so as to form a crude image of a buffalo, to which were hung strips of new calico, muslin, strouding, both blue and scarlet, feathers, and shawls of various lengths and colors. The longer and showier articles were placed near the end. This image was so placed as to face the east.

A screen was then constructed on the side opposite the entrance by sticking small cottonwoods and cedars deep into the ground so as to preserve them fresh as long as possible. A space was left, two or three feet wide, between it and the enclosing wall, in which the dancers were already preparing themselves for the dance. The Taime was already in place, but concealed from view behind the screen.

Above it was a large fan made of eagle quills, with the quill part lengthened out nearly a foot by inserting a stick into it and securing it there. These were held in a spread formation by means of a willow rod bent into a circular form.

Above this was a mass of feathers, concealing the image, on either side of which were several shields highly decorated with feathers and paint.

The ground inside the enclosure was carefully cleared of grass, sticks, and roots, awaiting a covering, several inches deep, of clean white sand, for the dancers were required to dance on sandy earth.

Marilla was in awe of everything and everyone as all around her singing, shouting, and chanting filled the air. She gazed at an old, old woman who moved into the enclosure with something on her back. Several boys went to assist her, removing the bag from her back, then emptied it of its contents . . . the white sandy earth.

The old woman held a digging tool in her hand. She turned toward the south and pointed with her lips. It was like a kiss and she began to sing: "We have brought the earth. Now it is time to play. As old as I am, I still have the feeling of play."

This was the true beginning of the Sun Dance. Slowly the

dancers began to take their steps, all the people were around, wearing splendid things . . . beautiful buckskin and beads. Some wore necklaces and pendants that shone like the sun.

Though Marilla did not understand exactly the significance of today's ceremony, she considered it, ah, so very, very beautiful. The Kiowa people were finally getting the opportunity to reaffirm their tribal unity, though it was being done without the buffalo bull.

Marilla had to wonder how a substitute would make things right for the Kiowa. But it was Kohanah's decision that this was the only way it could be done. Many Sun Dances would have to be performed in the future. This just happened to be the year they were forced to dance without a buffalo bull as the sacrifice to the sun . . . in their eyes, its strength and majesty regarded as the animal symbol of the sun.

If not this year, it would have been the next. Things did not go on forever in this world of trials and tribulations . . . not even spiritual beings, it seemed!

Rising to her feet, Marilla joined everyone within the dance structure. Reverently she took a seat among those who were not dancing, still looking around for Kohanah, wondering where he was, why he seemed to be the last to join in the celebration. Surely he was within hearing range of the singing. Did he not want to join in? Was he too ashamed of how the celebration was being forced to take place? Had he not accepted the absence of the buffalo bull all that easily, after all?

Clasping her hands on her lap, the softness of the doe-skin dress against her flesh comforting, made her feel closer to her husband. But if only he were here!

Where . . . oh, where *was* he . . . ?

Looking ardently at the activity around her, Marilla saw several Kiowa braves painting their bodies with bright colors. Other braves were dancing, always facing the sun. The dance was simple, the dancers merely rising on their toes in time to eagle-bone whistles, fulfilling their vows and seeking power.

Marilla had been told that at one time long ago at the

end of the dancing, the young Kiowa braves used to undergo severe torture in fulfillment of vows. But this had changed, just as so many of the customs had changed after the Kiowa were forced to bow down to the white man, to follow their harsh rules.

A great hush suddenly filled the holy dance structure as a figure darted into the room. Marilla turned her head and gasped when she saw someone prancing around the room hidden beneath a buffalo hide, with a stick holding the hide up over his head. As this person danced and swayed, everything became quiet, as though reverence was being paid the dancer.

Marilla's insides grew mushy warm when she began to suspect just who this was doing the fancy, even *erotic* dancing. Kohanah! Surely it was . . . Kohanah! And the way he kept swaying closer and closer to her, she knew that her suspicions must be correct.

When a hand snaked out from beneath the buffalo hide, offering it to her, Marilla's breath was momentarily stolen away.

Then, suddenly unaware of so many eyes on her, watching her, she intertwined her fingers through those that she was so familiar with . . . the fingers that could make her go mindless with pleasure, and rose to her feet and joined Kohanah in a gentle swaying motion. Though there was no music, the rhythm seemed to come to Marilla as if by magic. She found herself moving to her toes, then to her heels, then twirling alongside Kohanah. She held her head back and let her braided hair settle down to her waist. Then she gasped lightly when Kohanah lifted the buffalo hide over her head so that they were joined together in the darkness beneath it.

Thigh to thigh, chest to chest, they swayed and leaned. Unable to help herself, Marilla was beginning to become aroused. She could feel the tingling start at the tips of her toes and move upward, scorching her at the juncture of her thighs.

Knowing that her face must be flushed crimson from passion, she was glad that the buffalo hide hid her from those who were still observing the chief and his wife becoming too drawn into intimacy at such a strange time as this.

"Kohanah," Marilla whispered, breathing hard, her breasts pressed hard into Kohanah's chest. She could feel her nipples hardening. It was as though she had been fed some strange and potent elixir, causing her to become inflamed with hungry desire! "What we are doing is dangerous. If you asked me to, I would lie right down in front of everyone and let you make love to me. Oh, Kohanah, please. We must not go any farther with this."

"Tsonda, lovely one, just a while longer and then we must place the sacrifice at the feet of the Taime," Kohanah said huskily. "It is for Kohanah to reveal the Taime to his people. It is for Kohanah to present the sacrifice!"

"I feel as though I might *be* that sacrifice," Marilla said, laughing softly. "If you dare kiss me, I would even *allow* it. I am already mindless, my darling."

Still holding the buffalo hide up away from him with one hand, Kohanah defied everything Marilla had warned him against and swept his free hand down the front of her low-cut doeskin dress. Marilla's breath was stolen, the pleasure was so intense where his fingers kneaded and squeezed. Her hand was trembling as she slipped it down the full length of his abdomen and touched his hardness through his loincloth, this bold action also hidden from the viewers by the covering of the buffalo skin.

Kohanah slipped his hand away from her breast, then ground his hardness into her abdomen and gyrated his body as once again he urged her into dancing and swaying motions. Lips met in a frenzy. Passions mounted then peaked without a full sexual encounter even required. Together their bodies trembled as they found the ultimate of pleasure just being locked together in each other's arms. . . .

And then Kohanah placed an arm about Marilla's waist and guided her to the altar. Her senses reeling, shaken by how they had been able to communicate sexually without even having joined their bodies, Marilla willingly knelt down beside Kohanah, afraid that her passion-weakened knees would not hold her up much longer. She had never experienced such cravings, such hunger, as moments ago. Was that part of the power that was given to those who worshiped the Kiowa's gods? Or was it just because she was married to the chief, the leader of his people?

All of her questions were pushed to the furthest recesses of Marilla's mind when Kohanah slowly lifted the buffalo hide from over them. He handed it to Marilla to hold while he moved to his feet and slowly unveiled the Taime.

Marilla gaped openly at it, knowing how many trials and tribulations it had taken to finally get to worship the Sun Dance idol. It was fastened to a short upright stick planted in the ground near the western side of the dance structure. The Taime bundle was suspended by means of a strip of ticking from the fork of the stick.

Marilla studied Kohanah's face as he knelt down beside her and took the buffalo hide from her arms. Though this was a celebration, there was great sadness in Kohanah's dark eyes. He was surely feeling the wrong that had been done to him, making him have to offer the menial sacrifice of a hide when, in truth, it should have been the head of a buffalo bull.

This tore at Marilla's heart, and she felt Kohanah's pain . . . Kohanah's sadness. . . .

There was a great holiness all about the room when Kohanah meditatively laid the buffalo hide at the feet of the Taime, offering prayers in Kiowa to it. Marilla was recalling how Kohanah had said that the Taime was not very big, but full of power!

She could feel this power.

At this moment its presence overwhelmed the room. . . .

Kohanah placed a hand in Marilla's and urged her to her feet. With an arm about her waist, his chin held proudly high, he guided her from the holy place. Once outside, he lifted her up into his arms and carried her to their tipi. Without words, he disrobed her, then let her remove his loincloth.

Kisses became wild, hands became frenzied, as they fell to the floor beside the fire and began to make maddening love.

Marilla moved over Kohanah, straddling him. She

smoothed her hands over the sleek hard lines of his body
while his hands fondled her breasts. Then she lifted her
hips and came down onto his hardness, quivering with
bliss as he so wonderfully impaled her with his man's
strength, almost swooning with the pleasure it evoked.

Riding him, his body rising from the floor with each
thrust, stroking her within feverishly, Marilla fought the
urge to let her mind escape with the familiar explosion of
ecstasy this soon. She wanted to be a part of the foreplay
of lovemaking for a while longer, not take from it so
quickly, to have to wait until the next time to start all over
again.

She could not get enough of him. And that they were
man and wife, to share equally in such wondrous pleasures, made the rapture twofold!

Kohanah placed his hands on Marilla's waist and lifted
her from him and turned her so that he would be above
her. Again he slipped his hardness inside her and began to
pleasure her with his slow, easy strokes. His hands sought
and found her breasts, his mouth found her lips.

Kissing her heatedly, his tongue exploring between her
parted lips, he felt his passion mounting. He slowed his
strokes, wanting to prolong the ultimate pleasure. Loving
her was the final act of his celebration of the Sun Dance
this year. Years past, the celebration had gone on for days
and nights. *She* would be his celebration. He would go on
loving *her* for days and nights. She would never need to
beg. He would always be there to give her all that she
desired.

That she was willing to give him the same was wondrous in his eyes!

Happiness bubbled from within Marilla. She clung to
Kohanah, his lips now sending feathery kisses along the
column of her throat, his hands still fondling her breasts,
making her feel as though she were riding a wave of
rapture, perhaps never to return to earth, to be normal
again.

And then the great spiraling sweep of mindlessness
grabbed hold of her. She could no longer deny it. She
wanted to experience total bliss *now*. Trembling, she cried

out with joy as her body responded totally to Kohanah's searing thrusts.

His body stiffened, then shuddered, answering her in kind.

Spent, but wondrously so, Marilla kissed Kohanah's cheek as he rolled away from her. She turned to him and snuggled into his side, her hand touching his silken sheath still throbbing from the aftermath of ecstasy.

"Kohanah, everything is all right, isn't it?" she asked, softly enfolding his manhood within her fingers. "You seemed so sad when you were placing the sacrifice at the feet of the Taime. Your sadness touched me all over. But you no longer seem as sad."

Kohanah leaned up on an elbow. He traced her delicate jawline with a finger, reveling in the touch of her hand embracing his manhood. "You have filled the empty spaces left behind by my unhappiness," he said thickly. "When we make love, there is only you . . . only now."

"The Sun Dance was beautiful," Marilla said, unconsciously moving her hand on him, unaware that he was responding again so readily. "Your people are beautiful."

"Tsonda, you are beautiful," Kohanah said huskily.

He turned her so that his body was shaped into the back of hers. With skill known to him from the time he was a youth of twelve, he slipped his hardness into her this way. Her soft cry of passion was all that it took for him to know that she accepted his way of loving her even in this way. Her soft, warm womanly cocoon of love again welcomed him, opening all the way, then locking its walls about him, sucking, it seemed, as he began his gentle strokes within her again.

"Oh, Kohanah, love me all night," Marilla whispered, her face flushed red with ecstasy. "I do believe I could go on all night. Am I wicked? Do you consider me whorish?"

Kohanah chuckled against her neck. "My woman, you are what every man dreams of in a wife," he said, twining his arms about her, cupping her breasts, holding on to them, as though anchoring her to him in this way. "Relax and enjoy. Loving is beautiful this way. Beautiful."

He anchored her fiercely still, burying himself deeply within her.

Marilla found herself floating, drifting. . . .

And once again it was over and Marilla laughed to herself when she recalled telling Kohanah that she could last on into the night.

At this moment she was satiated.

Drawing a blanket around her shoulders, Marilla sat down by the fire as Kohanah banked it with more twigs, this day in May not feeling like May at all, but more like April, in its coolness. With lovemaking behind her, Marilla turned to serious thoughts. She was remembering Kohanah's promise to give the President some of his paintings. Now that the buffalo bull had not been used in the ceremony, would Kohanah feel the same? Would he still see the obligation here?

"Kohanah," she said, giving him a sidewise glance as he settled down beside her, drawing a blanket about his shoulders. "Will we travel to Washington soon?"

Kohanah weighed her words carefully, then nodded. "*Ho*, yes," he said softly. "Soon."

Marilla scooted over to him. Sighing with happiness, she leaned against him while he slipped an arm about her waist. "Kohanah, are you really excited about the possibility that I am with child?" she asked, giving him a lingering stare.

"Excited?" he said, forking an eyebrow. Then he laughed good-naturedly. "Kohanah is *happy*. Very, very happy."

Snuggling close, Marilla reached for his hand and placed it on her tummy. "We should know soon, darling," she murmured. "Soon. Oh, how I would love to have a son created in your likeness. . . ."

Thirty

Contrasting with each other as they sat on the train, Marilla
so white, Kohanah so dark, they were aware of eyes on
them. And Marilla understood. Surely it was rare for an
Indian chief to be a passenger on a train with a white
woman at his side in the capacity of wife.

For this journey to Washington, not wanting to draw
any more attention to herself and Kohanah than was absolutely necessary, Marilla had not worn the Indian attire
that she was growing accustomed to wearing while mingling with Kohanah's people and while teaching the Kiowa
children.

But she had made sure to wear a dress that was not
elaborate in design so as not to look so much out of place
as she sat beside Kohanah, in his attire of buckskin. She
had chosen a demure pearl-gray dress with little puffed
sleeves and a white collar at her throat. It was fully gathered and high-necked, covering her delicate shoulders and
her lovely breasts.

A bonnet hid her hair, which was drawn up into a tight
chignon on her head. A gray velveteen bow was tied
neatly beneath her chin.

Marilla glanced over at Kohanah, knowing him well

enough to recognize when he was uneasy. Yet this would not be noticeable to anyone else, for he sat with his shoulders squared and his dark eyes looking straight ahead, unwavering.

The knuckles of his hands were white from the force with which he was holding on to his canvases that he was supporting on the floor in front of him. He had absolutely refused to part with his precious paintings for even a moment while riding on the train, for he still did not trust the white man. He would guard his precious paintings with his life, if need be!

Oh, so adoring him, Marilla felt her insides grow warm as she saw how handsome he was in his new fringed buckskin outfit adorned colorfully with beaded designs, his greased hair braided, with the fur of the otter woven into it. His copper face was shining and devoid of any facial hair; his jaw was set determinedly as were his lips.

Marilla leaned closer to him. "I am so proud of you," she whispered. "I know this is only your second time on a train and you're accepting it so wonderfully." She giggled behind a gloved hand. "I must admit that the first time I traveled on a train I was petrified. The rumbling of the engine and the wheels along the tracks vibrated my insides out, it seemed! Thank goodness they have improved trains somewhat since then."

"Tsonda, no, it is *not* the first time Kohanah travels on a train," he growled. "But this time is different. The other time the purpose of such travel was filled with much sadness and hate. It was when Kohanah and other Kiowa were forced on a train to travel to their confinement in Florida. Some of my warrior comrades were so frightened they covered their heads with blankets! It was not a good time for me and my comrades!"

Marilla looked toward the paintings, wondering if Kohanah had chosen to bring the one that depicted the travels by train that he was describing. Or had he left it behind, as another bargaining tool with the President later, or future Presidents? Though the painting had been beautifully done, it showed nothing but sadness, hate, and the wrong done to the Kiowa.

Nausea spiraled suddenly through her, making Marilla's face become drawn and pale, banishing her smile as it caused her to wonder whether this feeling was caused by pregnancy or by sadness over Kohanah's losses and those of his people.

Yet she had to believe it was not because of the latter. She had discussed this matter of his imprisonment with Kohanah many times. She had been there with him while he was incarcerated and she had never become physically ill over it. Mentally, yes . . . but never physically. . . .

It surely was the same stomach upset that she had only recently begun experiencing. Though the trains had been improved somewhat, she was being joggled about just enough to cause her stomach to be uneasy.

Swallowing hard, straightening her back, she willed herself not to retch. She inhaled a deep, quivering breath, then became aware of a strong hand clutching hers where they lay resting on her lap.

"Perhaps it is not best that you make this journey with Kohanah," he said, his gaze shifting as he studied her with worry in the depth of his dark eyes. "You have so suddenly paled. Is it because you feel ill again? Is it because of the child you now carry?"

Marilla turned her head in a jerk, looking with wonder at Kohanah. "You are so sure I am with child?" she murmured. "You speak as though you are, Kohanah."

Kohanah's lips quivered into a soft smile. "Tsonda, how long have I known you?" he asked, squeezing her hand affectionately.

"Why, it seems forever," Marilla said, her eyes wide.

"And in this time, how many times has Kohanah seen you pale and weak from illness of any sort?" he said, chuckling low.

"Why, I believe none, until lately," Marilla confirmed.

"Then it is safe to say that you are experiencing the same sort of illness that women have been experiencing for as long as women have been on the face of the earth," he said, nodding. "Tsonda, you can expect to give birth to our child in eight months. Kohanah will be a proud father!"

In awe of his sureness, Marilla studied him for a mo-

ment longer, then laughed softly. "You are amazing, you
know," she whispered, leaning her face close to his, no
matter that those who still held ill feelings toward Indians
were watching and staring with pursed lips and tilted
chins. "Is there anything that you don't know? You are so
very, very wise. You will teach our children so much more
than I could ever expect to teach them in a classroom."

Once again Kohanah looked straight ahead, stubbornly
refusing to look from the window to see the land and trees
racing by beside the train. He could not show anyone, not
even Marilla, that seeing this made him quite nervous. It
was nothing at all like traveling on a horse, so free . . . so
wild.

In the train, he was confined, as though everything
outside of the train was trying to jump at him, to imprison
him there forevermore. In his heart and mind, trains would
always remind him *of* imprisonment because one *had* carried him to the dungeons in Florida.

Kohanah was proud of himself for deciding to travel on
a train again, to battle feelings that would always remain
bitter inside him.

Today he would win *many* battles.

One with the dreaded train.

One with the man who was called President of his
country!

"You call Kohanah wise. That is why Kohanah was
appointed chief of his band of Kiowa," he said un-
emotionally.

He gave Marilla a half-glance. He leaned closer to her.
"That is how Kohanah had the wisdom to choose *you* as a
wife," he said, smiling down at her. "Kohanah is very,
very wise."

Proud, touched to the core by Kohanah's tenderness and
his loving ways, Marilla wiped a sparkle of a tear from her
eye, then became excited when she saw the first signs of
Washington through the side windows of the train. Oh, if
only things could go exactly as planned, Kohanah could
finally live with some semblance of peace on the land that
he as now forced to share with the white man. Perhaps,

finally, with careful planning, the Kiowa would feel free of their dread *of* the white man.

President Hayes had a plan. He had wired Marilla, telling her of it, asking her advice.

She had sent an immediate reply, stating that the plan was wonderful!

It was generous, just like the man who offered it!

Marilla sat stiff-backed on the divan in the East Room of the White House, watching President Hayes and Kohanah talking over the paintings that were spread out, standing against the wall of the room. As the sun poured through the windows behind them, settling down in streamers onto them, it made the figures in the drawings look as though they were coming to life, their colors were so brilliant, the depictions of scenes so authentic. Even awesome!

"*Taka-i-taide*, white man chief, Kohanah has brought several for you to choose from," Kohanah said thickly. "It is Kohanah's way of thanking you for your kindnesses to me and my people. The cows will fatten the children. The buffalo bull . . ."

Kohanah's words trailed off to a nothingness. President Hayes stroked his neatly trimmed beard contemplatively, forking a gray eyebrow. He looked over his shoulder at Marilla, then back at Kohanah. "The buffalo bull served its purpose well, I presume," he said, now clasping his hands tightly together behind him. "It was my pleasure to send it to you, Kohanah. After much thought, I understood the position not having the buffalo bull put you in, in your people's eyes. It is important to keep face. I work at that, also. It is not my nature to want to disappoint. Especially my constituents who depend on me."

Kohanah doubled a fist at his side as he recalled the bloody bones that Jason Roark had left at the entrance of his tipi. His eyes became lit with fire. "Your gesture of kindness was appreciated," he said dryly, turning his gaze slowly to the President. "That is why I am here. To repay you. But it was impossible to use the buffalo bull in the Sun Dance ceremony."

President Hayes was taken aback by this. He tilted his

head, studying Kohanah, again caressing his beard. "What's that you say?" he asked. "Why *didn't* you use the buffalo bull? I sent it to you for that purpose. I thought it was necessary for the ceremony."

Kohanah knelt on one knee and began to fit his canvases together in one stack. "Kohanah learned at long last that the ceremony must be performed without the buffalo," he said icily. "There are no more buffalo. Now *or* ever. The Kiowa are learning to accept many sorts of losses. This is just one more. Kohanah understands now that this should have been one of our earlier lessons. Kohanah should never have planned to use the buffalo this year."

"But, Kohanah, you *had* the buffalo *for* this year's Sun Dance," President Hayes said, placing a hand gently on Kohanah's powerful shoulder. "I don't understand. Tell me why you did not use it."

Kohanah turned his eyes slowly up, to look at President Hayes. "That was not possible because Jason Roark stole the buffalo bull and killed it," he said, fighting to hold his anger at bay. "He not only killed it, he dismembered it, stripped the bones of the flesh, and placed the bones outside my tipi for me to find on the morning that had been set aside for the Sun Dance celebration, *and* he threw the head of the buffalo bull away, so that we could not use it for the ceremony. That is why there was no buffalo bull sacrifice at our Sun Dance."

President Hayes took a step back. He cleared his throat nervously, watching Marilla move to Kohanah's side as Kohanah rose to his full height. "That is unquestionably one of the most fiendish crimes I have heard of in many a year," President Hayes said, visibly shuddering. "This man who did this. You say his name is Jason Roark. He's the man accused of other atrocities in your area, isn't he?"

"*Ho*," Kohanah said, nodding. "He is the man."

"He's been on the run, hiding," President Hayes said. "I imagine he still is. His sort have ways of eluding the noose."

Marilla circled an arm about Kohanah's waist. She looked adoringly up at him, then smiled smugly at the President. "Jason Roark may have been clever enough to elude the

noose," she said, hoping that the disclosure of Jason's fate
would not sit wrong with the President. Something told her
that he would understand. He was understanding more and
more as each moment passed, it seemed.

"Oh? What do you mean, Marilla?" President Hayes
asked, looking from her to Kohanah, seeing similar looks
of triumph in their eyes.

"He has been dealt with once and for all," she said
guardedly. "You see, the Kiowa know the art of tracking
well. They found Jason Roark. He was dealt with in the
Kiowa fashion. Need I say more? Or had I best not?"

President Hayes squared his shoulders and cleared his
throat nervously, his face a sudden pink flush, caused by
uneasiness. "No, it's best that I hear no more," he said
hoarsely. He went back to the paintings and knelt on one
knee and again sorted through them. He stopped at the one
that had been done on a buffalo hide and set it aside, and
then one that depicted the Kiowa Sun Dance in all of its
excitement and grandeur.

"These are the two I would like to have for my private
collection," he said, giving Kohanah a quick glance over
his shoulder. "But if you wish to part with them all, I will
pay you a fair price. These are works of a genius at work
on canvas, Kohanah, I mean that from the bottom of my
heart."

Pride swelled within Marilla's heart; tears sparkled in
her eyes as she saw Kohanah's eyes mellow and his lips
lift into a slow smile. She anxiously awaited his response,
hoping that it would be the one that she wanted to hear
. . . the one that she knew would be the best for *him*. . . .

"In fact," President Hayes said, rising slowly to his
feet. "Kohanah, I would like to commission you to paint
several more paintings." He placed a hand on Kohanah's
shoulder. "These paintings will be placed in museums
across the country as part of a representation of our country's beginnings." He smiled over at Marilla, his eyes
twinkling, then again looked up at Kohanah. "Kohanah,
the Kiowa's rations will be doubled. More cattle will be
sent to your people. I will give you a promise of a buffalo
bull for your next Sun Dance."

President Hayes dropped his hands down and slipped them inside his trousers pockets. "What do you say, Kohanah?" he asked, slowly rocking his body back and forth on his heels. "Is it a deal?"

For a moment Kohanah was speechless. Then he fondly clasped his fingers onto the President's shoulders. "My friend, Kohanah will paint you many paintings," he said hoarsely, proudly firming his jaw. "It is good that you want the white community to see the ways of my people."

"Then I believe we've reached quite an understanding between us," President Hayes said, offering Kohanah a handshake of friendship. "This is a day I shall always remember."

Hands met in friendship. Kohanah embraced the President, then stepped quickly back away from him, embarrassed that he had shown his feelings so openly. He glanced down at the paintings. "These paintings that I have brought today," he said thickly. "They are a gift. You can send payment later, for others. Your gift of friendship and cows and the buffalo bull already sent to my people were payment enough for these."

"If that's what would make you happy, I will be happy enough with that arrangement," President Hayes said, giving Marilla a look of appreciation. "Now let's move our discussion away from business. You and Kohanah are going to stay for dinner, aren't you? Lucy would be delighted. So would the children. It's rare that we have such a guest of honor as Kohanah."

He smiled softly down at Marilla, leaning his face closer to hers. "And, of course, his *wife*," he said, patting Marilla on the arm.

Kohanah went to stand beside Marilla, possessively placing an arm about her waist. "Your invitation is a kind one, but we must return to our people," he said dryly. "It is not good that a chief be away so long." He gave Marilla a troubled look, his eyes wavering. "And my wife has not been well on the journey here by train. It is best to get her home, where she can rest."

President Hayes's dark eyes squinted, troubled. "Marilla, perhaps you should see a doctor before you leave Washington," he said softly. "I could have one here before you could bat an eye."

Marilla felt her face coloring with a blush. She cast her eyes downward, unconsciously moving a hand to rest on her tummy. "No," she murmured. "There is no need for a doctor. I believe my sort of sickness takes care of itself, in time."

"Well, whatever," the President said, softly shrugging. "Just remember. Whenever you want anything, all you need to do is wire me. I'm here at your beck and call. Always."

Marilla smiled up at the President. "Sir, how can I ever thank you for all that you have done?" she said, then moved away from Kohanah and gently embraced the President. "Thank you for everything."

President Hayes slipped an arm about Marilla and returned the gesture of affection. "My dear, it is you who deserves to be thanked," he said thickly. "Because of you, this peace and understanding between Kohanah and myself has all been made possible. God blesses you. *I* bless you."

*   *   *

Nine Months Later

Winter had passed without misfortune for the Kiowa. Hot tornadic winds were now sweeping along the land, arriving with spring. Marilla sat beside Kohanah in the medicine house during the naming ceremony for their one month old son. Old Man Trembling, the honored elder chosen to grant the name to the child sat on the west side of the lodge with the child to his left on a soft pallet of furs, the parents to his right.

Marilla's hand crept to Kohanah's and she intertwined her fingers through his, recalling how he had explained that a "good" name was derived from an important hunting or war feat. Names were felt to have supernatural significance. A person who experienced misfortune or a grave illness might change his name afterward.

But the name chosen this day for Marilla and Kohanah's *iapagya talyi*, baby boy, had a double meaning. It was part white, part Indian. *Kagya* Hayes was to be their child's name. The Kiowa name *Kagya* meaning "a triumph or rejoicing over a slain enemy," the other name assigned because of Kohanah's and Marilla's devotion to the President whose kindness would always affect their lives!

As Old Man Trembling raised his hands toward the heavens and began to chant a blessing in Kiowa to the child and its newly given name, Marilla's mind flashed back to the beginning, when she had first met Kohanah. Even when he had been imprisoned in that dreadful dungeon in Florida, she had known that their futures were to be interlocked.

And now they had a son!

A sweet whisper of joy touched her heart. She felt Kohanah's eyes on her. Slowly she looked toward him. Even without words, so much was being exchanged between them. Their eyes said it all. . . .